THE REMAINING

EXTINCTION

ALSO BY D. J. MOLLES

The Remaining

The Remaining
The Remaining: Aftermath
The Remaining: Refugees
The Remaining: Fractured
The Remaining: Allegiance
The Remaining: Extinction

The Remaining Short Fiction

"The Remaining: Trust"
"The Remaining: Faith"

THE REMAINING
EXTINCTION

BOOK 6

D. J. MOLLES

www.orbitbooks.net

Copyright © 2015 by D. J. Molles
Excerpt from *The Lazarus War: Artefact* copyright © 2015 by Jamie Sawyer
Cover design by Lauren Panepinto. Cover photos by Arcangel-Images. Cover copyright © 2015 by Orbit Books.

Orbit
Hachette Book Group
1290 Avenue of the Americas
New York, NY 10104
www.orbitbooks.net

Printed in the United States of America

First Edition: July 2015
10 9 8 7 6 5 4 3 2 1
Orbit is an imprint of Hachette Book Group, Inc. The Orbit name and logo are trademarks of Little, Brown Book Group Limited.

The Hachette Speakers Bureau provides a wide range of authors for speaking events. To find out more, go to www.hachettespeakers bureau.com or call (866) 376-6591.

The publisher is not responsible for websites (or their content) that are not owned by the publisher.

ISBN: 978-0-316-26164-7

This one is for the sheepdogs

ONE

TRICKERY

WE NEED TO DO this my way, LaRouche had told them. *No shock troop bullshit. Slow and quiet and then we take them quick. If you trust me, trust me to handle this.*

LaRouche threaded his way through cold, bare trees, trying to keep his feet light on all the dried leaves. First he would look around, standing as still as the trees around him. He would see if there was anything straight ahead of him, and he would listen to the woods. They were quiet in the way that only winter could bring. No insects to chirp. No night birds to call out. The odd, basal rumble of the world existing in silence. Like if you listened hard enough, you could just hear the gears in the center of the earth churning as they kept the planet spinning. The sense of some vast machinery. It was an odd noise that came in wilderness places, and it was a noise that LaRouche had never become accustomed to.

Then he would bring one foot forward and slowly ease it down into the leaves, watching where he was stepping, trying to decipher in the starlight the difference between leaves and branches in the jumbles of shapes underneath him. He would take a few slow steps and then he would stop again. It took time to make up distance this way, but that was what he had told them—slow and quiet.

Behind him, he could just barely hear the footsteps of Clyde, moving as stealthily as LaRouche was. LaRouche had not learned to move in the woods from the military—with so much taking place in urban environments or rocky desert, they didn't spend a whole lot of time teaching woodland movement. What he knew of moving through the woods he learned from a lifetime of bow hunting. It would be bow season right now, come to think of it.

After maybe an hour of moving this way, they came to the point where LaRouche was beginning to recognize things. The white farmhouse set back in the trees. The cluster of tents and campers and shanties. The dirt road that plunged straight through the trees to this little hideout in the woods. A single campfire smoldering. The shape of a man with his back to the embers.

Patterson Place.

LaRouche sank down into a crouch and looked behind him. A few yards back, he could see Clyde standing there, half concealed by the trunk of a tree. The lenses of his glasses shone faintly in the starlight—not enough to give him away, unless you were already looking for him.

LaRouche reached out a hand and motioned Clyde forward with a single wave of his fingers. The other man chose his footing carefully and made his way to LaRouche in a few steps, kneeling down close enough that their shoulders brushed. He knew as well as LaRouche that voices carried a long, long way, and in order for them to communicate, their whispers had to be quieter than rustling leaves.

LaRouche leaned in close to him. The man who had saved him. And cursed him all at once. Rescued? Captured? What difference did it make? LaRouche was a device that was useful for little else besides hurting and killing other people. It was his talent. It didn't matter whose hands swung an axe—it cut wood all the same. LaRouche was that axe, doing what it was made to do, but maybe providing fuel for the fires of the wrong people. Could you blame the axe for that?

You are not an axe, and you will burn in hell for the things that you do.

You are a man. A bad man.

With his mouth almost to Clyde's ear, LaRouche whispered, "We're going to do this a little different than what we said."

Clyde looked at him, alarm clearly on his face. His hand snaked up to his face, a single finger pushing his glasses back up. "LaRouche . . ."

"We're here for the guns and the food," LaRouche said firmly. "That's it. No prisoners. No women. Guns and food."

"So what are you gonna do?" Clyde's voice went scarily close to getting too loud, but he seemed to catch himself and brought it back down. "You gonna let 'em all go?"

LaRouche nodded. "The women and children."

"They're going to die without protection. Without food."

LaRouche considered this. It was true. Did it make a difference? Perhaps the women and children were better off being captured by the Followers. But was he capable of being the one that lined them up and turned them over? He didn't think so. Odd, where one sees fit to draw his moral lines in the sand.

"We should stick to the plan," Clyde urged. "Let's just take out the sentries and send up the signal for the others. If anyone finds out that you intentionally let them get away...fuck, man. You're gonna blow all that trust you just built up for yourself."

LaRouche chewed his lip. "Fine. But we're not...I'm not..." He growled and shook his head. "I'm not killing them if they run. If they run, they get away. Period. If anyone has a fucking problem with that, then they can stand me up in front of a firing squad. I don't give a fuck."

"Hang you from a telephone pole would be more likely," Clyde said.

LaRouche refused to acknowledge what Clyde had said. He rose from the ground. "Come on."

The two men began moving forward, but they split in different directions. LaRouche began to angle for the dirt road that the first sentry was watching, while Clyde began to swing out wide to LaRouche's right. LaRouche crept as close as he could, and when he was among the shacks and tents and campers that were sprawled through the trees, and perhaps ten yards from the sentry who was sitting, dozing off with his back to the fire, LaRouche stepped out from concealment, displaying an obvious limp, his rifle hanging loosely from his weak hand, while his strong hand was held palm up.

The sentry jerked when he saw LaRouche and started to open his mouth to sound the alarm.

LaRouche shook his head. "Sshh! It's Sergeant LaRouche...please...be quiet...I need help."

The sentry blinked rapidly. Recognition came over his face as the sleep fled from him. "Sarge? Is that you?" he said quietly. His near-sleep state was making him compliant. If he'd been more awake, he might have been more difficult.

LaRouche continued forward. "Yes...please... I need help."

The sentry stood up and moved quickly to LaRouche, reaching out a hand to offer support. His eyes were filled with concern, and for that LaRouche felt the tiniest measure of guilt, but he had not wanted to be friends with these people to begin with. That was Wilson and Father Jim. They were the ones that wanted to fucking befriend every goddamned lost puppy.

"What happened?" the man asked, looking over LaRouche's limping frame for a wound that wouldn't be there. As his hand touched LaRouche's elbow, a shadow slid out from between two tents. It swept the rifle out of the sentry's hands, then clamped a forearm over the sentry's mouth and nose to stifle any cries. The sentry's head was pulled back, exposing the throat.

LaRouche pulled a knife from its sheath on his

belt and inserted it into the side of the sentry's neck, then sawed across, cutting the larynx and the carotid arteries in a few quick motions. The sentry thrashed and jerked and made quiet choking noises, but Clyde held him and guided his weakening body to the ground. LaRouche stepped back away from the gouts of blood and immediately started scanning to make sure the other sentry had not been alerted.

There were no shouts of alarm. No movement save for the sentry's feet scuffing in the dirt, getting slower and weaker by the second until there was nothing left but twitches. LaRouche looked down at the man and tried to remember his name, but couldn't, and then thought that might be best.

The second sentry was easier. They were able to catch him unawares at the back of the farmhouse, keeping an eye on the forest. A strike to the back of the head with a rifle butt stunned him, and then LaRouche put the knife into the base of his brain.

Bad man. That's all you are.

The two men didn't die silently, but they didn't die with enough noise to wake the people they were trying to protect. LaRouche crept back through the camp with Clyde, looking at the little places where small families were holding on, and wondering if they would die. The men would die, that was for certain. But the women and children...

What do you care about women and children? Bad men don't care.

At the dying fire, Clyde slung off the satchel strapped to his back and opened it. The smell of pine forests wafted out. Fresh evergreen boughs were stuffed in the satchel, bristling with needles. They dumped them into the fire and then crouched down, scanning three-sixty. On the hot coals the green branches began to blacken and gouts of gray smoke started to waft up, carrying with them the scent of the trees that reminded LaRouche perversely of the holidays. Shopping for a live tree while the sellers stuffed the trimmed branches into a fifty-gallon drum and burned them, filling the air with pleasant-smelling smoke. But though this smoke smelled the same, it was a signal for the others that were lurking in the woods. A signal for them to come, and to kill.

It didn't take them long. They must've been close by. Within minutes the shapes of men armed with rifles appeared, slinking through the smoke like ghosts. They made very little sound, and Patterson Place kept on sleeping. The shapes all went to different places, some of them to the flaps of tents, others to the doors of the one or two campers, and still others stacked up on the front door of the farmhouse. LaRouche and Clyde watched them from where they stood by the fire, and the dark shapes of men watched them back.

LaRouche made the motion. He brought his hand up, and then down, almost lazily.

Tent flaps unzipped, camper doors were ripped open, and the front door of the farmhouse was kicked in. There were shouts, and then screams, and then gunfire, and all the little domes of tents and the windows of campers pulsed in the smoky darkness like luminescent fungus in a foggy swamp. There was wailing as women and children watched husbands and fathers die, and then were killed themselves, and probably for no real reason.

Bad men, one and all.

LaRouche turned away from the sights and sounds. His eyes fell to the corner of the house and he could see a woman and a child there, just stepping out and ready to make a break for the woods. There were no tears in their eyes, because they had not had time for tears. Only shock and panic. They stood there, stock-still, staring right back at LaRouche, as though they were trying to figure out whether he could see them or not. All around him the night was turning into hell. And he was the devil, standing with his back to the flames, the planner, the orchestrator, the executor.

He wondered if they recognized him.

Sorry, ma'am. Those guns I gave your people... I need them back.

LaRouche didn't raise his rifle. He stood as still as they did, a scene set in stone. Then he nodded to them. They broke and ran. Into the woods. The woman was barefoot. The child had no coat. Neither had a weapon or a pack. No food or water. Nothing to protect themselves.

They will die. You didn't murder them with your hands, but they will die all the same.

They disappeared into the trees. To freeze. To starve. To be eaten.

As suddenly as the chaos had erupted, it died. Or at least the gunfire did. All the threats had been eliminated. But there was still wailing. Weeping and gnashing of teeth. Now *there* was an apt description of what LaRouche had created.

Are you okay with this?

Of course I am. There's nothing to it but to do it.

LaRouche turned to face the fire where the green branches had all but burned away. He looked up at Clyde and found the other man's eyes fixated on the burned branches. Neither spoke. For a time they stood there, and the sound around them melted into a slurry that they didn't pay attention to. Eventually it felt normal again.

A man approached. One of the Followers. He stood between Clyde and LaRouche, looking rapidly between the two men as he spoke. "We've secured all the weapons. Still gathering the ammunition. So far we have ten of the M4 rifles, and about a half-dozen other long guns. And a few pistols."

Clyde didn't respond, so LaRouche took it upon himself. It was, after all, his plan.

He nodded to the man. "Good. Everyone did good. Gather the weapons and ammunition. If Chalmers wants the women and children, he can come back for them. If any of them are still alive."

Clyde looked up sharply at LaRouche.

"You mean . . . ?" the man stammered.

LaRouche's placid face turned dark. "Leave them. And if anyone has a problem with that I'll gut them. I promise you that." LaRouche leaned into the man. "What about you? You got a fucking problem with it?"

The man didn't cave like a coward. He stuck his chin out. But he also appeared to be seriously considering what LaRouche had said. Not many of the men truly knew LaRouche, but word traveled fast in the camp. Everyone knew what LaRouche had done to a certain commanding officer with a bottle of whiskey. They might not like it, but everyone knew that the new guy LaRouche might have a screw loose, and not many people wanted to fuck around with that.

Finally, the man nodded. "Fine. I'll pass the word along."

It's a trick, Abe kept telling himself. *It's a trick, it's a trick, it's a trick.*

Don't let your guard down.

He was finding it difficult to stay awake. The antibiotics weren't a cure-all, and the fever was still making him nauseous, and he would cough wetly every now and then. But he felt better knowing that the infection had at least been treated and he wasn't going to die of pneumonia. It was dangerous for him to be thankful for anything they had given him, including his full belly and the warm cell he was now sitting in. It was all too good to be true. It was just a trick to try to get him to relax.

He hated it, but the exhaustion was catching up to him and he thought that their plan might be working. His eyes kept drooping closed. It was so wonderful to be warm again. So wonderful to have food in your stomach, even if you felt like you might throw it up in a minute. It was the best he'd felt in days. Or weeks. However long they'd had him locked up in this place.

The man calling himself Carl Gilliard seemed to be saying that he was not aligned with President Briggs. And honestly, Abe's mind was so befuddled with everything that he was having a difficult time figuring out which way was up, never mind the delicate details of political intrigue. So he pretty much had to take Carl's word for it, though he still felt suspicious about it. Couldn't figure out why. Maybe it was the torture he'd endured. You just don't trust someone after they do those things to you. You can't become friends with them after that.

But were they allies?

Because an ally was very different from a friend. They say that an enemy of your enemy is your friend, but actually that person is just your ally. Useful. Sometimes faithful, to a point. But not your friend.

"He's not even an ally," Abe muttered, speaking just to keep himself from falling asleep. "He's just a guy...just a guy who wants to hurt me. No. Not gonna. I'm gonna..."

He realized he should be quiet, in case people were listening.

I'm gonna get out of here. I can't sit around and wait to see what's up this guy's sleeve. I need to get free or he's going to kill me. I don't know how or why, but I just know that it's going to happen. I just fucking know it.

But how? It was one thing to be determined to break free, but an animal in a cage can pace and growl and batter the bars all it wants and never really have a chance of breaking free. It wasn't about determination. That came after. Determination was what got you through the race. That was what he would need to get out of this compound once he'd busted out of his cell. Determination was what he would need to get through the guards and to get through the woods and back on the road. And determination was what he would need once he was on that road, to somehow find his way to friendly territory.

You have no friendly territory right now. No matter where you are, you're an enemy.

No, determination did him no good right now. Smarts. That was what he needed to summon up. Some clearheadedness. Some out-of-the-box thinking. Some cleverness. A little maliciousness. Find a way to get out of here. *Find a way. Find a way.*

Abe realized his eyes had been closed the whole time. He blinked rapidly and sat up, then scrambled to his feet. His head spun and his vision threatened to blacken. He tightened his core and grunted loudly to get some blood back into his head. He bounced on the balls of his feet. His heart labored to get moving. He shook his arms out, swung them back and forth, like a fighter limbering up in his corner. He needed to get his heart rate up. Blood flow equaled brain flow. Shit starts to get hazy when you curl up in a little ball. When you're moving you're thinking. It's all just a complicated mess of biochemistry. Ideas came from the brain, and the brain needed oxygen, and blood carried that oxygen, and movement forced more oxygen.

So move. Move!

He squatted down, then straightened up. Down, then up. He wondered if anyone was watching and if they were wondering what the fuck he was doing in there. A sheen of sweat had broken across his brow, and he was breathing heavily, even from that extremely small exertion. That just showed him how weak he'd become.

That's bad. That's real bad. Can I even overpower someone?

No. Obviously not. You're not going to muscle your way out of this situation.

It's brains over brawn, but you've done that before.

Abe was never big. Through every unit he'd ever worked with, he'd always been one of the smaller guys. The big guys tended to muscle their way through things, but Abe had always been forced to use his head. It was no different now.

Just remember who you're dealing with, Abe told himself. *These boys seem like operators. They know what they're doing. It's going to be tough to catch them with their pants down.*

His hammering heart and hard breathing were making his stomach fall into rioting. He gagged, burped, and tasted Salisbury steak and gravy, churned through with his own stomach acid. It burned in the back of his throat.

What are you gonna do?

I'm going to puke. And I'm going to pass out. And I'm going to hope to God that someone is watching . . .

Abe sank to the ground. He could see just under the door. A tiny crack, and on the other side he could see the bottoms of boots and the shadows cast by a pair of men. Probably Norseman and his smaller partner, if Abe were to take a wild guess. Maybe they were paying attention, or maybe they weren't. Maybe they had cameras in the room. In any case, there wasn't a whole lot that Abe had going for him. He was improvising with nothing.

He began to rock back and forth on his knees. Just the thought of it was already making saliva coat the sides of his mouth. He took a few short breaths, eyes locked on the underside of the door. He scooted a little closer. He made a strangled cry, and then said, "Help me...please..."

Then he shoved two fingers down his throat. His throat seized around them. Then he could feel everything opening up as Salisbury steak and gravy came rushing back up. He retched once with nothing, and then it all came out at once, a light brown chunky mess that spewed out onto the door and the floors. He retched two more times, and then collapsed in a puddle of his own vomit.

His eyes rolled back. His eyelids fluttering while his body shook violently. His face and lips were smeared with his own vomit. The pool of the mess he had just created began to seep under the narrow crack at the bottom of the door.

It took a moment, but then there was a cry of alarm from the other side of the door. Shuffling of feet, rubber boot soles squeaking on linoleum tiles. A few loud curses. Then the door was flung open. The air outside was noticeably cooler, and it chilled Abe's vomit-covered face. His eyes were still looking up into his own head, and he could not see who it was that was standing in the doorway.

"Holy fuck..."

"Hey! Get the fuck up!"

"Dude, he might be for real."

"God damn it...call the doc."

Abe coughed and spluttered and took shaky breaths. He blinked rapidly. It was Norseman standing over him, straddling the puddle of vomit, leaning down with his hands on his knees and inspecting Abe with a suspicious eye. His leaner partner was just outside the door, nose wrinkled in disgust, but eyes softened with pity.

The leaner one pointed. "Roll him on his side so he don't choke on his vomit."

Norseman avoided the puddle of vomit and stepped over Abe's legs, reaching for his right shoulder to pull him onto his side.

Abe did the only thing he could—he kicked with everything he had, and landed a hard blow into Norseman's groin. The air came out of the man's lungs in a *whoomph*, and he made a sound like groaning steel as he toppled forward onto Abe. The man was a righty, and his pistol was on Abe's left. As Norseman landed on him, Abe's left hand snagged the pistol from its holster on his belt—a simple quick-draw design with no safety retention in place. And then Abe was almost smothered by the man's 250-pound frame.

The lean man jumped forward, his pistol appearing in his hand, but then saw the pistol in Abe's hand, and jumped back out of the doorway. Abe was almost completely covered by the big man. Even a good pistol shooter would have had to take a second or two to properly aim at the inch of Abe's face that was peeking out from under the moaning form. The lean man hesitated, and didn't take the shot.

Abe did. Firing weak-handed with a man on top of him. He fired rapidly, hoping his volume of fire would make up for the lack of accuracy. But out of five rounds, four struck home except for the last one, which went high and to the left. The lean man, standing half in and half out of the doorway, yelped and danced as the bullets plunged through him and he fired reactively, the bullets slamming high into the wall behind Abe. Abe cringed when the man shot but forced himself to fire two more times, one striking the man low, on his thigh, and the other catching him right in the clavicle and cutting off his voice. The man tumbled against the wall, his chest still hitching for life though he was, for all intents and purposes, dead.

Abe heaved with everything he had and managed to get the big man off of him. Norseman's body was stiff, his arms beginning to work again as he was regaining some of his faculties. A blow to the testicles could be quite a shock to the system, but Abe needed to be out of arm's reach by the time the man was back into fighting capability, because he held no illusions that he would win a grappling contest with him.

Even as he was squirming, the man reached out and tried to grab hold of Abe's neck, cognizant enough to know that Abe was trying to get away. Abe managed to pull out of his reach and then the man's hand started grabbing at anything it could. Abe hit it hard with the slide of the pistol, right on the wrist where the nerve endings were. The Norseman growled and retracted his hand, but his body was rising up onto his knees, one hand still hovering protectively over his lower abdomen and groin.

Abe scooted back, his feet slipping in his own vomit, but he managed to get out of striking range, with his back up against the wall. He switched the stolen pistol to his strong hand, and sudden, full-blown panic hit him hard: What the fuck was he thinking? He just fired shots inside of a building. If there was anyone else in this building, they were coming, and they were coming prepared for war.

What the fuck was I supposed to do? I can't over-power them.

You needed strength to make a silent kill. Strength and endurance, of which Abe had neither in his current state. But whether or not taking shots was his best or only chance was a moot point now. It had happened. And he didn't have a lot of time. He had to assume the cavalry was already on its way.

He began to crawl up the wall and onto his feet, the pistol pointed at Norseman. "Don't. I'll fucking put one through your head."

The big man stared at him, still recovering, his face pale, but there was enough hatred in his eyes that Abe thought he could still be dangerous. If the man rushed him, he would have to take the shot. He wasn't going to risk a physical confrontation with someone close to twice his size.

"What are you doing?" the man said, accusation in his tone. "Same fucking side, you piece of shit. Unless you really are from President Briggs."

Abe shook his head, felt it swimming. He wasn't going to go down this road. Maybe the man was being clever and trying to set Abe off balance, or maybe he was telling the truth. There wasn't time to find out. "I'm not from Briggs. But I have no way of knowing if we're on the same side, and I'm not taking my fucking chances. Where is my friend?"

"Who?"

"Captain Lucas. My friend." Abe felt his voice rising. "I want to know where he is."

"I don't know who that is."

"The man that was with me!" Abe shouted. "He was with me when you took me prisoner! I need to know where he is!"

The man opened his mouth, but Abe could already tell that it was going to be another denial, and he simply wasn't going to have it.

Abe fired a shot that struck the big man in his shin, likely shattering the bone in two.

The man screamed and Abe felt panic rise again. *Another gunshot? Another one?*

Fuck it. If they're coming, they're coming. I'm completely fucked either way.

Even if he did make it out, what did he expect was going to happen? He was sick, partially starved, mostly dehydrated, with no transportation, no weapon save what he held in his hand, and barely any clothing to protect himself from the cold. He wasn't going to get far. But these were worries for another time and another place. Right now all that mattered was *momentum*.

"Where is he?" Abe demanded.

The big man had his eyes squeezed shut. The shot to the shin had been convincing enough.

"He's in the other detainee building. Across from this one."

"How many guards?"

"Fuck..."

"How many?!"

"Two. Just like for you."

"Where's the device?" Abe said, stepping forward, beginning to shake.

"I don't know..."

"No!" Abe bent down, still out of arm's reach, but close enough. "You need to tell me where the fucking device is. It is very, very important that I get it back. You don't understand what the hell is going on right now! You're fucking killing everybody, you stupid sonofabitch! Don't just follow orders—think for yourself! Think this shit through!"

"What is it?" the big man said through clenched teeth.

"It's something that doesn't belong to you. It belongs to someone else, and he needs it back. And if he doesn't get it back, lots of bad stuff is going to happen, do you understand me? Bad, bad things. And bad, bad people." Abe pointed the pistol at the man's other leg. "Tell me now, or you're not walking for the rest of your life. This ain't last year, big guy. These are the bad times now, when they can't fix shattered legs like this. You think anybody has time to teach you how to walk again, motherfucker? You want to walk, you tell me where it is."

"Jesus..." The big man was sweating profusely, rocking back and forth. "Carl has it. In his office. I don't know where."

"Where is his office?"

"I can show you..."

"You can't walk. Where is it? Tell me how to get there."

The big man took a few breaths to steady himself. "It's in this building. Top floor. Has a sign on it that says, BEWARE OF DOG."

"Good." Abe made a wide circle around the man. "Scoot in here. Scoot in."

The man did as he was told, the two of them trading places. Abe was now standing in the doorway. Abe bent down and scooped up the other guard's pistol, shoving it into his waistband. He turned back to the big man, who was leaning against the far wall of the cell now.

"I'm sorry about your partner here. I didn't want to kill anyone."

"You traitorous piece of shit..."

Abe closed the door on him, making sure that it was locked.

TWO

RUN

ABE RACED DOWN HALLWAYS that were unfamiliar as a labyrinth to him. None of the doors and long stretches of hallways seemed to be in the right spot. He had almost memorized the ones outside of his old, chilly cell, but now that they'd transitioned him to the new, warmer one, he was completely discombobulated.

He wanted to stop to listen and see if there were shouts, or the slamming of doors farther away in the building—the sound of people coming to take him out. But he didn't dare stop. He had to keep going, keep running, though his run was weak and he was finding his right hip felt somewhat painful and out of whack, though he wasn't sure why. It was causing him to lurch along like a man with a gimp leg.

He was looking for stairs.

Stairs. The Norseman said Carl's office would be upstairs.

And Lucas. He couldn't forget about Lucas. He had to get the GPS first—Lucas would have to understand that the mission came first—and then he would find Lucas. In the building directly across from this one. The *detainee* building, the Norseman had said.

How many detainees do they have?

Abe kept passing doors and not finding himself confronted by any guards. Unless they filled cells and then let people rot, he had to assume that perhaps he and Lucas were some of the only detainees that Carl had. Perhaps he just kept them in separate buildings to have an extra buffer against them working together.

What was it that Carl had said?

"We're what's left…"

So maybe there weren't that many. Maybe the majority of the Eighty-Second Airborne and Delta had packed up and ran off to hitch their wagons to President Briggs. But if they had, it was news to Abe. That was the part that bothered him. He'd never been told about the Eighty-Second Airborne or men from Delta being inside their base city, Greeley, Colorado.

But then again, Abe didn't put it past President Briggs and his Army lapdog, Colonel Lineberger, to hide them from Abe. Back in the Greeley Green Zone, it'd been a constant political battle between Abe, who had access to all the supplies, and Briggs and Lineberger, who commanded all the forces that were kept fed and armed by the Coordinators. It was a power struggle. They didn't like that Abe was the hand that fed them. And they'd slowly begun to squeeze him out, seizing more and more control of Project Hometown, until Abe finally read the writing on the wall and bailed.

Those sons of bitches, Abe thought venomously.

They were just waiting to get enough control of Project Hometown before they pulled the big red handle and sent their dogs after me. Well, fuck the both of you. I made the first move. And I'm keeping it alive. I'm keeping Project Hometown alive.

He stumbled to a stop, realizing that he was at the door to a stairwell.

Up. Gotta go up.

He pushed through the door and up the stairs. He stopped on the first landing, almost wheezing. He coughed to clear some air space in his lungs, then took a moment to listen. But the building seemed quiet around him. Maybe the shots had not been heard.

Up to the top of the next flight, where a door stood, closed and labeled LEVEL 2. He stopped again, trying to remember how far they'd dragged him up the stairs when they'd taken him to Carl's office. Above him, the stairs continued up to the third and final level. But he didn't think that they'd taken him up that far. He seemed to remember only one set of stairs.

"Go with your gut," Abe whispered, then yanked the door to Level 2 open.

The interior of this level was much different from the one below. Where the bottom floor had been cement floors and metal doors and glaring fluorescent lights, this one was soft incandescence and carpeted hallways and neutral colors. Still very institutional, but it was obvious that this was where the people that ran the building stayed.

Abe forced himself to move into this next long hallway, but he was racking his brain trying to remember when and where he had seen buildings like this at Fort Bragg. During his years in Delta he'd done time at Fort Bragg, and he thought that he'd been everywhere on base that there was to see, but he couldn't remember any three-story buildings with holding cells on the bottom. Of course, maybe they weren't originally holding cells. Maybe they had been repurposed. But they sure as hell seemed like holding cells.

The hallway here was another long one, similar in dimension to the detention level. But the doors here appeared to lead to offices, and they were wooden, with smoked glass panels. Text was scrawled on some of them. Various ranks and names. Captain Something. Lieutenant Whoever.

When they'd guided him up the stairs, they'd come through the door and hung a left, and then the office had been right there, and Carl had been inside. Abe mimicked the movement that he could remember, racing down the hallways and looking at the doors to his right, trying to see Carl or Gilliard in the name. But he wasn't even sure that was Carl's real name. And what if Carl wasn't an officer? What if he didn't actually have an office in here? Maybe he just took over someone else's office.

It's got a BEWARE OF DOG *sign on it.*

"Shit." Abe had completely forgotten that in his haste. He began running now, down the hallway, looking at every doorway he passed, every office, to see if anyone had a sign hanging. Some of them did, but none of them were the sign he was looking for. Typical stuff on the windows. Comics. Old printouts from the Internet with someone's face pasted obviously over the original.

He kept looking ahead, thinking that there would be another stairwell door ahead of him somewhere, and that it would open and men would come spilling out. But the hallways remained abandoned. It seemed to be just him in this building. All alone and running amok.

The hallway stopped abruptly, forcing him into a left turn. He took it and found another staircase straight ahead of him. Maybe that was the staircase he had come up. He ran to it and looked beside it. There was what appeared to be a utility closet, but then an office, and hanging on the door was a black sign with orange lettering: BEWARE OF DOG.

The name on the office door read MASTER SERGEANT CARL GILLIARD.

Guess he was telling the truth. Master Sergeant, huh?

Abe was breathing hard. He tested the doorknob, feeling sweat beginning to run down his face and tickle his bearded jaw line. The door was locked. Abe looked around, more out of reflex than out of any need to do so, and then turned his back to the door and mule-kicked it. The locking mechanism wasn't substantial and the door flew inward, the wooden framing splintered.

Abe rolled into the room, sweeping it from left to right with his pistol tucked in tight to his body, ready for a threat, ready for someone to be hiding. But the room was empty. Abe checked behind the door, but found only a filing cabinet with a set of pictures on it. One was of a young, scrawny-looking Carl Gilliard in his dress blues, fresh out of basic training and thinking he was bad as fuck, as all eighteen-year-olds in the military automatically assume. The others showed different Carl Gilliards of different ranks, in different countries, fighting different wars, and gradually growing older both in body and in mind.

Abe closed the damaged door behind him. It didn't latch but it stayed closed. That would have to be good enough. He ran to the desk sitting in the middle of the room. Yes, this was the room he had been sitting in when Carl had given him his little speech. But who was Carl? Good or bad? Abe had asked him whether they were friends, and though the question had been a sarcastic one, Carl had said the truth.

Hardly.

Standing at the desk and taking a quick look around, Abe immediately spotted some things of his, piled in the corner, just behind the desk. It was his pack, all the pockets open, the contents spilling out and obviously rifled through. But with the exception of a single black, electronic device, nothing inside that pack was of any import. It was all medical supplies and spare ammunition and food and water and a few changes of underwear and socks and some basic hygiene supplies. Abe had not stuffed himself full of military secrets before leaving the Greeley Green Zone, because he was well aware that something like this might happen. He might fall into the wrong hands. And honestly, everything he needed to know was locked up tight in his mind.

Except the GPS. That was the Achilles' heel of this whole goddamned thing.

He went to his pack. It was the most obvious place to start. He ripped through the supplies in all the pockets, starting with the one that he'd kept the GPS in, but it wasn't there. It wasn't in any of the pockets. He started grabbing the stuff and cramming it back into the pockets, haphazardly. He needed to take this pack with him. His chances of survival out beyond Fort Bragg were slim enough as it was. At least what was inside this pack would give him an extra day, maybe two or three. He had antibiotics in there, so he would be able to stave off the pneumonia, which was good. And food and water . . .

Don't put the cart before the horse. You need to get Lucas and get the fuck out of here first.

Well, I need to get the GPS, and then Lucas . . . if I can.

Abe hated it. He hated how that tasted in his mouth. But the rotten taste of it didn't stop it from being true. It didn't matter that he had basically forced Lucas into this situation. Lucas knew the risks. He knew that what they were doing was dangerous. Two men wandering across an unknown and enemy area by themselves? Risky.

But necessary.

And the most important thing was keeping Project Hometown alive. Lucas knew that. Abe would get him if there was any way on God's green earth that he could, but he hoped that Lucas knew how important it was that the GPS get back in the hands of Lee.

"It's the *right thing*," Abe said to himself. "The *right thing*."

He slung the pack onto his back and went for the desk. Only one of the drawers was unlocked, but it contained nothing of immediate interest to Abe. Some documents. Some maps. Some print-outs. Maybe if he had time for gathering intel, there might have been something useful there, but there was no time for that now. This was the equivalent of a smash-and-grab, and Abe was the burglar.

Nothing else in the unlocked drawer.

"Shit, shit, shit."

He yanked hard at the locked drawers, but they weren't budging. The desk itself shook and groaned at him. He looked around the room for something to pry with, but there didn't seem to be anything substantial enough to pry open a metal desk. He thought about shooting at the lock, but the results would not necessarily be what he wanted, and could quite possible jam up the desk drawers even worse. It also carried the unintended consequences of wasting valuable ammunition and calling more attention to himself. Just because no one seemed to hear the last bit of gunfire didn't mean they weren't going to hear it this time.

"C'mon, c'mon…" Abe searched the desk, the open drawer. He found a paper clip. A pen. That would work. Obviously brute force with a crowbar would be fastest, but it wasn't the only way to get into a locked drawer.

He straightened out half of the paper clip and slid it into the locking mechanism, using the tip of the pen to apply pressure to the cylinder so the tiny inner pins would stick when he punched them. Then he started working the paper clip. There was the slow and steady, surgical method of lockpicking, where you punched each individual pin until you had them all stuck and then you turned the lock cylinder. And then there was the panicked oh-shit method, which was less reliable but much faster, and entailed shoving the picking device into the lock and jiggling it around furiously while you waited for the cylinder to turn.

Abe had to adjust his sweaty grip on the paper clip three times, but after ten or fifteen seconds of working it, he felt that slight give in the turn of the cylinder. "Ha!" he said, cranking the cylinder all the way around with the tip of the pen. "I got you, you stupid sonofabitch."

The lock disengaged.

Abe yanked open the first drawer in the desk. Paperwork, paperwork, and more paperwork. An old Colt 1911 with pearl grips. It was loaded. It seemed like a personal weapon. Perhaps some sort of heirloom from Carl Gilliard's family. Abe appropriated it. Nothing else important in the drawer. He slammed it shut and moved on to the next. Lucky for him, this was a desk where the main lock was on top and locked or unlocked all three of the drawers below it.

The next drawer opened.

Abe's elation was short-lived but euphoric. It blotted out his pain and his sickness. He lunged into the desk drawer and yanked out a Project Hometown GPS device, though it was dangling in several pieces. *Repairable* pieces, though. Carl hadn't been dumb enough to destroy it, but he'd been smart enough to dismantle the power unit, because he didn't want to leave an activated mystery device lurking at the bottom of one of his desk drawers. Abe stared at the little black device and thanked God that it was such an innocuous-looking piece of crap, or Carl might have read more importance into it and locked it away someplace much more secure.

Abe made sure he had all the parts, but he didn't bother reassembling it then. He slung his pack off, stuffed the GPS securely at the bottom of the main compartment, then zipped up the pack fast and pulled the strap back onto his shoulder.

"All right, Lucas." Abe headed for the door, pistol in one hand. "I'm comin', partner."

Moving out of Carl's office, Abe could already feel the heaviness of the pack. He opened the door and scanned the hallway quickly before stepping out into it. He was weakened by torture and being cramped in a cell and his body fighting an infection, but he probably still had better conditioning than your average guy. Heavy packs and aching muscles were something he could work with. Even the sickness was retreating as his mind found its way back to thinking on its feet. The adrenaline was pushing everything down into a queasy undertone, and when he took deep breaths he could hear the rattle of the fluid in his lungs.

But I can work with this. You have to work with what you're given.

He stood at the doorway for a half second,

deciding to dig the other pistol out of the back of his pants. He had three pistols total—the two from the guards and the one from Carl's desk. The guards' weapons were both Beretta M9s, which shared the same 9mm cartridge. Rather than tote both of them, Abe left one behind after stripping its ammunition and putting the spare magazine in his pants pocket.

He moved quickly to the stairs directly to the left of Carl's office. He listened for a moment before pushing the door open, but the sounds of the stairwell beyond were empty. He pushed through. The stairwell was cold, as he remembered it being when they'd taken him through it blindfolded. He descended to the ground floor and peeked out.

More abandoned hallways.

No exit signs.

Maybe on the other side.

He jogged down the hall, tightening the straps on the pack as he went so that it wouldn't flop around so much. At the next end of the hall, he was forced to turn left, and there was the exit, a glowing red sign above it.

Abe moved to it, wetting his dry lips with his tongue. He was getting thirsty again. He wanted the water in his pack, but he didn't have time for it. Besides, Lucas might need it. He didn't know what condition he was going to find the other man in.

"Directly across," Abe mumbled to himself. "That's what he said."

Abe wondered if the man was going to bleed out before the alarm was raised and someone got help to him. He wondered if the shattered tibia was ever going to heal properly or whether he'd doomed the man to only one working leg. At the very least, a severe limp.

Better than dead.

He put his shoulder to the heavy, industrial outer door. He scanned all around it to see if the thing was alarmed, or if there were any placards that stated to use the door only for emergencies, but there were none. He pressed against the push-bar gently, until the door cracked open an inch or two.

Beyond, it was gray dawn shot through with the first rays of sunlight.

Abe blinked rapidly, suddenly disoriented. He'd been thinking it was in the dead of night, as quiet as it had seemed around here. But here was clear daylight. He felt suddenly exposed. He would have liked to make an escape at night. Maybe he had been picturing darkness because that's what he *wanted*. The light made things more difficult.

Work with what you got.

Out beyond the cracked door he could see gravel. And sandy dirt. A well-traveled drive, but otherwise there wasn't much else to be seen. The road led off into a rank and file of pines. There was an old pickup truck, painted in OD green. No one was in it. Abe pressed his face to the crack and he smelled the smell of the pines and the dirt and gravel and the frosty smell of a cold morning. He listened, but heard nothing. No voices. No rumble of engines. No crunch of footsteps on gravel.

He pushed the door open a little farther.

From deeper in the building, the guard he'd locked up began to pound on the door. The thumping was noticeable from where Abe was standing, but the yelling was muted and probably wouldn't be heard outside the building. Abe didn't have the time to go back and deal with that problem, and "dealing with it" would essentially be killing the man. Abe was on uncertain footing as far as whose allegiances he was toying with at the moment, and he didn't want to stack bodies on himself. The cleaner the getaway, the less pissed they'd be when they came after him, and maybe that would give him the edge. Maybe they would give up. Cut their losses.

He stepped cautiously out of the door, waiting for the shouts of alarm and gunfire.

Outside of the building it was quiet.

Directly across the long, narrow, gravel parking lot, there was another building that appeared to be of identical construction to the one he was stepping out of. They were both cinderblock, painted the same color as the sandy loam all around them. Green metal roofs about the same color as the surrounding pines. He got the sense that this was an out-of-the-way corner of Fort Bragg. Maybe some new addition. Clearly, from the offices upstairs, it had belonged to some aspect of Delta, but to what purpose Abe couldn't figure out. It'd been a while since he was among their ranks. He'd been Project Hometown for years. Clearly they were doing things a little differently.

Keep moving.

Abe stepped out of the building. He ran. He

figured it didn't much matter if he looked guilty at this point. His hair was a tangled mess, and his beard was still matted with his own blood. His clothes were torn and filthy and he had a gun in his hand. Walking calmly across the parking lot wasn't going to fool anyone, if anyone happened to be watching.

The two buildings sitting adjacent to each other were long buildings, as Abe had guessed from running around inside of them. He was facing the broad side of the building now. There were doors on both ends of the broad side, and he was directly across from the one on the far right of the building, close to the pickup truck.

Convenient.

He eyed up the truck, then changed direction and headed for it. Depending on what shape Lucas was in, they might not be able to hoof it out. And if things went bad, he didn't want to be hotwiring the damn truck while under fire. Best to do it now when things were relatively quiet.

Quiet outside. But inside his chest and head it was a panicked riot. His heart was hammering, his lungs pumping. His mind was trying to grasp all the thoughts that he knew should've come easy to him, but were now sluggishly bumbling into each other. He felt weak and unprepared and that he was flying by the seat of his pants, and he hated it to his core.

He gave the truck a quick once-over before looking cautiously around him and then yanking open the door and diving in. No need to hotwire it. The keys were in the ignition. Perfect. He cranked the truck to make sure that it wasn't just defunct machinery. It took a few turns, but the engine caught and rumbled, horribly loud. He killed the engine and plucked the keys out. He didn't want the truck magically disappearing while he was in the middle of springing Lucas.

This is good. This is good. You're thinking clearly. Keep it up.

Leave the backpack in the truck? It would lighten him up. He didn't know if he had the strength to carry Lucas and the pack together, if necessary. But then again, if they had to abandon the truck, they would lose what little supplies they had. He decided to keep it strapped to him. Hopefully Lucas would be able to walk under his own power.

He was worried about his partner. Worried enough to feel it like lead in his gut.

"It's gonna be okay," he whispered to himself, gently easing the truck door shut. "I'm gonna get him out of here and we're gonna be okay. I got this. All day long."

Two guards, the Norseman had told him. Two more guards that were sitting outside of Lucas's cell. Or maybe one was sitting there and the other was roving. Who knew? Certainly not Abe. Once again, he was going to have to just roll in and hope for the best. Momentum. He needed to keep momentum up. Stopping to try and plan things out would only create inertia. And that would be the death of him.

And Lucas, too.

He moved to the door, pistol held firmly in his

strong hand, tucked in close to him. He put his left
hand on the doorknob. *Kill the guards or give them
a chance? Killing would be easier and quicker. Giving them a chance might be better in the long run.*

He yanked open the door before he'd really
come to a decision. He moved through quickly.

A long hallway. Fluorescent lights. Identical to
the one he'd just come from.

He scanned right and saw the end of the
hallway—abandoned.

He scanned left and saw two men, sitting in
chairs, their heads swiveling in his direction.

Curiosity.

Then alarm.

Almost immediately, their hands went to their
guns. These were professional warriors. They did
not need minutes or even seconds to identify a target. They saw Abe and they saw a threat. There
were not going to be any words.

Shoot them shoot them shoot them.

Abe moved laterally as he fired, trying to get off
the X where he'd just been standing, but the hallway was narrow. He focused his fire. The first man
to move came up with a rifle. The second man had
a pistol. The rifle was the bigger threat, and the
man holding it was coming out of his chair and
sinking into a crouch, making himself as small as
possible in the narrow corridor. Abe knew the M9
platform as well as anyone that had ever touched it,
and he watched the sights falling and jumping at
the right moments—one-two, three-four—a double tap, followed by another double tap.

The man with the rifle got off a short burst

before crumpling into a half-split position, his right arm mangled while his left arm grasped the inside of his thigh, close to his crotch, and bright red arterial blood started spurting onto the wall.

Abe's right shoulder hit the wall hard. It pulled his sights off the man with the rifle, but the rifle had clattered to the ground, the man's hands instinctively moving to the wound that would most likely bleed him out.

The other man was standing tall in the middle of the hallway, pistol clear of its holster, centered in his chest, and then punched out. The second that Abe hit the wall, the guard with the pistol fired three times and Abe watched them as they lanced the wall in front of his face, right at eye level, each one closer than the last.

Abe dropped.

The fourth shot split the air above Abe's head as he hit the ground. He would have rolled, but the pack on his back pinned him still. He had made the move without really thinking it through. It was all or nothing now. He'd bought himself a microsecond, and the cost had been his freedom of movement. He needed a good shot...

A little gray puff from the end of the guard's pistol.

Abe's left shoulder exploded.

He fired with his right, but his aim was pulled off.

Something else tugged at his back, but he didn't hear anything now. Not even his own pistol reports. He forced his eyes to stay open, despite the fact that it felt like every muscle in his body wanted to contract itself around that spot in his shoulder, right at the joint. His eyes stayed open and he put his sights on the man, one-handed, with a scream working its way out of his belly.

Two trigger pulls as the air came out of him.

The last guard fell back.

Abe strained to keep his eyes open as he watched the man hit the ground. He watched long enough to see the pistol fall out of the man's hands, his hips bucking as he tried to stay alive. His compatriot with the rifle was lying still, eyes open but blank, staring at nothing. Abe realized he must've hit the man someplace else, possibly in the chest. It was unlikely that he'd bled out that fast.

Abe began to shake.

The pain hit him hard. His eyes slammed shut and he curled up into a ball, trying to keep himself from screaming. What little air he had in his lungs came out in a thin wheezing sound. When he had regained enough control of himself, he glanced at his right shoulder. There wasn't much to see but bloody fabric. But Abe could feel the damage. He could feel the shattered bones of his shoulder grinding together. The muscles sheared.

He felt winded. After the last, quiet scream, it seemed he couldn't draw a full breath.

You need to keep moving!

He rolled off his side, back onto his belly, and began squirming into a sitting position. His left arm was useless for the moment, there only to bring wracking pain into his body that he could feel, like lightning crawling over his skin and through his bone marrow, all the way from his shoulder down to his fingertips and along his spine.

He leaned against the wall for a moment, trying to breathe.

"Oh, fuck…" He stammered. "Oh, *fuck*…it hurts."

He worked his way upright again. His left arm was cradled limply against his body, the strap of his backpack feeling heavier by the second, more like it was made of razor wire now than padded nylon. His right hand still held the pistol. He looked at it, knowing it must be close to empty. He squeezed it between his knees, then pulled the magazine out. It had two rounds left. One more in the chamber.

He thumbed the two rounds out and then dropped the magazine. He fumbled into his pocket for the extra magazine he had with the five rounds in it. It took some maneuvering, but he managed to get the last two 9mm rounds into that magazine, for a total of seven. Plus one. He slammed it into the pistol and took it up again.

He slid along the wall. The passageway seemed dark one second and light the next.

"Stay with it. Stay with it."

He reached the bodies. The guard with the pistol was breathing out his last breaths. Maybe not even really alive anymore. Just the body trying to fight now. Chemical impulses forcing the muscles to move. His eyes were fixed and vacant-looking, unblinking. Tears were still streaming out of them, though.

Abe used his foot to push the pistol out of the man's grasp. He was standing in front of the door now. The one that they had been guarding. He summoned up a little strength and tried to make his voice strong, but failed miserably.

"Lucas! Hey! You in there, buddy?"

There was movement from beyond the door. It sounded like a hand slapping the door. The voice that came from the other side almost sounded as bad as Abe did. "Abe? That you?"

He's alive. He's alive. That's good. That's a start.

Abe was limited to one hand, but the doorknob was a latch, so he just used the muzzle of the pistol to swipe the latch down and push the door inward. He saw a disheveled man with blood and grime covering his face. Short-cropped red hair. Pale, gaunt features. A scraggly, unkempt beard. His partner was crouched on the floor, looking up at him, and for one bad moment it seemed like he was a lame beggar. Abe almost shook his head, certain that there was no way he was going to get them out of there.

Abe stood in the doorway, feeling his knees beginning to shake. The pain was incredible.

"Hey, buddy," he said around short breaths. "Can you walk?"

Lucas pulled himself quickly to his feet. "Oh, Jesus Christ, Abe!" He reached out to touch Abe's arm, but Abe moved back out of instinct to protect his already wounded arm. "You're shot. Are you okay?"

Abe nodded, though he didn't feel okay at all. "I can make it outta here."

"Lemme grab that pack." Lucas peered out of the doorway, assessing the two dead men on the ground. "I'm in better shape than you. I don't think they spent as much time on me as they did you. You look like shit."

Abe waved him off. "No. It's going to hurt like a motherfucker to get it off my arm. Let's just get outta here." Abe pointed to the pistol still lying on the ground. "There. That's for you."

Lucas scooped it up, transitioning smoothly from cowering prisoner to armed operative. He checked the magazine, then the chamber. He did a quick visual inspection of the two dead bodies and relieved them of their pistol magazines, then took the one guard's rifle. He had no spare magazines for it, though. But it still had twenty-some-odd rounds in it.

While Lucas worked quickly, Abe leaned against the wall, listening and looking for signs of trouble. He could feel cold sweat breaking out on his brow, and he still couldn't catch his breath. He was beginning to worry that the angle of the bullet strike had left that little projectile in him somewhere. Maybe had punctured a lung. Maybe that was why he couldn't breathe.

The only thing that seemed to be working in their favor was the fact that this was apparently some little out of the way Delta compound where the others dared not tread. *Detention buildings*, according to the one live guard still sitting in Abe's cell. And maybe there were people in Fort Bragg that didn't like Carl's methods of detaining everyone. Maybe that was why he kept it quiet and guarded by so few men. Or perhaps that was just how many men they had to stand guard. He had mentioned that they were the remnants of the Eighty-Second Airborne and Delta. And Fort Bragg would be a big place to keep secure. Maybe there just wasn't the manpower to have the two detention buildings guarded like a super max prison.

Two per prisoner, Abe thought. Probably would have been sufficient for any other prisoners. But they hadn't realized who they'd taken captive. Perhaps they'd taken him for some inexperienced officer that had been sitting up in an office during war times, staring at satellite images and telling others what to do.

"You ready?" Lucas had the rifle in his hands, the pistol stuck in the front of his waistband, his pockets laden with extra magazines. He held the rifle one-handed while he sidled over and put Abe's arm over his shoulder to help support him.

He's right, Abe thought. *They didn't go after him as hard as they did me*.

"Let's go," Abe said, and they started moving down the hall toward the door. "I got a truck outside. Hopefully it's still there. Not surrounded."

"What if someone pulled the handle and we're surrounded?"

Abe locked his jaw against the pain. "Then they're gonna lose a few more guys."

"Did you get the GPS?"

"Yeah, I got it."

"You got the ball, then, brother." They reached the door and Lucas looked sideways at him. "I'm just here to make a hole for you."

Abe looked at his partner, his only friend through the end of everything he knew, and he felt his throat tighten up. "You should take it. You're in better shape than I am."

Lucas shook his head. "With your shoulder busted you won't even be able to hold the fucking rifle with two hands, bro. You try to hold them off for me, you're just gonna get yourself killed. I can still move and shoot. I can create a hell of a problem for them. Give you some time."

"Fuck." Abe wanted to kick something. "This is only if we're fucked. It's a nonissue if we can get to the truck and get out of here."

"Right." Lucas unhooked his partner's arm from around his shoulder. "You ready?"

"Move."

Lucas pushed open the metal door to the outside. Cold air squeezed in. Bright sunshine again. The sound of engines that hadn't been there before. The crunch of tires on gravel. They had just enough of an angle to see out the door, beyond where the green-painted pickup truck was sitting, down the gravel drive that led into the woods. And coming their way were two more pickup trucks, their beds bristling with men and weapons.

Lucas shut the door.

Abe felt a horrible, sinking feeling.

Lucas didn't waste time on sentiments. "Back door. Now. We need to get in the woods."

Overhead, they heard the roaring of a helicopter.

THREE

CONSEQUENCES

THE FLIGHT FROM CAMP Ryder to Fort Bragg was short. Lee was strapped in with other men carrying rifles and dressed in fatigues. Tomlin was beside him, and on the other side of Tomlin, the sullen man named Carl Gilliard, master sergeant and Delta operator.

When they lifted off, Lee thought it was one of the best things he had felt in a long time—to be aboard a modern piece of military technology. To be ripping over treetops and across roads and small towns that would have taken them hours to clear or circumvent if they were traveling in vehicles.

He might've grinned if he hadn't known who was waiting at the other end of that short flight.

Fucking Abe Darabie. Goddamned backstabber.

The conversation that led to Lee being in the helicopter, roaring toward Fort Bragg, had been short and perfunctory. Tomlin had pulled him up into the office and explained the situation, right there in front of Carl, Staley, Brinly, and Angela. He made no mention of Nate and Devon, and this he seemed to do deliberately. Lee became maddeningly curious about what had happened to them, but all he had was an educated guess: They were hiding somewhere nearby Fort Bragg, in case all of this went south. Lee had the presence of mind not to mention them if Tomlin didn't. He figured there was a reason for it.

Tomlin had known Carl Gilliard from their time together in the Seventy-Fifth Ranger Regiment. Tomlin had gone on to Project Hometown, and Carl had gone on to Delta. The two had not crossed paths in the intervening years, save for a few phone calls and e-mails. But apparently their relationship had been close enough that Carl was willing to take a leap of faith and trust Tomlin after he'd captured him at one of the gates at Fort Bragg. Tomlin had convinced him to meet with Lee and the Camp Ryder leadership to talk of joining forces.

Sometime during the flight from Fort Bragg to Camp Ryder, it had become clear that Carl was in possession of two detainees who were either fleeing from Acting President Briggs or acting on his orders. And when Tomlin learned their names, he'd gone wide-eyed and openmouthed. Then they'd arrived at Camp Ryder and all further discussion had to be put on hold.

"Abe Darabie?" Lee had demanded when he'd learned the news in the office. "You have him in custody?"

Carl had nodded. "And a friend of his, Lucas Wright. Mr. Darabie claims the rank of major and Mr. Wright claims the rank of captain. Is this correct, to your knowledge?"

Lee had nodded, bewildered. "How long have you had them?"

"Six days," Carl said, after a moment's calculation.

Lee's decision was almost instantaneous. "You have to take me to him."

Brinly was the only Marine to accompany them. Staley agreed to remain at Camp Ryder for one more day, but he wanted a liaison to stay in contact with him while Lee was in Fort Bragg sorting things out. Lee had agreed without much debate—Brinly seemed solid, and Lee figured an extra gun couldn't hurt. It had not escaped him that he knew nothing of Carl Gilliard or the man's loyalties. He might profess to be opposed to Acting President Briggs, but the truth was usually more complicated, and Lee did not know whether he was wading into a nest of enemies or a possible alliance.

Dawn broke by the time they made their way out of the Camp Ryder building and the helicopter started spooling up. It was full light when they were halfway to Fort Bragg and the copilot reached back into the cabin and tapped Carl on the shoulder. Lee watched the movements, trying not to look suspicious, but not really being able to help himself. He was suspicious of everybody, and he damn well had a right to be.

When the copilot had Carl's attention, he made a motion that mimed putting a headset on. Carl then grabbed one of the headsets that was hanging just over his shoulder and put them over his ears. He adjusted the microphone so it sat in front of his mouth. Over the thundering rotors and the wash of wind in the open cabin, Lee couldn't hear what he was saying, but he could see his mouth moving.

Then Carl listened.

He leaned forward, his face becoming stony.

He spoke quickly into the microphone again, this time glancing up at Lee.

Something bad. This is something bad.

Lee's hand moved to the grip of his rifle. He shifted, tucking his elbows in. He wasn't sure why he assumed that somebody was planning something treacherous—aside from reoccurring experiences. But if they wanted a goddamned shootout on a helicopter, that was fine. He would punch holes in Carl first, then the pilots. The helicopter would crash and maybe Lee wouldn't make it out. But then again, maybe he would. He'd survived worse.

Lee stuck his jaw out and held Carl's gaze, hoping his thoughts came through clearly: *Motherfucker, I've been shot, stabbed, beaten, bitten, and blown up. What the fuck you think you're gonna do to me that hasn't already been done?*

But after a moment, Carl snatched the headset off and leaned partially across the cabin, yelling just loud enough for Lee to hear him. "Captain Harden! Our two detainees just busted free. They're on the run right now. And they're armed."

"What?!" Lee's hand flew to his head. He swore loudly and started thinking fast. He looked at Tomlin briefly, not sure what expression he would find. Tomlin's face was tight and tense. "Pull your men off of them," Lee shouted. "Drop me and Tomlin. We know them. We'll handle it."

Tomlin shifted uncomfortably.

Carl looked half amused, half irritated. "Not a chance, Captain..."

Lee reached out, wanting to grab Carl by the collar and haul his ass onto the deck of the Black Hawk, but he thought better of it and retracted his hand. "Carl, you don't understand. I need those men alive."

Carl considered it coolly for a moment then shrugged. "I'll put my men on the perimeter. They're not getting out of Fort Bragg." He pointed to Lee. "You can go after them, but if they reach that fence, they're fucking dead. No questions asked."

Lee nodded. "Fine. That works."

Carl put the headset back on and began speaking into the microphone more words that Lee couldn't hear. Lee turned to Tomlin, found his old friend looking at him a little unsurely.

Tomlin raised a single eyebrow. "This personal, or business?"

Lee shook his head. "Everything's fucking personal at this point, Brian."

"You gonna kill him?"

"No." Lee checked his rifle again. "Maybe."

The Black Hawk banked right, then left, and Lee was looking down at the earth, at rows and rows of pine trees crested in green and below that a never-ending carpet of burgundy needles and pale yellow sand. He could see trails cut through the woods. Some of them were foot trails. Others were for vehicles, and he could clearly see tire treads. Then there was a gravel path and a little compound, tucked back into what looked like hundreds of acres of woods. Two plain, long buildings sat there in the clearing and the helicopter began to slow and to sink toward the ground.

There were men on the ground. Dozens of armed men. Three pickup trucks. One was green and looked as if it had been sitting there for a while, all covered in melting frost. The other two were newer, and they were running, and there were men with rifles in the beds and in the cabs. Most of them wore MultiCam pattern fatigues.

Lee looked at Carl, who pointed to the ground and shouted, "This is you, Captain. Do what you need to do. If you catch either of them alive, bring them back to me."

The Black Hawk dropped below the trees, then the roofline of the two long buildings, and then it was hovering over the gravel and then touching down. Tomlin slid out first, and Lee followed quickly. Brinly came out with them, and Lee did not object. He felt that Brinly would likely follow their lead. And Lee knew the training that Abe and Lucas had. No matter what shape they were in, they were more dangerous than any of these people realized.

Then why are you going after them with only three guys? Why not just let Carl's men rake the forest with fire? Why not let the superior force handle this?

Because the superior force probably didn't know what they were up against, though they probably had a better idea now that Abe and Lucas had managed to get free. And because Lee didn't necessarily trust Carl, even if Tomlin did. And because Lee wanted a chance to see Abe face to face.

He pictured Abe as he'd last seen him: Dark complected, with a face that could easily switch between somber and cheerful. Always clean shaven. Always neatly put together. A model soldier. You had to be, if you wanted to be of Middle Eastern descent and still do well in the US military, though Abe was born in the US and was more American than a lot of others who served.

Then Lee pictured what that face would look like when he was finished with him. He didn't intentionally do it, but his mind summoned the images on its own, and now he saw Abe's face in ruins, flattened in places and swollen in others, blue blood bulging beneath the brown skin and red blood spurting across the face and lips.

Why did you do this? Lee thought to a man that was not there. *Why did you force me into this? You did the things you did, and now I have to do the things that I have to do. And everything that came before is reduced to nothing because of this. Because of you. Because of what you did. This is your fault, Abe. Everything I do to you will be your own fucking fault, you backstabbing piece of shit.*

Lee hit the corner of the first building, Tomlin and Brinly close behind. Beyond the building, there was only the pine forests. One of the Delta men was standing at the corner, his rifle at a low ready, peeking out from the corner and into the woods.

"Comin' up on you," Lee said quickly.

The man turned and looked at them. His beard was shorter than most of the other guys. He looked younger, too. He had longish hair, held out of his face by a black bandanna. "Who the fuck are you?" he asked.

"Friends of Carl's," Lee said shortly. "Where'd the two men go?"

The man with the black bandanna gestured into the pine forest. "One of 'em has a rifle. The other one has a pistol. The one with the pistol is hurt pretty bad."

Lee grimaced. His concern wasn't for their well-being. But in addition to the thoughts of vengeance that he could not keep from crawling into his mind, he knew that both Lucas and Abe would have valuable information about Briggs and what his intentions were with Lee and the Camp Ryder Hub. But they had to capture them first, and that was going to be difficult. It was easy to catch a man unawares. It was very difficult to catch him when he knew he was being hunted. And it was even more difficult to interrogate a man with wounds so grievous he knew he was going to die anyway.

Hopefully that's not the case.

Lee looked around the man and into the pine forest. All seemed still. "How long ago did they hit the woods? How far in are they?"

Before the Delta man could respond there was a burst of automatic fire and the ground to Lee's right erupted into particles of dirt. A quick follow-up burst skittered across the metal siding of the building and all four men ducked back around the corner.

The Delta man sank onto his haunches. "About that far."

"Fuck me running," Lee swore, wiping dirt and sand from his face and neck. He turned partially and looked at Tomlin and Brinly. "You two hold them down here. I'm gonna flank on the left."

Tomlin nodded. "We got you."

The Delta man scooted out of the way, recognizing when the fight was somebody else's, and wise enough to remove himself when that seemed to be the case. Lee made for the other side of the building and Tomlin slid into place at the corner, popping out just long enough to return a few potshots into the woods.

Lee hit the other side of the building then hung a sharp right, sprinting along it until he was at the opposite end. Once again, there was nothing but the ubiquitous pines. At the opposite corner, Lee was careful to look out slowly. He could hear the chatter of Tomlin's fire, and the even, steady response of whoever was in the woods.

Holding down a base of fire, Lee was sure of that.

Letting the other one get away.

But who gets away? Abe or Lucas?

Abe gets away. Lee wasn't sure how he knew, but he just knew that it was Abe running and Lucas bedded down, holding them back. But Lucas was running long odds, and he had to know it. Plus, the likelihood of him having a good ammunition store was low. Which meant he would be running dry in just a minute.

Or, if he was smart—and Lee knew that he was—he wasn't going to try for suppressive fire. He was going to give them a few bursts to let them know he was there, to slow their progress and make them careful, and then he was going to lie in wait. He was going to take shots at them as they tried to sneak into position.

When Lee looked around the corner of the building, he could see the little puffs of smoke that came with each rifle report, issuing from a copse of bushes that sat between two close-set pine trees. That was Lucas, he was almost positive.

Lee waited until Tomlin and Brinly were firing again, and then he sank down to his knees. His joints complained like an old man's, but he achieved a stable shooting position. As Tomlin littered the trees indiscriminately with rounds, Lee took long, slow breaths and sighted into the copse of bushes. In the forefront of his mind were the imperatives: *Control your breathing. Good cheek weld. Steady trigger pull, straight to the rear. Take out the base of fire. Advance. Overtake Abe. Capture him.*

But in the back, behind all the conscious thought, there was a soul sickness that he couldn't deny. An utter disgust and the image that went along with it was the image of Abe with his face battered and bloody at the hands of Lee, and with it came the image of Lucas's body, riddled with bullet holes and bleeding from his nose and mouth. These were not enemy combatants. They were not random men from some third-world country that he happened to encounter in the middle of a night, inside of a pitch-black thatch-roofed hovel while they fumbled for their AK-47s.

These had been friends. These were fellow soldiers. These were men that he had known. They'd

shared food and drinks and laughter and cama-
raderie. Project Hometown had chosen them
because none among them had family, none of
them were committed, none of them were tied
down. But they'd become a sort of small family
unto themselves. And this...

This was like killing his brother.

*Not my brothers. Not my friends. Men who wanted
me dead. Men who sent others to kill me.*

*They wanted me dead. They picked the fight. Now
they deal with the consequences of that action.*

Sickening or no, Lee did not pause to think
it over. The decision had already been made. He
had not made it; they had. They had chosen who
they wanted to ally themselves with, and it was not
Lee, and it was not the mission. It was not Project Hometown that they were implementing. They
called him a traitor, as he called them the same,
but in fact it was all just words.

They were enemies.

When he had a good sight picture, and his lungs
fell into their natural respiratory pause, Lee fired.
Four shots, evenly spaced and cold to the bone.
Deliberate. Deadly. He would have no excuses to
assuage his conscience. He gave it no room for
such frivolities.

The bushes shook and trembled.

Lee was moving again. Out from the corner of
the building, out from cover. He shouted, "Crossing! Crossing!" as loud as he could, so that the
others knew not to continue shooting as he moved
into their lanes of fire. He was about seventy-five
yards from the bushes where the shooter had been,

and still advancing. In his peripheral he could see the corner of the building, behind which Tomlin and Brinly had been firing, but he stayed focused on the bushes.

From around the trunk of one of the pines, Lee saw movement.

A man, going into the "urban-prone" position, the muzzle swinging toward Lee.

He could only see the rifle and the top of the man's head. A shock of bright red hair.

Lee dove to the side. Bullets peppered the ground just behind where he'd been standing, a few sizzling past his head as he hit the pine needle carpet and scrambled gracelessly to a tree trunk. Lee gasped for breath, his heart pounding. The air came out of his lungs colored with curses. He glanced to his left, deeper into the forest, hoping to catch a glimpse of Abe on the run, but there was nothing.

Lucas was delaying them more than Lee would have liked.

Tomlin and Brinly were firing again.

Lee rolled partially out of cover so he could see Lucas's hide. Bullets were smacking the wood on the trees, stripping the bark almost completely off the first four feet. They were stout trees, but the bullets would eventually go through. They all knew it, including Lucas. Which meant Lucas would be looking for a way out right about now.

Lee came up to his feet, rifle at the ready, and he began walking laterally, gaining more and more angle on Lucas, and getting closer in the process. Now within twenty-five yards. Tomlin was keeping up a steady suppressive fire on Lucas's hide, keeping the man's head down and letting Lee creep closer and closer.

Movement again.

Lucas peeking out. He saw Lee, and his rifle came up.

But this time Lee was ready for it. Finger already on the trigger. Lee fired once, watched Lucas jerk, but stay on his feet, then fired two more times, and he couldn't tell whether he fired the shots out of anger or necessity. The rifle was already dropping out of Lucas's hands when Lee fired those last two shots. And when the third shot had been fired, Lucas's legs went out from under him and he hit the ground in a heap of limbs.

Lee ran to the body, keeping his rifle trained on it. Conscious of the fact that the man he'd just shot was still moving, might be reaching for a secondary weapon. He could still be a threat. *You should just shoot him again, shoot him now, shoot him for the things that he did...*

Lee reached the man on the ground. It was Lucas, just like Lee had thought it was, though almost unrecognizable except for the bright red hair. His features were sunken and sallow. His eyes were dark and hollow-looking. He had a scraggly, unkempt beard, darker red than the rest of his hair. Almost auburn. Blood was coming out of his mouth and nose. He was struggling to keep his head up, but he was looking at Lee, and his eyes registered shock.

"Lee..." His voice was just a wet croak. "I can't believe you're here." He sounded almost dreamy and Lee got the uncomfortable sense that Lucas thought it was a good thing that Lee was here.

Then some other realization clouded Lucas's face. He looked confused. "You shot me, Lee. Why'd you shoot me?"

Lee could feel his head buzzing unpleasantly. His stomach slip-sliding around like a bowl of live eels. *Shoot him. Shoot him and kill him. He's just going to lie to you. He's just going to confuse the issue.*

Don't. Don't. Something is wrong.

"Where's Abe?" Lee said. He'd meant for it to sound stern, but it came out gentle. There was something roiling around in the back of his mind, something that he didn't typically feel. When you shot a man, there was no redo switch, no way to put the bullets back in your gun. So you found ways to rationalize it. Sometimes it was easier than others. But here and now, for the first time, he felt *terror*. True fear that he had just done something that he should not have done, and could not be taken back.

Lucas glanced into the woods. "He ran that way. He's hurt bad, Lee. He needs help."

"Help?" Lee was incredulous, but it was hollow.

Lucas frowned up at him, his confusion almost childlike. "I don't understand...we came for you."

"To kill me?" Lee said. "On Briggs's orders?"

Lucas seemed to realize something he had not seen before. His head relaxed and he looked skyward, and for a moment, Lee wanted to grasp that silence as an admission of guilt. But Lucas would not even give him that. The man on the ground just coughed, then spat blood. "I don't believe this shit..." His voice sounded far away. "...Not supposed to happen this way..."

Lee knelt down, the terror making him shake. He grabbed Lucas's shoulder. "Lucas. Lucas. C'mon. Stay awake. What are you talking about?" He kept looking down at the two bullet holes, just an inch or so from each other, both punched neatly in the center of Lucas's chest.

Good aim.

Bad shots.

What did I do? Is this right?

This isn't right. This is a mistake.

Lee could hear Tomlin and Brinly running up to his position.

"What are you talking about?" Lee said desperately. "Why'd you come here?"

"To find you," Lucas said, frowning again.

"To kill me..." Lee said again, but knew it wasn't true.

"To help you." Lucas grit his teeth together. "It's about...it's about what's right."

Standing over Lee, Tomlin swore. "Oh fuck, man...Oh, Jesus. Lucas...what the fuck were you thinking?"

Lucas closed his eyes. "Don't let 'em get Abe. He's...he's got something of yours."

Lee felt his throat tightening. He stood up, blinking rapidly as the world blurred and turned quickly away from Tomlin and Brinly. He pointed to Lucas. "Brian, stay with him. Don't let him die."

Too late! It's too late for that!

Lee took off through the woods before Tomlin could respond.

FOUR

TIES

ABE RAN, HEARING THE smattering of gunfire far behind him. Pausing, hesitating, pushing back and forth, like an argument spoken in the tongues of burning propellant, sonic cracks, and copper-jacketed lead punching through trees and dirt.

The running was painful. His hip still felt out of whack—some strained muscle from the electrocutions, he had to assume. But the shoulder...the shoulder felt bad enough to make him curl up in a ball, but he knew he would die if he did that. He kept forcing his unwieldy legs to move, and every time his foot hit the ground, his shoulder threatened to make him faint. He kept telling himself it would go numb eventually, that the pain wouldn't feel so bad, but it didn't. It was getting worse. A slow, harsh, aching pain, and a fast, beating, spiking pain, intertwined with each other.

The forest ahead of him was deep and flat and neverending. But he knew that it ended. It would end in a road, and that road would lead out of Fort Bragg. And maybe they would have the road cordoned off, or maybe not. There was always the possibility that Abe could make it through. Shot shoulder and all, Abe *had* to make it through.

Keeping Project Hometown alive. That's what I'm doing.

The gunfire had stopped.

Abe halted in the forest, stumbling to a stop and leaning his good shoulder against a tree. The breath came out of him in hot, steamy plumes. The momentary respite made the pain in his shoulder cease for all of two or three seconds, and then it was back, worse again. Abe winced and looked back into the forest in the direction he'd just come from.

No more gunfire…

Abe's eyes kept staring into those endless pines, hoping to see Lucas running toward him. Surely he'd just given up his firing position and was backing up to…to…

"C'mon, buddy…" Abe realized his throat was almost clamped shut. The words came out of him choked and stricken. Pain weakened everything about a man. His physical strength, his mental strength, even his emotional strength. And here Abe might have given it more time before he let despair take him, but he was sick and he was beaten and he was in agony. And he knew damn well what the silence in the woods meant.

"No…" He faced into the looming woods, the direction he was supposed to be running, but the energy and the fight were bleeding out of him fast. He looked back toward the sound of silence. "C'mon, man. Fuck you, Lucas. Come the fuck on."

Am I going or am I staying?
Lucas is dead. He died for you. For this.

What Abe really wanted was to fling the backpack off of his shoulders and sit down at the base
of the tree, his wounded arm tucked against his
chest, his good arm gripping a pistol, and wait
there for whatever bastard was on the way to fight
him. His chances of ending the fight with the
rounds that were left in his M9 pistol were probably just as good as his chances of getting out of
Fort Bragg and to Camp Ryder in one piece. What
the fuck was the difference?

"No difference at all," he muttered. "This is all
a goddamned joke."

Still, he turned back into the woods and put one
leg in front of the other. Not running anymore.
Just a slow, painful jog. His wounded arm hung
limp. His good arm, still holding the pistol, was
also clutching his wounded arm, trying to hold it
in place while he jogged, to keep it from flopping
around, to keep the bone fragments from grinding
together. Just the thought of it made him sick.

"Maybe they just took him captive again," Abe
said. But he knew Lucas wasn't going to let that
happen. Lucas would have fought to the very last,
trying to give Abe every second he could to get
away.

That thought spurred Abe's feet to moving
faster. He needed to get out of this fucking shit-
hole. He needed to get out of Fort Bragg. He had
the key to everything, the key to Camp Ryder surviving, the key to Lee Harden being able to save
these southeastern states from total destruction.

The key to Project Hometown. And it was the only way they were going to keep Briggs from consolidating his power and becoming the president of a United States of America that was very different from the country that Abe remembered.

No more moping. No more thinking. You're just acting. You're moving. Just keep moving. That's all. When you encounter an enemy, you will kill him. Otherwise, you will keep moving. Until you reach Camp Ryder. You know how to survive. Just do it. No more thinking.

So he kept going.

The world got dark. In his mind, not in reality. In reality, the sun was climbing, and great beams of bright light were piercing through the canopy of pine needles and illuminating great glowing swatches all across the forest floor. But Abe's body was spent and on the verge of shutdown. He was running on autopilot. The only thing keeping him going was his own will.

His mind was going to other places, way down deep inside of him.

And his sight felt like it was dimming. The edges were dark and shadowed. Only the small space in front of him seemed to be bright. Overly bright, in fact. Everything was stark whites and deep dark blacks. He felt the same now in these woods as he'd felt when he was sitting in the pitch blackness of his cell. It was cold and hot and full of disorienting pain and no concept of when it was going to end so the body just kept going, because that's what it did. It survived.

He lost track of how long he'd been running.

He heard a noise behind him that at first he thought was a hallucination.

Then he turned. Back behind him, a dark figure slid behind a tree, perhaps a hundred yards away. Maybe a little more.

Abe swung his pistol up and cranked off two rounds that he was sure went wide, off into nowhere, but hopefully kept his stalker's head down long enough for him to dive for a tree and get into cover. He hit the ground awkwardly and had to bite his tongue to keep from screaming. He tasted blood.

This is it. This is it right here.

Abe crawled farther behind the trunk of a large pine tree, wriggling his way out of the backpack as he did. He was gasping for air. The world was coalescing. He could hear and feel the rattle in his lungs, and again he hoped the bullet that had entered his shoulder wasn't rattling around in there, poking holes in his lung tissue. He hoped it was just pneumonia.

Interesting, to hope that something was *just* pneumonia.

He put his back against the tree, trying not to cough.

Somewhere back in the woods he could hear the stealthy movement of feet slipping quietly over the pine needles. Pine needles had always been Abe's favorite for practicing woodland movement. They were quiet and soft. Abe remembered stalking through them himself, somewhere in these very woods, when he was in the Operator Training Course. It was a trick, though. The pine needles just deceived you into thinking you were stealthy. It was close to impossible to be stealthy in a deciduous forest, with all the dried, broad leaves sounding the alarm at every step.

Abe tried to get his left arm to work, but it just wouldn't.

One-handed, he ejected the magazine in his pistol and looked at how many rounds he had left.

Not many. That's the official count. Not Fucking Many.

He put the magazine back into the pistol. Felt the click as it seated.

This is it.

More shuffling behind him. How close was it? Less than a hundred yards now, for sure. Maybe closer to fifty yards.

He stuck the pistol out of cover and emptied the magazine into the woods. Then he tossed the gun off to his side. Reached awkwardly around his back and drew out the Colt 1911. He would have eight rounds in this one. He checked the chamber. *Eight plus one.*

In the woods, there was no more shuffling noises.

A voice called out. "Abe? That you?"

Something about the voice was passingly familiar, but not strikingly so. Abe didn't give it a second thought. He gripped the 1911 tight and slipped his finger onto the trigger, making sure the hammer was back and the safety was on. "Just let me go. We don't have to be enemies. I'm leaving and I won't come back. You should have never captured us in the first place."

"Abe, it's Lee. It's me, buddy."

Abe's face twitched, but otherwise he remained very still, as though he had not heard. His mind started to race. He tried to piece things together that just wouldn't fit in any logical way. He realized he was shaking his head. "No. You're not Lee."

He glanced around, suddenly aware that whoever was talking to him might be trying to keep him distracted while the flankers moved up to either side so they could gun him down. Or worse, imprison him again and torture him. But there was no movement and no rustling.

"Look out and see for yourself, Abe. I'm standing out in the open. Don't fucking shoot me."

Trap, it's a trap, just like I knew it was a trap before.

Abe kept looking right and left, waiting to see the movement of a flanker slipping through the trees. And this stupid ploy to get him to look out...

"You want me to look out?" Abe said, hating how his voice reflected his weakening body. "So you can put a bullet through my brain? Fuck you."

Abe leaned left, poking the .45-caliber pistol out from cover and cranking off three rounds. *Save the rest,* he told himself. *You have six more to fight with when it comes down to it. And you will fight. You will go down fighting. With six bullets. Like an old-time cowboy. Six-shooter style.*

His heart was hammering noisily. It sounded almost mechanical in his ears. But he could hear the woods well enough, and they were silent. No response from his three wild shots. No shuffling of feet moving for cover. No yelling or exclamations. Just the sound of the three shots echoing out through the woods and dissipating within a second or so.

Maybe I got him, Abe thought cautiously. *Stranger things have happened.*

Funny, if he'd managed to sling out that unaimed shot that travels thirty yards and strikes someone in the head—there was always stories quietly circulating around Iraq and Afghanistan about some lucky goatherd who cranked off a round from a hip-fired AK-47 from over a hundred yards away and managed to catch some very unlucky GI in the face.

Maybe Abe was that lucky goatherd.

Do I move or sit tight?

If he moved, there was a chance there was someone still waiting for him to pop out and gun him down. But if he stayed still, maybe he was missing a valuable opportunity to run. What if he was that lucky? What if one of those three rounds had managed to punch a hole through his attacker's brain? What if *now* was his chance to run and he was wasting it, sitting there behind cover and ruminating about the best course of action?

Shit, shit, shit…

Very slowly, Abe leaned to his left again, trying to keep his wounded arm from touching the ground. His neck was cranked all the way left and steadily he let an eye break the plane of the tree trunk to see out into the forest.

Brown tree trunks. Rust-colored pine needles. Low, green bushes.

No body lying on the ground. No movement.

Abe realized his mistake a half second too late.

"Drop the gun, Abe," the voice behind him growled.

Whoever it was must've known that Abe wasn't likely to do that.

Abe rolled quick back to his right, holding the pistol in tight, aware that if he extended his arm, the pistol might get stripped from him. But whoever it was had already thought one step ahead and as Abe turned and saw the figure standing over him—a tall man with a grizzled beard and gaunt features, not so different from himself—the man kicked out fast with his boot. Before Abe could even get the pistol on target, the toe of the man's boot caught him on the outside of his forearm, right on the radial nerve. The pain spiked up and down his arm, turning his fingers to rubber, and the pistol tumbled clumsily out of his grip.

Abe snatched for it, but the man was on him quick. He grabbed him by the collar and pushed him onto his back. The man's hand was on his chest, pinning him to the ground. He was holding a pistol of his own, Abe realized, but he also had a rifle slung to his back. Abe made a desperate grab for the man's pistol, but it was tucked in tight and not going anywhere.

The man pulled away from Abe's grab and then smashed a knee into Abe's wounded shoulder. The pain nearly caused him to collapse. He couldn't cry out. He couldn't breathe. He could only lie there, stiff as a board, with his eyes open wide, locked onto the man standing over him. Like he was being electrocuted.

"Stop it!" the man shouted again, and his voice

was desperate. "It's me! It's fucking me! Do you recognize me, Abe? Do you recognize me?"

The coursing pain retracted enough that Abe was capable of some conscious thought. The man standing over him…the tall man with the lean build, like tall men often are. The man with the slightly Southern accent. The man with the placid face and the sharp eyes, though now the face was different. Now it was shrunk of all fatty tissue. Now it was twisted with desperation and anger. Now the eyes were sunken in and there were dark circles under them. Now the face was covered with the beginnings of a wild man's beard. Now the eyes were more than sharp. They were hard. They were cold.

Abe knew this face. He knew it, and he didn't know it. It was a brother and a stranger all at once.

"Lee." Abe's voice came out flat. The single word was almost an accusation, rather than a realization. Because Abe wasn't just recognizing the voice. He was trying to cram that bastard puzzle piece into places it didn't fit and the frustration was growing, along with the realization that no matter where he put the puzzle piece of Lee being right there in front of him, he wouldn't like the image that it created. How was Lee here? How did Lee know where to find him? Why? When?

But most of all, if Lee was standing before him now, then where was Lucas?

Abe's body tightened against the pressure Lee was putting on it to control him.

Lee must have felt it. He pushed back, his face showing strain. And some anger. Lee was making his own calculations, Abe realized. And maybe the things he was computing were not flattering to Abe. Maybe they both wanted to rip the other's head off.

"Where's Lucas?" Abe said, halfway between a whisper and a growl.

Lee's face seemed to tremble. His eyes said it all.

He may have felt Abe's body shifting underneath him, but if he did, he reacted too late. Abe latched onto Lee's arm, holding it tight to his chest while he simultaneously brought both of his legs up. Quick as a snake striking, he had one leg under Lee's pinning arm, and the other up against Lee's neck. Lee tried to pull out of the triangle choke hold, but Abe had sprung it too quick. He ratcheted his legs down, crossing them behind Lee's back, creating an enormous amount of pressure on Lee's neck.

Lee let out a gagging noise and twisted.

Abe rolled onto his right side, thankful that he hadn't rolled onto his wounded shoulder.

Lee didn't try to get out of the triangle. It was locked too tight. But he brought one of his legs up and put the boot against Abe's shoulder, then started hammering it with his heel. Pain brought stars to Abe's eyes, but he stayed clear long enough to see Lee bringing the pistol up, pointing it at Abe's face.

Abe swept out with his hand, seizing the pistol's slide and muzzle and yanking the aim off. At the same time, the pain from Lee's kicks to his shoulder made his legs numb, and all of a sudden Lee was swimming out of the choke hold Abe had put on him.

Abe still had a grip on the pistol. He yanked and wrenched, putting his body into it.

Lee pulled the trigger. The gun fired, but the round went harmlessly into the dirt. Abe's grip on the slide prevented it from cycling. He worked his hip, rolling onto his knees as he did, so that his back was to Lee and Lee's gun arm was wrapped around his waist, and the angle of the pistol was suddenly too sharp for Lee to maintain a grip. The pistol slipped out.

Abe turned, ready to smack Lee in the head with the pistol.

Lee was rolling out of Abe's reach, then sliding for the 1911 that he'd kicked out of Abe's grip.

Abe knew the spent round was still in the chamber and he would have to work the slide manually to get a new cartridge in. He also knew he wouldn't be able to do it with his wounded left arm. He reached behind him, watched Lee slide across the ground, pine needles scattering everywhere. Lee's reaching hand found the grip of the 1911. Abe put the slide of the pistol against the heel of his boot and pushed. The sights caught on his heel, racking the slide back and ejecting the spent round, then slamming a new one into the chamber.

Lee was turning, rolling onto his side, the 1911 in his grip, already getting on target.

Abe knew he was on the defensive now. He threw himself backward, kicking his legs. He felt his back hit the ground, saw the pine tree he'd used for cover looming up over him, felt his right arm brush against the rough bark. There was the clap of a pistol and Abe saw the bark split and splinter.

He scrambled behind the trunk of the tree. But this time he was on his back, the tree at his feet. On the other side, Lee was kneeling on his knees, but neither man could see the other with the tree directly between them. The sudden momentum of the fight was gone. Now it was back to a stalemate. On either side of the tree, the men moved like reflections of each other, though Lee was kneeling and Abe was on his back. They both were pointing their pistols out, scanning back and forth, each waiting for the other man to make the first move and pop up in his sights.

"Where's Lucas?" Abe rasped. It was hard to find air in his lungs enough to talk. "Did you kill him? Did you kill him, Lee?"

There was silence from the other side of the tree. Then the sound of a few deep breaths. The man that was both strange and familiar spoke, and Abe could hear that he was gratifyingly just as out of breath as Abe himself was. "I don't...I don't know if he's still alive, Abe. I shot him. Twice in the chest. He didn't look good."

How did that feel? Abe's mouth opened, but no sound came out. How was this supposed to feel? At first, it was nothing. Like being shot, Abe recalled. At first there was just a tremendous reality that seemed very unreal. Something difficult to accept. But then... *Oh, there it is. There's how it's supposed to feel.* Like something cold and sharp in your guts.

Abe choked. Coughed. "God damn it, Lee... you sonofabitch..."

Lee's voice sounded far away. "I didn't want to. He was shooting at me. What the fuck was I supposed to do, Abe? What would you have done?"

Abe's teeth were grinding together.

"Why'd you send the men to kill me, Abe?" Lee's voice went from faint to full of anger and resentment. "As long as we're airing grievances, why don't you tell me about that shit? You tried to have me fucking killed, you piece of shit! Then you come in here, for God knows what reason, and you expect me to welcome you with open arms? What the hell were you thinking?"

"It wasn't me!" Abe barked back. "It was...it was..."

He wanted to blame it on Briggs. Place the blame squarely onto the acting president and his lapdog, Colonel Lineberger. But they hadn't forced Abe to do it. He had objected, of course, but they had cited Lee as a *nonviable asset*, and technically he was. And no matter how wrong it felt, Abe had toed the line like a good soldier.

"You broke the rules," Abe said lamely.

"The rules?" Lee sounded on the verge of insane laughter. "The fucking *rules*? Oh man, Abe. Where the fuck have you been for the last four months?" Now he did laugh. A bitter sound. "You want to talk about rules? How about common fucking decency? How about ethics? How about morals? How about not leaving the entire eastern seaboard to die while you huddle your resources out in the fucking Rockies?" Invisible behind the tree, Lee made a tired, raspberry sound. "Rules. Listen to yourself. Trying to tell me you wanted me killed over a set of goddamned rules. What about rescue? What about rebuild? What about those rules, huh? *Subvenire refectus*? You remember that, Abe? I followed *those* rules. But those weren't the rules that Briggs wanted me to follow, so you sent men to kill me. Well I fucking killed them all and now you come knocking. You tell me what the fuck I'm supposed to think. I didn't want to kill Lucas. I don't want to kill you. But you keep putting me in these fucking situations, Abe. You keep forcing my hand. And I'm tired, man. I'm so, so tired. You don't know. You just don't fucking know."

"Abe..." This was a new voice from off to Abe's left, and behind him.

Abe twisted to look. About fifteen yards away, he could see the figure behind a tree; the only things protruding were the rifle that was aimed right at Abe and the side of the man's face who held it. But the voice was distinct, floating through Abe's recent memory, and the eyes were in his memories as one of the men he had sent and never heard from again.

"Brian?" Abe said in one heavy breath. "Is that you?"

A slight nod. Very calmly: "Why don't we stop pointing guns at each other?"

Abe's head was swimming. He glanced down at his shoulder, at his side. It was a magnificent amount of blood he'd lost. Surprising that he was still up and talking. Even now the whole left side of his body was soaked in blood. It coated the surface of the pine needle carpet underneath him.

And that wasn't counting what had dripped off of him while he was running.

Abe looked back toward the pine tree that stood as the only barrier between him and Lee. "I thought you were dead, Brian. I thought he killed you."

"No. We worked things out," Tomlin said from his position of cover.

"I..." Abe blinked rapidly. His scalp felt hot. His extremities cold. *That's not good*, he thought.

Lee's voice. "Why are you here, Abe? You tell me that. You tell it true and don't try to fucking lie to me. Then we'll talk. You lie to me and I'm going to kill you. No questions asked."

Abe felt his lungs getting heavy, and it was hard to draw enough oxygen from the air. His vision was down to little pinpoints in front of him. He could barely even feel the pistol in his grip anymore, and he could see it wavering. He was on the verge of passing out. *I lost too much blood. Too much. Too much blood. I'm going to pass out, and then they're going to kill me. I can't believe that Lucas is dead. And now they're going to kill me. I'll be dead. This is the last thing I will see. Fucking pine trees in Fort Bragg. God damn it.*

He laid his head back and looked up. Above him the sky was clear blue.

"I...uh...I brought your GPS back."

Then he groaned and collapsed.

FIVE

ALLIES

LEE HESITATED, CROUCHED A yard or so on the other side of the tree from Abe. He heard the words, then the groaning sound of someone losing consciousness, and then silence. He leaned to his right, so he could see around the tree, but all he could see was Tomlin, standing in cover several yards away, rifle still trained in the direction of Abe.

Lee scrambled to his feet and pied the edge of the tree quickly. He could see Abe's form lying on the ground. It was moving. More twitching, actually. In that way that people do when their mind has disconnected from their body for a moment. It was difficult to fake that. But he wasn't putting anything past Abe at this point. He wanted to trust someone that he had considered his friend, but that ship had sailed a long time ago. And Lee knew better than to trust.

He closed the distance, still pointing the pistol at Abe. The same pistol that he'd knocked from the man's hands only moments ago. His pace quickened as he got closer, and when he was within a few feet of him he kicked the pistol out of Abe's limp hand and sent it skittering across the forest floor.

Abe remained on the ground, his eyes wiggling weirdly underneath his eyelids. Chest hitching up and down in an unnatural rhythm.

Tomlin emerged from his spot of cover. "He's gonna bleed out."

Lee stared down at his old friend across the tops of his pistol sights. One pull of the trigger would end it all right now. And even if he didn't do anything, Abe's blood pressure was clearly dipping to dangerous levels. Already his dark complexion was turning to an ashen color and the blood was standing out in stark contrast. Lee didn't have to pull the trigger. He just had to sit there and let it happen.

"Lee...we gotta do something."

"Why?" Lee looked at his partner. Another friend. One that he had believed betrayed him, but had proved himself a friend. Did Abe deserve the same consideration? In the case of Tomlin, he'd been sent along with other teams to try and assassinate Lee. But he'd never tried himself. He made himself known and he suffered through Lee's interrogations and he proved himself to be a friend.

Abe, on the other hand, had actively tried to kill Lee. And that was a very different animal.

"What about your GPS?" Tomlin said quickly. He pointed to the base of the tree where the fight had occurred. "Check in his bag."

Lee looked at the bag and hesitated for a moment. Should he rush? Should he look for proof? Did it matter in the end? But he couldn't help himself. He needed to know the truth. But he also realized that he didn't want to find the GPS. He didn't want to prove Abe and Lucas right. Because he'd killed Lucas, and Abe was dying in front of him. And the weight of all of that was a terrible thing.

He moved to the bag that lay tossed against the tree. He yanked it off the ground and unzipped the main compartment, then upended it so the contents went spilling out onto the ground. He shook the bag a few times to make sure the main compartment was empty, and when he did, a familiar piece of disassembled electronics came tumbling out.

Lee dropped the bag, almost shocked to see the GPS device lying on the ground at his feet, the power unit disconnected and hanging. But it was there. It was not destroyed. It was not in Briggs's hands. It was not halfway across the country. It was right there in front of him.

Unless it was a trick.

Unless this was a different GPS device.

"He needs help," Tomlin said, his voice urgent.

Lee looked back at the fast-fading figure of Abe. He reached down swiftly and snatched up the GPS device. "If it works, we'll save him."

Anger flashed across Tomlin's face. "He brought it to you! We can always tinker with it later!"

"It's no good to me if it doesn't work!" Lee shouted. "How do I even know it's mine?"

Tomlin balled his fists and knelt down at Abe's side. "He's gonna die, Lee. You don't want that.

If we turn it on and it's not your GPS, you have my full backing to execute Abe. But right now all we know is that he risked his life for this shit. Save him now and we'll figure it out later."

Lee stood there thinking, *Maybe I do want it. Maybe that's exactly what I want. People have died because of the decisions that Abe made. Good people. My people. The people I'm supposed to protect. Can you absolve all of that by bringing me the fucking GPS?*

Tomlin turned Abe over, inspecting the heavily bleeding wound in his left shoulder. Then he looked up. "Lee! Let's fucking go!"

Lee stuffed the GPS into his cargo pocket, still in pieces. He made sure that his pocket was closed and buttoned. He felt like he was carrying something precious. Like he had just tossed a priceless diamond into his pants pocket. It didn't seem like it was enough. He wanted to put it in a guarded vault. Having it again only refreshed the nightmare of possibly losing it.

When it was secure in his pocket, he pointed at Abe. "Cut those clothes away. Find the wound. We'll need to stabilize before we move him out of here." Then he stooped and began snatching up a few medical supplies he'd seen fall out of the pack. Some gauze, some bandages, some medical tape. That was as good a wound treatment as Abe was going to get right now.

And if his words didn't turn out to be the sparkling, golden truth, Lee was going to finish what was started.

When they had his wound wrapped up, they

hauled Abe's limp body out toward the edge of the woods where they could see the two tan buildings rising up out of the forest. A hundred yards inside the edge of the pine trees, Lee could see men gathered around where he'd left Lucas's body. As Lee and Tomlin came into sight, both huffing and chuffing as they struggled with their unwieldy burden, two of the soldiers broke off from the huddle and ran to help them the rest of the way.

At the tree, Lucas's body lay staring blankly at the sky, his skin even paler than usual and bloodless. Lax in only the way that a dead man's face can be. And Lee tried not to feel the hard heaviness of that death, but it found a way into his chest anyway, like it was constricting his rib cage. An invisible pressure.

I couldn't help what happened. He forced me into it. He forced my hand.

But I still feel…unjustified.

A medic was there, or at least someone that filled that role. He was putting his instruments back into his pack, clearly having done what he could for Lucas. Brinly was also there, along with Carl and a few others that Lee did not recognize.

Lee and Tomlin set Abe down in front of the medic.

"He's still alive, but fading," Tomlin said, breathing hard. "He's lost a lot of blood. Gunshot wound in the shoulder. I think it may have clipped the axillary."

The medic gave Abe a quick looking over, pulling Lee and Tomlin's impromptu bandage work away to inspect the entry wound to the top of the shoulder. He shook his head. "Maybe. But I think if he'd clipped the axillary he wouldn't have gotten that far. Still...no exit wound. Could be in his chest. He might have internal bleeding as well." He looked up at Carl as he pressed his fingers in for a pulse. "He doesn't look great. He's gonna need to get to the infirmary or he's fucked."

Carl looked down at Abe and Lee could sense the coldness in his gaze. Then he looked up at Lee. "Three of my guys are dead. What the fuck am I supposed to do about that?"

Tomlin raised his hand. "Carl, we don't have time for this right now."

Carl looked at him. "Explain to me why he deserves to live."

Tomlin licked his lips. "If it were you sitting in one of those detention cells, what would you have done? Would you sit there, Carl? Would you sit and wait to find out what was going to happen? Or would you try to escape? Wouldn't you kill your captors? Isn't that what we're supposed to do if we get the chance?"

Carl scratched at the bald spot on top of his head, looking down at Abe's body with a grimace.

"Get him help," Lee said quietly. "They risked their lives to bring me something. If it is what I think it is...it could be well worth it."

"Worth three of my men's lives?" Carl asked.

Lee nodded without hesitation. "Worth enough to keep the rest of us alive."

Another moment's thought. On the ground, Abe started to make an unpleasant breathing noise. The medic looked up at Carl. He probably didn't care whether or not Abe lived, but he knew that if the decision was made to keep him alive, then they would need to do something immediately.

"Fine." Carl nodded. "Get him to the infirmary." Four men stepped forward, each grabbing a limb and lifting Abe up smoothly, jogging for one of the pickup trucks. Carl started walking, but looked over his shoulder at Lee. "I need a better explanation, though."

Lee pointed for the helicopter. "I'll explain on the way back to Camp Ryder."

"That your way of asking for a ride?"

Lee stopped and looked at Carl. "You got a fucking bone to pick, that's just fine. Pick away. But I ain't got time for dick measuring right now. We're either on the same team and working to survive, or we all might as well lay back and enjoy the last week we got until we're completely overrun. You want to survive? You want your people to survive? I know I do. I know I have people counting on me, just like you have them counting on you, just like Colonel Staley and Brinly have people counting on them. You wanna be a part of the team or should we end this relationship right now?"

Carl clearly didn't like the tone, but he was smart enough to hear the words. He glanced at Tomlin, a look that said, *We might be friends, but I'm not sure about this guy you brought me to.* But eventually he nodded and started walking for the helicopter again. "Your point is made, Captain. Let's get going, if it's that goddamned urgent."

"It is," Lee assured him. "I promise you it is."

* * *

Nate and Devon pulled up to the gates of Camp Ryder at nine o'clock in the morning. They'd left their hiding place in the woods just outside of Fort Bragg several hours earlier, making their way to the pickup truck that they'd stashed among all the other abandoned vehicles and pulling quickly out onto the road. They had hiked in complete silence, grim expressions on their faces. Then in the pickup truck, the only sound was that of the engine roaring. Nate drove, and Devon rode shotgun with his rifle out the window, as usual. Nate knew the way home, and neither needed to stop and converse about how they were going to get there.

When they pulled up to the gate, they noticed the big tan vehicles that could only be military but were of a make that neither Nate nor Devon was familiar with. The second that Nate saw the vehicles, he slammed on the brakes, fear shooting up his spine, ready for an ambush, for the bullets to start flying. He shoved the truck's shifter into reverse, and almost slung gravel to put distance between him and the camp, but one of the guards that he knew opened the gate partially and waved.

Nate opened his mouth, but remained silent.

Devon had his rifle ready, finger already on the trigger. He spoke the first words of the day: "You think it's safe? Big fucking vehicle. Never seen that before. Maybe they came in and took over."

Nate closed his mouth, causing his teeth to clack. He put the shifter back in drive. "Well..." He eased forward, letting the transmission trundle them slowly toward the gate. "Keep an eye out and be ready. You see something up, we'll make like rabbits."

As he spoke, he scanned all around. Looking for the snipers. For the men about to spring the ambush. For the wires that led to the claymores that would blow their doors off and punch steel balls through their bodies. But everything seemed normal. The man at the gate kept waving them forward.

By the time the gate was fully open and they were rolling—still cautiously—into Camp Ryder, a few people had gathered to see who the new arrival was. One of the new guards, Brett, saw that it was Nate and Devon and ran back inside the Camp Ryder building, returning a moment later with Angela.

Nate and Devon met her in the middle, their rifles hanging dejected in their hands. Nate noticed that Lee's dog, Deuce, was tagging along beside Angela.

"We lost Tomlin," Nate said in a low tone. "He tried to make contact, but whoever is running shit at Fort Bragg took him and he didn't come back out again. He told us to wait a little while and if he didn't come back for us, to return to Camp Ryder. So here we are." He glanced down at the dog standing beside Angela and frowned, seeming to notice the dog for the first time. "Where's Lee?"

Angela looked at them with slight amusement in her eyes. "Yeah, Lee's in Fort Bragg right now. Flew out at first light. He's with Tomlin."

Nate and Devon looked at each other, extremely confused.

"Why's Deuce still here?"

Angela shrugged and looked down at the dog, touching the top of his head. "Apparently Deuce is not a big fan of helicopters. He's been splitting his time between running the fence line and helping me watch Sam and Abby." She looked up and then motioned for the Camp Ryder building. "Come on. I'll fill you in while we walk. I've got to see to Jenny. She's taken on a nasty fever right now." She gave Nate a sidelong glance. "Might need you guys to find me some medication if we can figure what's wrong with her."

"Probably the pneumonia that's going around," Devon said offhandedly. "So what the hell is going on?"

Angela brought them up to speed as they climbed the steps to the building and shoved their way into the doors. The interior was crowded with strangers. Nate almost froze in the doorway, he was so shocked to see that many people hanging around. Angela had to backtrack and explain that as well.

"Jesus Christ," Nate griped. "I'm gone for forty-eight hours and everything's different."

The interior of Camp Ryder was a mess of tables and chairs and circles of people sitting on bed-rolls and milling about, finishing late breakfasts or scrounging up something to cook for lunch. People that he didn't recognize. People with hard faces and ragged clothes, worse off than many other groups of survivors Nate had seen. There was also a sense of unpleasantness to them, some-thing just below the surface, and Nate gathered from what Angela told him that there had been a minor run-in with this group, and then an uneasy truce.

Angela stopped at the stairs, looking up them toward the office. When Nate stood beside her, he saw three men descending the stairs. All three were in uniform. One was old, and the other two were young. They were moving with some urgency in their step, but not quite running.

As they hit the bottom of the stairs Angela gestured to the older man. Nate knew little of military ranks but it seemed like this man was the one in charge. "Nate, this is Colonel Staley and the Marines I told you about."

The older man named Staley gave Nate a curt nod, then turned his attention to Angela. "First Sergeant Brinly just contacted me. Captain Harden and the others are on their way back as we speak, probably within an hour or so. We're leaving immediately for Lejeune."

Angela glanced between the Marines, concerned. "What's wrong?"

"Nothing, actually." Staley gave a small smile. "It seems like your Captain Harden has a plan to get us out of this shit storm." He waved his hand dismissively. "I'm sure he'll fill you in."

Angela eyed the other man. "I'm sure he will. Travel safe."

Staley nodded. "Always."

And then he and his Marines were walking on, heading for the doors to the Camp Ryder building. Angela and Nate and Devon watched them go, their expressions matching.

"A little rude, isn't he?" Devon asked.

Angela shrugged. "Beggars can't be choosers," she said. "If he's willing to lend a helping hand, then I won't turn him away because he's a little rude."

"What was he talking about?" Nate asked.

Angela started walking again. "I'm not privy. I suppose we'll find out when Lee gets here."

She answered other questions and filled in small gaps from the last two days that Nate and Devon had missed. As she talked, they made their way through the crowd of strangers and into the back of the Camp Ryder building. Finally they came to a blanket that had been laid out and obviously tossed around, but was now sitting empty.

Angela approached it with her hands lifted in question. "Where the hell did Jenny go?"

Nate eyed the blankets. "Maybe she's feeling better."

Angela didn't seem so sure. "Yeah. Maybe she is."

Jenny sat in darkness. She had some faraway concept of where she was. She'd been in the place with the people and the stink of them had been both incredibly interesting and incredibly suffocating. The feeling of sickness was beginning to go away, but in its place was rising another feeling. Something very different. Something different from anything she'd felt before.

The world was becoming strange. All her life it seemed that language had tied everything together. Her thoughts came to her in words and phrases. Things were identified by their English names. Now it seemed that nothing had a name.

Words were becoming soft and pliable and diffi-cult to grasp. People were no longer people. They were colors and shapes and smells. The gravel in front of the Camp Ryder building was no longer gravel; it was the hard, painful stuff that smelled of stone.

Still, there were little spots and moments of clarity that came through to her.

Inside the place with all of the people, sitting on the soft thing...the soft thing...the thing she couldn't remember the name of, it had suddenly occurred to her that the strange feeling she had, the one that she had never felt before in her life, was the desire to kill something. There was no simpler way to put it, and those were the words that came to her in that small moment of clarity, though they soon dissolved. And then the same concept rolled through her head, but instead of words, it was understood in the image of her chasing something, the thought of how it would feel between her jaws, the taste of blood, the feel-ing of its pulse. Some primal connection that she shouldn't have had.

The dark place where she now sat was...was...

Rust blood sharp painful cold hard.

Hard. Metal. Steel.

Dark. Dark. Grease and dark. The place where the rolling beasts sleep.

Garage, she thought, but it didn't seem right. It smelled like a garage, but that was not where she was. A small space. Not open like the woods and the fields. Confined like a building. Like a small building. *Cage. No, not cage. Box. Metal box.*

She saw faces that she knew but had no names. She could see them running from her. They stank like fear in her fevered imaginings. Their fear made her heart race. But she was not afraid. Not afraid of anything. She chased them in her mind. Felt the feeling of them trying to get away. They were people. And they were animals. It made no difference. She wanted to catch something and rip its life out.

Not you. Sanity like a flickering lightbulb. *This is not you. You are not an animal. You don't want that. You are in the box with all the metal parts because you need to stay there until you can control yourself. Can you control yourself?*

I can't control myself.

It's not me.

It's just IT.

I can't control IT.

I don't want this.

I don't want this.

"Ah doh wan' dis." She was terrified of her own voice. The words were thick, her tongue unwieldy. She began to weep, curling into a little ball, closed up inside the shipping container with all the spare engine parts. The same place that Captain Tomlin had been held. The same place that Angela had been held. The place where Jenny was holding herself. But she could not lock herself in. If she wanted out, she would get out.

She cried for a time, desperately sobbing. In her brain, a tiny organism was eating away her memories and her thoughts and every part of her that made her who she was, and it was leaving very little behind. But she could remember Gregg, and though it made no sense to her fast-fading consciousness, the feeling that rose in her when Gregg's face flashed before her eyes was one of intense desire. And then she saw Lee's face, saw an image of him, scrambling through the dirt with Gregg, biting at Gregg like an animal and eventually taking the life out of him. Killing Gregg. And the feeling that was left was one of barrenness and bitterness and anger. Lee was an animal, and she was becoming an animal just like him.

She was becoming an animal.

SIX

COORDINATING

FOR ONCE, LEE LET himself feel hope. It was a cautious hope. A bridge made of old, frayed ropes that had proven itself untrustworthy in the past. But as Carl's Black Hawk lifted off from Fort Bragg and Lee pulled the disassembled GPS out of his pocket, he wanted it to work so badly that he thought it might just happen. With the bird in the air, roaring toward Camp Ryder, Lee's sense of urgency was growing right along with his hope that things would work out.

He reconnected the device's wires to the battery pack, and then seated the whole power assembly back into the guts of the device. He snapped the cover back on. Then he turned the screen to face him.

Tomlin huddled close, looking over his shoulder.

Across from them sat Brinly, Carl, and two of the Fort Bragg soldiers.

Lee glanced up, a little nervously. "Moment of truth," he said, but knew he was barely audible over the sound of the rotors.

Then he pressed the power button and waited.

The dark screen flashed, then blinked, then glowed mutedly. A status bar crept across the screen.

Lee's pulse was hammering. *It works. It actually still works. I can't fucking believe it.*

Still, he held back rejoicing just yet.

The status bar reached the other side of the screen and an image of a map sprang to life in full, vivid colors, and it was a map of North Carolina. A window popped up, partially covering the map, asking for a password in order to access the application. Lee typed in his password and pressed Enter.

The screen went black.

Lee almost screamed.

But then the map came back again, this time without the password prompt to block it, and at the top of the screen were the words, *WELCOME, CAPT. HARDEN.*

He breathed and grinned. The smile stretched his face in a way he wasn't used to. It'd been so long since he'd smiled so fully and so genuinely. He looked at Tomlin, who was grinning just as foolishly as Lee, and then he looked across to Carl and Brinly.

"We're in business!" he shouted loud enough this time for them to hear.

For the remainder of the short flight, Lee donned a set of the headphones that Carl offered him and explained in detail everything that had led them up to this point. Carl remained stoic when Lee explained Project Hometown, though his eyebrows had twitched up just slightly. He seemed to look at Lee and Tomlin with more intense focus, as though he had just realized that he should take them seriously. He didn't seem at all surprised when Lee explained how President Briggs and Major Abe Darabie had sent men to kill him, to prevent him from using the bunkers. He did, however, seem very surprised to learn about the infected hordes coming out of the northeastern states.

"And you have a plan to deal with this?" Carl's voice came over the headphones with a tinny, electronic quality.

Lee nodded. "Yes, we do. If we can get rolling on it immediately."

"Time sensitive?"

"Extremely."

As they came into view of Camp Ryder and started to slow, the rush of positivity that had overcome Lee was tempered by the realism of the situation. Getting the GPS back was a big step in the right direction and made him feel like he was getting control of things, but in reality, he was still behind the ball. A lot of men had already died, and their deaths would only be worth it if Lee could pull this off. Not to mention the lives that depended on it. The people of Camp Ryder that *knew* their lives depended on Lee being smart and quick, as well as hundreds if not thousands of others strewn across the state that knew nothing of Lee and the Camp Ryder Hub, but would be wiped out nonetheless if Lee's plan to stop the hordes failed.

And there was Abe. And Lucas. One dead, the other lying in an infirmary somewhere in Fort Bragg, close to dead, if he was not already there.

They were both where they were at Lee's hand. He had fired the shots. He had chased them down. He had been so damned convinced that they were the enemy.

Is that where I'm at now? he thought, feeling the positivity bleed away. *I can't tell the difference between friends and enemies?*

Tomlin put a hand on his shoulder. Lee turned to look at him. He must've known what Lee was thinking, must have seen the elation fade from Lee's face. He shook his head slowly. "There was nothing you could have done about that, Lee. It's a shitty situation. No other way around it. No way you could have made it turn out different."

Lee looked down at his hands. They were filthy. Bloody.

"Focus on what you have to do right now. You can have your regrets later."

Lee nodded. *He's right. Regrets later.*

They landed at Camp Ryder amid a crowd of people that shuffled in close and then realized how big the helicopter truly was and decided to give it a wider berth. The pilot set the Black Hawk down in almost the exact same spot he'd arrived in earlier that morning—right in the middle of the Square.

Before the bird settled onto its tires, Lee was already out.

Nate and Devon shouldered through the crowd first. Both looked concerned, perhaps slightly irritated. They were looking over Lee's shoulder at Tomlin. Nate raised his hands in a *what the hell?* gesture. Tomlin smiled and took Nate by the shoulders.

"Sorry, gents. It was for your own safety."

Nate rolled his eyes. "Oh, Lord..."

Lee grabbed Devon as he walked. "Get Angela. And Old Man Hughes. And Brett. I need all the leaders up in the office, immediately."

"Okay." Devon nodded quickly and took off running to find them.

Five minutes later they were packed into the office-turned-war-room. They encircled the small desk, on which the big map of North Carolina had been laid. Lee, Tomlin, Angela, Old Man Hughes, Brett, Marie, Carl, and Brinly. Even Mac and Georgia were there. Nate and Devon hovered near the door, unsure whether they were a part of this meeting or not.

Lee waved them in. "Come in and shut the door. You're a part of this."

They exchanged a glance, then slipped in and shut the door. They made their way to the desk, directly across from where Lee was standing, and they pressed into the narrow spot between Brinly and Carl so that they could see the map that everyone else was looking at. That, and Lee, who everyone could tell was moving with some urgency and impatience. Everyone was accustomed to Lee being intense, but even in that focus, he had a laid-back way of operating. It was clear now that time was of the essence, and the urgency was contagious through the group. They were listening.

Lee looked to Brinly first. "Did you pass the word along?"

Brinly nodded once. "Colonel Staley's on his way back to Camp Lejeune as we speak. Birds should be in the air soon." He pointed to two points on the map. One was the bridge over the Roanoke River where Wilson and his group had been overrun. The other was the town of Eden. "These are the two known collapse points, correct?"

Lee bobbed his head. "That we know of."

"Right. So that's where we're gonna start." He drew two quick lines on the map. "First sorties will begin from these two points and start blowing bridges, moving toward each other until they meet up in the middle."

"Good. What's the ETA on that?"

"Until all the bridges are blown?" Brinly shrugged. "I'd say within twenty-four hours, if we run sorties constantly."

"Okay." Lee touched his lip with the tip of his finger, staring at the map. "Okay. Okay."

Carl looked somewhat dubious. "How exactly are my guys fitting into this?"

Lee met his gaze. "What's your fuel situation?" he asked. "Aviation fuel, specifically."

Carl tilted his head. "Enough."

Lee smiled. "Enough's enough." He pointed to a black dot in the eastern section of North Carolina, near to the coast and south of the Roanoke River. It had been drawn there in marker. "This is bunker number three. I've got two more in eastern North Carolina, but this one is closest to Camp Lejeune." Lee looked at the only Marine in the room. "Now, First Sergeant Brinly, if Carl can get me flown out to bunker three, can you get one of your Chinooks to meet me there to pick up the guns and ammo?"

Before Brinly could answer, Carl held up a hand. "Why am I using my fuel to fly you out there? If the Marines have birds, why aren't they flying you out there?"

Lee looked briefly exasperated. "Because they barely have enough fuel to blow all the bridges along the Roanoke. I need you and your birds and your fuel to get me there. I need to get the guns and ammo to the Marines. Once they have the guns and ammo, they'll be able to run their artillery pieces out of Camp Lejeune and get them to a point where we can use them."

Carl frowned. "For . . . ?"

"I'm getting to that." Lee pointed at Brinly. "Can you get a Chinook to me?"

"If you can get yourself out there, I can get a Chinook to pick up the supplies. But that is literally going to bleed us dry." Brinly looked pained. "We'll have virtually no air power after that."

Lee nodded. "I know. I know. But I don't see another way to get those guns and ammo to your men in the time frame we need." He didn't wait too long for Brinly to agree. Lee was on a roll, and Brinly knew that his crew had to make some sacrifices here. They were all making sacrifices, because they all understood the gravity of the situation.

Lee looked at Nate and Devon. The two men stared back intensely. "I know you two guys have been run pretty hard, but that's what you get for being so damn reliable." Lee earned himself a smirk from Nate and a grin from Devon. "I've got a job for you guys. And it's not gonna be nice."

Lee planted his two index fingers on the two

points that he had already indicated where the infected hordes had made it across the Roanoke River. "These two hordes are moving south. I don't know how big they are, but from the little information we could get I would estimate... big. They are going to follow lines of drift—the easiest path possible. This means roadways, fields, flatland, wherever it's most convenient to put one step in front of the other. And then they're gonna start to spread out through North Carolina. And I don't think anybody at this table wants to see that happen."

No one did.

Lee continued. "The only way they will divert from just following the path of least resistance will be if they have their eyes on something. And the only way this plan is going to work and we can stop the advance of these hordes is going to be if we can draw them into one area."

Nate made a quiet hissing sound through his teeth. "You want us to lure them."

It was insane. Lee knew it. And dangerous. There was no denying. But it made sense, if you could get past how uncomfortable it made you to dangle your own limbs out as bait. Lee smiled grimly. "Like an Old West cattle drive, my friend. Except they won't be running from you—they'll be running *for* you."

Nate took a few more breaths. Finally he nodded as he stared at the map. "Okay. We can do that."

"We can?" Devon didn't seem so sure. But Nate gave him a stern look, and he just stood up straight and accepted it. "We can. We can do it."

"Good." Lee looked at Old Man Hughes. "I need two more. Nate and Devon will be drawing in this horde"—Lee indicated the one that had overrun Eden—"which we will just call 'the western horde' for now. I'm going to need two more men to draw in the eastern horde."

Old Man Hughes nodded. "I can get you two men, that's not a problem. But how is this gonna work? We just gonna ride out there and try to get them to follow us?"

Lee nodded plainly. "Yes. That's exactly it. Two men in a pickup truck. One driving, one in the bed. From what I can tell, these hordes operate off of a fairly herdlike mentality. If you can get one or two chasing you, the rest of the horde is coming along for the ride. All we need is for one of the guys to stay visible. I feel like if they can see us, we've got a better chance of them running after us. Then we just drive them in."

Old Man Hughes looked at the map. "Drive them into where? And why?"

Lee spread his palms around the area of the map north of Camp Ryder and south of the Raleigh-Durham area. "The plan is to have them converge into one single area. One single horde. We need a relatively open area. But it needs to have a point of high, defensible ground where a small element can stay in view of the infected but not be in danger of getting overrun. It also needs to be pretty much between the two hordes so that they can meet in the middle at the same approximate time. And also be away from Camp Ryder enough that we're not catching the outer rim of the horde."

Mac had been growing increasingly fidgety as Lee spoke, his face clouding with every second. Finally, he seemed to burst. "Excuse me. Why the fuck are we luring them anywhere near us? Why aren't we luring them off? Out of the way? Over to a different area? Putting two huge hordes together to make one even bigger horde?" Mac was shaking his head vehemently. "That seems like a horrible idea."

Lee exercised patience. He took a moment to tone down his response. "You know how we cleared the towns we hold now, Mac?"

Mac sniffed loudly, insolently. "How?"

"We figured out that the hordes inside the cities liked to bed down at night when the temperature got cooler. So we'd sneak into town in the middle of the night. And we'd pick a point in the town where we could sit on a rooftop and look down on a big, open area, like a large intersection, or a four-lane street or something. Then we'd line that street with claymores and explosives. And then right before dawn, we'd take a bag full of deer guts and we'd throw it on a frying pan, on a little camp stove, and we'd just let it burn. The smell would waft all through the town, and before you knew it the infected would come running for their next meal. Herd instinct. They all just crowded around the burning guts, trying to get a piece. And when we had them all right there in our killbox, we'd light 'em up. Pick off the stragglers with rifle fire from the rooftops where we were hiding. We could knock out hordes of hundreds in a matter of minutes."

Mac clenched his jaw. "That's clever, Captain. But hundreds ain't millions."

"You're right." Lee nodded. "That's why the bait's gone from deer guts to men, and the killbox has gone from an intersection to an entire town. And the claymores have been upgraded to howitzers."

"The Marine artillery," Old Man Hughes said.

Lee snapped his finger. "Exactly. And back to your question about where..." Lee pointed at a familiar town. "I think Smithfield meets our needs best. It's directly between the two hordes, it's got major roadways that feed it but don't run through big cities, so it should be easy for our... *bait trucks* to get through safely. It's got high ground at the hospital where we can put a small element to keep the infected's attention. Plus, we already own it. It won't take any clearing operations to secure it. We can have people in the hospital by the end of today." Lee shifted his hands to an area southeast of Smithfield. "Out here we have some natural high ground. It's just farmland, but it's accessible, defensible, and you can park artillery there and be within perfect range of Smithfield. Brinly, we need to get your arty right there."

Brinly eyed the spot on the map. "Yeah. I can get my guns there. But I'm gonna need a path cleared if you want us there quick. If we gotta roll slow, looking for ambushes, then you can expect it to take a few days."

Lee looked back at Mac and Georgia. "Folks, this is where I need you."

Mac did not look pleased. "For what? I'm not making any promises..."

Lee spoke over him. "We need to get the Marine artillery from Lejeune to this overlook east of Smithfield. First Sergeant Brinly has passed on some reports from his men back east that the Followers have very rapidly started pushing west. I don't know how far they intend to push, or whether they will reach us. But I need some people to keep an open door for the Marines." Lee traced a finger from the overlook to another dot on the map. "Newton Grove. We've traded with them very recently and maintained open roads between them and the Camp Ryder Hub. Unfortunately, we haven't had any contact with them within the last week, so I'm not sure what's going on there." Lee straightened his back and made eye contact with Mac, and then Georgia. "I need that town secured. I need it secured and I need a scouting party to continue to keep the roads cleared for the Marines and keep an eye out for the Followers. I'm not sure what's up with Newton Grove, but the roads have been traveled recently, and I still feel like they should be the best bet as a highway for the Marines."

Mac was scratching his face, his lips pulled down into a grimace. "Why the fuck we gotta clear the way for the Marines?" He took a sidelong glance at Brinly. "I mean, no offense, man, but aren't you guys, like, bad motherfuckers and all that? Captain, you're giving them weapons. I thought that was the point in giving them the weapons in the first place. So they can clear their own way."

"Because we need those artillery pieces in place ASAP," Lee said simply. "No matter how much I despise a time-sensitive plan, that's exactly what this is. We draw the hordes down into Smithfield. We'll need to have a team posted on the hospital. They will be the ones to keep the attention centered on them so we keep the hordes in one place. But we can't leave them there. So we fly in a helo to extract them from the hospital. And then we have a very small window for the artillery to take out those hordes before they start to disperse."

Georgia cleared her throat, irritated.

Mac looked away. "You're asking us to infiltrate and secure the whole town of Newton Grove. But we're not soldiers."

Lee crossed his arms. "Old Man Hughes."

Hughes raised his bushy white eyebrows. "Yuh?"

"You a soldier?"

"No, Cap. I surely ain't."

"What about you, Angela?" Lee looked at her.

Angela hooked her fingers into the gun belt around her waist. "Nope. Housewife."

"Nate? Devon?" Lee turned to them. "Either of you got prior military experience? What about you, Brett? You a closet Navy SEAL I never knew about?"

Brett was looking right at Mac and Georgia. "Computer programmer."

Nate just shook his head. "I sold cars."

"Drywall," Devon said. "I hung Sheetrock for a living."

If Mac's face could have tightened any further it would have shattered from the strain. Whether out of shame or pure anger, or perhaps a little of both, he finally looked away from the others that had gathered around the desk and the map that was laid across it. He and Georgia faced each other, and Georgia did not look any happier than he did. She tossed her head toward the door.

Mac nodded, then looked back at Lee. His voice was ice-cold. "We need a minute."

Then the two of them walked out of the room without waiting for another word to be said.

Lee looked to Angela. "You think they're gonna leave?"

Angela looked at the closed door with consternation. "I don't know where the hell they think they're gonna go." Behind the frosted glass of the office door, Lee could see the shadows of the man and woman hunched close together in quiet but intense conversation. "Let me talk to them," Angela said.

She went to the door and went out, closing it again behind her.

The room stood in silence for a brief moment, Lee trying to figure through how he was going to split his manpower up if Mac and Georgia's group decided to split. Honestly, he wouldn't be sad if they did. He needed to make use of them if they were going to sit around and soak up resources from Camp Ryder, but he didn't trust them after the display the other night. Hell, he'd almost executed one of them on the spot. He had to imagine their feelings for him were similarly dismal.

There were the soldiers out of Fort Bragg, though. Lee trusted them only marginally more than he trusted Mac and Georgia's group, but he was being forced out of the comfort zone of his trust in their current situation. He needed people to hold guns and pull triggers. He needed warm bodies, and he needed them badly. Whether or not he truly trusted any of them was beside the point.

He looked to Carl, but before he could open his mouth, Brett spoke up.

"Captain, I've got twelve good people in my group that are in good fighting shape. And they all got a bone to pick with the Followers." Brett was nodding, his eyes alight with some unforgotten rage. He had come from one of the small towns out west that had been destroyed by the Followers. He and a portion of his group of survivors had managed to escape with their lives, though many of them had not managed to save members of their families. Lee imagined Brett and his friends did have quite the bone to pick.

"If you'd let me," Brett continued, "I'd like for myself and my group to take Newton Grove and scout those roads for you. I don't care what you do with Mac and Georgia's people, but let me and my people handle that for you. I promise we'll do it right."

Lee only had to consider it for a moment. Brett and his small group of survivors had wandered to Smithfield looking for refuge and had met Jacob. They'd helped Lee take back Camp Ryder from Jerry, and they'd volunteered for things at every turn. Brett had a good handle on them, and for the most part the people in the group tried hard to contribute. Lee trusted them more than he trusted some of the original Camp Ryder folks.

"It's all yours," Lee said. "Whatever happens

with Georgia and Mac, whether they're in or out, we're gonna hit it tomorrow. Brett, you'll secure Newton Grove. I need to find a small team to secure Smithfield, too. Carl, I'm gonna need a ride out to that bunker ASAP. Brinly, I need your cargo bird to meet me there. And Nate and Devon—you guys and the other team will be heading out to try to make contact with those infected hordes." He paused for a breath and looked at them sternly. "Find pickups that are in good working order. Don't take some fucking beater that's going to break down on you. Take some extra gas with you. Keep in mind you're not going to be going that fast. You have to stay in sight of the horde."

"Carrot on a stick," Nate said with a nervous smile.

"Carrot on a stick," Lee agreed.

Sam held his rifle steady. Quiet. Still.

Beside him, Deuce was also still, sensing the tension. The dog's golden eyes were watching the same thing that Sam was watching. Sam couldn't figure how Deuce knew when to be still and when it was time to move. Instinct, maybe. Or maybe he could just sense that Sam was being still for a reason.

Unlike Abby.

Sam glanced over the stock of the rifle that he'd already brought to his cheek. Abby was crouching there, on his right. He'd already gone over the basics with her, but she was clearly too excited to contain herself. He didn't know how excited she was going to be in a moment.

"Stop squirming," he whispered.

She froze with an eye roll and a huff.

"And don't breathe so loud," Sam said. "You're gonna scare him off."

"Are you gonna shoot him?" she said, her voice wrenched tight.

"If you don't scare him off first."

"Okay."

"Sshh."

Up until a few days ago, Sam had enjoyed games of soccer with some of the other kids in Camp Ryder. But since "the Caleb Incident," Sam didn't feel like he would be welcome to play with the other kids. They were all frightened of him, which was irritating just by itself. But on top of everything else, he didn't want to do much lately that would take him more than arm's reach away from his little .22 rifle.

He wished Mr. Jenkins was still alive. Wished that Kyle and Arnie hadn't bashed his brains in with a pipe. Wished even more that he'd never seen it happen. But he had. And Mr. Jenkins was gone. Just like his father. Because people died. People died a lot.

A good way to spend his time was hunting. And it didn't even require going out past the gate. On the back side of the Camp Ryder building, in the area they referred to as the backyard, there was a big tree that Mr. Jenkins had taught him was an oak tree. And oak trees had acorns. The long limbs from the tree hung over the back fence and dropped loads of acorns on the ground there. And the squirrels made a habit of coming by to pick them up.

Sam and his two companions were huddled against an outcropping of weeds that had turned into something more like bushes. They really didn't have a way of keeping weeds and cutting grass—no one was wasting resources on making lawnmowers run. But Sam didn't mind. It provided perfect cover.

About twenty yards from him, a fat little squirrel sat on the fence, its tail swishing back and forth. It had been on a mission, making its way from branch to branch, before Abby had started moving around. Now it was eyeing them from across the twenty yards and chattering nervously.

Sam could have taken the shot. Twenty yards was a casual distance with his little .22 rifle. But he didn't want the squirrel to topple back over the fence. Because he might not be able to get it.

They waited, and eventually the squirrel either forgot that they were there or decided that they were not worth worrying about. The bounty of acorns strewn about the backyard of Camp Ryder caught its attention again, and it began to descend the fence.

"Shoot it!" Abby urged breathily.

Sam shushed her again.

The squirrel navigated the chain-link fencing expertly. It reached the ground. Looked around. Twitched its tail. Then it hopped down. Face to the ground. Started looking for acorns.

Abby made an exasperated noise.

Sam held on for a moment more. He waited for the squirrel to wander just a little bit farther from the fence. Then he closed his left eye. Sighted through his right. Down the barrel. Good sight picture, just like Mr. Jenkins had taught him. Slow, steady trigger pull, just like Lee had showed him. Let the rifle go off. Let it surprise you...

CRACK!

The squirrel jumped, spinning in the air.

Sam saw the tail twirling, flying, and knew that it was a good hit.

The squirrel bolted for the fence.

"He's gonna get away!" Abby squealed in Sam's ear.

But the squirrel only made it about halfway up the fence before it stopped. Even from twenty yards away, Sam could see its tiny chest heaving, breathing rapidly. It looked like it was hanging on to the chain-link with one paw. Weak and dying.

"C'mon," Sam said, and rose from his position.

Deuce bolted out of cover and raced toward the squirrel.

"No!" Sam ordered, jogging behind, and Abby bringing up the rear.

When they reached the squirrel, it was still alive. Chest still heaving. Tail twitching. Tiny black eyes regarded Sam, and they were oddly emotionless, as Sam had found wild animals to be. Wild animals didn't beg for their lives, or feel guilt or pity or sadness. They just fought to survive, until they could not fight any longer, and then they simply died.

Deuce was on the fence, directly underneath the squirrel, trying to get his mouth on the tail.

"No, Deuce," Sam said sharply.

Deuce backed off, but clearly didn't want to.

The dog watched the squirrel on the fence, his tail wagging furiously.

"It's still alive," Abby observed, her voice sounding far off.

Sam looked at the younger girl. She was standing in an odd posture, like she didn't quite know what to do with her hands. The look on her face had gone from excitement to a little bit of disgust that she was trying to hide. Sam thought that was odd. Odd that she had seen the things she'd seen, and yet was still shocked by the killing of an animal.

"It's just a squirrel," Sam said suddenly.

Abby's eyes jagged to him. She seemed unsure of herself.

Sam looked back at the squirrel. He could see the bullet strike now. Cleanly through the chest. Just a little bit of blood leaking out and matting down the fur on the squirrel's back. The squirrel shivered, then tried to make another go at the fence, only to lose its grip and fall to the ground with a soft *plop*.

"Just a tree rat," Sam said, stepping up to it. "You shouldn't feel bad about killing it."

"I don't," Abby said, but it was obvious that she did.

"We killed it, and now we have to eat it."

Abby shook her head. "I don't want to eat it."

Sam bent down so he was kneeling over the squirrel. Still hanging on to life. "Abby, you wanted me to kill this squirrel, and I did. Now you're going to eat it. We're both going to eat it. Do you know what disrespect is?"

Abby couldn't take her eyes off the dying animal. "It's when you're rude to someone."

"Right. And it's rude to kill animals and not eat them."

"Isn't it just rude to kill?"

Sam looked at her, gauging her words, measuring his own reaction to them. But he decided to be silent. He reached down and took the squirrel by the head. Then he swung it sharply in a circle, breaking its neck and finishing it off for good.

SEVEN

KENSEY

HARPER'S GROUP CLEARED THE narrow gap of highways between Burlington and Greensboro around midday. Harper rode shotgun in the lead Humvee, with Sergeant Kensey in the backseat, tending to Julia, who was still in and out of painkiller-induced sleep. Charlie drove the Humvee and Dylan sat in the turret, for all of the good it would do with the fifteen rounds that remained in the M2's ammo box. Behind them, their convoy kept an even spacing, and they didn't slow down as they passed through this more populous area.

Off to the right and left, Harper saw more glimpses of infected. Small groups of them stood at the edge of wood lines, warming themselves in sunlight and watching the convoy pass with unreadable faces. There was no human thought behind them, and no human interpretation could be made from their expressions. It still bothered Harper when he saw these infected watching them, tracking them with animal eyes, and Harper with no real concept of what was going through those half-eaten brains.

As they cleared I-40 and continued south on

Highway 61, the number of infected he saw began to dwindle. In the backseat, Julia began to make muttering noises. The sound of someone in the throes of a nightmare that they can't seem to wake up from.

Harper turned to look at her. Humvees were anything but roomy, and Julia was laid out in the back area where normally they would have stored their packs and supplies. Kensey negotiated himself with a few curses so that he could reach into the far back and shake her by the shoulder. She started and her eyelids fluttered open for a moment, but she was still too far under the drugs to come back awake. She settled back and was asleep again within seconds, but at least now she was not whimpering.

They'd had a later start that morning than they'd anticipated. Kensey had not wanted to get the column moving before scouting out the roads ahead, and Harper had been forced to agree that it made sense. They didn't want to pack up, thinking they were making an escape, and then just end up running into the massive horde they thought they were escaping. He wasn't sure whether the majority of the horde was still milling about Eden, or whether they had moved farther south already, but aside from the few small packs they saw between Burlington and Greensboro, the countryside had been empty.

Kensey situated himself back into his seat and leaned forward. "We need to find a place to stop."

Harper turned to face him, incredulous. "Stop?"

"Just for a little bit," Kensey said, as though there was no argument to be made. "I've got to check in with my command. And I don't think Julia has pissed or taken a shit within the last day. I'm a little concerned about her fluid levels. Might need to give her an IV before we roll on. Besides, we should probably give her the opportunity to relieve herself before loading her up with painkillers again. Or she's gonna end up pissing her pants. I'm surprised she hasn't done it already."

Harper's nose wrinkled. That would make for an unpleasant drive back. Harper was no medical expert, but he knew that Kensey was right. Someone under the influence of that many painkillers was usually hooked up to a catheter. Julia was not and she still hadn't wet herself, which probably meant she was extremely dehydrated. He tried to think about the last time she'd eaten or had anything to drink. It must've been more than a day ago.

Harper glanced at the woman laid in the back of the Humvee. The bandage around her leg was just barely bled through, which was good. Last night it seemed to be bleeding through completely within minutes. At least that had stopped for the most part.

"How long will it take to give her the IV?"

"Well." Kensey considered it. "It'll only take me a few minutes to hook it up, but I'd like to give her an hour to get rehydrated. Once the IV is finished and she's more awake, she'll probably need to piss like a racehorse."

Harper didn't like having to wait for an hour, but he relented for Julia's sake. "Fine," he said.

"Charlie, find us a place to hide out for an hour or so."

Several miles south of I-40 they found an old, abandoned granary. Sets of silos, most of them short and squat, stood together with vines crawling up them and weeds clinging to their bases. The tops were worn and rusted in places. Still, except for the overgrowth, Harper would have guessed that the granary had been in use as little as a year ago.

The granary was surrounded by six-foot-tall chain-link fencing, with a gravel road leading in through a pair of gates that appeared to have been rammed open some time ago. There was also evidence that someone had attempted to get the silos open—large pieces of the steel siding had been cut through and pulled back. The interiors were dark and empty. Harper suspected they'd been dark and empty when whatever hopeful individual had tried to scavenge from them.

There was a large, metal barn with stalls for vehicles and tractors and implements. A defunct, rust-red tractor sat in one of the stalls, along with a few moldering bales of hay, and some implements that looked much newer than the tractor. No vehicles save for an old pickup truck with no tires that was likely being kept for spare parts.

They pulled the convoy in and tried to secure the gate behind them as much as possible, though the bent bars made it pointless. They drove behind the barn and parked. The doors to the vehicles popped open, Harper's along with them. He stepped out and watched the others do the same.

He was glad to see the few people left to his group helping the Marines with securing the area. They moved quickly through the interior of the farmhouse, while the Marines swept the rest of the granary, looking between the silos and small outbuildings and sheds for anything unpleasant that might be lurking.

Harper and Kensey stood beside their Humvee and watched the clearing take place. Harper had his eyes on his own team and waited for them to emerge from the big metal barn. One of them held his arm up, his thumb protruding from his fist.

"Barn's good," he called.

Kensey watched his own Marines and nodded at some signal that Harper had not seen. "Rest of the area's secure as well. Help me get her out. I'll start the IV and then try to radio command while she soaks it up."

"All right." Harper went to the back of the Humvee. They opened the fastback and pulled Julia out. She was almost awake by then, but still groggy, and her muscles must have felt like putty to her, because she seemed limp and loose. She squinted at Kensey and Harper as they helped her into a sitting position, and then down off of the bumper of the Humvee and onto the ground, taking care to avoid jostling her leg.

Charlie and Dylan stood close by and watched. Harper glanced up at them with a little annoyance, but he supposed he couldn't blame them for hovering. They were just as much friends with Julia as he was, and Charlie had seemed a little sweet on her sometimes, though he hid it well. Just like

Harper, they wanted to help her but really didn't know how. So they just stood idly by while Kensey worked.

While Kensey prepped an IV line, Julia glared up at the bright sky and seemed to find some use for her arms. She held them up above her, shading her face from the sun. It was cold, but the sun still managed to be cloyingly bright. Her arm wavered unsteadily in the air above her. Her eyes lolled about but then managed to anchor on Harper.

"Where the fuck are we?" she mumbled.

Harper smiled. "There we are. Not awake for two seconds and you're dropping f-bombs. I expect no less." He squatted down at her side. "We're on the way back, but we stopped here. It's just some sort of farm or something. Grain farm."

She cleared her throat with some effort. "Why are we stopped?"

Kensey pulled the sleeve of her jacket up to expose her arm and started swabbing the skin with an iodine patch, staining her pale skin a dark yellow. "I think you're pretty dehydrated. Have you had to pee since you broke your leg?"

Julia closed her eyes tight, then opened them again, as though she were trying to clear her vision. "Um ... I dunno."

"I'm hooking you to an IV right now. Get some fluids in you."

"Okay." She nodded and watched him stick the needle in without blinking. She was a nurse, after all, Harper remembered. He didn't suppose there were very many nurses that were uncomfortable with needles. Kensey had to poke around some, but Julia just stayed still until she watched the tip of the catheter fill with blood. Then she relaxed.

Once he had the catheter in, he hung the bag from the antenna on the back of the Humvee, connected the lines, and then set the drip. When he was finished, he knelt down beside her, stripping his latex gloves off and tossing them to the side.

"How you feeling?" he asked.

Harper could see the discomfort on Julia's face, the edge of pain just barely dulled by the vestiges of the painkiller rolling through her blood stream. But she put on a haggard smile that came and went on her face like the brief sighting of a rare bird.

"Fine," she said with a little strain. "Better, I think."

Kensey nodded. "I'm not giving you any more painkillers until you void. It might be a bit and you might start to hurt, but hang in. I need to make sure you got enough fluids to get your plumbing running before I drug you up again." He patted her shoulder gently. "You were a nurse. You know how it works."

"Yeah," she said. "I'll be okay."

Kensey stood and turned to Harper. "I need to put a call in to my command. Just keep an eye on her, will you?"

Harper watched him go. Kensey walked across the gravel and dirt and joined his group of Marines, which crowded around him and began speaking in hushed tones. Harper eyed them for a minute. Maybe they were discussing how the hell they were gonna stop the millions of infected from wiping out the entire state, and them along with it.

Maybe you should have listened in the first place, Harper thought bitterly.

But he knew it wasn't their fault, specifically. They were not the ones calling the shots. They were following orders, like the good Marines they were. The fault lay with this fabled Colonel Staley, whom they all spoke of in terms of reverence, and who had decided to promise with his mouth and hold back with his hand.

And now here we are.

"You're pissed about something."

Harper looked down at Julia, who was staring at him, her face still pursed into that look of concentration that people get when they are trying to read reality through a filter of drugs or drunkenness.

Harper realized he was scowling and shook the expression off. "No. I mean...nothing new. Same old shit to be pissed about."

"Oh," she said. "You mean, like, the end of the world and stuff? Shit like that?"

He smirked. "Yeah. Shit like that."

Julia made a rude noise and closed her eyes, resting her trembling hand on her brow. "End of the world. It ain't gonna end. Never will. We're living through it right now. And I think some of us will make it to the other side. Not all of us. Nope. Not everyone. But plenty of us. There is no real *end of the world*."

Harper sniffed and looked off at the abandoned farmlands that surrounded them. "That's very philosophical for someone that's high."

She opened one eye enough to glare at him. "Ass."

"I meant it as a compliment," he defended himself. "It's a very astute observation for someone in your condition."

She closed her eyes again. "Yeah. The world goes on, Harper. It goes on. And on. And on and on and on. Never fucking ends."

"You say that like it's a bad thing."

"If an asteroid were to strike and wipe us out in the blink of an eye, would you really be all that disappointed?"

"If I was wiped out in the blink of an eye I don't think I would have time to feel disappointed."

"You know what I mean. Jesus, you're an ass right now."

Harper smiled at her but she still had her eyes closed. "I know what you meant. And no. I guess I wouldn't be all that disappointed."

"God, you're depressing," she sighed.

"You were the one that brought it up."

"Whatever."

They sat in silence for a time. Harper cast his eyes around the granary but found only the evidence of things left behind. He kept glancing at the bag, wondering when it was going to be empty, and then felt slightly guilty. Making sure that Julia didn't die of dehydration was not an inconvenience. And there was no real reason to be feeling urgency at the moment. They were in the middle of rural nowhere, with a good line of sight almost all the way around them and fields of wheat stubble, sprouting with tall weeds. They extended for hundreds of acres in all directions. The fields were only broken by thin stands of wood that separated one field from the next. There was nothing around them. And even if there was, they would know about it long before it got to them.

Safe?

Don't be ridiculous, Harper chided himself. *But it's safe enough to relax for a minute.*

He looked over to his left, where the Marines had been gathered, discussing things in their small committee to which Harper and his group were not allowed entry. Or maybe they were. Harper had never asked. He figured they had military things to discuss and didn't want to be the prying civilian. Silly thought, really, since all their survivals were codependent from where Harper was standing. Harper supposed he just didn't want to be "that guy."

The group of Marines seemed to have dispersed. Three of them stood where the whole squad had stood. Kensey was not in sight, nor were the other five. Harper's own people were milling about, closer to him than to the Marines. There was a clear delineation there, but nobody seemed to mind it, least of all Harper. The Marines were the Marines. Harper's group was Harper's group. Each set of people knew their set well, and the other set not as well. You couldn't just expect them to mix it up like a Sunday social.

The three Marines still standing in the open seemed to realize that Harper was looking at them. One of them turned and glanced at him. Harper nodded respectfully. The three of them broke apart, like a trio of teenagers trying to find a spot to smoke their cigarettes away from adults.

They moved to the rear of one of the LMTVs and walked out of sight.

Harper brushed it off. He glanced over at the IV bag. The fluids were half gone now. Julia was still lying with her arm over her shoulder, but she was clearly awake. Her face was a full-on grimace. Her eyes squeezed shut. Wakefulness had brought pain back to her.

"It's gonna be all right, Julia," he said quietly.

She nodded, still with her eyes closed.

He heard gravel crunch behind him. He turned and found Kensey there again, his rifle in his hands. Harper looked the man in the eyes and saw something strange. The way Kensey was standing. The body language. The way he was holding his rifle. The way he had locked eyes with Harper.

Harper shifted, feeling suddenly uneasy. "Kensey..."

The man raised his rifle, pointing it at Harper.

Blooming alarm in Harper's chest, like a match on gasoline. Instinctively, he turned his body to shield Julia on the ground, reaching an arm out and touching her good leg. It must have got her attention and she must have opened her eyes, because Harper heard the sharp intake of her breath.

"What the fuck?" she coughed.

"Get on the ground," Kensey said, almost casually.

Harper looked to his left, trying to see if Dylan or Charlie could see what was happening, but they were on the other side of the Humvee, not paying attention to what was going on. And by the time that Harper looked back, Kensey was on him, grabbing him by the shoulder and smashing him down into the ground. Harper grunted as he struck, tried to call out, but felt Kensey's knee in his back, pressing the wind out of him.

Kensey's voice: "Don't resist. I'll kill you both, Harper. You know that I will."

"What the fuck are you doing?" Harper strained to get the words out.

"Harper!" Julia was trying to sit up and failing.

With his face smashed against the ground, Harper could not see Dylan's and Charlie's faces, could not tell if they were registering what was going on. But he could see their feet. Underneath the Humvee, he could see their boots. And the sound of footfalls, pounding quickly across gravel. Someone else was there, on top of him, and he felt his rifle being stripped off of him.

Julia was screaming, and then her screams became muffled.

Don't hurt her, Harper wanted to say, but couldn't find the air in his lungs.

He could see, and from this low perspective the gravel parking lot seemed like an endless range of jagged mountains. He could see tires. The bottom of the Humvee's bumper. He could see Julia, or at least her legs and arms, kicking as someone wrestled to restrain her. Someone in digital camouflage and tan boots.

Then there were gunshots. He heard the first two, and then the rest seemed inaudible for some reason. But he could *feel* them. The pressure. The sharp jab on his eardrums. And the smell—tangy, and black, and dirty. And when he looked underneath the Humvee he could see Charlie falling to the ground, still trying to get his weapon up as his torso kept twitching and red holes kept appearing. Then he tried to get up and run, but his legs would not work. He clawed with his hands, trying to get away, trying to live. More holes sprouted in his back and they just kept appearing until Charlie stopped moving.

Harper was screaming. The knees in his back kept pressing down, and the cold steel of Kensey's weapon kept pressing into the side of his face, but he kept thrashing, trying to get free. *These are the only ones left!* Harper kept thinking, feeling a very real pain in his guts. *They're the only ones left! Don't kill the only ones I have left!*

Julia was still fighting, but they'd restrained her. And beyond her, Harper could see the big metal barn and the red splashes against the stainless steel siding and the crumpled bodies that were dead and dying and begging for mercy and trying to get away. And the gunsmoke, the gunsmoke, the smell of it, the taste of it, and the sight of it puffing out, and the way that each gunshot poked his ears even though he couldn't hear it.

"Don't kill them!" Harper screamed. But the gunshots kept going and the smoke kept leaping out and the blood poured right along with it. The people dying along the wall of the barn kept dying, and then they were dead. Dead, dead, dead. Just like Gray. Like Mike and Torri. Like Josh. Like Annette. Like everybody else.

Harper's screams became unintelligible. For

a moment he fought so hard that he thought his rage, or his grief, the way that it exploded in him, he thought that it might just break him apart. But he stayed right where he was. Pinned to the ground. Staring at Julia as she was turned over, crying out in pain and anger and looking at him through tear-streaked eyes.

"What the fuck are you doing?" she yelled at whoever had Harper held down. But no amount of yelling was going to change anything, was it? You couldn't scream your way out of this. And you couldn't scream the pain out of yourself. It was an immovable object that settled on you, immense and implacable, and it could not be denied.

Harper closed his eyes, unable to look at Julia's face.

"Don't kill them," he kept mumbling.

But he knew that they were already dead.

EIGHT

DISTANCE

LEE FOUND HIMSELF ALONE.

Night was drawing in, and it seemed the teeming urgency to the day was suddenly gone from the camp. But it wasn't gone from Lee's mind. Brinly had retreated to the company of his Marines, who had been given a few of the shanties that no longer had occupants but preferred to lounge and sleep in their MATV. Carl and Tomlin had left for Fort Bragg again, Carl to prep what needed to be prepped, and Tomlin to check on their wayward friend, Major Darabie, who was sitting in an infirmary somewhere. Mac and Georgia had gone off somewhere into their group, trailed by Angela. Old Man Hughes, Brett, and Nate and Devon were gone to find food and sleep. But Lee was still there, staring at the map by the glow of an electric lamp.

The marrow of his bones seemed to ache. The day had been full of violence and sudden, stark realizations. His mind had yet to wind down. His head felt buzzed and out of sorts, his ears ringing annoyingly in the silence of the room. He felt utterly spent, but was unable to simply close his eyes and turn it off. Not now. Not when things were finally getting back into hand.

It felt as though he had dreamed this current turn of events. Like he was asleep in that moment and knew that it was going to be stripped away from him if he moved, if he blinked. He didn't want to breathe too hard or the thin veil of possibilities hanging in front of him would just shatter and fall to the ground. He had lost it once—his GPS, his plan, everything—and now he had it back in hand.

I can't lose it again. The first plan is scrapped. We're hanging on by a thread. You got your life back by the hair on your chinny-chin-chin. Now there's a new plan. And it actually has a chance of working. You cannot let this one go. You cannot lose it again. You have to maintain this one. You have to hold on to it. You have to make sure this shit happens the way that it's supposed to happen. You have to think of everything…

And the thoughts went on. And on. And on.

He leaned forward, finally daring to move. He planted his elbows on his knees and buried his face in his hands, shutting the world out for a moment. Maybe what he needed right now was not more planning and thinking. Maybe he just needed to sleep. Maybe he needed some goddamned rest, because tomorrow it started for real. The great, big freight train of his plan was going to start rolling, and it wasn't going to stop. The only problem was, the tracks weren't laid just yet, and it was up to Lee to make sure all those iron rails got into place by the time the locomotive came bearing down. Because there were no brakes on this one. It was do-or-die time.

His hands smelled of sweat and dirt and pine needles. It was a grungy, earthy smell. Almost unpleasant. He could use a bath. He hadn't bathed in... *Shit, how long has it been? You're filthy.* There came a certain point when you really couldn't smell yourself anymore. Lee was not quite there just yet. He could still smell the sourness of his own body, but just barely. Not that it was any different from anyone else. They all smelled ghastly by the old standards. Now he supposed it was somewhat normal.

He pulled his hands away from his face and stared at the map again, as though it had other secrets to tell. Secrets it just wouldn't spill. No matter how long Lee looked at it. Part of that was just plain old pessimism—so sure that he was missing something—but most of it was just the usual befuddlement of a tired brain.

In the quiet, in the half light of the lamp, Lee felt suddenly abandoned. The world outside was a cold and lonely place filled with dangerous things and people that might as well be strangers. Not even the ones that knew him truly knew him. Not even Angela. Not even Tomlin, though he knew him more to an extent, because he knew how Lee's mind worked. But who among them could he talk to? Who among them could he go to and say, "Sometimes I want to give up"?

None of them. They would not be able to hear that. Not from him. Not from the great Captain Harden, who kept them safe, and kept them fed, and found medicine for their sick children. Not him. He couldn't have moments of weakness. It was not allowed.

"Sometimes I feel guilty for the things I've done," he wanted to say, to vent. "Sometimes I think it's all useless. Sometimes I fail to see the purpose in any of this. Sometimes I look at my rifle and think about the easy way out. Sometimes I think the things that I've done will send me to hell. I think that I've damned myself for the sake of this mission, and then I wonder if it was ever worth it. If the mission ever even had a chance."

But who would be able to hear those things and still trust him? Still follow his lead?

No one.

And it didn't matter how many people out in that camp knew his name and followed his lead or thought good thoughts about him, or thought that they truly knew the man that he was...none of them really did know. None of them could see the doubts he had inside. None of them could see the animal in him. The fearful one, or the one that raged. The one that threw up its hands and called it all hopeless, or the one that bared its teeth and took the lives from people.

They only saw what he let them see.

There had only ever been one person in the world he thought would ever understand anything that was crawling around in the corners of Lee's soul. But his father had been dead for a long time. Lee's parents had always joked that he'd been a carbon copy of his father, but it was less of a joke and more of the truth. As he grew older, he began to see more and more similarities, and the two men identified with each other. Ron Harden was a man that Lee could talk to, freely, and without fear of reproach. But he was gone now. And what little of him that Lee had left came in dreams, like ghosts and whispers, though lately his dreams seemed to have been too dark for even Lee's father to find his way in.

Sleep could be a punishment all its own.

But you need it, he told himself, rising from the desk. *You need it, or you're going to drive yourself insane with all of these nonsense thoughts. Quit focusing on the past. Quit reliving painful things. Stick your chin out and look straight ahead to what's right in front of you. All that other shit can wait. And everything in the fucking world can wait and give me four hours to catch some damn sleep before I eat my gun.*

He walked around the desk and almost made it to his bedroll before someone knocked on the office door. His rifle was propped against the wall between the desk and his bedroll. He stopped there and reached out to touch the barrel of it.

"Yeah?"

The door opened and Angela stood there. She looked around the room, seeming to make sure that they were alone, and then she slipped in and closed the door behind her. Lee released the barrel of the rifle and took a seat on the edge of the desk, eyeing Angela and trying to take a read off of her. She wore a strange half smile on her lips, a *grin-and-bear-it* type of smile. Her hands were stuffed into her coat pockets. Her cheeks were flushed red from being in the cold outside. She was giving him an odd, evaluating look of her own.

"What's up with Mac and Georgia?" he said, breaking the silence before it could linger. "They in or out?"

Angela looked down through the door, as though she could see through it all to the inside of the Camp Ryder building, where Mac and Georgia and their thirty-some-odd people were housed. "Yeah, they're in. Partially."

Lee quirked his brow. "Partially?"

"Mac and fourteen others. That's all they're willing to give." She came over to the desk and sat on it, beside Lee. She sighed with a shake of her head. "They still don't trust us. Most of them think we're holding them prisoner, I guess because of the guards. I had to explain to them that it's not the case. They were free to leave. And then Mac and Georgia explained to them why they'd stayed this long. Because of the hordes coming down out of the north. And I don't think many of them want to keep running."

"Did anyone leave?"

"Some of them wanted to. But they went by consensus, and they're staying. So I told them they were free to go, and free to stay, but if they chose to stay, they had to contribute. And I told them we didn't need scavengers and woodcutters right now. We need fighters."

"Fifteen ain't bad. I can work with that." Lee nodded and looked at Angela. "Good work. You don't give yourself enough credit, but people listen when you talk. You should have more faith in yourself."

That tired smile again. She tilted her head as she looked at him. Like you might to change your perspective so you can decipher the image in an optical illusion.

Lee sighed lightly through his nose. "You're giving me that look."

"What look?"

"Like you're about to ask me questions... about me."

She made an amused sound. "Captain Harden. The man who can put himself in danger and fight all the bad guys, but utterly terrified of having an honest conversation with someone."

He looked away from her, didn't want to see her eyes, because he felt that they could surmise things that he was intentionally leaving unsaid. The blank wall of the office was a safer place for his gaze to wander. She was something strange, something different. Something he was not accustomed to. Unlike so many other people in his life, she could be both a chink in his armor and the patch welded over the holes. Because he cared about what she thought, oddly enough. And if he told her the truth...well, she would either side with him, and then the relief of the stress of secrecy would strengthen him, her support would strengthen him, and he would be more focused. Or she would revile him.

There was a part of him that resented both her and himself for this. Her, because he had never allowed another person to factor so heavily into his thought processes. And himself for letting it happen. He'd never intentionally given this type of power to her. It was something that had happened under his nose, without his knowledge. The heart was a traitorous thing, and often operated in secret.

"What's going on with you?" she said, her voice quiet.

The quiet was worse to him than if she'd been demanding. The quiet suggested she could understand, that he could tell her things he did not want to tell her. But that was just a trap. Wasn't it? He hated how secrets degraded willpower over time, particularly with people you cared about. He'd been so long without anyone that he cared about that his previous, quiet, solitary life had been easy to maintain. But now he'd gone and fucked that up, hadn't he?

"What do you mean?" he said, lamely.

She chuffed. "Oh, Lee...what a stupid question."

He stayed silent.

"Ever since you came back..." she started, then stopped. "I don't know. I thought that we had an understanding." She didn't seem to like the words that she'd chosen, and scrambled for better ones. "What happened in here, when you were gone...I did some things I never would have thought I was capable of doing. Not good things. Things that still wake me up at night. And I thought to myself, if anyone ever understands that, it's gonna be Lee. And I could see it in your eyes when you came back. I could see you'd had to do some things, too. But I thought that we were going to be able to...to..."

"Talk about it?" Lee said, and didn't like the near-sarcastic edge to his voice.

Angela glanced at him and he could tell that he'd made her feel foolish when she was only trying to be open with him. She pressed her lips together and looked elsewhere. "Is that such a ridiculous thought?" she said with a little bitterness creeping into her voice. "That we could actually talk about something? Rather than sitting in silence?" She laughed suddenly. "No. You're right. That is ridiculous. What the hell was I thinking? It's not like we're in some normal relationship. We're in *this*. Whatever *this* is."

"Angela..."

"What is this, then?" Her hands supplicated, palms up. "What are we doing? We're together but we're not. You sleep in my house, but we never talk about anything. I worry about you when you're away from me, but when you're here it's like you're not. So tell me what this is."

Lee wanted to fight this line of questions but didn't have the energy for it. He just felt that empty feeling of knowing a conversation was going down paths he didn't want it to. He looked at her, hoping that she would not expect an immediate answer. But she only sat there and waited for his response. Her question was earnest, not rhetorical.

"I don't know what this is." He shook his head and the silence stretched. "I wish I knew. I'm in the same boat as you, Angela. I really am. I've never been here before. Even before all this shit went down, it'd been a long time since I'd had a relationship with anyone. And now this? I mean...how are we supposed to be? I don't know how this works any more than you do. I know that

I worried about you when I was gone. I worried about you, and I can't explain how relieved I was when I saw that you were okay." He rubbed his face and beard. "I care about you. More than I wish I did."

Angela planted her hands on her knees, and remained pensive.

Lee felt like he was empty of high-minded words. All he had left was the truth, take it or leave it. "What do you want me to say, Angela? That I love you? Yeah, I guess I do. I don't know what else to call it. I've tried to find another word. Because how does that shape out for you, Angela? Have you ever thought about that?"

She looked at him. "What do you mean?"

"I mean that everything about this is fucked up. You already lost your husband—I was the one that killed him. And then there's me. And how likely do you actually think it is that both of us make it out of this? Everyone around me keeps dying, Angela"—*you said it yourself in my dream: "Everyone around you dies."*—"and I've come damn near close more times than I care to count. So how's that shape up for us, huh? I'll tell you how it shapes up. More heartache. More loss. And I can't afford any more of that. I don't think you can, either."

Angela's mouth came open to argue, but then it froze, and after a moment it snapped shut again. Her expression went from reproachful to ... almost placid. If not for the hard edge of it. An edge that had not been there months ago.

Lee shook his head and swore. "And this is why I don't talk." He looked right at her and waited until she returned the eye contact. "Angela, you're a *good person*. You are. Things have been tough for you, maybe a little tougher than some other people around here. But inside, you're still good. And I think everyone around here knows that, and that's why they trust you."

He stood up from the desk, for no other reason than to put distance and meaning into the words he had to say. He didn't want to say them, but they needed to be said. "You think that you want to be in my head, but you don't. I promise you, Angela. You don't. I'm not a good person."

Her face screwed up. "Because I'm too fragile to handle it?"

"You think I don't want to tell you?" He felt his anger level rising. He was trying to keep himself level, but she just kept pressing. "You think I like keeping shit to myself? I don't. It wears on me. But what I have to say, no one wants to hear, I promise you that. And I made my peace with that a long time ago. Because it's not my job to make my voice heard and be understood as a person. It's not my job to be happy and cheerful and friendly and appreciate the fucking beauty of the world around me." He shook his head. "No. It's my job to do all the ugly shit that needs to be done so that all the other people can go on about their lives with some semblance of normalcy. That's what I do. That's what I'm good at."

Angela raised her own voice in turn. "What are you even talking about? What'd you do?"

"Do you really want to be a part of that, Angela?"

"Lee!" She came off the desk. "What'd you do?"

He just stared back at her.

Her eyes narrowed. "Julia told me that you were hiding something. She told me and I didn't believe her because she's been acting so weird. But you *are* hiding something from us." She looked suspicious. "Where'd you go all those mornings? What'd you do?"

"This...this..."

"Tell me!"

And Lee wasn't sure why he said it. Maybe just to watch her jump, to see her react, the base desire to prove himself right: *You're not ready for this. You don't understand men like me. You don't understand having to do bad things for the greater good. You don't understand how negatives can turn into positives. How cold-blooded murder is sometimes the best and only option.*

"I killed them, Angela," he said, his voice dropping back down again.

She paused for a long second. Processing. Computing. "Who?"

Even though she knew. She *had* to know.

Deadpan, Lee said the names like any old list on a piece of scrap paper: "Arnie. Kyle. Connor. Zeke. Jody." He took a breath. Let it out. "I killed them."

She was still looking at him, like she was trying to turn what he was saying into something acceptable, something that fit her worldview. But it would not. Lee saw things from a very different perspective than her. And there were miles and miles to cross before the two vantage points converged.

"I don't..." she started, then stopped. "I don't understand."

"There's nothing to understand, Angela," Lee said tiredly. He found the exhaustion coming back over him in waves. Did it feel good to have the truth out? No. It felt like he was vulnerable. It felt like he had taken that little chink in his armor and pried it open until it was a big, obvious gash. He felt weakened. Foolish. But he went on. Might as well get the whole thing out. No use telling half truths when the full truth was just a few more words away.

And miles and miles more between them.

"I went out, every morning that the trials were held. I waited under a tree, because I knew the road they were going to take. I made sure it was far enough that no one in Camp Ryder would hear the gunshots, but close enough that I could get back quickly. And I waited for them. And when they came walking up the road, I gunned them down. Killed them. And then I left their bodies there. And the infected ate them."

Angela placed her hand over her mouth, but otherwise her face was still. She did not cry out, or show any other form of outward emotion. Still, though...Lee could feel the anger in her. The resentment. The disbelief. Possibly even disgust—and that hurt him the worst. Even sitting there, hardhearted as he'd become, that still struck him.

He shook his head. "I told you..."

She held up her finger with a jerk. The cords in her neck were standing out, but her skin was oddly bloodless. She looked around the room, then finally came back to him for a moment. "I don't believe this."

Lee grabbed his rifle off the wall and shook his head. He went to his bedroll and stood there, aimlessly. "What do you want me to say, Angela? This entire time, I just don't know what you want from me. You say you want the truth, but every time you get it, you spit it right back out. I told you not to pry, and you kept prying."

She looked aghast. "This isn't about me! This is about you killing...unarmed people!"

"Yes," he said. "I did."

You're damn mighty good at burning those bridges, aren't you, bud? His father's voice echoing in his mind. *Gotta be the loner. Gotta carry all the groceries at once. Can't let nobody else help. Always got something to prove. You never could. Your damn pride, son. Your damn pride is gonna leave you a bitter old man and it ain't gonna keep you warm at night, I promise you that.*

"Why did you do that?" she demanded. "We'd already kicked them out! It doesn't...It doesn't... I don't understand."

He jabbed his finger in the air at her. "Because loose ends always come back to bite you in the ass, Angela. If I'd put a bullet in Shumate's head a few months ago, my life would've been a helluva lot easier these past few weeks. If we'd gotten rid of Jerry as soon as he started acting up, then we wouldn't have fifteen more bodies in the ground out back! Every one of those motherfuckers that fought with Jerry should have been executed. Lined up in front of a firing squad and goddamned *executed*. But everyone wanted to hold a trial. Everyone wanted to feel fucking good about themselves. And they don't give a shit that all those warm fuzzy feelings are putting them and everybody else in danger. Fine. You people do what you need to do to make yourselves feel better. I'll keep seeing the world like it really is and do what needs to be done to keep everyone safe. It's what I've always done for civilians, and nothing's changed. Even at the end of the fucking world, when you think people would take some responsibility for shit, nothing's changed."

He sat down and put his back to the wall, rifle over his lap. "Is that what you want to be a part of? I didn't include you for a reason. People need me and what I do. Society has always needed men with blood on their hands. But they need you, too. They need the good people to lead them. And they need the bloody ones to clear the way. And if you try to help with clearing the way, you're gonna find out that it changes you. And you're not going to be the person you were."

He laid his head back against the cold cement wall and looked up. It felt like lead in his gut. Like killing a friend. Like burning bridges. But that was what needed to happen. People's survival outweighed Lee's personal relationships. Angela needed to be away from Lee. For her own good, and for the good of what he was trying to accomplish. He had tried to keep that distance physically, but now he had to put it into words.

"I don't know what we are," Lee said quietly. "Or were. But it was foolish, Angela. I killed your husband. Abby hates me. And you yourself are never going to understand what I do and why I do it. And I can't continue to do what needs to be done if I'm always taking into account what you might think of it." He looked at her. "You're going to lead this place. You already are. And you're going to need men like me to keep doing the things that we do, or this place has shit chance of making it. But neither of us can do what we need to do if we're together. Do you understand what I'm saying?"

She wasn't meeting his gaze. She apparently preferred to stare at the door. She gave no indication that she had heard anything he had said, but Lee knew that she had. Lee could see it in the set of her mouth. He could almost read it like words on a sign: *Fine. If this is the way you want it. But I can't believe the words that you're saying.*

"You should leave," he said, like pounding the last nail in the coffin of a loved one.

She crossed her arms over her chest, and Lee almost wanted to tell her to stay, but the words had been spoken and could not be taken back. *And they're for the best. It's for the best that she leave and not keep trying to attach herself to me. We're so close to winning the fight, why weaken myself now? This is best. This makes the most sense.*

She hesitated at the door and looked over her shoulder, but never quite looked at him. And then whatever she had wanted to say she let die in her mouth and closed the door behind her. And then she was gone. And Lee had managed to make himself alone again.

This is best, he kept telling himself. *This is best.*

NINE

Cause for Concern

LEE SLEPT IN FITS and starts. His dreams were all of blood and terror and the feeling of being lost. As he wandered, he found a road and began to walk it. To either side, the grass had grown high and was encroaching on the cement. Beyond the grass, the forest stood silent, watching him breathlessly. The trees were barren of leaves, and yet the whole woods was dark and black as a midnight shadow. He feared the woods, but they were all around him. The only safe way was straight ahead. One foot in front of the other on this old and empty road.

He began to run, but mile after mile he was not putting any distance between himself and whatever was in the woods. It was still there, all around him, and one mile of this long, flat road looked just like the next. And the black woods were beginning to laugh at him. The trees had faces and they sneered, and the trunks were scarred and slashed as though some huge animal had sharpened its claws on them, and sap that looked like blood trickled out of these marks.

Finally, he could run no more. He stopped and

stood. For as far as the eye could see, his path remained the same. And behind him the view stretched, just a mirror image.

"This is only a dream," he told himself, and he could remember the nightmarish Father Jim coming into his bunker after him, screaming some prayer of damnation over him. That had been so real, but it had been a nightmare. Just like this. "I'm sleeping."

But his heart would not slow down.

He closed his eyes, trying to picture the office that he knew he was lying in. His bed roll. The desk where only hours ago he had sat and pushed away one of the only people left in the world that cared for him. Pushed her away because *that is what's best*. And when he opened his eyes, he did not see the trees anymore.

But he was still on the road.

He could not see the trees, because it was completely dark. He was standing in the middle of the road, in a ring of light, like a spotlight was shining down on him, center stage, all the world a dark, invisible, faceless audience, watching him in rapt silence. He looked up to see the spotlight, but there was only darkness in the sky. Not a single star to give him direction.

When he looked back down, he could see shapes in the gloom just beyond the ring of light in which he stood. Dark silhouettes that did not move and were almost as black as the emptiness beyond them, and he felt more than saw them. There was one directly in front of him. And another to his left. And to his right. And he knew that if he turned, they would be behind him. He got the sensation that there were many of them.

"Go." His voice was a threadbare croak. "Leave me be."

Murder, they screamed, but yet it was as quiet as wind. *Murder for the killing kind, the killing man, the man that kills, the one with blood on his hands.*

Lee looked down and could see that he was naked, and that his entire body was splashed with gore. Not only blood, but bits and pieces of bone and brain matter and ligaments and muscles. And his hands and arms were coated in it, up to his elbows, like a crimson pair of gauntlets.

"Not real," he said. "Not real."

But his heart did not believe him.

The voices became louder, more distinct, and at the same time they seemed to be filtering down, at first spoken by the many, and then by a dozen, and then only by a few, and then by one: *Blood for the one that does what he has to do. Kill another's body. Suicide by your own mind. Blood and murder for the one that does what he has to do . . .*

The single speaker stepped out of the gloom now.

It was Kyle. Not as Lee had left him, dead in the roadway with a bullet hole. But after Lee had gone away. After Lee had left him in the hands of the infected hunters. After he had been eaten and torn apart. This Kyle was not a whole body, but more of a skeleton with meat and organs still clinging to it. But the face remained intact, grinning at Lee.

Maneaters acquire a taste for human flesh. Murderers acquire a taste for murdering. Killers kill.

Animals eat. Everyone just does what they do. And you will do what you do, you big hero you, you man of the hour, you big swinging dick. You kill everyone you need to so you can complete your mission, but you love it, don't you? You love it, but you just hate how much you love it.

Lee stared and felt the fear melting into anger. "That's unfair, Kyle," he said in a voice carved of stone and ice. "I don't enjoy killing. But there is a . . . certain satisfaction when I get the job done."

And then he had his KA-BAR in his hands.

He reached out, seizing the corpse by the throat and ramming the knife into its guts. As he jammed it repeatedly into Kyle's masticated torso, he could hear the body whispering something very odd: *Where's Harper?*

Lee came awake to a cold dawn. Flat and gray, it bore the shaky, queasy feeling of nights spent awake with nerves and anticipation. People were already moving about, Lee could hear. He knew many of them probably had slept very little, and finally given up as soon as the sky had started to lighten, thanking God that the endless night of waiting was over.

Nerves, nerves, nerves. They robbed sleep and sanity and Lee wished in vain for the day when it would not be his lot to feel them so often. The day when he might know peace and rest. Wherever that place was, on whatever day it began, he felt that he was far away from it now. Many days and many miles.

He sat up on his bedroll, trying to rub some

life back into his face. His stomach still squirmed. Part hunger and part nausea from fitful sleep and a mind filled with nightmares. The anger he'd felt in the dream, the thing that had consumed his fear like a flash fire, it was still burning down inside of him.

Where's Harper? a stranger's voice in his head had asked. *Where's Harper? Where's Julia?*

Lee threw the blankets off himself and went to the office window. The pain in his side, the pain in his ankle, the general feeling of being beat to hell—he barely noticed it anymore. He still walked with a little limp in the morning, but the pain was just a distraction. The buzzing of a fly.

At the window he looked out. Two pickups. The Marine MATV. A few other small cars huddled in the Square, coated in frost. No sign of the vehicles left to Harper's care. The Humvee and the LMTVs and the HEMTT with the wrecker attachment. They had not returned in the night.

Lee tapped the windowsill aggressively with a single finger. *They should've been back already. They should've been back. What does that mean? Why haven't they checked in? Are they dead? They're fucking dead. That's what fucking happens around here. People don't forget to check in. They just get killed.*

But Lee didn't know that. His thoughts erred on the side of the negative and pessimistic, having just been dredged out of dreams of murder and death. Perhaps he was just rushing to conclusions. There were a million and one reasons why Harper and Julia might not have made it back yet. Not all of them included death and dismemberment.

Down in the Square, the two pickup trucks were attended by a group of men, one of which was Old Man Hughes, standing and talking. Two of the others were Nate and Devon. The remaining two were from Old Man Hughes's group, which had come out of Dunn. The pair was young and old. Father and son, Lee remembered, though their names were escaping him.

He pushed away from the window and gathered his things from his bedroll. He stepped into his boots and laced them up. His back, stiff and twisted, complained when he yanked to tighten the laces, but that was nothing new. He worked his way into the chest rig that he'd scavenged, and then slung into his rifle. The rig only had four full magazines left. But that would change soon.

Lee reached deep into the backpack that sat next to his bedroll and extracted the GPS device. He pressed the main button and watched the screen come to life, only to switch it off again. He kept thinking that it wasn't really going to work. That when he walked up to the bunker, it would betray him and not turn on. But so far it had worked.

"It's gonna work," he told himself. *You can be pessimistic all you want, but I won't have you prophesying doom over everything. This shit can still get done, and you're going to make sure that it does. That's all you can do.*

Tucked against the cabinets where they had erected the main radio station for the Camp Ryder Hub, Lee found the four "manpack" radios. They were as valuable to him as gold might've been in another life, and when he'd believed that he would never access another bunker for more equipment, he had guarded them jealously. They were the only manpack radios he had, and he wouldn't just hand them out for every scavenging or scouting mission. But this was a little different. Not only would he have access to his bunkers again, but what they were trying to do would require a little coordination, and without Harper's vehicles with the SINCGARS radio mounts inside, Lee would have to rely on the manpacks.

These were smaller but more powerful than the manpacks he had seen used in Iraq and Afghanistan. Rather than having to strap it into a small backpack, Lee was able to hook it to an empty spot on his chest rig. It fit awkwardly, but it fit. He grabbed two more, then looked over everything to make sure nothing else was needed. Then he left the office and closed the door behind him.

In the Square, Lee stood in the center and called the gathering volunteers to himself. Hughes stood with his two men—introduced as Paul and Junior. Tomlin had appeared with three more. One of them was from the Fuquay-Varina group, but the other two were original Camp Ryder folks. The one from Fuquay-Varina was a younger guy that had toed the line with Professor White, but since had been making himself useful. He just went by Joey. Lee wasn't sure if anyone had got a last name from him. The other two were just a couple that had been around Camp Ryder since its inception. They had followed Bus, dealt with Jerry, and fought back when the opportunity arose. His name was Jared and he had been an electrician, if Lee recalled correctly. Her name was Brandy, and Lee wasn't sure how far back before the collapse Brandy and Jared went, but they'd been together ever since Lee could remember.

This mismatched crew was joined by Brett and his dozen others that had a bone to pick with the Followers, and Mac and his fourteen, who would be going with them to secure Newton Grove and make sure the way was clear for the Marine artillery. Brinly and his three Marines pressed in to Lee's right.

Lee looked to Brinly. "Did Tomlin get comms with you guys?"

The older Marine nodded. "He's got one of our radios. Won't pick anything up until we're in position with the arty, though. Too far to reach Camp Lejeune on that frequency."

Lee turned to Tomlin. "So you've got both radios, right? Camp Ryder and Marines, right?"

Tomlin gave him a thumbs-up. "As soon as we're clear from the hospital, I'll make the call and let the arty do its job."

Lee directed his attention to his bait trucks. He gave the first manpack radio to Nate, and the second to Paul. "Frequency should already be set to the main communications channel," he told them. "So you don't need to mess with any of the buttons or knobs. Just report in every so often to make sure everything is good, and obviously when you make contact with the hordes, or if you meet any sort of resistance."

He looked between Paul and Junior, and then Nate and Devon. "It's not your job to fight if you hit something that wants a fight. A roadblock. Another crew. Whatever. You retreat. You go around. Keep pushing, but don't get caught up in a fight. We don't have the time or resources to come back you up. You're pretty much on your own. You guys understand that, right?"

Paul and Junior nodded and shuffled their feet, but did a good job of looking confident. Devon blew a breath out of pursed lips and looked nervous. Nate seemed to be calm. But surfaces didn't reveal much. Most folks had violent rivers flowing under seeming stillness.

Lee turned to Mac and Brett's group, the largest group by far. "I already said it once, but it bears repeating. We have not had contact with Newton Grove in a bit. That worries me and it should worry you. Be on your toes when you get out there. If any of the Newton Grove folks are there, they aren't going to recognize any of you guys, so don't provoke a fight if there isn't one. On the same note, though, we need to hold Newton Grove. I-40 runs straight through it, and that's the path the Marines are going to be taking in. It's gotta be held."

Brett seemed sure of himself. "We'll take care of it, Captain."

Beside Brett, Mac remained silent and somewhat sullen.

Lee felt uncertain about Mac and his group, but his reservations had to be put aside. There was no time for them. "Our hand is being forced

here, guys. I don't like it any more than you do.
I like a plan that I can control. Not one that I'm
forced into. But this is the hand we've been dealt,
so we're gonna play it the best we can. We get one
shot at this, guys. One shot to coordinate this shit
before . . ." He sucked air through his teeth. "Well,
I don't need to tell you everything that will happen if we strike out. I'm sure y'all have thought
about the consequences plenty enough for yourself. Probably why most of you look like you didn't
sleep last night. So just focus on what you have to
do to get it done. Do whatever it takes to make
this happen. It has to happen. We have to pull it
off. And I believe that if anybody can, we can. We
managed to build the Camp Ryder Hub—one
of the safest places in the state—in the middle of
complete chaos. And even if you weren't here for
building Camp Ryder? Hell, you're still alive."
There was a brief, nervous chuckle. "That counts
for something in my book. That lets me know the
quality of people I'm dealing with. Survivors. And
that's all that I can ask. Keep making sure that we
survive."

Lee gestured to the group at large. "Look
around, folks. This may not seem like much. Just
a bunch of tired people standing in a gravel lot in
the middle of Bumfuck, North Carolina. But if
this state still exists a week from now, it's gonna
be because of everyone standing in this group. We
made it happen. We are *going* to make it happen.
And that's all I gotta say about that."

Through the cold stillness of the morning
air, Lee could hear the beat of helicopter rotors.

"That'll be my ride. Does anyone have any questions? Need any clarification on anything?"

Nobody said anything.

"I'll have one of the radios with me at all times." He looked to Nate and Devon and stepped a little closer. "I'm not sure what's going on with Harper and Julia's team. They were supposed to have made it back here by now. You're essentially going to be following their path north and west, so...I know it's a long shot, but if you stumble across them, let me know immediately."

Nate clapped Lee on the shoulder. "Will do, boss. I'm sure they'll show up."

Lee turned to Brinly. "You goin' back to Lejeune or staying with me?"

Brinly pointed at him. "We're stickin' with you."

Lee addressed the rest of the gathering as the sound of rotors grew louder and forced him to raise his voice. "Every one of you knows what's up. It's do-or-die time, folks."

The crowd split and headed for the vehicles, Nate and Devon to one of the pickup trucks, Paul and Junior to the other. Brett's and Mac's groups made for an assortment of larger and smaller vehicles, managing to cram into three cars and a large van.

As the gathering dispersed, Lee could see Angela and Marie standing a few yards back from where they had gathered. They both looked worried. Angela's face still bore an edge from the previous night. Lee wouldn't fault her that.

He approached, giving a nod of greeting to Marie.

"Nobody's heard anything from Harper or Julia?" Marie said. She was one of the toughest people in Camp Ryder, and Lee could probably count on one hand the number of times she'd showed concern for her sister being out and about and in danger. Even when she'd been the medic for Lee's team, back when it was LaRouche and Wilson and Father Jim, and they'd been infiltrating cities and trapping the hordes...Marie had always just shrugged it off. Lee imagined that she was worried all the time, or maybe she managed to put it out of her mind. But she didn't let it show.

It showed now, though. And all that Lee could do was shake his head. "They were supposed to be here yesterday evening. I'm not sure why...let's just hope they're running a little late."

"Yeah." She nodded once. "Sure."

Lee looked at Angela and searched his mind for softer words, but had none. Perhaps that was best. If he showed kindness or tenderness, it would only undermine what he had so painfully accomplished the night before. He needed Angela to leave him alone. He needed her to forget about him. It would make things easier.

Carl's bird came over the treetops, the sound suddenly becoming loud and overbearing and directly on top of them. Lee wanted to reach out to Angela but resisted that urge. She would likely pull away, anyhow. So he just gave her a grim nod and shouted over the roar of rotorwash, "Camp Ryder's on you now, Angela. Stay on the radio. Keep everyone safe."

If she even heard him, she gave no acknowledgment of it.

Good. It's better that way. Let her stay angry. Let her stay mad at me.

Lee turned away without another word shared between them, and walked stoop-shouldered into the rushing wind as the helicopter from Fort Bragg touched down to pick up its passengers and make their last gambit for survival.

TEN

INFIGHTING

HARPER TWISTED TO TRY and relieve some of the pressure on his shoulders. He was bound by the wrists and by the ankles and lying in a dusty corner of the metal barn where they had parked their convoy the previous day. He'd been sitting in that same position, thinking about how uncomfortable he was for at least the last hour. But no matter how much he tried to turn himself around, one position was as uncomfortable as the next.

Inside the big metal barn were stacks of tractor implements fallen into disrepair. Entire racks filled with various tools. Shelves filled with everything from antifreeze and oil to insecticide and fertilizer. Harper stared at the fertilizer and thought about all the diesel fuel lying around and how he would love to blow this place to smoking bits, with Kensey and his goons still inside.

They had cleared an area to put their prisoners—leaving no tools or sharp objects within reach. They would have to cross the entire barn to get to anything that might be used as a weapon. And they had chained him and Julia to one of the columns that held up the roof of the barn. They weren't going anywhere.

In the center of the barn, Kensey's men had built a small fire. The barn's roof had a skylight that they managed to open to let the smoke out, but the inside of the barn was still hazy and acrid when they threw some unseasoned wood on the fire. Two or three Marines would huddle around the fire while the rest remained on the perimeter outside. They swapped out at intervals of three hours. At least it was what Harper figured was three hours.

He had not slept the entire night. He'd just lain there the whole time, back up against the wooden post, and sometimes he dozed, but he was too damn cold and too damn uncomfortable and too damn enraged to fall asleep. He kept thinking about it over and over, and every time he thought about Charlie and Dylan and the others that had been gunned down against the side of the barn, his heart rate would spike and he knew there would be no sleep.

Before the sun had set, Harper had stared at the wall and he could see all the little bullet holes, like pinpricks of light, in the side of the barn. The places where those little projectiles had punched through his people, and then through the thin metal walls. As darkness fell, the little holes that marked the places where his team had been murdered slowly disappeared. But dawn was coming, and he could see them again.

His tongue played at the empty space in his gums where one of his incisors had been until only several hours ago. When they had cleared the barn and chained them up, Harper had started yelling at them, trying to figure out what the hell they were doing, but it only earned him a spectacular right hook from Reilly, the Marine with the acne scars.

Since then, he'd kept his silence.

But he'd brooded.

Internally, he wasn't sure whether he wanted to scream in anger or weep for the people he had lost. But he thought that maybe he was far past weeping. The last time he had, it was after Mike had killed Torri and then took his own life, right in front of everyone. Now there was just anger. The sense of being cheated. Being wronged. The feeling that none of this made any sense at all. Not the deaths of his people, and not Kensey's sudden betrayal. None of it seemed logical. It just seemed cruel.

He knew there was a reason. There had to be a reason.

After all, me and Julia are still alive.

As dawn broke and the bullet holes in the wall became a visible reminder again, two voices became audible, coming from outside of the barn. The Marines around the dwindling fire were asleep in their bivy sacks, except for one, who was watching them. When he heard the voices, he glanced at the door to the outside with some irritation, then back to Harper.

It was obvious that the voices were in disagreement. At first, Harper could not hear what they were saying, only that it was an apparent argument, but as they drew closer, the words became more distinct.

"...I was with you from the start. But this isn't what we fucking talked about. This wasn't what you fucking described, man." A sound of irritation. "This is some fucked-up shit."

"This is how it's going down. Don't go all queasy on me now."

The door to the barn ripped open harshly. Baker, the light-skinned black guy stood there, looking immensely pissed from under the brim of his floppy hat. Close behind him was Kensey. Baker took a step into the barn, and then stopped and turned to address Kensey.

"Don't play that with me, bro." Baker put a finger in Kensey's chest. "You know the shit I've done for you."

Kensey glanced at Harper, then swiped the finger from his chest. "Hey, why don't you lock it up, jackass?" He nodded fractionally in Harper's direction. "You want to talk, we can do it outside. Quietly. Don't get all black and loud on me now."

Baker eyed Harper with some annoyance and then reversed himself, stepping back through the door and outside. He shouldered Kensey and said, "Fuck you, mick."

Kensey locked eyes with Harper, as though the whole disagreement was his fault. He spat into the dirt and then closed the barn door again. The voices were quieter, but Harper could still hear most of what was said. The rest he intuited from context.

"So what are you saying?" Kensey's voice. "We gonna have problems?"

"Nah. You're the one makin' a problem. I just said that shit was fucked up. You got a problem with me sayin' the truth, it's probably 'cause you got a guilty conscience about it."

"You pulled the trigger just as much as I did."

"Nah, I didn't shoot them dudes up on the wall. That was all you."

"What'd you think was gonna happen, big boy? We were just gonna order 'em to lay down their weapons? We were gonna babysit ten dudes? Fuck that. We got the two important people. The rest were just wasting space. And you were on board with this twelve hours ago. You wanted this just as much as everyone else in this squad, so don't act all high and mighty 'cause you got a little dirt under your fucking fingernails."

"I went along with it because you're my boy. But I'm starting to think that was a bad fucking idea."

"Which part? Going along with it or being my boy?"

"Yeah. Both."

"Really? You wanna walk?"

"Maybe. Maybe."

"Then walk, motherfucker. But that'd be pretty fucking dumb at this point, because nobody else is going with you. You already did the work, even if you think it was too damn dirty for your black ass. Might as well reap the rewards."

There was a moment of silence. Harper glanced at the Marine who was sitting by the fire. He was staring into the fire, shaking his head slowly.

Something banged up against the metal wall of the barn loud enough to make Harper jump. There was the sound of scuffling feet. A few grunts and grumbles. More scuffling, shuffling, scrambling. Then it got quiet for another long moment. There was a gagging sound.

The Marine at the fire stood, but didn't make a move for the door.

The silence beyond stretched. Harper began to imagine.

Then the door opened and Kensey stepped through, looking a little dusty, a few scratches on his neck, sucking the blood from a split lip. He held his rifle with one hand and was breathing hard through his nose. He looked hatefully at Harper, and then turned to the fire.

The Marine at the fire looked outside. "Baker all right?"

"He'll be fine." Kensey raised his voice a little bit, as though he were saying something for the benefit of someone still outside the barn. "I think everyone's just goin' a little stir crazy. We only got a little while longer to wait. They should be here any time now. So let's just calm the fuck down."

Harper stared at the Marines as they switched out who was resting and who was watching. None of them made any eye contact. Whatever was going on, Harper didn't think the Marines really wanted anything to do with Harper and Julia.

We got the important ones, Kensey'd said. *What the hell was that supposed to mean?*

Seated almost back-to-back with him, Julia stirred awake. Kensey kept her drugged, whether out of mercy or strategy, Harper couldn't tell. He wished that she was awake more often, but he was glad that she was not in pain. He felt her fingers touch his, and both their hands were cold from lack of circulation. He squeezed her finger to let her know that he was with her.

But for how much longer?

Not much longer until they get here, Harper thought obtusely. *Whatever the fuck that means.*

Not much longer…

Brett ended up in the van with Mac and Georgia and a mixed assortment of both their groups. Brett thought that was interesting. Maybe it was the sense of desperation hanging thick like a fog over everything. Even survivors could be cliquish at times, but here and now they were crammed together and not saying a word about it. The people from Brett's group were seated with the people from Mac and Georgia's group and they spoke to each other, swapping war stories and gloomy premonitions.

Brett was by no means the leader of his group. They didn't really have a leader, but if they'd gone around and polled them all on who they thought was their leader, Brett might have the winning vote. He had come along late to the party, joining their group only a few weeks before their little farm camp was razed by the Followers. Brett had arrived with only the clothes on his back, and he'd escaped the destruction much in the same manner—piled into the back of a pickup truck with everyone else, clutching a rifle, his face soot-stained from the fires he'd choked through while he fled.

It wasn't until that day that it seemed those people started to trust him. And maybe it was because they had no choice. The people they saw as their leaders had been murdered and burned and hung from telephone poles, or enslaved, either to fight or to breed. They were scared and lost. Brett must have seemed confident to them. Maybe that was why they clung to him.

The day that he'd come across the man named LaRouche on the road, as they'd fled from the Followers with only an hour between them and the destruction they had left behind, Brett had cemented his spot in the bedraggled vestiges of that group. He had been the one who told them about the Camp Ryder Hub. He had been the one that had spoken with LaRouche. He had been the one that had taken them to Smithfield, seeking asylum. He had been the one that had dealt with Jacob, and had fought alongside the exiles from Camp Ryder to take it back.

Now, when Brett asked for a few bodies to help hold Newton Grove, in order to save the Camp Ryder Hub, nearly everyone capable of holding a rifle and pulling a trigger had volunteered. He'd actually forced a few of them to stay behind.

And now here he was. Driving down Highway 50, straight toward Newton Grove, not knowing what was ahead of them. Not knowing how many of these people were going to be alive in another twenty-four hours. Only knowing that he had a job to do. It didn't matter that he was scared near to the point of trembling—in fact, his legs were trembling, but he hid it well.

It would be good to get out of the van, he knew. Once he was moving, once he was doing what needed to be done, then it would not be so bad. But nerves always festered in the stillness of waiting. Left at idle, the mind could make a coward of even the bravest man.

Mac drove the van, with Georgia in the passenger seat, looking as gray and curmudgeonly as ever. Brett knelt between the two front seats and watched their progress. In front of them was a flat road that rarely curved. Just two simple lanes with yellow paint between them, barely visible now over the leaves and branches that clogged the road. To either side, fields sat looking sadly abandoned, the dirt and dead weeds as gray as corpses. The stands of forest were similarly colored. A herd of deer watched them from the center of a field and darted away skittishly as the van drew parallel with them. Every mile or so there was a farmhouse, sometimes close to the road, and other times tucked back away with a long gravel driveway leading to it. From what Brett could tell, almost all of them looked like they'd been looted. As they passed at forty-five miles per hour, Brett noted small details: a missing door here, broken windows there, fire damage on many of them.

Someone must've set the houses just to watch them burn, Brett thought. There didn't seem to be any legitimate reason to burn a random farmhouse in the middle of nowhere.

As they drew closer to Newton Grove, the

scenes started to change. Some of the evidence of looting was not as prevalent. Most of the abandoned cars had been pushed out of the roadway, or in areas where there was a slight snarl, they had at least been pushed far enough to clear a path. There were several places that caught Brett's eye, and he thought that these might have been used for sentry outposts to guard the roads. A small embankment that provided high ground, with beaten paths through the overgrown weeds, leading to the top. A box truck with a ladder against the back and sandbags on top—that one was obvious.

Brett saw them and pointed them out, and Mac would slow the van. But the nests and lookouts were never occupied, and the convoy would continue on. Everything seemed to be abandoned.

"This doesn't look like a place where people are living," Brett commented.

"We're not even there yet," Georgia said. She had a gruff way of talking. She reminded Brett of an old washerwoman, the way she walked around with stooped shoulders and glared at people, her haggard face framed by her stringy gray hair. Centuries ago she would've been accused of witchcraft and burned, Brett thought.

Brett shifted his weight, relieving some of the stress on his knees. He was tense. Jumpy, even. He couldn't seem to sit still, and both Mac and Georgia seemed to have already taken notice, though they hadn't said anything. When he fidgeted they just kind of gave him a sidelong glance, their faces somewhat annoyed.

"You guys are some pretty cool customers, huh?" Brett said, only half antagonizing.

"What do you mean?" Mac asked, keeping his eyes on the road.

"I mean..." Brett glanced between the two of them. "Neither of you seem very nervous."

Mac shrugged. "Well, you heard the good captain. He thinks this place is abandoned. What's there to worry about?"

Brett almost laughed, but caught himself. "So it's only people that worry you?"

Mac nodded. "Most of the time. The infected? We can drive away from the infected. They aren't gonna shoot at us, and they ain't gonna drive after us. But people...people are more dangerous."

Brett considered it. "Yeah. I guess you kind of have a point. On the small scale, that is."

Georgia looked at him, perpetually irritated.

"I'm just saying," Brett explained. "People don't band together in massive hordes and strip the countryside clean and kill everything in their path. Like a fucking...a fucking plague of something."

"A plague o' locusts o'er the land?" Mac said with a half smile.

"Sure. Yeah." Brett nodded. "But seriously."

"I know." Mac's face dropped the smile. "We're serious. We just...we try not to get too worked up."

Brett pointed through the windshield. "That it?"

Straight ahead the road ended in what looked like a barricade of some sort. There was a substantial amount of Jersey barriers, which made Brett think that there had been some state-sponsored barricading going on before the survivors took over. But as they drew closer, he could see that there were also cars, tires, and fifty-gallon drums that he assumed were filled with something heavy—either water or dirt. Brett couldn't really see beyond the barrier, but he could see the limbs and upper branches of a stand of large trees.

Mac stopped the van about a block from the barricades and the giant turnabout that marked the dead center of Newton Grove, North Carolina. To either side were dilapidated buildings. To the left it was brick with chipping white paint revealing dusky red underneath. To the right it was regular redbrick storefronts. A gas station. A Hardee's restaurant. An automotive store.

All of them very still and quiet.

"Creeps me out sitting in the middle of all this shit," Brett said, unconsciously lowering his voice.

"Yeah," Mac seemed to actually agree, and the van crept forward another few feet before he stopped it. "Maybe we should get out and walk."

"That sounds good," Brett said, nodding.

Georgia already had her door open. "Leave the engine running."

Brett and his people were the only ones with weapons, though they didn't have enough to even fill the hands of every person in his group. Lee had given them six rifles, which were the only ones they had to spare. He'd given them a total of twelve magazines, so each person had enough to refresh their rifle only once. Everyone already had a passing familiarity with the M4 platform— Lee had taught it to them shortly after he'd taken Camp Ryder back.

Mac and Georgia's group was largely weapon-less, unless you counted various cutting and blud-geoning instruments. A lot of machetes and axes, Brett noted. There was a shotgun and a hunting rifle in the mix somewhere, but in a show of soli-darity, Mac and Georgia both had gone without firearms. After shoving some supplies off to the Marines so that they could get their artillery con-voy rolling, Lee's first stop would be right here in Newton Grove, to arm Mac and Georgia's group, and the rest of Brett's.

But for now, it was up to Brett and the five oth-ers in his group that were armed. So when the convoy stopped and the doors opened, Brett's people moved up first. They were undisciplined and clumsy, and they were scared. But they formed a loose line out in front of the rest of the people who had no weapons and they started moving for-ward, very cautiously.

As he got closer to the concrete barriers, Brett smelled something that had become very famil-iar to him. He wrinkled his nose and stopped dead in his tracks. A glance to either side revealed that Georgia and Mac were smelling the same thing, too.

"That's not a good sign," Brett whispered.

After a moment's hesitation, he pushed forward. Here, directly in front of him, the walls around the Newton Grove camp were only barriers, and they were only chest-high. From about fifteen yards away, Brett could clearly see down into what had once been the town of Newton Grove. What had once also been the group of survivors that had gone by the same name. The details seemed too big to gather, but Brett comprehended what he was seeing in broader strokes.

The camp inside of those barriers seemed to be a sister city to Camp Ryder's own Shantytown. Just a bunch of cobbled-together structures that nearly filled the entire space inside of their hastily erected walls. But it was obvious that they had not built the walls high enough. They had not built them with barbed wire and spikes of metal and broken glass, like Camp Ryder did. And something had gotten inside.

There were some bodies, but mostly there were just parts.

Black blood.

Bullet holes.

"They had a hell of a fight here," Mac said.

"With what?" Georgia croaked, hand over her nose.

Brett didn't say so, but he was looking at one of the bodies. Not one of the people that had belonged to the group, he didn't think. This body was whole, rather than ripped to shreds. It was completely naked. Bloat and rot had taken it, but Brett could still see the face. The ghastly face with its hollowed out eye sockets and the jaw that hung open just a bit too wide to be normal. The long, lanky arms. The overgrown, clawlike fingernails.

He didn't say so, but he thought he knew what they'd been fighting.

ELEVEN

THE HOSPITAL

IN THE TIME THAT he had been with Lee at Camp Ryder, Tomlin had yet to go to Smithfield, or to see the Johnston Memorial Hospital, which had become a sort of medical way station for the Camp Ryder Hub. According to Lee, it was still full of supplies, but had yet to be taken back after Jerry had pulled everyone out, leaving only a skeleton crew to research the infected woman that Jacob had captured. Then Jacob had met with Brett's group, fleeing from the Followers and coming to Smithfield on the advice of a long-lost LaRouche, and Jacob had left the place abandoned.

Tomlin's team needed very little, except for the ammunition they carried for their own defense. It was Tomlin, and the three people he had garnered as volunteers for this particular aspect of the mission, and they could all fit into a small, older model sedan with a squeaky fan belt and a puttering engine. They each took a small pack with them, mostly containing some food and water that would hopefully last them until the bait trucks could get the hordes into Smithfield. But food and water wasn't a big concern.

Joey-the-college-student was up front with Jared-the-electrician. Tomlin and Brandy-the-waitress sat in the backseat. Jared had taken the wheel and was driving with both hands on it, leaning forward in his seat and scanning all around as the four-banger putted down Brightleaf Boulevard at a steady thirty miles per hour.

Tomlin knew none of them well, but he felt like that was going to change. You can't be stuck on a roof with someone and not get to know them a little bit. These were simply the people he had talked to that had heard the call and volunteered. He wished he could say that he chose them specially for this part of the mission—people with nerves of steel and good skills, that were going to watch his back and their teammates' backs. People that would make him feel more confident.

But what he got was volunteers. A student, an electrician, and a waitress.

I can make do, he told himself, sitting upright in the backseat with his rifle in his lap, looking out the back driver-side window at the carnage of the small town known as Smithfield. He'd never gotten the full story, but Tomlin could intuit from bits and pieces of conversation that he picked up from others. Smithfield had been a bloodbath when they'd found it months before, when Lee had first come to Camp Ryder. And it had been a bloodbath again when they'd cleared it of the thousands of infected that were milling about in the streets.

They'd made an effort to clean up the bodies to prevent the spread of disease, but even so you couldn't erase scars like that. On the road that they traveled there were still patches of skin and bones and clothing that clung to the concrete. To the sides, where massive funeral pyres had been lit, scorched tangles of bones remained behind like monuments. After several operations to reclaim the city, there had been so many bodies that most of them had just been pushed into uncovered mass graves. The stink of them still tainted the air, though Tomlin understood that it had been much, much worse in the previous months.

Jared dodged around a mass of tangled something lying in the middle of the road. Up ahead, Tomlin could see the top of the hospital looming. It was a four- or five-story construction, with a parking deck attached to one side. Ground-floor access from several points. Not to mention the access doors at each level of the parking garage. It had been sitting abandoned for a little over a week now. And like a boot left outside, it needed to be shaken out to make sure there were no biting things inside.

Tomlin leaned forward in his seat. "Take us right up to the front, Jared."

"The front?"

"Yeah." Tomlin checked his weapon—not out of any real necessity but simply out of habit. "We gotta clear this entire structure. The late great Jacob left this fine establishment abandoned to the elements, so it's up to us to make sure there ain't nobody creepin' around in the halls, takin' us unawares. We're gonna start from the front door— the most likely point of entry—and we're going to clear and secure as we go. Once everything is safe, we'll set up our post at the top."

"Okay," Jared said, steering the sedan around a dilapidated barricade and into the parking lot of the hospital.

"Okay," Brandy echoed.

Joey-the-student just nodded.

I can make do, Tomlin reminded himself. "Any of you guys seen any shit?" he asked hopefully. "Get in any shootouts?"

They looked between themselves as though they were all mysterious strangers to each other, though Tomlin got the impression that they knew each other quite well. None of them spoke up. Tomlin's heart dropped just a tiny bit. He supposed it would be a little too much to hope for to get a few seasoned fighters in his group of volunteers. But the seasoned fighters were all dead or used up on other aspects of the mission.

There's old survivors and there's bold survivors, Tomlin thought with some irritation. *But there ain't no old, bold survivors. Is that the shape of it?*

"Okay then," he said, shouldering his rifle. "You already know the basics of how to use that rifle Lee gave you. All I can add is . . . watch where you put your muzzle—not into my back, please—and make sure you ID a target before engaging. I think everything else is pretty much common sense. I hope." Tomlin sniffed. "I'll go point. Y'all just follow me and do what I do."

They pulled to a stop at the front of the hospital. The sliding glass doors were open. And that did not make Tomlin feel any better. The engine in the little old sedan died and the doors popped open. Tomlin stepped out into cold sunshine. The sun hanging in its low winter arc. Everything seemed alternately golden and gray.

Tomlin took a brief moment to listen to the world around him. The ears were one of the more underutilized tools, but they had so much information to give. If you just sat still for a few moments, you could often get a sense of what was going on around you. Small things made noises. Other things were noted by their lack of noise. Just like right at that moment as Tomlin stood there. Everything was silent. Silent save for the ticking of the old four-banger engine. The sound of engine fluids. A slight gust of wind.

No birds.

No people.

No other cars.

It felt like the surface of the moon.

Tomlin looked at the sliding glass doors to the hospital. They were southern exposed, and the sky was reflecting madly off of them. It was difficult to see inside. Tomlin started moving. Stillness was death. He always felt awkward standing in one place too long. Habits developed in third-world countries with enemy snipers were difficult to overcome. Behind him, his three inexperienced partners followed.

Tomlin angled himself as he moved, trying to defeat the reflection of the sky while trying not to stay directly in front of the doors and the fatal funnel they created. It wasn't just infected creeping around in the darkness that concerned him.

Other things had been known to take up residence in the abandoned places of the world. Things with guns.

About a yard or two from the front door, he was able to see into the building. His eyes went deep into the atrium of the hospital, looking behind desks and pillars. It looked clear, for the most part. There was a bad stench coming from inside, but it wasn't until Tomlin drew his focus a little closer that he saw what was making the smell.

He had looked over them, thinking they were small piles of trash that the wind had blown in. But when he looked harder at them, he could see the red-brown of blood, the tatters of clothing, the shards of bones. Three of them, all just inside the entryway. The sliding glass doors were painted with old gore from these bodies, and their deconstructed state was not from a week or two of corruption, but because something had gotten to them when they were still fresh. There wasn't enough between the three piles to piece together one person.

"Infected must've got 'em," Tomlin said, wrinkling his nose and aiming his rifle into the shadows of the atrium. If an animal found an abandoned building that yielded a meal, wouldn't it peruse the rest of the building? But these bodies had been ravaged some time ago. Perhaps the infected had moved on.

"Who were they?" Brandy said, her voice hollow and flat.

Tomlin shrugged, then stepped into the atrium of the hospital and around the bodies. He lowered his voice. "Best guess? Doc Hamilton and his two guards. Jacob never said what happened to them."

"I guess this happened to them." Her voice sounded a little tight. Then she gagged, audibly, and moved past the bodies. "Sorry. I'm fine. It's just...the smell."

Tomlin didn't mind. Nobody got used to that smell. The smell of dead flesh was a warning sign that went straight down deep into your DNA and rang a bunch of warning bells. It was not only a putrid odor; it disturbed something inside the mind as well. A way for your animal brain to shout at you, *Don't go in there! People die in there!*

"Guys." Tomlin pointed behind him. "Slide those doors shut for me. We gotta secure as we go. Any open door needs to be closed and locked. And barricaded, if we can manage it."

Tomlin motioned Brandy to move with him while Joey and Jared muscled the doors shut and manually locked them. The atrium was mostly empty. No furniture. Nothing that could be moved in front of the doors to block them. There were several large support pillars with fancy tile work on them that a few anonymous bullet holes had ruined, just a reminder from some little forgotten spat, that nothing and no place was truly safe. There was a large front desk area. A few doors that remained closed. To the left, Tomlin spotted the doors to the stairs that would take them to the upper levels.

Tomlin looked behind the pillars, behind the desk, and in utility closets and bathrooms with push-open doors. The interiors of the bathrooms were lightless like dungeons. Each stall sat in murky pools of shadow. He listened hard at the entryway, but inside was only silence. A deep breath through the nose revealed only a dank, musty smell. Not the smell of rot, or the smell of long-unwashed bodies. He glanced behind him to make sure that Brandy was close.

"Hold the door," he whispered.

He moved in, navigating by the light coming in from the open bathroom door. Unlike Lee, Tomlin still had his original rifle—the one he'd come out of his bunker with—rather than the stripped versions that were handed out to everyone else. Tomlin's still had the items he'd customized it with, including the light kit.

He swept the white beam of light over the stalls. He used it in flashes and quick sweeps. You never just left your gunlight on. It gave you light, but it was also a beacon for people and things to shoot at. Besides, using it sparingly conserved the batteries.

He went to the stalls randomly. The middle one first, then the two sides.

They were unoccupied.

The women's bathroom was similarly empty, though he found a pile of clothes in one corner and an empty can of black beans. The inside of the can was old and dried. The clothes were matted down from lying there for a while. It looked like someone had slept there for a night, but not recently.

He wondered how many single survivors there were, wandering around out there. He imagined that there couldn't be many, but perhaps there were. This could not have been more than one or two people. Maybe a small family at the very most—two adults and a child. He imagined them huddled around that single can of black beans, sharing it. He wondered if they knew how close they were to Camp Ryder when they'd stopped here for the night, or if they'd just kept going whatever direction they were heading, hoping that safety lay in some direction. But besides Mac and Georgia's group, no one had come to Camp Ryder within the last week or so. Whoever this had been had not found Camp Ryder.

Back in the atrium, Tomlin found Joey and Jared standing in the center, looking about warily. They had successfully closed the door. Joey looked a little green in the face. Tomlin noticed what looked like a fresh puddle of vomit near the sliding glass doors.

"They locked?" Tomlin asked.

Jared nodded.

"Okay. We've got to clear every single level of this hospital." Tomlin looked above him as though he could see the challenge that awaited them through the ceiling. "It's going to take a while, so we might as well get started. Stick together. No breaking up. In every room we go into, I'll be point, then Brandy, then Jared. Joey, you're going to stand in the door and watch our backs, make sure nothing comes at us from behind or tries to sneak around us. Got that?"

"Yeah." Joey nodded, swallowing. "I got it."

"Finger off the trigger and outside the trigger guard until you see a threat." Tomlin had already told them this, but it was just one of those rules that needed to be repeated, especially when he was standing in front of them. "And try not to muzzle-sweep each other."

Nods all around.

"All right, then." Tomlin headed for the stairs to the second level.

Lee wasn't doing it consciously, but he kept catching himself gripping the GPS in white knuckles. Only when his hands began to tremble with the strain did he realize it and force himself to relax. It reminded him of when he was ten years old and his father had let him shoot his shotgun for the first time. Not a youth shotgun. Not a shotgun chambered for a light round. A hunting shotgun loaded up with double-ought buck. He'd been so simultaneously thrilled and terrified. He had clutched that shotgun in a similarly intense grip, partly because he feared it would buck out of his small hands, and partly because the opportunity was so unexpected that he thought if he put the shotgun down, his father would never let him pick it up again.

On the screen, his life was held in the balance of pixels. One blue dot moving toward a stationary waypoint marked *B#3*. And coming in fast. Closing the distance quickly. Below them, the eastern North Carolina crop lands were a jumble of geometric shapes.

Sitting directly beside Lee was Carl and a few of his Delta boys. They'd been introduced quickly, and Lee hadn't remembered their names, but he'd been able to pick them up by listening to what Carl called them.

Rudy was a bald man with a pale, blond mustache, and pale skin. The only one that stuck to a mustache instead of a beard. He had the disposition of an old hound dog, and despite being young, he had a sort of jowly face that heightened the hound dog illusion. Lee wondered how many units during his military career had dubbed him Huckleberry Hound. Lee had yet to see the man move or say anything with more vigor than one might expect from a backyard barbecue. He spoke straight Texas with no affectations of anything else to water it down.

The man sitting next to Rudy was called Morrow. He was a big, serious man, with a swarthy complexion and large eyes that soaked up and evaluated everything. He wore what had to be the oldest hat still used in the world—a tattered old ball cap in sun-faded MultiCam, with rips and tears and salt deposits ringing the brow. Thick, black hair curled out from the edges of the ball cap, long enough to cover the back of his collar.

The last of Carl's crew was Mitch. He was quiet, but Lee could sense the humor in him. He had that slight upturn to his mouth, like he was constantly thinking of something amusing, but held it back. He was smallest of the three men, but stoutly built.

Directly across from Lee was Brinly and his three Marines. Nine men total, all of them experienced fighters. Aside from the fact that he didn't really know them, Lee had never felt this confident in the competency of a team. They had already flown across the Roanoke River and were on the other side. The side that wasn't protected and wasn't patrolled. No one quite knew what to expect when they touched down.

"We're getting close," Lee called over the noise inside the cabin of the helicopter.

Carl saw that Lee was speaking, but he had the crewman's headset on and looked like he was listening, the face of a man absorbing information. He said something into the mic, then pulled one of the ear cups away from his ear and inclined it to Lee. "What?" he said loudly.

Lee tilted the screen of the GPS toward Carl. The dot and the waypoint were nearly on top of each other. "We're almost there. Probably less than a minute out on this course."

Carl nodded, but even as he did, Lee felt the helicopter banking to the left. Carl pointed out the right windows. "Look out that window when we come back around. Pilot wants you to see something."

Lee kept Carl's eyes for a moment, but the other man remained aloof, and his stare was already directed out the window, his lips compressed into a thin, harsh line across his face. Lee felt the Black Hawk level out, and then bank again, this time to the right. Lee looked out the windows.

The earth and sky were rolling. The ground and horizon seemed to lurch up as the helicopter flew nearly on its side. Out the windows, he seemed to be staring directly down at the ground. And below them the ground was overgrown croplands, and in those lands, like pale spots of mold springing up in a dark petri dish, were hundreds of faces staring up at him.

"Fuck me!" Lee's breath fogged the window.

The horde below them was scattered, rather than jumbled up. But even scattered, Lee could take a quick count and didn't like the numbers he was coming up with. They milled about in singles and in groups of a dozen or more, most of them standing in the sun, like they were warming themselves. There must have been at least a thousand there, and Lee could see that there were more in other fields, spread out across God only knew how many miles. Lee could not see a definitive end to them. For all he knew this could have been one of the hordes of millions. There was no way to know.

I should've fucking figured, was his first thought. The second was more resolute, and he spoke it aloud: "Well, there ain't shit we can do about that right now. Still gotta get those supplies. If we gotta land in the middle of them and fight a little bit to the bunker doors, then that's what we'll fucking do."

Lee could see Carl's jaw muscles bunching. "That might be difficult. You'll need to guide us right onto your bunker."

Lee shook his head. "Bunker'll be in the woods. We may or may not be able to get your bird close to the doors. Probably going to have to move on foot."

Carl rubbed his face. "I can't leave my fucking bird in a field, surrounded by infected. We'd have to fight our way to the bunker, and then fight our way back and clear the fuckers off, probably damaging my equipment in the process. No way. We're not doing that while carrying crates of guns and ammo."

Lee snapped his teeth together a couple of times, thinking. "Okay. Okay." He started nodding rapidly. "We can work around this. Stay with me on this, Carl. Trust me. I ain't gonna sacrifice your bird. I need it just as much as you do."

Carl didn't look very trusting.

Lee consulted the GPS. "Tell your pilot to keep circling." He looked up at Brinly. "You and your men will be with me. We're going to dust off and hoof it in. If we hit contact at the bunker doors, y'all are gonna have to keep 'em off me until I get those doors open. There's a few security procedures. It's gonna take me . . . thirty seconds or so."

Brinly gave the thumbs-up. "We can do that."

Their location dot was directly on top of the waypoint on the map. The rest was visual. Lee looked out the window, feeling sick and almost giddy all at once. The chopper was cutting a constant circling pattern over a section of woods. Lee looked for the access road—there was always an access road to the bunkers. This one was no different. It cut the border between two fields and fed into the plot of woodland that could not have been more than ten or fifteen acres. And it looked thankfully sparse. The road had a turnaround, something like a cul-de-sac cut out of the trees. The bunker door was camouflaged well enough, but Lee knew this was where it would be. Lee peered into the trees, but couldn't see any movement or pale, naked bodies. The fields looked empty as well.

The horde's north of us. Maybe five miles?

Lee could also see the spire of what looked like an antenna rising up out of a blank spot in the trees. All of the bunkers were designed to fit in. This one was clearly designed to look like a public service radio repeater station, of which there were several dotting the countryside. Something that a farmer or a kid on an ATV would likely not think twice about.

Lee turned back to Carl. "Can your pilot fit in that turnaround? That clearing?"

Carl grimaced at it. "That's tight." He pushed the microphone in front of his mouth. "Hey, Biggins, can you get this bird down in that clearing?" A pause, and then a nod. "He says he might shave a few branches off the trees, but he can do it."

Brinly spoke up. "If this thing barely fits, that Chinook definitely ain't."

"I know," Lee said. "We're gonna deal with that in a minute. Right now, get in communication with your people and get that thing en route. Tell them to load a truck on the back. I don't care what kind it is. They're gonna have to park that thing outside of the woods, and we ain't humpin' crates of ammo three hundred yards. We need to get this shit done before that whole horde wanders its way down here to check us out."

For once, Carl seemed to agree. "Biggins, put her down," he spoke into his mic.

The helicopter came out of its circling pattern and hovered for just a moment before Lee felt the descent. He looked out the windows and watched trees looming up at him, waving in the rushing wind of the rotors, looking like writhing creatures in pain, trying to grasp at the helicopter. The closer they got to the ground, the faster they seemed to be dropping.

Lee felt his whole body clench, and he wanted to look away but couldn't. The trees were so close it seemed like there was no way the bird was going to get in without crashing. But he just had to hold on and trust this helicopter pilot, just like he'd trusted every other helicopter pilot he'd ever ridden with. And he'd ridden with some real risk takers who could do uncanny things with the machine that they loved so much.

Brinly seemed to share Lee's fear.

Carl seemed calm.

"Carl," Lee called out. "Keep your bird on the ground as long as you can. Try to conserve your fuel. But if we start taking contact, lift off but stay close. We might be able to fight our way to a better spot, if all else fails."

"We'll cross that bridge when we come to it," Carl said, then pointed. "We're here."

The helicopter touched the ground and shuddered. True to the pilot's word, he had managed to squeeze it in this unlikely place, even if there were a few freshly chopped tree branches lying at the edge of the clearing.

Lee took one big breath and pulled the Black Hawk doors open.

TWELVE

___

CONTINGENCIES

THE RUSHING AIR FROM outside suddenly filled the cabin of the helicopter. Instead of the metallic, oily stink of military machinery, this smelled of wet woods and dirt, and it was cold enough to water his eyes.

Lee felt a hand slap him on the shoulder and a voice yell, "Move!"

He rolled out, felt his boots hit the ground—gravel with some weeds growing through but pressed flat by the downdraft. He brought his rifle up to his cheek and started moving, scanning left, then right as he kicked out about three yards and took a knee. All around him the woods were moving with the wind, but the whine of the engines was dying and the rotor was slowing to an idling speed. Lee tried to see *through* the woods, *through* the shaking trees and underbrush, to what might be lurking inside. What might be in the shadows.

The battering winds and the roaring rotors blanketed everything so that the only sense he had to his advantage was sight. He would not smell the infected, and he would not hear them coming. He would have to see them. He would have to keep looking.

Keep that head on a swivel.

Another hand on his shoulder and Brinly's voice again: "We're good! Move!"

Lee hauled himself out of his kneeling position, scanning the woods one more time before he turned that over to his Marine escort. The woods were just as empty as they had been a moment ago. But the helicopter was making a shitload of noise, and it was like a goddamn beacon when they were flying in. The infected had seen them. Lee had watched them staring up at him. They knew they were here.

He moved for the fenced-in area. It was topped with liberal amounts of concertina wire and hung with placards threatening jail time, fines, and accidental death by electrocution. The big metal construction of the radio tower sprouted up from the center, surrounded by what looked like a small utility building and a large diesel generator. None of it was actually what it appeared to be. Like so many things having to do with Project Hometown.

The gate was secured with a monstrous-looking padlock, and a chain that could have been used to tow heavy equipment. Lee let his rifle drop to his chest and then withdrew the GPS out of the pouch on his chest rig. It was already powered up. He punched in his access code and swiped the device in front of the padlock. The lock popped open and Lee pulled it out of the chain.

"That fence still electrified?" Brinly said, eyeing the menacing-looking wiring.

"Shouldn't be anymore." Lee reached out and shoved the gate open. It did not electrocute him. Lee knew that the GPS being there deactivated the protection measures for him, but it was still a little nerve-wracking touching a fence with so many black lightning bolt placards and stick-figure pictures of people being shocked to death.

Lee looked behind him. The Marines were facing outward in every direction, a solid three-sixty security. Brinly had his satellite phone pressed to his ear, his hand cupped over his mouth and the mouthpiece to block out the rotor noise. He was speaking rapidly to someone.

Lee jogged into the fenced area, closing the gate behind him after the Marines followed. He went to the little construction that appeared to be just another utility shed to house circuit breakers and emergency shutoffs and other such nonsense. This door was also padlocked, and the padlock popped just like the other one. The door to the shed opened up, but there was no interior to the shed, as Lee knew there would not be. There was only another door, recessed about two feet. A door that looked like it led to a vault.

From here, the procedure was identical to every other bunker. The GPS device activated the security panel, and from there it was mnemonics and alphanumeric codes. When all the security hurdles had been run, the vault made a threatening hissing sound and then slid open with the sound of heavy-duty hydraulics. What lay beyond was a cargo elevator.

Lee looked behind him.

Brinly was no longer on the phone. He eyed the elevator. "That's quite impressive."

"Smoke and mirrors," Lee said, then stepped onto the elevator.

Brinly and the others came in behind him. "The chopper's on its way from Camp Lejeune."

"Good," Lee said shortly. He pressed a button and the vaultlike door slid closed again and the elevator descended with the whirring of massive machinery. Lee looked at Brinly's Marines. "When we get down there, just follow me. We're going for guns and ammo. That's it. Guns and ammo."

"What else do you have down there?" one of the Marines asked.

"Stuff," Lee said as the elevator slowed. "But we only care about the guns and the ammo."

Brinly gave the Marine a *stand down* look. The Marine looked vaguely irritated. "Roger 'at."

The doors opened and Lee was out, his feet moving with purpose. As they stepped out into the bunker, the whole system came alive, burning lights, air-conditioning, computers, electronics. There were the showers in the back living area, and Lee yearned for that. *A hot shower, good God, how amazing would that feel right now? I could pretend I wasn't here. Wasn't doing this. If I could just stand under some hot fucking water…*

But there wasn't time for that. No time for anything but movement.

Lee hung a left and reached the armory door. The door was secured with a simple four-digit code, which he punched in quickly and then pushed the door open. The room sparked into light as the overheads winked on at the detection of movement. The room was filled, wall to wall. All crisp black polymers and glinting blued steel and dull, flat green. To the left was a wall of M4 rifles. The rest was crates upon crates of ammunition and ordnance.

Lee pointed to the wall of weaponry. "Start grabbing the rifles and stacking them up in the elevator. Don't take them topside just yet. Just stack 'em in there. I'll start pulling boxes of ammunition and mags." Lee motioned out the door. "We'll get a nice little assembly line going. Let's work fast, gentlemen."

And they worked fast. Brinly grabbed rifles and tossed them to a Marine at the door, who alternately caught the rifles and then the boxes of ammunition and magazines that Lee was sliding to him. Then he would toss the rifle down the hall, or slide the box along to the next guy.

Lee was sweating within a few minutes. A little more out of breath than he would have preferred, he looked to Brinly. "What's the ETA on that chopper?"

"They said thirty minutes ten minutes ago."

"Okay." Lee bent, ignoring the splitting pain in his side. "I can work with that."

He separated another box of ammunition from the boxes of gear and explosives and shoved it to the Marine at the door. He thought he felt one of the stitches in his side busting loose, but he had no time to stop and inspect it. He only had time to work.

Time to work. Get it done. Get this shit done.

It didn't take long to fill the elevator.

"Ain't gonna fit no more if we want to ride it too," the Marine loading the elevator shouted out.

Lee hopped down off of a pile of crates and stalked to the door. He was burning up but hadn't taken off his jacket. Inside, he was soaked with sweat. Maybe a little blood from his side. "It's full?" he called out.

"Full. No more."

Lee looked back at the room. The wall of rifles was only half-depleted. There were still crates upon crates of ammunition. Lee wiped a trickle of sweat from his eyebrow. "All right. What are we looking like?" Lee tried to do a quick estimate based on how many gun racks were empty. "Uh...thirty? Thirty-five rifles?"

"Yeah." The Marine looked into the elevator. "About that. And probably fifty thousand rounds of ammunition."

Lee looked at Brinly. "That work for you guys?"

Brinly gave a thumbs-up. "Works for us, Captain."

"They should be here any minute," Lee said. "Let's get topside."

The elevator rumbled up easily under the weight of the load. The five of them were crammed in, straddling crates of ammunition and standing almost shoulder to shoulder. At the top, Lee tapped the button and the big, heavy doors slid open. As they cracked, Lee heard the sound of beating rotors, and saw the big black helicopter still sitting there.

Lee huffed relief. "All right. We're good." He bent down and grabbed a case of ammunition.

"Start stacking this stuff near the gate so we can load it on the truck quickly when it gets here."

"Hey." One of the Marines held up a radio handset. "I'm pickin' them up now."

Brinly grabbed the handset. "This is First Sergeant Brinly. Where're y'all at?"

The sound of rotors got heavier and deeper and was suddenly coming from above them. Brinly looked straight up and Lee followed his gaze. The Chinook helicopter roared over their heads, low enough to see the rivets on the fat-bellied beast of a machine. Brinly watched the big, double-rotored aircraft slide smoothly over their heads, and then looked back down at Lee, his face grave.

"Roger that. Brinly out." He shoved the handset back to the Marine. "Pilots spotted that horde. It's about a mile from us and closing. Fast."

Lee picked up his crate. No more time for talking. The Marines left their rifles slung and started grabbing boxes and armloads of weapons. Lee didn't know what "fast" meant, but he imagined they were closing at a good pace, over fairly level terrain. He started a mental clock at ten minutes.

"What happens if they get here before we can finish loading?" Brinly dropped a case of ammunition and a pair of rifles at the gate.

"We'll get the Chinook loaded," Lee said, more trying to convince himself than anything else. "But I don't know if we'll be able to do the Black Hawk in time."

"So..."

Lee jogged back for more supplies. "I'll handle it."

"You'll handle it?"

"I'll handle it."

There wasn't much else that Lee could say. What if they swarmed the bunker? He ran through scenarios in his head. If he reactivated the physical security, such as the electrified fence, then they'd probably be okay. But the Black Hawk wouldn't be able to get them out. Even if it could lower ropes for them, which Lee didn't even know that they had, it still couldn't get in close enough to the fenced-in area because of the radio tower. And that wasn't even counting the cargo. That was just extracting the men.

I've got some tricks, Lee told himself. *Don't know if they'll work, but I'll sure as hell give 'em a whirl.*

They had half of the cargo transplanted to the gate by the time they caught sight of the truck roaring down the gravel access road and skirting around the bulk of the Black Hawk, skidding up dust and dirt as it went. It was a regular Humvee with a truck bed. Barely big enough to cram in the cargo, but they'd have to figure it out. The thing was moving fast. The driver was well aware of the situation.

Lee threw open the gate as the truck came to a halt, flinging pebbles. No orders needed to be given. The driver jumped out, along with two passengers and they immediately started grabbing crates and rifles along with Brinly's Marines. Lee worked fast, feeling the warmth in his side turn to a sticky sort of wetness that could only be blood.

Good job. You busted your stitching open yet again.

He kept looking over his shoulder as he worked,

looking through the fence and the trees, knowing that at any second there was going to be a mob of skinny, bedraggled creatures coming for them. Starving creatures. Ones that would rip them to shreds and leave nothing but bloody patches where they'd been standing.

The truck was loaded within five minutes. Lee did a mental check. Maybe they had a few minutes left. If they were lucky.

Brinly grabbed the open driver-side window of the Humvee and spoke loudly to the Marine behind the wheel. "Get this shit on the chopper yesterday, Marine. Don't stop for nothing."

"Aye, First Sergeant."

And then the Humvee tore away in the same direction they'd come from.

Brinly was clearly doing his own time calculations. "Captain, we ain't got time for another load. They're gonna show up in a minute. We need to dust off."

Lee shook his head. "No, I got this."

I think I got this.

Brinly looked at him hard. "I'm not risking my men for a fifty-fifty shot at success. We're getting on that bird and flying out of here."

Lee matched his gaze and leaned in. "No. I need your men. This has to happen. You need to trust me."

"I don't fucking trust you!" Brinly suddenly shouted. "I don't even fucking know you!"

Lee was an officer. Brinly was enlisted. He could've pulled rank and made it an order, but Lee got the feeling Brinly wouldn't give two shits about protocols, and frankly Lee wasn't one to judge on that front. Everyone was just trying to do the best thing for their people. And the Marines were Brinly's people. But the folks at Newton Grove and Camp Ryder, who needed the rest of those weapons, they were Lee's people. And Lee could not do it on his own.

"The bunker," Lee said resolutely. "It can defend itself, I promise you. We can still do what we came here to do. And I just gave your people half of the weapons in this bunker. I'd say that counts for a little fucking trust, don't you?"

Brinly's jaw worked. Eyes glared.

Lee nodded rapidly. He wasn't sure whether he had Brinly or not, but he pointed for the bunker and started stepping backward for the Black Hawk, still facing the old Marine. "You have to trust me, First Sergeant. This will work. I promise it will work. Get your men ready to get on that elevator. I'll be back in just a second."

Lee took off running, not waiting to see if Brinly was going to ignore him and head to the Black Hawk himself with his Marines in tow. But when Lee glanced over his shoulder he saw Brinly still standing there, his Marines fanning out into a defensive position around the small, fenced-in area.

Making promises you can't keep.

You can. You will. You have to.

Lee ran up to the open doors of the Black Hawk. He opened his mouth to speak.

Carl was already yelling, and pointing into the woods behind Lee. "Contact! Right there!"

Lee ducked as he watched Carl bring his little subgun up to this shoulder and let out a burst. He looked behind him as he ducked and watched an infected stop in midsprint, about fifty yards shy of the fence. It spilled to the ground, spinning streamers of bright red.

Lee came up again and just pointed up. "Get in the air! Hover above the trees! I'm gonna clear the area!"

"You're gonna *what*?" Carl yelled, incredulous.

"Just fucking do it! And when you see the area clear, you gotta drop this bird right back in place, because we're comin' to get on board and time is fucking tight, you got it?" And then Lee was sprinting back without waiting to see if Carl actually got it.

All around him the woods were suddenly alive. The smell was not just of jet exhaust and wet leaves, but now had that peculiar unwashed smell that always rode the wind like a banner in front of the infected hordes. The noise of the rotors winding up was suddenly drowned in a cascade of rifle reports. The Marines in the fence held like rocks, rifles up, spitting flame.

Lee didn't bother going for his own rifle. His only objective needed to be to *get inside the fence*. Everything was lost if he didn't *get inside the fence*. As he sprinted, the distance between the helicopter and the gate seemed impossibly long, and the infected seemed impossibly close. Lee grabbed the GPS from his chest rig, felt his heart squeeze its way into his throat as he nearly dropped it, then held on tight.

Ahead of him, Brinly was standing with a look on his face that was some dark place between determination and pure hatred for Lee. He had decided to stay, and no matter what happened, now he was going to deal with the consequences. Maybe he was regretting listening to Lee, maybe that tiny bit of trust had already been retracted, but those were peripheral concerns.

He swung his rifle in Lee's direction and Lee didn't break stride. He could see the first sergeant's eyes weren't locked on Lee, but on something behind him. Lee didn't take the time to look. Brinly's rifle barked, the concussion of it smacking Lee full in the face and the sound of bees buzzing by Lee's head. Something behind him yowled.

Lee hit the gate and shoved it closed. Brinly rammed his entire body against the gate along with Lee, pinning it closed as three infected hit the other side, pressing their fingers through the fencing, their teeth trying to bite through like wild animals, chipping and breaking off in the process.

Lee felt terror. They were close enough to him that he could smell their breath as they screeched. He forced himself to grab the latch of the gate and slam it home—a temporary fix, but all they needed was a second, just a second for the gate to hold while they stepped away from it.

"Get off the fence!" Lee bellowed. "Everyone off the fence!"

Brinly might have known what Lee was about to do, or maybe he didn't, but he echoed the order to the few Marines that were posted right up against the chain links. "Get off the fucking fence, Marine!"

And then he stepped clear of it himself.

Lee staggered back two steps and hit a command on his GPS device.

There was a sound like a clap of lightning and all around them the fence let off showers of sparks. The infected that had been pressing the gate were jolted back in a cloud of smoke, their screeches suddenly cut off by instantaneous death.

Lee felt elation, and then immediate dread again. The woods were filling, like the fenced-in area was an island sitting in the middle of a rapidly flooding riverbed. They were crowding in, pressing in, and they seemed to sense the electricity coming off the field, or maybe they could feel the thrum of it somehow, but they didn't touch it. At random spots around the entire perimeter, the crowd of them pushed in and caused one to stumble into the fence where it died in another cloud of stinking smoke and sparks.

"Holy shit!" Brinly coughed. "That thing's got some juice."

"Into the bunker." Lee was already running for it. He looked up and over his shoulder and could see the Black Hawk hovering above them at about two hundred feet. The noise behind them was swelling like the cusp of a riot breaking out, the voices of hundreds, and more every minute.

As the bunker doors slid closed and the elevator descended, Brinly let his anger flare up again. "So how the fuck do we get out now?"

Lee was breathing heavily. He forced himself to

take a breath through his nose and regain control of his respiration. There were only a few autonomic functions of your body that you could control to help bring yourself back out of the black, and one of them was breathing. Slow and steady. In through the nose, out through the mouth, even when your lungs were burning for more.

As the elevator slowed, Lee spat some gummy saliva into the corner of the elevator. "Like I said. The bunker can defend itself. Let me worry about that. You worry about getting this lift loaded up with more rifles and ammo. Load as many rifles as you can carry on your persons and sling into them. Load up a bunch of magazines and fill up your pockets and pouches with them. Then grab a case of ammunition, or two if you can manage it. But whatever you carry on you is all we're getting. We're only gonna have one shot at this and we can't make trips. Everyone understand?"

"Aye."

"Yeah, we got it."

Brinly's lips pulled back like a growling dog's. "Fine."

The elevator opened and Lee ran out first while the Marines made for the unlocked armory. The bunker could defend itself, but it could not do so indefinitely. And the more infected arrived on scene, the harder this was going to be, so the sooner they got back up top, the better chances they had to actually make it work.

To actually survive.

Because now they were committed. It wasn't just about the cargo now. They'd had a chance to board that helicopter and get gone, but they'd passed on it for the chance to grab the weapons and ammunition. Now it was all or nothing.

Lee stopped at a door just prior to the living quarters and punched in the code on the keypad to access it. The door opened just like the armory and inside the lights came on to reveal a small room with walls and banks of computer screens. The bunker's command module.

Lee moved quickly to the main console and pulled out the keyboard. The screen in front of his face came to life. The others were already switching on all around him and he was surrounded by images from the outside. The horde had grown, just in the time it had taken them to get down into the bunker. But it was milling; that was good. The ones closest to the fence still seemed enwrapped with the possibility of prey still being on the inside, but the outer edges of the horde that surrounded them seemed to be losing interest and were milling about.

"Good, good, good," Lee said quietly to himself. "Walk away."

Maybe if they were losing interest, more of the infected horde that arrived wouldn't crowd around the fenced-in perimeter. But this whole thing had him on edge. He'd never been through this. He'd never dealt with a horde of this size. He'd thought that the worst were the ones that ran in packs through the rural areas. And then he thought that it was the hunters, the larger, more adaptable ones that were not only getting by, but thriving with the sudden and dramatic changes occurring in their bodies. But this…this seemed unstoppable. Like water. Like waves. Like an avalanche. It was just so huge, so vast, there were simply so many of them, that he feared these hordes more than he had feared any other infected.

He tore his eyes away from the video monitors and ran through a few command sequences, pulling up the bunker's online security systems and activating the ones that were not already activated. He rolled through a series of command protocol options and found the one labeled *SIEGE PROTOCOL*. When selected, it prompted for target identification and discrimination—the computer's way of asking for rules of engagement.

Lee selected the option that said *ALL*.

Then he transferred command of the execution from the console to his GPS device. It took a maddening moment for a status bar to finish creeping its way across the screen, and then the image that had just been on the console monitor came alive on his handheld device, with a new button that simply said *EXECUTE*.

"Okay," Lee breathed. "We got it. We're good."

He ran out of the command module, letting the door swing closed behind him.

At the armory door, the Marines were strapping three and four rifles to their backs, all fully loaded. One Marine was on the ground, hammering stripper clips of cartridges into magazines and handing them to his buddies, who stuffed them in their pockets.

Lee stepped in and took his fair share of the load. He quickly loosened the straps on four rifles so that they would not choke him when he slung them crosswise on his back. He loaded each of them up and then stacked them onto his back. Then he started grabbing magazines and filling his own pockets and pouches.

The Marine filling the magazine looked up, grinning, as he worked. "You know, I always thought stripper clips were fucking bullshit. But seriously...thank God."

The last of them finished loading up. Lee took a good look at the men, mostly young, skin and bones, and weighed down by a ridiculous amount of gear, their pockets bulging with filled magazines, the weight causing them to have to hitch their loose fatigues back up onto their hips.

"Y'all ready?" Lee said, clutching the GPS again.

Brinly nodded once. "It would seem so."

They loaded quickly into the elevator and Lee hit the button to ascend. He turned to the Marines. "When the doors open, we're running for the gate. Hopefully the bird will pick us up and we can get the fuck out of here in time."

"I think that sounds like a great idea," one of the Marines said, hitching the awkward weight of the weapons around and adjusting his grip on the wooden crate of ammunition.

For a moment the elevator whirred on, the sound of cables winding and gears turning. The interior of the elevator was filled with the smell of gun oil and sweat and dirt. Lee repeated his breathing—in through the nose, out through the mouth—trying to force his heart rate down.

Always best to be clearheaded. You never knew when a split decision would have to be made. When something important will be playing at the edge of your vision that just a few deep breaths would have allowed you to see.

The elevator slowed, then stopped.

Brinly stepped up to the door.

Lee consulted his GPS device.

"You gonna open the doors?" Brinly asked hotly.

"Hold on," Lee said, distractedly. He accessed the screen and then tapped the *EXECUTE* button. A prompt for a security code came up and Lee entered the digits steadily and deliberately. *Clear thoughts. Clear mind. Slow is smooth. Smooth is fast.*

The code prompt disappeared.

"What…" Brinly began, but was cut off.

The heavy doors of the bunker muffled the sound, but they all could feel the vibration, rumbling through their feet, and the sound, the very distinctive sound, like a giant buzz saw chewing through hardwood trees. Then explosions shook them, rapid and steady, *boom, boom, boom, boom, boom*. The Marines looked around, their faces displaying shock. Then they all looked at Lee.

But Lee was focused on the GPS device, his hand hovering over the elevator control panel, poised next to the button to open the doors. Outside, the buzzsaw ripped through trees and the explosions kept pounding, pounding, obliterating. Lee felt sweat at the top of his brow, gathering at his hair line. He rubbed it away.

The explosions suddenly stopped.

The buzzsaw paused, then started again, then paused and started again.

It went on like this for another few seconds, the noise starting and stopping, and Lee standing there, sweating, with his eyes affixed to the GPS screen. *Lord, let this work, please let this work, this has got to work. Good God this is so damn risky, please don't punish me for being so fucking risky. I'm just doing what I gotta do...*

The GPS screen flashed. A window appeared: *PROTOCOL TARGET ELIMINATION "ALL" COMPLETE. RUN AGAIN?*

Lee clicked *NO* and pressed the Open Door button on the elevator console. "Get ready, guys."

The doors opened.

Smoke washed in. The heavy smell of spent casings and blood. The sound of wailing. The beating of helicopter rotors. Lee took a big lungful of it. Felt it burn his throat and cauterize his mind. The wind from the rotors was pushing the smoke away. The scene was outlandish in how suddenly it had changed from only moments ago. The electrified fence sat in sparking shreds. The bodies beyond lay in squirming heaps, ripped into sections and pieces. The Black Hawk helicopter was lowering its bulk out of the sky, directly ahead of them, emerging out of the smoke like a dragon from a fog.

"Holy fuck me running," someone behind Lee muttered.

Lee broke out of the elevator, heading for the gates. There was an odd, chaotic, horrific beauty to scenes of destruction like this. Something that

Lee would have never admitted, but he felt it like wonder and awe in his soul. It was not a good feeling. It was an otherworldly one.

To his right, the giant, rusted drain grate in the center of the concrete island had been pushed aside, and the huge drainpipe beneath had sprouted some contraption full of barrels and hydraulics and thermal imaging lenses. But Lee could see the guts of the machines that had been cyborged onto this contraption—an M134 Minigun and an Mk-19 grenade launcher. The weapon system sat there, silent now, though smoke was still rolling off of it like someone had poured water on a fire.

A long time ago, Harper had asked Lee what would happen if you entered the wrong code when trying to access one of the bunkers. Lee had told him that they should definitely avoid that.

The bunker defends itself.

Lee deactivated the electrified fence, though he was sure all the bullets ripping it to shreds had already done that for him. Behind him, the doors to Bunker #3 slid shut, and the whole thing sealed itself off from the world. Ahead of him, the Black Hawk lowered itself to the gravel. Lee ripped open the gates and ran for it, with the Marines in tow. All around them the infected were dead and dying, but there were more coming. There were always more.

In the woods beyond the smoke and mangled bodies, shadows shifted and screeched.

The five heavily laden men clambered and clattered their way onto the Black Hawk, and as the second to the last set of boots left the ground, Carl shouted into his microphone, "We're good! Dust off! Dust off!"

Lee lay on his back, staring up at black metal rivets. He breathed deep of the smell of the helicopter, the fuel, the exhaust, the oil. He felt the gravity pulling him, the force of the helicopter's sudden ascension pressing him. He let out one big breath as the tops of the trees slipped by underneath them.

Carl was sitting there, calm as ever. He nodded in Lee's direction. "I gotta tell you... that was some impressive shit. Good job."

"Yeah," Lee said, a little shakier than he would have liked. "It got the job done."

Brinly slid himself up into a seat and hiked a foot up onto the crate of ammunition he'd carried. He looked at Lee, and Lee couldn't tell whether he was irritated or grateful. Maybe both. The first sergeant huffed air and then grabbed the satellite phone and dialed it. He seemed to gradually relax as the helicopter banked away. They could all look out the windows below them and see more of the infected, trampling over the dead, many of them falling to feed on them.

"Yeah," Brinly said into his satellite phone. "We're clear. We got the guns. The chopper on its way?" He listened for a moment, nodding in thought. "Okay. Rog. Thank you, sir."

He hung up and rubbed his brow, which was still sweating despite the cold. "That cargo chopper is en route back to Camp Lejeune. Colonel Staley says they plan to move the artillery convoy out within the hour." A pause to collect his thoughts. "He also said that our scouts are reporting zero activity from the Followers, even out past Wilmington. They've been pressing and not making contact. It looks like they've all just up and left."

Lee righted himself off of the floor and sat his butt onto one of the bench seats, again next to Carl. "Well...that sounds like a good thing...I guess."

"Maybe," Brinly agreed hesitantly. "Hopefully."

THIRTEEN

HOSTAGES

HARPER MANAGED TO DOZE off somewhere around noon. His dreams were half real and half manufactured. The Marines that were holding them would be walking around, changing their guards, and a fight would break out and Kensey would be there with an axe, hacking one of his comrades to pieces, spraying blood across Harper's face. But then the body on the ground wasn't a Marine anymore; it was Julia, and Kensey was speaking reassuring tones as he hacked away at her legs.

"We have to amputate the leg," he would say quietly. "Here's something for the pain. How are you feeling?"

Julia looked up dreamily at Kensey as he chopped her right leg off and moved to her left. She smiled tiredly and nodded. "I'm fine. I'm just fine. Never been better."

"You need to drink something," Kensey said. "Hey. Hey."

Harper snapped awake.

It was not Kensey that stood in front of him, but Baker. The Marine had long, slender arms and long, skinny fingers that gripped a green plastic canteen, held out to Harper. "Hey. Harper. Wake up."

Harper blinked a few times. "I'm awake." His eyes jagged to the floor where moments before Kensey had been making a bloody mess of Julia's legs, but there was nothing there. He felt behind him with tingling numb fingers and felt Julia's hands, still bound to the same wooden post as he was.

Harper coughed. His tongue was dry. "I'm awake."

"Thirsty?" Baker said. "You should drink."

Harper looked at the young Marine. The boonie hat that he tended to prefer was swept back and hanging from the lanyard around Baker's neck. His crew cut was extending out into a short, nappy afro, pressed down in a ring where the hat had been sitting. The Marine's light brown skin was showing the contusions he'd received from Kensey: a scrape on the left cheek, some bruising and swelling around the left eye.

Harper nodded slowly. "Yes. Thirsty."

Baker put the canteen to Harper's lips and tilted. The water was cool, but it tasted stale and plastic. Still, he was parched enough that he didn't care. He drank deeply, four long gulps, before Baker withdrew the canteen and capped it.

Harper licked the dribbles of water off his lips and cleared his throat again. "What was that earlier? With Kensey?"

Baker just smiled, like he was considering how to explain an adult concept to a child. "You know, my dad used to tell me, 'When words fail, blows must follow.' Sometimes brothers fight."

"Brothers?" Harper half-laughed at him. "I don't know if Kensey considers you a brother, given what he said."

"Ha." Baker just shook his head. "You mean all the racial shit? You think me and Kensey ain't brothers 'cause he's white and I'm black? Marine Corps don't care whether you're black, white, brown, or yellow, my friend."

"Kensey seems to care." It was the only button Harper had to push. Driving a wedge was pretty much his only way to fight back when he was tied up to a wooden post in a barn in the middle of nowhere.

Baker looked thoughtful. "You know, I'm light-skinned. When I first got to Kensey's squad, everyone called me 'the little mixed kid.' But it's cool. I call them cracker and honky and redneck. None of it fucking matters, bro. All that matters is that we have each other's backs at the end of the day. Civilians don't get that. That's all just words. They leave bananas in my gear bag, I leave saltines in theirs. But when the bullets fly, they got my back. And I got theirs."

"Maybe you got theirs. Maybe they don't have yours."

Baker sniffed, becoming slightly irritated. He stood. "Ain't no color around here, Harper. No color but green. In the eyes of Uncle Sam, we're all just olive drab."

Harper grunted. "Uncle Sam is dead, last I checked."

"Nah, you're wrong about that." Baker shook his head. "Why do you think we're here?"

Baker turned to walk away.

"You said you didn't think this was right," Harper said desperately.

Baker hung his head but didn't look at him. Harper felt his pulse quicken. Could he have pushed the right button? Maybe Baker was the only ally that they had. He'd been the only one to verbalize any sort of objection. And was it coincidence that he brought Harper water?

"You didn't think it was right," Harper said again. "You guys murdered my team, Baker. You fucking murdered them. Your *brothers* murdered mine. We trusted you guys. We put our faith in you. And you waited until our backs were turned and you gunned my people down." Harper had to stop because he could feel the memory of it tightening his throat. He didn't want to sound weak or emotional. He choked off the rest of his words.

Baker nodded, slowly. "Yeah. That was badly done." Finally he looked at Harper. "But it's been done. And this? Right now? This is necessary. This needs to be done. Because there's a whole lot more going on out there than just your little camp of survivors. There's a whole nation."

Harper shifted against his restraints, frustrated. "What are you even fucking talking about?"

Baker turned away. "I'm sorry about your people, Harper."

Harper sat there, sullen, quietly shoving down the rest of those emotions, whitewashing the images of his team out of his mind. There were only a few dead faces that he clung to—Annette, Miller, and sometimes Mike and Torri—but the rest he cast aside. He did not have room in his soul for so many ghosts. He could only stand the company of a few at a time.

Julia stirred behind him.

Harper turned his head. He could not see her, but he could press their numb fingers together. Baker was the only Marine in the barn at the time and he was standing over by the smoldering fire. "Jules," he whispered. "You awake?"

Her voice was scratchy and dry. "Yeah."

"You okay?"

"No. We're still here."

Harper put his head against the wooden post and took a deep breath. "I know. I know."

"Are we gonna get out of here?" she said.

Harper didn't know. It seemed a far-gone hope at this point. He was no special forces soldier. He did not know the things that Lee and Tomlin knew. He could not even figure out how to get out of these ropes, let alone how to overpower a squad of Marines. Were they getting out of there?

No. No, we're not.

His silence was his answer.

Julia sighed heavily. "Shit."

The silence dragged for a while. Harper's mind wandered. At his back, Julia breathed heavily in discomfort and fidgeted a lot, trying to relieve some of the pain in her leg. She seemed determined not to request more morphine, though.

Good job, Jules. You keep a clear head, Harper

thought. *I don't know what good it will do us, though. Maybe you should just take the drugs and live comfortably for however long we have left to live. Because I'm not sure what the fuck we're doing here and I feel like I could scream, I'm going mad, but it's best to be quiet. Just be quiet and watch.*

The first sign that Harper had that anything was happening was the rattling of some tools against the steel siding of the barn. He perked up, searching for the source of the vibration, thinking maybe some Marines were on the outside of the wall, banging on it. But there was no banging noise to accompany the vibration.

"What's that?" Julia asked.

"I dunno…"

Their question was answered. The vibrating turned into a rumble and then the very clear sound of a helicopter came through to them. At the fire, Baker stood up and slung into his rifle. He did not move quickly. He moved as though he was not surprised that a helicopter was on top of them. He'd known that this was going to happen.

Is this their helicopter? Did they call for it? Is that what they've been waiting on? That would make sense. Where are they taking us? Camp Lejeune? Fuck. Does Lee know about this? Is Lee still working with the other Marines? Why have they taken us captive? Jesus, maybe they've taken Camp Ryder…

The noise became overpowering. Dust thrown by the rotorwash crept in from under the walls where there was a one- or two-inch gap from the ground. The door to the barn was flung open, and wind and dirt came sweeping in. Kensey stood there, a shemagh pulled up over his mouth and nose, his eyes covered by goggles. He yanked the cloth down from his mouth.

"Baker! They're here."

Baker threw a thumbs-up. "Roger."

Kensey disappeared outside again, leaving the door open. The sound was much louder, thunderous. And then it began to wind down. The whine of turbine engines overtook the chopping sound of the rotor blades, and then that too began to die.

Harper realized his pulse was beating hard.

They're here. Who's "they"?

"They" are whoever wants you, Harper. You and Julia. Though I have no idea why. Why do you want me? What good am I to anyone but Camp Ryder? I don't know anything special. I serve no practical purpose. I'm just another guy with a gun. I'm a dime a dozen. Who wants me?

There was the sound of talking from outside. The voices were raised, but the dying helicopter engines made it so that Harper could not tell what they were saying. The voices were drawing closer. They seemed to be all business.

A shadow fell across the barn door. Kensey stepped through, then stepped to the side. He looked first at Harper, and then to someone standing outside the door. The sergeant made a gesture with his hand. A welcoming gesture as though to say, *Come and see what I have for you.*

The next man to step through was not a Marine, Harper didn't think, which only confused him more. He was a tall man with a shock of blond hair that was close cropped and looked like it was recently trimmed. He wore a uniform and gear, though Harper could not identify any of it. The uniform was camouflage, but different from what the Marines were wearing. It was the same camouflage he'd seen Lee wear when he first got to Camp Ryder, and Captain Tomlin as well. The gear and the uniform had some wear to it, but not to the battered level that he'd seen the Marines' equipment in. The rifle that the man had slung on his left side looked to be similar to an M4, but with some slight differences, and some things attached to the rails that Harper didn't recognize. It, like the rest of the man's gear, was in better shape.

He stood there for a moment, sizing Harper up, just as Harper was sizing him up. The man did not appear malignant, or cruel. Harper could not see in his eyes any harshness. Honestly, he looked on Harper with what looked like regret and pity.

"What are their names?" the man asked.

Kensey pointed to them, each in turn. "The man is Harper. The woman is Julia."

The man nodded and stepped forward. He kept his distance from them, standing several feet away. Even if Harper lashed out with his legs, he wouldn't be able to reach the man. Not that he would. It would be a futile effort, and if he didn't get killed for it, he'd be beaten senseless at the very least.

"Harper. Julia," the man said in an even tone. "My name is Major Tyler Bowden. I'm a Coordinator for Project Hometown. I've been sent here by President Briggs to deliver a message to Lee Harden. You are going to help me do that."

* * *

Lee stood in the center of Newton Grove. All around him was the evidence of a group of survivors that had been there once, and were no more. Brett's and Mac's groups had cleared the worst of the carnage when they'd taken the town as their own, but like a crime scene, Lee could still see the blood and bullet holes.

Brett, Mac, Georgia, and all their people had gathered in the center with Lee. They had been able to carry twenty rifles—four strapped to each of them—and a decent amount of ammunition and magazines to load them with. There were still a few people that did not have firearms, but they could make themselves useful in other ways.

"Does anyone have any questions about how to use these rifles?" Lee asked, loud enough for the whole group to here. "Everyone have a good understanding?"

There was a lot of mumbles and nods of assent. Nobody appeared to have any questions. Lee had been told that a few of the people from Mac and Georgia's group were former military and had experience with the weapon system. If anyone decided they had questions, or if there was trouble with one of the rifles, Lee figured these people would have to step up.

"All right." Lee nodded. "You got your guns and ammo, and you got a base for your operations. Start hitting the roads and patrolling." He turned to Brinly. "Your convoy on the road yet?"

Brinly had just got off the satellite phone again.

"Yeah. They were Oscar Mike about ten minutes ago."

Lee nodded, doing some quick calculations. "I don't know how long it will take them to get here, but I anticipate it will be before nightfall. Hold this town. Hold the roads to the east and the west, leading toward Smithfield. That's all you folks have to do."

Brett gave a thumbs-up. Where Mac and Georgia seemed reticent, Brett seemed eager. "We got it locked down, Lee."

"First Sergeant Brinly," Lee addressed him for the huddled gathering. "Could you pass along the reports of the Followers?"

Brinly folded his arms across his chest. "Our Marine reconnaissance patrols have been pushing out around Camp Lejeune, where historically the Followers of the Rapture have been camped around us. So far, they've made zero contact. All the usual places are abandoned. There's a lot of directions they could have gone, but we all know that they've been moving east. So there's a good possibility they might be heading this way."

Lee nodded along with him until he was finished. "If you guys make any contact with the Followers whatsoever, I want to hear about it over the command channel, okay?"

Brett was the one Lee had provided with a manpack. He slapped the gadget that hung on his side. "I got it, Captain."

Lee looked to Brinly. "Anything else you can think of before we head out?"

Brinly considered it for a few beats.

As he stood there, watching Brinly, Lee heard a squawking from his shoulder where the radio handset was hooked. It almost took him by surprise to hear the radio going off. He didn't anticipate that either of the bait trucks had made contact yet, but perhaps they'd made quicker progress than he'd thought. Or maybe it was Angela, back at Camp Ryder, trying to hail him for some reason.

His mind coursed through myriad nightmares in the time it took to grab the handset and bring it to his ear. Nobody ever had good news to say over the command channel.

As he brought the earpiece to his head, the squawking became a voice, and the voice became familiar. Lee caught the very tail end of the transmission.

"…anyone on the command channel. I'm trying to reach Captain Harden."

Lee almost fumbled the microphone. He clenched the PTT button. "Harper?" he almost yelled. "Is that you? This is Captain Harden to the last transmitter. How copy?"

"Yeah," the voice came back. "This is Harper." The voice was heavy.

Something's wrong. Something is really wrong.

There was silence and static. Harper was still holding the transmit button, but he was struggling with words.

Julia's dead. The crew is dead. Everyone's dead.

"Lee…myself and Julia have been taken hostage…"

Lee's ears were humming. He looked at Brinly and found the man staring back expectantly. *Taken hostage taken hostage taken hostage—but who were they with? They were with Marines. They were with Brinly's men...*

"...Everyone else is dead. It's just me and Julia..."

...the Marines, the Marines, does that mean they're dead, too? Everybody died...?

"...It was the Marines, Lee. They took us hostage and killed the rest..."

Lee held Brinly's gaze. Since he was holding the handset to his ear, Brinly could not hear the transmission. The two men stared. *He knows. He knows.* Lee felt cold and prickly hot. Like his skin was ice-cold under hot water.

"...There's someone else that you have to talk to." Harper's voice sounded dead and cold. "I'm handing you to him now."

Still and silent. Thrumming, humming, buzzing, blackness turning to red. Lee looked away from Brinly for a second, doing another head count. One, two, three, four, plus Brinly made five of them. Five Marines. Versus Lee, four Delta operators, and all of Brett's and Mac and Georgia's people. Lee felt his hand sliding toward the rifle strapped to his chest.

Brinly was trying to speak to him. "Everything okay?"

Lee didn't respond.

On the other end of the radio transmission, there was rustling, crackling, and then a new voice came on. Another voice that was familiar and unfamiliar at once. Lee knew it, but it did not fit into the files of his recent history. He knew it, but he didn't know it from Camp Ryder.

"Lee, there are men holding guns on Harper and Julia. Do not react poorly. When I ask you if you are copying this transmission, that is not your opportunity to get mad at me. Just say whether you understand my transmission, and then let me speak again. Do you copy?"

Who are you? I know you. I know your voice.

The line went dead. Lee pressed the transmit button. "Copy" was the only word he sent back.

The transmission came back again, unmerciful. "Lee, this is Tyler Bowden. I've been sent by President Briggs. We know what Abe did. He killed Eddie Ramirez and took back your GPS. According to our systems, you just accessed one of your bunkers earlier today, so I can safely assume that he made it over to you and delivered the GPS. Is all of that true?"

The Marines. The Marines. How are we going to take them without a firefight? Or maybe we should just do it. Gun them down...

"Yes," Lee said. "That's true."

"Lee, we have more things to discuss...but Abe and Lucas were friends of mine. And of yours. They still are, just like you are. No matter what. And I'll get back to business in just a minute. But right now I need to know..." For the first time, Lee could hear what sounded like fear in Tyler's voice. Not fear of Lee, but fear of the truth. "Are they still alive? Abe and Lucas?"

"Abe is injured. He might be dead by now," Lee said, feeling detached. "Lucas...he's dead. I killed him."

There was a long pause on the other end.

Directly in front of Lee, Brinly shifted his weight on his feet, looking uncertain.

He must know by now. He must've figured out what has happened. They were probably in communication. Hell, he's been on the sat-phone all day.

When Tyler's voice came back, the fear was gone, replaced by the same level of calm that he'd spoken with before. "I'm sorry that it went down this way. But we all have a job to do. This is about doing what we were supposed to do—rebuilding the United States. President Briggs is the lawful president. I'm sworn to obey my commander in chief. So are you. In order to support the interests of the new United States, we need that GPS device back. You're going to stop accessing bunkers and surrender your GPS within twenty-four hours, or I'm going to kill Harper and Julia. Just like you killed Lucas. Do you have any questions about that?"

"Why are you doing this?" Lee said quietly, almost in a whisper. "Why didn't you just come after me?"

"Because you were my friend. You were my brother. That doesn't change for me, though apparently it does for you. I don't know why you killed Lucas. But it doesn't matter. I just want the GPS device. Once I get it, I don't care what you do after that. I don't care if you keep trying to establish your little dictatorship out here or whatever it is that you're doing. All I know is that you're not welcome west of the Appalachians. And eventually your time will come."

A pause, but Tyler held the line open.

"We could argue all day. Maybe one day we will hash this out. But not today." Tyler's voice became cold and hard. "You know what the deal is, Lee. I'm disconnecting this radio, so don't try to reach me on it. I have nothing else for you right now. You'll receive further instructions in a moment."

The line went dead.

Lee kept holding the handset to his ear. Then he gradually pulled it down. He looked to his left. Carl was standing there, watching Lee with a look of reservation, eyebrows knit together as though he wasn't sure what mind-set Lee was in at that moment.

Lee hung the handset back on his shoulder. As calmly as he could manage, he stepped to Carl's side. He didn't look at Brinly, had to fight every instinct to look at him and his Marines. They were the threat now. They were the enemy. He leaned into Carl and spoke in a bare whisper.

"We need to detain these Marines."

Carl pursed his lips, but nodded. "Okay."

"I'll explain in a minute."

"Okay."

Lee turned and swung his rifle up. Beside him, it was a chain reaction. Carl initiated off of Lee, and then Rudy, Mitch, and Morrow reacted off of that. None of them knew what was going on, but they knew their lead man was pointing his gun at someone. And when the friend that you trust points his gun at something, you point your gun at it, too.

Lee sighted his rifle at Brinly's head.

"Let me see your hands, Brinly! All your Marines! Hands up!"

To Lee's right, Mac and Georgia stood, stunned, but Brett swore and swung his rifle on the Marines as well, and then a few of his people followed suit, and then all of them. In the matter of a single second, the four Marines had more than twenty rifles trained on them.

"Hands on your heads," Lee said again. "Do it now, Brinly!"

Brinly showed his palms and raised them. His face devolved into a look that seemed to be made from shards of volcanic glass. His voice ground like boulders rubbing together. "You stupid motherfucker. What the fuck is the meaning of this?"

Slowly, the Marines beside him complied.

Lee didn't respond to Brinly. He felt the urge of violence, but that wasn't the purpose of this.

"Brett," Lee called out. "Remove the weapons from those Marines."

Brett took a step forward, but Brinly's voice stopped them.

"Negative!" Brinly bellowed. "You take a step back, you boot-fuck piece of shit. I'll stand here and put my hands on my head, but you ain't takin' my goddamned weapons. You get close to me again and I will hollow that disgusting fat body out like a fucking canoe." Brinly turned his wrathful gaze on Lee. "You. Explain yourself."

"Explain Sergeant Kensey," Lee snapped back.

Brinly's jaw jutted. "You better make more sense than that or this shit's gonna go south real quick."

Lee spoke through clenched teeth. "Explain why Sergeant Kensey is holding my people hostage."

Brinly looked taken aback. "Jesus Christ..."

Lee lost the grip on his restraint. His finger went to the trigger. "I need some fucking answers here, Brinly!"

"I've got nothing to do with that!" Brinly shouted back. "I have no idea what the hell that idiot is doing, but it certainly wasn't on my orders! I don't know what the fuck is going on right now!"

"What about Staley?" Lee demanded. "Does he know?"

"No," Brinly said. Then, "I don't fucking know."

One of the Marines stepped forward, hands still raised. "The colonel don't know about it. Neither does the first sergeant."

Lee stared at the younger man. The Marine stood there, that same stupid smirk on his face that had been there all day. This was the one that liked to talk. The one that liked to joke down in the bunker. His eyes were bright with secret knowledge. He seemed pleased with himself.

"Who the fuck are you?"

"Lance Corporal Turner, Captain Harden. And before you think about killing me, let me tell you that I'm the only one that can get that GPS to them in twenty-four hours. I'm the only one that knows where they are."

Brinly had put his hands down and looked like he was about to latch them around Corporal Turner's neck. "You a part of this, Marine?"

"Yes, sir." Turner nodded. "I'm sorry, sir. I

have nothing but respect for you, but I'm done with what we're doing here. We're not serving the United States anymore. We're serving Colonel Staley. And me and some of the other Marines are tired of sticking around, just to look for Staley's daughter. She's fucking dead. The colonel burned our chance to go west and join up with President Briggs and the rest of the fucking military. Now we have a chance to make that right, and I intend to do so."

Corporal Turner had grown serious as he spoke. He turned to Lee again. "All you have to do is give me the GPS device and let me leave. Give me a car. Don't follow me. I'll get it to them before the twenty-four hours is up and you get your people back, along with the truckloads of supplies they had. If you kill me, then the GPS will never show up, and your buddy, Major Bowden, he's gonna kill your people and burn those trucks."

Lee realized he was trembling. He wanted to kill; he wanted violence and blood so bad in that moment that it seemed the only possible thing in the world. He felt like bombs were going off in his chest and he was having a hard time containing it. His breathing had become quick and strained. Behind his eyes, he could feel the dull ache coming on.

Not now. No time for this now.

"Where?" he said. "Where are they?"

Turner just smiled. "You know I can't tell you that."

Lee took two steps, dropping the rifle and letting the sling take it. With his free hands, he grabbed Turner up by the throat—he was surprisingly light—and planted his left leg behind Turner's feet and whipped the man over his hip in a vicious throw. Turner hit the ground, choking and coughing, grabbing at his throat. But he was breathing, so Lee supposed he had not crushed the man's larynx. It had not been his intent to do it, but Lee still wanted it bad. Kensey and his fucking buddies were miles and miles away and they couldn't be touched, but this shithead was right here right now.

It only felt right that he pay for everyone's sins at once.

Lee put a knee in Turner's chest, continued to grip him by the throat.

Without being asked, Carl had leapt forward as soon as Lee got Turner on the ground and was removing the man's rifle, and the large combat knife he kept in a shoulder-mounted sheath. Carl flung them away and Lee heard them clatter across the ground, far away.

Turner coughed and gasped and Lee forced himself to let up on his throat. The man below him looked up, eyes red and face redder, his expression one of anger and determination. That was fine. Everyone was determined at the outset, but pain had a way of robbing you of that determination. They would see how determined young Turner truly was.

Lee bent down, eyes locked and spoke quietly to Turner's face. "This isn't going to go the way you want it to go, Turner. This is not going to end well for you. I am not the one to fuck with. I do not let people like you stand in the way of my mission. And I will accomplish my mission. I don't care what I have to do, or who I have to destroy. You will learn this. Because your chances for mercy died as soon as you stepped forward."

He didn't want a response from Turner, so he pressed his throat a little harder to keep him silent and leaned in even closer, his voice just a whisper: "You're going to see who I've become, Corporal Turner."

FOURTEEN

CONTACT

"OKAY, STOP HERE, STOP here." Devon was struggling with reading the road map as the icy wind from his rolled-down passenger-side window ripped it around. His rifle was sitting between his legs, propped on the dash with the barrel pointed up. He muttered a few curses and cranked the window up.

Nate sat in the driver's seat. He pulled to a stop in the middle of the road.

Devon flattened the expansive paper out and hunched into it, muttering to himself. "Goddamn maps. Maps. Who uses maps anymore?" He looked at Nate grudgingly. "You know what generation I come from, don't you, Nate? We had smartphones. I don't know how to use this thing."

Nate had heard this complaint before. "I swear to God, a three-year-old could do this." He leaned over the center console and splayed his palm onto the map to angle it in his direction. "We're on Highway 421...Highway 421...right there. Here's 421. And we're near Julian. Which puts us here. Coming up on Highway 62."

Devon did not look pleased. "You should have let me drive."

"You drive for shit." Nate traced his finger along Highway 62. "See? This heads north. This is what we want."

"It goes right into Burlington. Burlington hasn't been cleared."

"Well, we just turn off before we get to Burlington, then."

Devon leaned down, almost to the point that his nose was touching the paper.

"You need glasses or something?" Nate asked.

"Just . . . just let me do this." Devon waved him off. "Focus on driving, if you're so damn good at it."

Nate shrugged and accelerated. "You told me to stop."

Up ahead, he could see the signage for the Highway 62 interchange. He took the exit and then they were heading east, and then southeast, and then Highway 62 made a left-hand turn and went north, as intended. There wasn't a whole lot around. The usual gathering of gas stations that had been looted, the tanks drained dry and all the windows smashed in. The houses were spread far apart, though occasionally they passed a subdivision. Several subdivisions made Nate take a second look—there were smoke trails and signs of use in some of them. Perhaps small pockets of survivors that had banded together as a neighborhood. But it wasn't Nate's job to find people right now.

He was trying to find a horde.

They drove on in silence for a while. Devon seemed to find what he was looking for on the map. He folded it back together with that section up, though the fold was haphazard and lazy, and tossed the map on the dash so that he could reassume his position in the shotgun seat. The roadblocks that plagued the highways in the first month or so after the collapse seemed to have died away. Most of the people that could be robbed had already been robbed and many of them killed. Nate guessed that in the beginning, the roadblocks were easy because the victims were easy. Now everybody traveled warily, fingers hovering over triggers, and cautious when they went around bends and curves. Robbing by way of a roadblock had probably just become more dangerous than it was worth.

Nate didn't think things were settling. The dangers were still there. The people that had manned those roadblocks in groups of three and four were now parts of larger groups, he imagined. Groups like the Followers.

No, things were not settling. They were growing. From small spats between small groups to something like tribal warfare.

Tribes. Bunch of fucking tribes. Like the Middle East or something.

Devon directed him to take a left on a road as they began to close the distance to Burlington. Nate didn't demand to double-check the map for himself, but he hoped to God that Devon wasn't taking them the wrong way. Some risks you just have to take if you hope to maintain a good relationship with someone. And Devon was not an idiot. He was a smart kid. But his calling was definitely not topography.

Nate took the left as instructed, hoping they were going to pass between Burlington and Greensboro, as he knew had been Harper's plan when they'd set out. But with each mile, Nate grew more nervous about what was around the next corner. With each mile, his certainty that Harper and Julia were dead was growing. And each mile brought him closer to a horde large enough to swallow a city whole.

Devon seemed to have an uncanny ability to sense what Nate was thinking about. "You think this will work?" he asked.

"What?"

"You think this horde will just up and follow us?"

Nate tapped the steering wheel. "I dunno. Seems consistent with the behavior that I've seen. You've seen it, too. You get one chasing you, they all want to chase you. Even the packs are like that. The packs just try to flank you. But they're just running on prey drive. They see food and they go after it."

"So you think it will work?"

"I just told you I don't know."

"You said—"

"I said we've both seen how they act when they're in a horde. But we've only seen hordes of what...couple thousand at the most? Who knows what they do when there's fucking...a *million* of them." Nate realized he was gripping the steering wheel a bit aggressively. He relaxed. "We'll just have to see."

The last few visible houses passed them by.

Ahead, the road extended out onto a bridge. The trees ended, and the water began. Nate slowed as he approached the bridge. There was the cluster of an uncleared accident up against one of the bridge abutments and it sprawled out, taking up much of the two available lanes.

Nate edged to get around it and onto the bridge. Then he stopped.

In the passenger seat, Devon stiffened, then grabbed for his rifle.

"Oh, Jesus…" Nate breathed, losing his voice in fear.

The bridge was swarming with them. From the halfway point and on, he could not see concrete from the number of bodies that had crowded onto the structure. And far beyond, the opposite shore was a moving mass of bodies, as far as Nate's eyes could see. They seemed to swallow the world on the other side of that bridge, and they were beginning to consume the bridge.

There was a brief moment in time, just a half second or so, when they were stopped there at the foot of the bridge, that there was a sort of pause. Only the sound of the engine. Nate and Devon, staring out at the mass of people that crowded onto the bridge and the opposite bank, and all of those people, those infected people, those crazy people, they were staring right back.

Then, almost at the same instant, every one of those infected that saw them started screaming.

The sound of it hit him like a physical thing. Rattled in his eardrums.

"Go, man!" Devon was shouting. "Fucking go!"

Nate fumbled with the shifter. It seemed his entire body was made of senseless rubber. He managed to get the pickup truck into reverse, then jammed the gas and jerked the wheel. The truck burned rubber backing up and slammed into the side of one of the abandoned vehicles. But Nate wasn't stopping. He could look out his window and see them, pouring toward him across the bridge, more infected than he had ever seen. More infected than he had ever anticipated.

And they were all coming for him.

"GO NATE GO GO FUCKING GO!"

Nate put it in drive and squealed tires again. And when he saw the road racing underneath them, a little piece of his brain managed to make itself heard over the tumult of instinctive fight-or-flight. *This is why you're here, Nate. You're not supposed to RUN you're supposed to LURE.*

He slammed on the brakes. "Get in the bed!"

"What?" Devon seemed aghast. "Why?"

Nate put a hand on the younger man's shoulder and shoved him into his door. "Because that's the fucking plan, jackass! Get in the fucking bed!" Nate looked into the rearview mirror. He had put up maybe a quarter mile before steadying his mind, and behind him, the infected had just crossed the halfway point of the bridge. "You can do it. You got time."

Devon looked behind them, not making the same estimate that Nate had, but he opened his door anyways and hopped out, swinging hurriedly into the truck bed. "Okay! Now can we go? Can we go now?"

Nate accelerated, but then backed it off to twenty miles an hour.

Lure, don't run.

In the rearview mirror, the very first waves of infected began to flow off of the bridge and onto land. They spread out, taking up the shoulders of the road, filling the entire opening and even spilling into the trees. They stumbled and scrambled over each other. Some of them tripped and fell and were trampled by others. They ran shoulder to shoulder, all huffing and screaming and howling as they did.

All coming for me.

"Carrot on a stick," he said, his voice tremulous.

It looked like the plan might work after all.

Lee threw the doors to the Camp Ryder building open. His head was full of burning steam. His chest was full of fire. In the background of his mind, something like panic. Ahead of him, the people stood, their faces turning in his direction as the doors rebounded harshly off their stoppers. Behind him, Angela was calling out to him over the sound of the helicopter idling down in the Square.

"Everybody out!" Lee shouted, stepping deeper into the building and hiking his thumbs behind him. "Now! Out!"

The people began to head for the doors. They skirted wide around Lee, giving him sidelong glances full of wariness and fear. They were seeing the man that he had become, and that was okay, because he had to do what he had to do. And he was not their provider, their solace, their elected leader. He was a soldier. He was a fighter. He was a killer.

As the crowd filtered past him, Angela caught up and touched his arm. "What's going on? What happened?"

Marie was trailing in, close behind Angela.

Lee looked at Angela, but then fixated on Marie, because it was her that needed to hear this news. "The group of Marines that were with Harper and Julia...they turned on us. They're trying to buy their way back into President Briggs's good graces by holding Harper and Julia hostage for the GPS."

Angela put a hand to her mouth, then looked at Marie, gauging the other woman's reaction.

"Oh my God," Marie muttered. She put her hand out to brace herself against the wall. "Julia? Is she okay?"

"As far as I know, yes." Lee looked away. "But they are threatening to execute Harper and Julia both if I don't have the GPS to them in twenty-four hours."

Marie was in a daze.

Angela was not much better. But she processed through it quicker. "Well, what're you going to do? What's this about? I don't...what's going on?"

Lee pointed outside. "The squad of Marines that did this was working independently. Brinly didn't know. But one of the men in his squad was in on it. He fessed up right after I got the radio transmissions. And he's the one that's supposed to take the GPS to them. He's the only one that knows where they are."

"So...I don't understand." Angela blinked rapidly. "Is he working with us?"

"No," Lee said. "He's not. But I'm going to change his mind."

"What are you going to do?" Angela said, and then stepped back, as though she knew the question was a bad one.

"Do you really want to know?" Lee asked.

The doors to the outside slammed open again and Rudy and Mitch walked in, each holding one shoulder of Lance Corporal Turner. They had bound him with wire and blindfolded him with a bandanna. He'd also been dealt a hard blow to the face by one of his fellow Marines, and the bottom half of his face was caked in blood.

Lee looked into the Camp Ryder building. It was empty. All the people had fled. Lee pointed into the center of the main open area. "Put him there."

Behind Carl and his operators came Brinly and his two remaining Marines. Brinly's face was pinched up tight like a drawstring bag. He glared at the back of Corporal Turner as Rudy and Mitch led him into the center of the Camp Ryder building.

Lee caught Brinly's gaze. "First Sergeant, you okay with this?"

"No," Brinly said, almost immediately.

Lee sucked his teeth for a moment. "Maybe you should wait outside, then."

"Is that gonna make it better?" Brinly snapped. "For fuck's sake." He held out a hand in the direction of Turner. "You got one of my men! One of my fucking boys. God damn it, I know he fucked up..." Brinly trailed off. His hand closed into a fist in midair and then dropped. "I don't know what to fucking do with this." He looked up sharply at Lee. "Don't kill him. Promise me that."

Lee looked at Turner's back as they led him into the center of the room. There was a part of him that understood where Brinly was coming from. And there was another part that wanted blood. Why was everyone else so soft? Why could everyone else spare lives for people that had been their friends in the past, and Lee just found himself pulling the trigger? Was there something wrong with Lee? Was something broken inside of him that wasn't broken in everyone else?

"Fine," he said. "I won't kill him. But you need to wait outside and let me do what I need to do to find my people."

Brinly's face looked bitter and conflicted. But then he nodded. "Yeah. Okay." Then Brinly motioned his Marines to follow him, and he turned and left the same way he'd come in.

"What about the rest of Harper's group?" Angela asked, worried.

Lee's stomach clenched when he said the words. "They're all dead. They were killed."

Angela closed her eyes, touched her forehead. "Oh, Jesus."

Marie drew herself up. The emotion had run down her face like water breaking a levy, but it suddenly dried up, just as quick as it had burst from her. She stood up straight. Her wide eyes relaxed. Her lips were tense and tight. "Lee... that's my sister. I already...I already lost her once.

You brought her back to me. And I thank you for that." Her eyes flicked to his and he could feel the rage in them. He could feel it in himself. "But you cannot let her die. Do you understand that? That is my sister. You will not let her die."

Angela looked rapidly between the two of them. "Marie, wait a minute." She stepped in front of Marie, facing Lee, full on. "Think about what you're going to do. Think about all the people that are outside. What they're going to think about this."

Lee laughed, a bitter sound. "You think I give a shit what they think?"

"Remember what we talked about."

"I do," Lee said. "I remember every fucking word. I do what needs to be done. That's it."

Marie reached up and grabbed Angela's shoulder. "Angela. You need to step back away from this." Marie's voice trembled with anger. "That's not your sister. It's mine. My sister. And she is not gonna die. And Harper. He's my friend. And your friend, too. You walk away from this if you don't have the stomach for it. But don't you try to stop Lee from doing what he needs to do."

Angela and Marie looked at each other for a long, stretching moment. Lee watched Angela's jaw tensing, clenching, the cords in her neck pressing out against her skin. Finally, she turned back to Lee. She searched his eyes, but she must not have found what she was looking for. She only found exactly what she'd seen in Marie.

"Fine. You're right." She withdrew from him. "You do what needs to be done, Lee."

And then Angela put a comforting arm around Marie and led her from the building.

LaRouche and Clyde stood at the edge of the woods, looking out across I-40. They'd left their car parked among a jumble of other abandoned cars, where it would be camouflaged, and then they'd hiked down south of Newton Grove, where they'd already seen an armed presence. Here on the interstate, LaRouche watched the beat-up red pickup truck pass by for the second time.

"That's twice in an hour," LaRouche murmured.

"They patrolling," Clyde responded.

LaRouche agreed with a nod. "Out of Newton Grove, I'd guess."

A minute out of sight and a blue car came rolling on, going the opposite way as the truck. This was the second time it had made an appearance as well. LaRouche growled at the sight. "Well this is interesting."

"How's that?" Clyde asked, shifting his weight.

LaRouche rubbed his beard, scratched it. "Newton Grove was always quiet. Kept to themselves. Not into the whole patrolling thing. Either they've expanded, or they got taken. Either way, might be a good lick for us. If they got enough resources to be putting out patrols like this, then I imagine they have gas and guns. Might be tough to take, though."

Clyde regarded his partner and raised an eyebrow. "You think we should do it?"

"Well, that's not really up to me," LaRouche said with some irritation. "We're just scouting."

"Hey, you hear that?" Clyde held up a finger, inclining his head to the roadway.

"What?" LaRouche held very still, listening into the silence.

No, not silent. Something in the distance. The whistling, growling sound of diesel engines in the distance.

"Yeah, I hear it." LaRouche rose from his position and worked a little closer to the edge of the woods for a better view. He couldn't quite tell which direction the noise was coming from, but as he got closer, and the sounds drew nearer, he could tell they were coming from the southeast.

"You see anything?" Clyde asked, close behind.

"Mmm..." LaRouche leaned out, still conscious of remaining in cover. "Okay. Yeah. Let's get back into the woods."

"What is it? What'd you see?"

"You'll see in a minute." LaRouche turned into the woods and pushed himself up the incline back to where they'd been hiding a moment ago. He chose the same spot, but hunkered down farther into the leaves. Clyde followed suit. Only their two heads would be visible from the roadway, peeking out from behind a few tree trunks, but you'd really have to be looking for them.

The noise of the engines grew louder and louder.

The blue car sped past, back toward Newton Grove.

"Is it running away?" Clyde asked.

LaRouche didn't know, but he didn't think so. "I think he's leading them."

Closely following the blue car came a multitude of green and tan vehicles, one after the other.

"Marines," Clyde said, his voice tainted with disgust. "What are they hauling?"

LaRouche watched the bigger trucks and the guns they were towing. "Artillery. Lots of artillery."

"What the hell are they doing this far away from Camp Lejeune?" Clyde shook his head. "They've never come this far west before."

"Coming after us?" LaRouche offered.

"Come on." Clyde stood up as the last of the Marine vehicles roared by. "Let's get back to Chalmers. We need to figure out how we're going to handle this Newton Grove issue."

Lee gave himself some time to cool down, but not too much time. They didn't have much to begin with. It wasn't smart to enter into these types of things with your temper already lost. You could be angry—angry was fine. But your temper needed to be in check.

He looked into the dim interior of the Camp Ryder building where the three Delta operators and Carl stood surrounding a young man in a battered Marine Corps uniform. Corporal Turner was doing a good job trying to seem brave, but even in the vague lighting, Lee could see the man's breathing was rapid. He could see the sheen of sweat on him. No one, no matter how brave, wanted what was about to happen.

Lee felt sick to his stomach. Queasy. Jumpy. There was a part of him that kept asking, *Is this right? Is this the right thing to do?* But sometimes it wasn't about right and wrong. He knew that now. Sometimes you had to look at the bigger picture. No matter how much people hated it, sometimes the ends justified the means.

You are not what you once were.

Fine. I don't have to be.

How long? It's been an hour, maybe a little more.

They did this. They forced me into this. They are starting things and they are going to fucking hate how I finish them, but it's out of my hands. I'm not responsible for this.

Lee approached the young man kneeling on the floor with his hands tied behind his back. He had to look down on the man. Turner craned his neck to look at Lee, but then looked away. Lee rubbed the fingers of one hand together, feeling the grit of dirt caught between them. The rasp of callouses bought by pain and toil.

"What's your first name?" Lee said, keeping his voice level.

The Marine hesitated. "Luke."

"Luke. Why are you doing this?"

Turner took a deep, settling breath. "Because I'm a patriot, Captain. What you're doing here is against the command of the president. It's against the United States. In the middle states, they're rebuilding America. They have a safe zone. Those are the people that I'm loyal to. That is who I fight for. Not for warlords or self-imposed dictators. Not for Colonel Staley. Not for you."

Lee looked briefly pained. "Corporal Turner, listen to yourself. Think. I used to be a blind patriot, just like yourself. But the thing that we serve isn't an office, and it's not a name. Anyone with enough power and guns can come along in this collapsed nation and announce themselves president of the United States of America. Besides the part of your oath where you swore to obey the commander in chief, what was the other thing you were sworn to uphold?"

Corporal Turner knew, but didn't answer.

"The Constitution," Lee finished for him. "An idea. A concept. Not whatever person props himself into a leather chair and claims to be runnin' shit. And when that person comes along and tells you to abandon an entire coastline because it's 'not worth the resources,' what would you do?"

Turner looked up sharply. "You're making things up now."

Lee shook his head. "Why do you think Major Darabie and Captain Wright and Captain Tomlin defected? Why do you think these Delta boys and a bunch of the Eighty-Second Airborne defected? Why do you think your own unit hasn't gone over to President Briggs? 'Cause they're smart enough to spot a lie when they see one. Briggs isn't the president of anything but a bunch of desperate people, willing to give their liberties away for some peace of mind. Are you one of those people?"

"I know what I believe," Turner said flatly.

Lee knelt down so he was at eye level. "You're going down a road that you can't turn back from. You're not going to get the GPS. It's not going to happen. Remove it from your mind. Those are my friends that are being held hostage. And I'm going to find them, and I'm going to keep them from being executed. And I don't care who throws themselves on the tracks in front of me—it ain't gonna stop shit. You're not gonna stop shit. All you're gonna do is earn yourself a bad death, fighting for the wrong side."

Turner closed his eyes. Lee watched the pulse in his neck throbbing rapidly. "Captain Harden. Just give me the GPS and let me go."

Lee stood up. "Tyler knew I wasn't going to give you the GPS. He knew this was going to happen to you. But he's such a goddamn pussy he wouldn't come fight me himself. So he put you in this position to assuage his own guilt, even though he knew I'd never give the GPS to you. So as this happens, just remember who fed you to the wolves. Maybe that will shed some light on your *loyalties*."

Lee looked at Rudy and Mitch. "Strip him down naked."

Turner didn't fight, but he didn't cooperate, either. He stared balefully at Lee, but Lee could feel the fear in his eyes, and he thought that maybe Turner could see the pity in Lee's. And maybe that scared him more. The two big operators pulled out knives and cut off the clothes they couldn't pull off of him.

Lee faced him, clenching his fists. "Where are they?"

Naked and trembling, Turner breathed heavily through his nose, making a fierce sound. He shook his head vehemently.

Lee leaned down and seized the man by the

back of the head. He grabbed the man's face with his other hand and yanked his head back so that he was looking up at Lee. His neck and hair were sweaty, despite the chill in the air. Turner grunted, but otherwise refused to open his mouth.

"Well...you know what I want."

Then Lee hauled him up off of his feet and started dragging him across the floor.

Now Turner did fight, but only by trying to dig his heels in. He bore his teeth and let out an animal growl, but Lee just gave him a hard knee into his kidneys to soften him up. Turner yelped and Lee dragged him again, stumbling bare feet and all. And now Lee's blood was getting up again. He could feel the anger that had become so familiar to him, like a fully choked engine.

"Don't try to fight it now!" Lee yelled as he dragged the man across the floor, kicking and screaming. "You know what's fucking coming! You don't want it, then you tell me where the fuck my friends are! You fucking tell me!"

Lee dragged the man into the makeshift kitchen.

Turner must have felt the heat coming off the firebox on the opposite wall.

"No! No!"

Lee grabbed Turner's arm and slung him against the wall, then pinned him there with an elbow up against his face. "You see that? You see that shit? That's been burning nonstop for months. The only reason that stove ain't red hot is because it's cast-iron."

"No no no, don't do this..."

"You ever been burned before?"

"Don't do this, please!"

"Where are they?"

Turner had his eyes clenched shut. His teeth clenched together, spit flying as he screamed wordlessly through them.

Lee looked behind him where Carl and the operators were standing close by, weapons ported, watching. Lee nodded to them. Two of them stepped forward and took Turner by the shoulder while Lee applied downward pressure on his head. There was a moment when a little part of Lee raised its hand in all the chaos and said, *Do you really want to do this?* But it was too little and much, much too late.

Turner screamed through his teeth.

Lee slammed his face onto the stove and pressed it down.

It was like suddenly connecting two live wires. Turner gasped and started bucking so violently that Lee thought he might throw all three of them off. His feet started running in place, his hands clenching and unclenching, his torso ripping back and forth, every muscle in his body doing everything that it could to get his face off of that hot metal. And then the air he'd taken into his lungs came out of him in a blasting scream and right along with it came the smell of charred skin and burning hair. Lee just held on; he held on and kept pressing that man's face down and thinking of Harper and Julia, Harper and Julia...

I will not let them die. I will bring them back alive.

The scream seemed like it wouldn't end.

Lee realized he was screaming along with Turner.

He yanked the man up from the firebox. Patches of skin were left behind, still smoking and blackening. Lee threw the man down onto the floor where his body curled up like a pill bug and the breath was coming in and out rapidly, hyperventilating with short, sharp little barks of hysterical pain. Turner's sudden and monumental effort to get away had been so taxing that his legs cramped up and Lee could actually see the muscles binding up under the man's pale skin. The entire right side of Turner's face was a mess of wet-looking whiteness and bright, angry red. It was unrecognizable.

Lee steadied himself, swallowing down the sickening feelings. None of the pity that came over him in that moment could be heard. He forced his voice to be as hard and angry as it had been before. "Where the fuck are my friends? Where are they? You wanna lose the other half of your face? Do you?" Lee waited only a half second for a response, before snatching Turner's arms up. "Fine. We'll do it again."

"No!" Turner melted, every muscle in his body going limp. "No don't…don't don't…I'll tell you…"

Chalmers looked down at a map of North Carolina, finger planted firmly on Newton Grove. The Followers encampment, since removed from the town square farther east, had parked itself in a shopping mall, sprawled out and unprotected and daring the world to make a move against them.

There were hundreds of men there, and all of them were armed. They felt confident en masse.

LaRouche knew the truth, though. But he kept it to himself. Armies were not made up of numbers; they were made up of discipline. And the Followers were not particularly disciplined. But he had yet to see them in any real action, aside from the quick sneak attack that the Marines had mounted on their camp, just before the helicopters had razed it. He'd seen large armies routed by a much smaller but well-disciplined force. But maybe he was not giving the Followers enough credit. They were undrilled, but they followed Chalmers with religious zeal, and that might do in a pinch.

Chalmers looked up from the map, seeking eye contact with LaRouche. "And in your professional opinion, where were these artillery pieces going?"

LaRouche didn't particularly know. All he could offer was process of elimination. "They're not at Newton Grove, I can assure you that. On the way back, we checked. It was a pretty big convoy, so we should have been able to at least see a few of the vehicles if they were parked at Newton Grove or nearby. But we saw nothing. No Marines. No evidence of the vehicles."

"So they continued north on I-40."

"They could have gotten off any number of exits. But the people in Newton Grove were clearly working with the Marines, and they were patrolling I-40 pretty hard. It would be my guess that I-40 was the main corridor the Marines were taking, rather than hopping off onto some surface streets. Which would mean their objective was somewhere northwest of us."

"Any idea who they're allied with?"

"I don't know," LaRouche said. "I tried to recognize the faces of the people in civilian clothing that were holding Newton Grove, but the few I could get a clear enough look at I didn't recognize."

"Is it possible that this all has to do with Camp Ryder?"

LaRouche thought for a moment. "Yes. It's possible. Camp Ryder takes in a lot of people."

Chalmers smiled knowingly. "Yes, we know. They're very lax about who they allow in." He stood up from his seat. "Clyde. LaRouche. You both have done stellar work. I need more from you, though. I'm going to send you with a small detachment. You're going to go to Newton Grove, but hold position far enough away that you won't be noticed. And then I want you, LaRouche, and you, Clyde, to go out ahead of your detachment and watch Newton Grove."

LaRouche absorbed this.

Clyde asked the question that LaRouche was thinking: "Okay. What are we looking for?"

Chalmers smiled. "You both are good soldiers, but you lack faith. Particularly you, LaRouche. So I want you to go, and I want you to watch, so that you can have faith. The Lord clears a way for His people, I promise you. And when the way is clear, I want you to take Newton Grove with your detachment and send word back to the rest of us."

"Okay." LaRouche shook his head. "But what are we looking for?"

Chalmers sighed. "Always the doubtful one. Doubting Thomas. Just trust in God, LaRouche. Have faith. You will know it when you see it."

FIFTEEN

___

WOLVES

THE DOUBLE DOORS TO the Camp Ryder building burst open. Lee emerged, his pace clipped, his jaw set. Outside in the Square, the people were standing, still as stones, their faces paler than usual. At the bottom of the steps stood Brinly and his remaining Marines, one of which looked pissed, another very distraught. Angela and Marie stood near them, taut as high-tension wires.

Lee walked straight to Brinly. "We need to talk."

Brinly looked inside as the doors began to close slowly. All was very quiet. He nodded once, then followed Lee a few paces away from the others. "Is he still alive?"

"Yes." Lee folded his arms across his chest. "Scarred, but he'll live. I'm sorry that had to happen. He's yours. You can do what you want with him."

Brinly sniffed. "Did you find out where your friends are?"

Lee nodded. "I did."

"What do you need from me?"

"Why didn't Colonel Staley leave North Carolina? The real reason."

Brinly looked directly at Lee, searching his face.

"Turner mentioned something about Colonel Staley's daughter," Lee pressed. "He said it right in front of you. You heard it. I wasn't concerned with it at the time, but now..."

"Now you are?"

Lee frowned. "Now it has to do with loyalties. What happened with Colonel Staley's daughter?"

The whole time that Lee talked, Brinly continued to size him up, taking the measurement of him. Whether or not he had been found wanting in those measurements, Lee never knew, but finally Brinly broke the long-held eye contact and gazed back at his Marines.

"She was taken. By the Followers of the Rapture. That's why Colonel Staley never left North Carolina. It's why he's been so...passionate... about hunting the Followers down. He knows she's in one of those cages, with all the other women. Or at least, that's what he believes."

"You don't?"

"No." Brinly shook his head with a sigh. "She's dead. We've hit too many of their encampments and never caught a single trace of her. She's fucking dead. She was stubborn as her old man and probably was more trouble than she was worth to them as a captive. Probably got herself executed."

"Probably."

Brinly shrugged. "We don't have a body. All I can do is play the numbers."

"So Staley's only here because he hopes his daughter will show up?"

"You're asking about the internal workings of

Colonel Staley's mind. I'm his second in command, but that doesn't mean he tells me everything. I know that searching for his daughter kept him here. Whether there are other factors—particularly concerning President Briggs—all I can say is what he already told you. We severed communications with them."

"Apparently not all of you severed communications."

A nod. "I suppose not."

"Speak to me honestly here, Brinly." Lee dipped his chin, looked at the first sergeant earnestly. "How many other people do you think are on board with Kensey and his group?"

"No idea." He looked visibly distressed. "Kensey was a solid Marine. But not the most charismatic person. I can't see a bunch of people going down with him on this one. But then again, I didn't see him even pulling this shit in the first place."

"Did you notify Colonel Staley?"

"Yes. He's circling the wagons, so to speak. Just in case."

"Where is the artillery?"

"Convoy just moved past Newton Grove. Should be in place by the end of the day."

Lee nodded. "I'm running short on time and long on problems here."

Brinly looked at the captain. "As far as Kensey goes, he's in the same boat as Corporal Turner. Ain't no Marine of mine ever swapped sides on me. They can all go to hell for pulling that shit. You do what you gotta do to get your people back. We can stick around if you need."

Lee felt the offer like a fish might feel about a worm on a hook. Tempting, but risky. He was beginning to doubt what might actually be going on with the Marines. He wanted to trust First Sergeant Brinly, and believed that at least *he* was on the up-and-up. But Colonel Staley and the rest of the Marines in his command...that became dicey. Three Marines and an up-armored MATV could wreck a lot of shit inside Camp Ryder if they chose to.

Long on problems, Lee thought again.

"No, you should meet up with the artillery units," Lee said. "Don't take this the wrong way, but I want to make sure those guns are pointed in the right direction."

Brinly grunted and Lee could tell he was a little miffed. But given the evidence at hand, he kept silent. There really wasn't a case he could make for himself at this point.

Lee clapped him on the shoulder, trying to display some warmth and goodwill, but it came off stiff. Lee turned and walked away from him. He went to Angela and Marie. Their backs were to the crowd of people and Lee could see them between Angela's and Marie's bodies. They were still staring, but Lee thought they were showing less horror on their faces and more concern and curiosity now.

Marie grabbed Lee's arm. "Did he tell you?"

Lee nodded and turned his attention to Angela. "I'm sorry..."

She held up a hand and he wasn't sure whether her dismissal was sympathetic or angry. Her face didn't give much away. "I didn't have a chance to tell you earlier with all of this going on, but Nate and Devon and Paul and Junior radioed in when you were on your way back. Did you catch any of what they said?"

Lee shook his head. "No. I must not have heard them inside the helicopter."

"I figured that, when you didn't respond," Angela said, then cleared her throat. "Both teams have made contact. The basic gist of what I got was that they're not sure if the entire horde is following them, because of how big it is, but they definitely have a lot strung along behind them. They're working their way back toward Smithfield now."

"Shit." Lee touched his head.

"Isn't that what you wanted?"

"Yes, it's good. But there's too many things happening right now." He rubbed his eyes. "I've just got a lot of pans in the fire is all." He looked at Marie. "Getting Julia and Harper back is priority number one right now, okay?"

Marie nodded stiffly. "Okay."

"We're gonna get 'em back."

"Okay."

Lee looked to Angela for a moment. He waded through murky waters of unsaid words, but was unable to find the right ones in all the silt. An apology was pointless, and she was right to cut him off for trying to give her one. What was the point in apologizing for something you didn't intend to change? Besides, Lee couldn't change what he'd done to Turner. This was a fight to the goddamn death, and Turner had gotten himself in the way at the wrong time.

Someday she'll understand it.

The doors opened again, and this time Carl emerged, alone. Lee waved him over to where he was standing with Angela and Marie. Carl made his way to them, eyeing the Marines as he passed. "Your friends only got about twenty hours left. Might want to get this train rolling."

"Angela just informed me that the bait trucks have already made contact and are on the way to Smithfield."

"Damn."

"Yeah. A little quicker than I anticipated. But we can still work it." Lee looked over his shoulder to the Black Hawk that took up the vast majority of the open area in the Square. "How's the fuel situation in the bird looking?"

"Fine. What you need?"

"I need a fast way to get to where they got my people, and a fast way to get out. Also need your boys with me."

"I can do that." Carl made another glance in the direction of the Marines. "Don't trust 'em?"

"Don't trust anyone," Lee answered. "But I have particular doubts about them now. Besides that fact, Tomlin vouched for you, so I guess that counts for something."

Carl cracked a rare smile. "I'd hope so."

"I need something else from you," Lee said, then looked at the two women. "And this pertains to y'all as well."

"I'm listening," Angela assured him.

"What're you thinking?" Carl asked.

"I'm thinking that when those hordes hit, that's going to be a couple million infected, just thirty miles north of us. If anything goes wrong with the plan, or if we don't kill them all, or if some of them get distracted, and keep heading south before we can splash rounds, then they're gonna be coming straight this way."

"I'd considered the same," Carl said darkly.

"Wait." Angela held up a hand. "You want us to leave?"

Lee nodded. "Angela, we can't stay here. It might just be a few stragglers that make it out of Smithfield alive. Or there could be entire sections of thousands that wander off before we can hit them. If a horde of a thousand were to come here, they would wipe Camp Ryder off the map. These fortifications won't hold."

"What do you need from me?" Carl asked.

"I need you to send an escort up here. Get these people out of here. Take them back to Fort Bragg."

"Lee!" Angela hissed. "You can't be serious! You're going to transplant the entire group over a possibility that something bad might happen?"

"No," Marie said suddenly, putting a hand on Angela's arm. "He's right, Angela. These fences barely keep the infected out anymore. It's been a long time coming, but we knew this was going to happen. This was a good place for us to get a start and be secure. But it didn't hold back the hunters, and it sure as hell ain't gonna hold back a horde of a thousand if they come knocking."

"But..." Angela stammered, but couldn't seem to find a convincing argument.

"I'm not talking about a permanent shift," Lee said. "But until we have everything sorted out, I don't think this is the safest place for everyone. People wanna come back after everything is said and done? That's fine. But right now? It's just dumb. Especially if Fort Bragg is willing to house us for a short time." Lee glanced to Carl with the last part.

Carl considered it, and to his credit, it didn't take him long before he nodded. "Honestly, I'm surprised you guys are still standing in this place. We have barracks and army houses that have been empty for months. More than enough room to house every person here and then some. Plus we're secure and insulated. It won't be a problem. I can put the call in right now and get a detail working on escorting you folks to Fort Bragg."

Lee nodded. "Angela. Marie. You guys are the leaders here. I just advise, and I'm strongly advising you to do this. But you gotta make the call. What do you say?"

Angela and Marie shared a look, and then Angela turned partially outward so that her gaze fell on the crowd of survivors that stood around at the front of Shantytown. Lee looked out at them, too, and thought he knew exactly what was going through Angela's head. *We lost so many people, we sacrificed so much for this place, and now we're going to abandon it. Sure, we can come back to it, but realistically, are we going to? Is it practical? Our houses are made of tarp and wood. We're cold and wet half the days. Most of the people that fought for this place are gone or dead. And most everybody that remains is new, or a stranger. There's no reason to be here. There's only misplaced emotional attachment.*

Angela turned back and nodded. "Okay. Yes. We'll do it. I don't think it will take much convincing." She looked at Carl. "If you get your men up here, we'll be ready to go."

"I'll start working on it," he said. "But right now, I think we need to come up with a plan to get your people back, yeah?"

Lee nodded. "Turn the corporal over to First Sergeant Brinly. Then we'll get going. You okay with an in-flight plan?"

"I've been known to wing it from time to time," Carl admitted.

"All right." Lee pointed to the Black Hawk. "Let's roll."

Brett extracted himself from the uncomfortably small interior of the blue car. The Jersey barriers didn't completely surround the nucleus of Newton Grove, so they were able to pull the vehicles into the protected interior. He stepped out into the cold air, stretching his legs as the next shift gathered around to take the vehicle from him and his partners.

It just so happened that he'd gone on patrol with Mac this past time.

Mac's people were the ones standing there, waiting for the blue car.

"Mac, didn't the Marines already come through?" one of the men asked.

"Yeah. Why?"

The man looked irritable. "Then why are we still out here doing this? Isn't getting the Marine convoy through the whole reason why we were here?"

Mac looked at the others as though he were considering it.

"Let's get the fuck back to the camp," another man urged. "This place is creepy as shit."

Brett looked at them all like they were idiots. "Mac. And you—I don't even know your name— were you guys not fucking listening? Captain Harden said that after the Marines passed through we were supposed to watch their back. The Followers are pressing west and there's a good chance they might start showing up along our route. If we're not here to sound the alarm..."

The man who had wanted to go rolled his eyes. "I don't give a shit about no fucking Followers."

"Well, you should," Brett said sharply.

Mac addressed his man. "You're talkin' out of your ass, Bud. Why don't you hit the road. Let's just stick to the plan, okay?"

The man called Bud heaved a heavy sigh, and he and his three companions took to the vehicle. Four people in a scout vehicle seemed like a bit much to Brett. What was this, a fucking social call for them? Or were they really, secretly scared of the Followers? That was probably more likely.

Brett smirked to himself as they closed the doors and headed out to do their patrol. As they squeezed through the opening in the barriers, he watched the van come around the corner. Brett arched his aching back and nodded to Mac. "Why don't you go ahead and grab some food. I'll watch the perimeter first. Need to take a walk and loosen these legs anyways."

Mac nodded tiredly and headed off toward the center of the ring of barriers, where they had stored most of their junk: sleeping bags, bedrolls, food and water, and extra fuel. Some of the people had helped themselves to the abandoned shanties. But many of them were unsettled by the empty shanties, as though they were haunted by the ghosts of their previous owners. Some chose to sleep in the open, despite the cold air. They'd built several larger fires around the camping area to keep them warm. But Brett got the sense that Mac's group had been somewhat nomadic until very recently and was used to laying their heads in odd spots wherever they could find a place.

Brett turned his attention outward and scanned the buildings that surrounded them. They really should have posted lookouts in the buildings, he thought. But they had the work divided in half already. There were twenty-four of them, total. Twelve were on patrol at a time, taking six-hour shifts. It was supposed to be two in the car, two in the truck, and eight in the van as a sort of quick reaction force.

Apparently Mac's brilliant people decided to go four to a car, for whatever fucking reason.

Whatever. Brett shook his head. It didn't bother him that much, but for the fact that these people refused to stick to a plan. They were highly undisciplined. Their randomness created a lot of concerns for Brett. He propped himself up against the cement barrier that was almost as tall as he was. Across the expanse of what had once been a prospering group of survivors, Brett watched the van roll through the gap in the barriers and pull to a stop. The truck was close behind.

The sun was just now beginning to head for the horizon, but the night watch was taking over. They wouldn't really watch it all night long. More like second-shift hours. They'd keep patrolling until about midnight and then turn it over to Brett's half again.

Brett watched them while they unloaded. The Marine convoy had passed, and now they were waiting for the Followers. Brett had a job to do, and yet he was strangely calm. Peaceful. Even in the midst of all this wreckage, his back against a cement barrier pockmarked with bullet holes and stained with blood that could have been from the people trying to survive here, or from whatever had attacked them.

He wondered if there'd been any survivors after the infected had attacked. Maybe they decided to up and leave when most of their friends had been killed…and probably eaten. But wouldn't they have headed for Camp Ryder? The next closest safe place? Maybe. Maybe not. Sometimes people made decisions that made sense only to them.

The squads swapped out. The van pulled out and left them. Then the pickup truck.

Brett continued on his walk around the perimeter. He found another guard standing watch on the opposite side of the ring of barriers. He hadn't been able to see him through the trees and tents and shanties that took up the center. The man was from Brett's group, an older guy named Roland. Trucker. Transplanted out of Ohio when the collapse happened. Found his way to the same little group of survivors in the woods that Brett had.

Brett waved to him with a smile. "Roland. You doin' okay?"

Roland wasn't a fan of the cold, despite being from Ohio, which was much cooler than North Carolina. He was hunched in his jacket, his arms wrapped around his rifle, looking miserable. He managed a perfunctory greeting to Brett. "Fine. You?"

"How long you been out here?" Brett asked, looking back toward the fires that Mac was stoking back to life.

"Couple hours."

"Why don't you go take a break. I'm walking the perimeter anyways. No point in you being out here."

Roland didn't need any extra encouragement. He flicked up a finger to acknowledge and then was gone, walking back to the camp and the fires that would warm him. Brett stood in the spot that Roland had been in and took another good survey of the buildings around them. Except for the scorch marks and bullet holes, everything looked relatively peaceful. A few decayed bodies up against the bases of buildings, or huddled in ditches, but you found your eyes glossing over them after a while. Bodies were commonplace inside the cities and towns. A lack of them would be something to be concerned about.

Brett kept walking clockwise, with the wall of

cement to his left side. The conversations of the people in the center of the fortifications seemed quiet and far away. They paid Brett no mind as he continued on to the opening where the vehicles came and went. By now they would be several miles away in either direction.

Brett patted the pocket of his jacket to reassure himself that the spare mag was there before he stepped through the opening and out into the town beyond so that the wall of Jersey barriers was between him and the camp.

His eyes traced over the buildings, but they were just as quiet and abandoned on this side as they'd been on the other. But somehow, he knew that they were not. He couldn't quite put his finger on it, but he knew this was it. This was the time they had told him about.

Go and be a part of this Camp Ryder Hub. And when you know that we are coming, open the way for us.

And they were coming, Brett knew. They were coming for Camp Ryder.

Brett pulled the spare magazine out of his pocket and set it on the top of a Jersey barrier so that it would be right there when he needed it. Then he laid the muzzle of the rifle gently over the top of the cement, pointed inward. He took a deep breath and sighted the rifle at the dozen people, clustered in the center of Newton Grove. He sought out Mac first, though he wasn't sure why.

Then he started shooting.

SIXTEEN

HARD PLACES

WHEN IT WAS FINISHED, Brett stood behind the wall, looking over at what he'd done. He took a moment to evaluate himself, both physically and mentally. Physically, he'd taken some shrapnel from return rounds spat out by a few of the more heads-up people in the group that had sprayed bits of concrete into his face. He could feel the blood trickling down from the half-dozen little cuts on his forehead, around his eye, and his left cheek. He didn't think any of the shrapnel had gotten into his eye—at least it didn't hurt if it did—but it was difficult to see out of his left eye because of all the blood dribbling into it.

Mentally, he felt rock-steady. He gave himself time to feel remorse, or even just a pause, but there was none. This was what he'd been sent to do. Chalmers and the Followers knew about the Camp Ryder Hub. They'd heard about it from people they'd captured and from people that had joined them. They knew that if they ever had to move west, it would become a problem. So they sent him out, among others. To join small groups that would be overrun by the Followers and then seek asylum in the Camp Ryder Hub.

Brett had done his job. He'd executed it flawlessly. Chalmers would be proud. They would bless him. His place in heaven would be a high throne for the things he had done for the Kingdom of God and for the Lord's Army.

He stepped back into the ring of Jersey barriers. Not everyone inside was dead. A few still clung to life. He went to them, because even a warrior of the Lord's Army was required to show mercy. He was no barbarian. He did not want them to suffer.

He thought about the men hung on crosses, but those men had refused to bend the knee. He could not fault Mac and Roland and all the others in this group—they'd never been given a chance to bend their knee and submit. Therefore, they did not need to be punished. They only needed to die.

Brett walked to the center, where most of them had fallen. A few had made a run for the copse of trees in the center, but Brett was a good shot. He'd taken them out on the run, and they now lay unmoving in the dirt and grass. Brett was very conscious that any of them lying still could very well be alive, waiting for a moment to surprise-attack him. He was on the side of God, but that did not mean that God made him invincible. He still needed to be cautious.

He went to Roland first. It was unfortunate that it had to be this way. He had always liked Roland. He wished that Roland had been given the chance to kneel, to submit. He would have made a good soldier for the Lord's Army. Brett would have been proud to serve next to him.

Roland was squirming, bleeding from the gut, but his hands were clamped around his own neck, where a bullet had clipped him. Blood was still pulsing from his carotids and Brett did not think that Roland had very long to live.

"Roland, I am sorry it had to be like this. You seemed like a good man, even in your sin."

Roland's voice was barely audible. Just a gurgling whisper. "You son of a bitch..."

Brett was disappointed in Roland, but he understood that pain and blood loss sometimes made people say things they didn't really mean. Brett gave the man on the ground a serene smile to let him know that there was peace between them, and then he finished him off with a shot to the head.

He continued on, finding three more people that were not completely dead. One attempted to make a go for the rifle that had fallen from their grip and was lying several yards away, but he could not out-crawl a bullet. Brett put them all down without much effort.

As the last shots faded, Brett heard another sound: engines.

He peered over the top of the barrier and watched a vehicle approaching. A truck, but not the truck that had so recently departed from Newton Grove. That truck would not be back for quite a while. This was a different truck, one that he did not recognize, but somehow knew who was in it. He stood in the center of the camp, surrounded by his gory work, the smell of fresh blood and bowels mixing with the rot from the old carcasses.

The truck pulled up to the Jersey barriers. It was a large one, full of armed men in the cab, and in the back. None of them pointed their weapons at him. They all wore the white armband and black cross of the Followers.

Brett smiled broadly.

Two men exited the passenger's side of the truck and approached him as the others began to fan out. One seemed very rough. His eyes were not full of peace but a sort of reptilian coldness. Something that said he would kill if and when he damn well pleased, and that emotions and morals and sympathies did not make an appearance in that decision-making process. Still, there was something vaguely familiar about him.

Brett recognized the other man as he drew closer, though he was now a little worse for wear since the last time that Brett had seen him. His hair was longer, pulled back into a ponytail, and his glasses were scratched and bent askew on his head. It took him a moment before recognition broke out across his face.

"Holy..." the man said, bewildered.

"Clyde," Brett said, opening his arms and embracing the other man. "It's been a long time."

"I thought you were dead," Clyde said. "Where have you been?"

"On a mission," Brett said, feeling satisfaction flood him. Victory. Completeness.

The rough-looking man regarded Brett with that cold look. He was a distrustful one. "Who is this?" he said, pointing a casual finger at Brett.

"Brett," Clyde introduced. "This is LaRouche, one of our newest men. LaRouche, this is Brett, one of our best."

LaRouche narrowed his gaze. "I recognize you from somewhere."

Brett squinted back, feeling that same sense of familiarity. "Yes. Where are you from?"

LaRouche considered for a moment, still taking the measurement of Brett, it seemed. "Camp Ryder," he finally said. "I was sent east to blow the bridges…" He trailed off. Then he lifted a finger.

Brett remembered as well. "Ah yes, *LaRouche*. How could I forget? We met on the road. You told me to go to Smithfield. Your name was the whole reason I was even able to get into Camp Ryder. 'Tell them LaRouche sent you' was what you said to me. And it worked! It worked quite well."

LaRouche lowered his upraised finger. Something hot flickered behind all that ice in his eyes. "Yeah. I remember now."

Brett then took the measurement of LaRouche. "You're quite new to be riding in the front and conducting operations with one of our oldest lieutenants," Brett said, casting a glance at Clyde, for whom he had tremendous respect.

Clyde held up a hand and spoke for LaRouche, and for the first time Brett got the sense that LaRouche might be volatile. Clyde seemed to be treating him like a dog that liked to bite. "LaRouche has proven very valuable to the Followers. Chalmers has already used him in several important situations. Such as this one."

Brett felt almost giddy. "We're taking the Camp Ryder Hub?"

Clyde nodded, then turned to LaRouche. "Send the men to get Chalmers. Tell them we own Newton Grove and all roads are clear to Camp Ryder."

Not much left. Not much left. Not... much... left.

Three words of the English language, the only ones that remained solid and substantial in her mind, and they looped endlessly through Jenny's brain. She knew these words, and she knew what they meant. She knew that she had known many other words, many other sounds that could be used to express herself, but they were all gone now. She tried hard to make them come back, but there just was *not much left*.

She felt frustration. Incredible frustration, though the concept was just a concept. She knew that she had once been able to find the things making her frustrated and make them better, but all she could do now was *feel*. Her brain was an instruction manual written in a foreign language. And because she could not make it better, it only made it worse. Fluttering, beating, roaring frustration.

And anger. She felt that, too, again without words. Just the hotness in her chest. The quickening of her pulse. The way her entire body was locked up and tense. She used to have command of it, but now it seemed to have a mind of its own, and hers and its were not in communication. More and more of her was being turned over to autopilot, as her logical brain made its last death throes and kept thinking, *Not much left*.

Not much left, and soon there would not even be those words. The captain would be dead in the cockpit. The machine would be running itself. Already there was no forethought. There was very little memory outside of clips and images that made no sense and were completely disassociated, like photos of another person's life stuck in her neural passageways, and they only made her more angry. Because sometimes they blocked the NOW. And the NOW was the important thing. There was nothing before or after that concerned her. Just NOW.

Now she was cold and hot. Cold outside, hot on the inside.

Now she was hungry. A pain that drove her in the pit of her stomach. There were images, and these few were welcome. Something bloody. Juice and gristle in her teeth. Satisfaction in her guts. The pain would go away.

Now she was frustrated and angry. She punched walls and felt bones crack, but it only made her more angry, so she kept doing it.

Now there were noises. Noises that she'd heard before. No pictures to go along with them, none that made any sense to her, but a feeling. A feeling of fear. Once the noises didn't mean fear, but that was before the NOW. The noises made her want to run. Made her want trees and leaves and places to hide. She sank low and circled around in the semiblackness, feeling cold hardness all around her. Sharp hardness. She pictured rocks and stones, but that was not right. This cold hardness was a different kind of cold hardness.

When she banged on the walls, it was very loud.

She screamed, and it was louder. She waited to hear another scream—another thing like her that had heard her and knew she was here, to answer back, to make a connection. She knew the screaming was wrong. She knew she shouldn't do it. But she could not control the urge to be heard, to rage, to vent.

Not much left—her secret words slipped away. The meaning of them was becoming strange, black like the darkness around her. Other things were more important. Smells. Noises. Feels. With the meaning of the words went the importance of them, the fear that they brought to her belly. Thinking them no longer made her stomach twist. That was good. Her stomach got twisted a lot from things that were outside of the NOW. She didn't like the twisting. It was good that it was gone.

The NOW was good.

Sam followed Deuce around the corner of the Camp Ryder building. He was on the side of it now, right next to the big water containers that they'd built. Sam could smell the cold, blank smell of the water in the square bins, almost as tall as he was. Ahead of him, Deuce was scenting the air and growling low in his throat.

Sam heard the shuffle of feet on gravel behind him.

He turned. Abby was standing there, caught trying to follow him. Her blond ringlets framed a guilty face and wide blue eyes.

"I told you to wait on the steps!" Sam said.

"Mom told us *both* to wait on the steps," Abby insisted.

"Deuce is growling."

"So?"

"So he only growls when there's infected somewhere around."

"So why didn't you tell one of the grown-ups?"

Sam looked back over his shoulder and saw that Deuce had advanced to the second water container. The dog was moving slowly. Cautiously. But if Sam waited around too long, the dog would go and he wouldn't be able to...to...

To handle the problem.

He felt it like tightness in his chest. His pulse working a little harder. His breath coming a little shorter and sharper now. He wanted to find what Deuce was growling at. He wanted to be the one to do it. Not run to one of the adults and cry to them about it. He had his rifle. He'd killed before. And now everyone looked at him like he was some poor wounded boy.

He was a man. He could handle this.

It was probably just an infected on the fence anyways. Sam could just sight the little rifle from twenty yards away, just like he'd done with the squirrel, and put whoever or whatever it was down with a shot to the eye. It wasn't even dangerous.

Deuce crept forward a little more, almost to the back corner of the building.

Full-on growling now.

Sam said the bad word that Abby had been trying to get him to interpret. Then he looked back at her. "Fine. You can come along if you stay quiet. And if there's something bad, you have to run. You have to run back to the Square. Okay?"

Abby nodded fiercely.

"Okay," Sam said. "Be quiet."

Then he started moving again.

Deuce stopped at the corner of the building, looking left into the backyard. Sam could see the dog's hackles were up, his tail stiff and level with the ground, his teeth starting to show as his lips curled back a bit. Then he looked back at Sam, as though to say, *Are you coming to take care of this or what?*

Sam brought his rifle up to his shoulder and stepped wide around the corner of the building. He took it in slow, side-straddling steps. He watched his sight picture swing over the back fence, then the open area of the backyard, then the big steel container, and finally the wall of the Camp Ryder building itself.

Sam lowered his rifle, confusion playing across his face.

"What's wrong?" Abby whispered. "What's he growling at?"

Sam glanced down at the dog. Deuce was still standing stock-still, growling quite loudly now. "I dunno," Sam said. "There's nobody back here. Nothing."

Deuce barked once, making Sam and Abby jump. Then the dog looked up at him and whined. Then back to the object of his concern, growling again. Sam followed the dog's gaze, but the only thing there was the big steel container. Just like all the other steel shipping containers scattered around the interior of Camp Ryder.

Abby was craning her neck around the corner. "I don't—"

Something rattled. Clanked.

Sam felt like he'd taken a little jolt of electricity. There was something both good and bad about that feeling. He raised the rifle and stepped farther around the corner. "Stay there, Abby. I mean it."

The girl sidled closer to the wall, putting a hand out to touch it for reassurance.

"There's something in that container," Sam said.

"You should call someone," Abby replied, her voice almost begging.

"It's fine. Just stay right there."

"Sam..." Abby whined.

Sam looked back at her, perturbed. "I can handle this, Abby."

"But Deuce only growls if it's *in-feck-a-tid*."

"Why would there be infected in a shipping container?"

Another sound, like someone pounding on the inside of the metal. And then a distinct creaking noise. Like rusty hinges.

Sam spun back to the shipping container.

Deuce started barking madly.

The door was open.

Sam lifted his rifle up. He felt his legs suddenly heavy and unwieldy. Like they were just hollow sacks of flesh filled with dead, lifeless sand. *It's not locked in, it's not locked in, it's not locked in, what do you do? What are you gonna do?*

Something moved in the shadows of the container.

Deuce had pressed himself against Sam's leg and would not stop barking.

"Sam!" Abby was frightened. "Sam, let's go!"

Be a man. Handle this.

He moved one leg in front of the other, a halting, shaky twitch of his body. He struggled to make his mouth work in conjunction with his throat, his diaphragm. *Don't be scared. Nothing to be scared of. You have a rifle. You've shot people before. You've killed things before.*

He finally found his voice. "Hey!" he called out, trying to sound like an adult. "Who's in there? Come out! Let me see your hands!"

The door to the shipping container swung open a little farther. Something—*someone*—edged out. Pale skin. Blond hair hanging lank around a slack face. She looked sickly. Like she might keel over at any moment. Like she'd looked when Lee and Angela had carted her into the Camp Ryder building the other night, so sick she could barely walk on her own.

Sam felt relief flood him so hard, his knees started to wobble. "Ms. Jenny?" he called out, his voice shaky and cracking.

Ms. Jenny looked at him from where she'd stepped out of the shipping container. She tilted her head slightly, like an animal hearing a strange noise. And Deuce was still at Sam's leg barking incessantly. Sam nudged the dog with his leg, trying to get him to be quiet.

"Deuce! Shut up! It's just Ms. Jenny!"

But Deuce was unconvinced. He was barking so hard that his entire body was almost lifting off the ground every time he did it.

Abby was still peering around the corner, but now she was shaking her head. "Sam..." Her voice wavered.

Sam raised his voice, trying to be heard over the dog's barking. "Ms. Jenny? Are you o—"

Then Ms. Jenny made a noise that she'd never made before, but one that was so very familiar to Sam. And it made every muscle in his body lock up. The electric shock again, but this time wholly unpleasant. Terrifying. Gut-wrenching.

She had crossed half the distance before Sam realized what was happening.

Deuce was snarling, still leaning against Sam's leg, refusing to run and leave his two human companions by themselves. At the corner of the building, Abby started to scream. And Ms. Jenny was making that sound, that sound, that horrible sound.

Sam snapped his rifle up and cranked off a single round without thinking. Ms. Jenny reached out for him, only a few lunging strides away. The single round shot out of the rifle and it lanced through the air, perfectly aimed, and snapped right through the bone of her forehead.

She landed at Sam's feet, still twitching.

* * *

Camp Ryder was a mess of activity. Even with the Black Hawk helicopter and the Marines' truck both gone from the Square where they'd been parked, with everyone running around, it still seemed crowded.

Everything had been rushed. She'd barely been able to wrap her head around it when she turned around and the Marines were gone and Lee was in the helicopter, already lifting off the ground. She felt something pull loose in her, like it had been tethered to the belly of the aircraft and now was yanked out of whack. The feeling of anger that she'd had against Lee, the feeling of coldness toward him, was suddenly crippled and then there was only the fear that he would not be coming back.

But there was no time for her. No time for Lee. The people stood around, not knowing what to do, formulating plans of their own, many of which wouldn't be divergent. All the big guys with the guns were gone, and now it was just civilians, looking to her, though she didn't want them to. Waiting for her to knit them all together and come up with a workable plan.

They didn't like the workable plan. They didn't know Fort Bragg or the people in it. They didn't trust them. Lee was wrong. Angela was wrong. Marie was wrong. It was dangerous. It was foolhardy.

Their objections were numerous.

But when Angela nodded to them, heard them, and then told them the plain truth of the matter, the reality of the situation, so bluntly put to them as Lee had put it to her, suddenly their objections were not so numerous. She assured them it was not permanent. She assured them that the people from Fort Bragg were worthy of their trust—though she didn't know any of them except Carl, and him only in passing for the last twelve hours. She assured them that this was the best course of action.

They were assured, although begrudgingly.

Now they were milling about, gathering the things they feared they might never see again, trying to prepare themselves for some exodus to Fort Bragg. And as much as she liked the sound of it not being permanent, she knew that, in a way, it was. Maybe they would come back to Camp Ryder, but would anyone want to live here after she'd just pointed out the things that were so weak about it? They'd been lucky so far. They were off the beaten path, and the few bad elements that had managed to find them were rebuffed. But how long could they expect that to happen?

Lee was right about that one thing, at least, Angela admitted to herself as she walked briskly toward Shantytown. *This has been coming for a long time. Camp Ryder has become our home, it's become a place full of emotion, but in reality, there isn't much here for us. And it's always been the plan to link up with other groups of survivors. Would we just insist on staying here, even if they have room for us and better protection? No. Not likely.*

Now, she had another worry, besides the imminent journey from here to Fort Bragg.

Where the hell was Jenny?

She hadn't seen her since she slipped out of the

Camp Ryder building the previous night. She'd been busy all morning and into this afternoon. And then she had searched the crowd for the woman while she'd been convincing everyone to pack their things. She'd seen no trace of her. And given her condition yesterday, Angela was right to be concerned.

She could be fucking dead in her shanty right now. Can you die of the flu? Yeah, of course you can. There was that old lady that died because of the flu. But she was old. Jenny is young. I don't think young people are supposed to die from the flu.

As she was about to turn onto Jenny's row of shanties, she heard the gunshot.

Just one. The sound of a small caliber. Like a .22.

She immediately halted in her tracks and turned back toward the Camp Ryder building. Her first thought went to Abby and Sam. Her eyes shot to the front of the Camp Ryder building, the steps, the fucking steps where she told them to be! Why weren't they there? Where the hell did they go?

When she heard her name being yelled out in a panic, her fear drove deeper, like spurs into a horse. She started running for the building. Everyone else had heard the noises, too, and they'd perked up, stopping where they were to try and figure out what was going on. Angela pushed passed them all and only when she got to the edge of the building did her heart stop having conniptions in her chest.

Abby and Sam were standing there side by side, as they were so often found these days, looking at something on the ground that was very nearby to them, but which Angela could not see from where she was. Sam had his rifle in one hand, the other held protectively around Abby.

Angela knew the look on Abby's face as she ran up to them. Abby was terrified, and just now beginning to cry, the tears spilling over. Abby saw Angela coming and any semblance of control fled her. "Mommy! It was Jenny! It was Jenny! I thought it was...I thought it was something else!"

Still standing there with her, Sam kept staring at the thing on the ground that Angela could not quite see. Not until she reached the two children. Then Sam looked back at Angela and their eyes met. Whatever was going on inside of his head, it was flowing under a thick layer of ice.

The form that he'd been staring at was stretched out, facedown on the ground, not five feet from where Abby and Sam were standing. Angela couldn't see the face, but she could see the stringy blond hair, the clothing, the small frame of the person underneath. The tennis shoes that she insisted on wearing, despite everyone else wearing boots. She knew who it was. She understood suddenly what her daughter had been screaming about.

"Oh my God." Angela grabbed Abby without thinking. She wasn't sure what she was hoping to accomplish, only that she needed to take her daughter in her arms and make sure she was okay. She didn't think about the fact that maybe Sam was holding her just as much as Abby was holding him. And when she took her daughter out of

his arms, he looked like he snapped back into real
time. His eyes sharpened, then stretched wide and
fearful. His mouth worked. His body looked like it
was starting to tremble.

"I'm so sorry," he stammered breathlessly. "I
didn't know. I didn't know."

"What happened?" Angela said, trying to keep
her voice from yelling and realizing that she was
failing miserably.

Sam winced when she spoke, like he'd been
stung. He spoke rapidly, haltingly: "Deuce was
growling and I didn't know what it was, so I came
back here with Deuce, and then she...it was just
Jenny, but she was sick, she was infected, and she
started coming after me, and I didn't know, I
didn't know, I didn't know what to do!"

Angela struggled to comprehend him, like he
was speaking some other language. Inside of her
chest, her pulse was pounding hard. And Sam
was speaking so fast and panicked, and Abby was
clinging to her, starting to wail loudly. Behind
her, other people were starting to talk and shout
over each other as they came within view of the
body. And highlighting everything, Deuce was
standing there with Sam, barking savagely at the
body.

Jenny. That's Jenny on the ground.

Angela stared at the body as Sam continued to
repeat the things he had already said, his voice spi-
raling out of control, now fully shaking and cracking, tears springing into his eyes. She stared at the
body and thought for a second that there was no
bullet wound, but then she could see the little exit

in the back of Jenny's head, where the .22-caliber round had broke free of her skull and spilled just the tiniest bit of blood and brain matter into Jenny's hair.

She was shot in the head. Sam shot her in the head.

"I didn't know it was her!" Sam was yelling now, like he was trying to convince everyone. Like nobody believed him. Sweat was joining with the tears on his face. His dark complexion had suddenly turned ashy and pale. His feet moved like he was thinking about running.

Why did he shoot her?

Deuce barking, barking, barking, refusing to stop. Refusing to leave Sam's side.

Deuce only barks when there's infected.

And there was infected. Angela suddenly saw everything correctly and she felt surprise and shame, because she should have put it together long before. But how the fuck would she have known? Who would have thought that Jenny had been infected? She was in so much contact with all the sick people with the flu, everyone was just counting the days until she caught the flu, that no one thought twice about the symptoms she was displaying. Of course it was the flu. Just like everyone else. She hadn't been bitten! She would have reported it! It didn't make any sense!

But the proof was right here in front of her.

If you could call a dog barking proof.

Jenny was sick. That's where she disappeared to. She must've known that she was infected. She must have known she was going to turn and that the only thing we would be able to do was kill her. She must have been trying to hide. Maybe she was trying to protect us. Maybe she was just trying to keep us from killing her when we realized it.

One of the adults in the crowd was weeping now—someone that had known Jenny, Angela thought.

Sam heard it. Angela could see it on his face, the look of guilt, like he'd been caught red-handed at a murder. And Angela had rushed in and snatched Abby from his arms, like he'd done something wrong. Like he was dangerous. Angela had taken the one person that Sam found comfort in. She'd made him vulnerable.

She had a million questions in her mind. Where did Jenny come from? Where had she been hiding? Did she say anything? Why didn't Sam call one of the adults? Why weren't he and Abby where Angela told them to be? Why the hell did he let Abby tag along with him? Why was Sam always shooting things with that goddamn little rifle of his...?

But any of those questions would have been devastating.

Sam didn't need to answer questions right now.

Angela reached out and grabbed him, pulling him in with Abby. He didn't resist, but he felt stiff. Encumbered by shock. Angela put her face to his ear and spoke the only words that she knew made sense in that moment: "It's okay. It's okay, Sam." Then she put her hands on his shoulders and held him tightly by his arms, looking right into his face. She couldn't believe the words when they exited her mouth. "You did what you had to do, okay?

There's no shame in that. You did what needed to be done. And sometimes that thing is ugly, but it's okay, because you had to do it to keep people safe. You were just keeping Abby safe and everyone else safe. It's okay."

SEVENTEEN

INFILTRATION

AT THE CENTER OF Newton Grove, the Followers of the Rapture gathered. Deacon Chalmers, and every one of his lieutenants, around a campfire stolen from people they'd killed. LaRouche stood with the others, wondering if his specialty was wearing thin. He wondered how much use they would have left for him once they had taken Camp Ryder. But they would always have a use for people like LaRouche, wouldn't they?

He looked off into the growing darkness where the van, the truck, and the blue car sat. And beside them, a pile of bodies stacked up like cordwood.

It had not been very difficult. They let the vehicle pull in, and the men get out, and then they shot them where they stood. The van had more people, so they had shot them while they were still in the van, starting with the driver. Because of this, the van was still workable, but covered in glass. And blood. The truck and the blue car had come away without too much damage and might still be used.

But the biggest bounty was not the vehicles, of which the Followers had plenty. The boon of the day was from the twenty-some-odd rifles and cases of ammunition that they'd scored from the people that had been supposed to be guarding Newton Grove. Good rifles. Good ammo. Better to help them take Camp Ryder.

"Clyde and LaRouche," a loud voice called.

LaRouche snapped his attention back, getting the sense that it was not the first time his name had been called. At the campfire, Deacon Chalmers was waving them forward, closer into the light, where the battle plans were being actively discussed. Clyde was already halfway there and looked back over his shoulder to see why LaRouche was lagging behind.

LaRouche stepped forward quickly into the warmth of the fire. A man on the other side tossed fresh wood on the fire. Sparks flew up in gouts and then disappeared as they got higher and the cold air snuffed them out.

"Yes, sir?" LaRouche said quietly when he was inside the circle, shoulder to shoulder with Clyde.

Deacon Chalmers looked at them seriously. "It is clear to us all that God has His hand on you. Both of you. I trust you, Clyde. And LaRouche? I haven't known you for long, but you've proven yourself over and over. Now, I have a job for you both. One of great importance."

Clyde bowed his head, honored.

LaRouche just felt his gut clamping up.

Chalmers looked out beyond the fire. "Our scouts are working their way through the countryside as we speak. They're looking for the Marines, and I feel that we are close to finding them. It is obvious to me and to all of the lieutenants standing at this fire that the hand of God is being shown to us right now. God has delivered this town to us. And He has delivered us a convoy of Marines—these soldiers of a sick, bastard country. It is clear to me that we have the impetus to strike, to surprise, and to overtake them. And when we overtake them, we will have control of their artillery. And when we have control of their artillery, we will return east and level their opposition once and for all."

LaRouche looked around at the encampment. There were many of them, probably many more than the Marines. But that didn't make him confident. The Marines were a trained fighting force. These were just...pirates. Thieves. Bandits.

"LaRouche, you disagree?" Chalmers said, somewhat coldly.

LaRouche realized he'd been shaking his head. He looked at Chalmers. Did he disagree? Of course he disagreed. It would be much smarter to ignore the Marines and continue on to Camp Ryder. They had the numbers and equipment to take Camp Ryder now, LaRouche thought. If they sidetracked and tried to take the Marines, they would only hurt themselves. It would be smarter to stick with the plan. Gain strength. Then try to hit a hard target. Chalmers's zeal was getting the best of him.

But then again, do I actually care?

LaRouche sniffed. "No, sir. I don't disagree. What would you have me and Clyde do?"

The smile returned to Chalmers's face. "You're going to lead the attack."

LaRouche bowed his head. But inside, he could feel the acid burning its way up his stomach, and he was thinking, *Suicide—that's suicide!* But along with those negative, fearful thoughts, there was also a sense of justice that came to him, a sense of rightness. He would only get what he deserved. And at least he would die fighting.

Clyde seemed dumbstruck. "We'd be honored," he said.

Lee found himself in a strange place in his mind. One that was unfamiliar to him. He sat in the roaring darkness of the Black Hawk's belly and he felt very still. It was exhaustion; he knew that much. Not just physical, though it was there as well—the pain in his side, in his legs, the solid ache like heavy metal injected into his marrow, it bled the energy out of him. More than that, though, it was mental. It was emotional. He did not feel as wound up as he thought he should.

The place that he found himself in was one of an odd sense of flatness. Emptiness. His heart wasn't racing; his mind wasn't rolling through the nervous procedures that it should have been just before an operation. He knew that he was going into a dangerous situation, he knew that people's lives depended on him just as much now as they had before, but it all just felt two-dimensional. The dangers became peripheral. It became more about the goal. And perhaps his goal was skewed, but it was not Harper and Julia he thought of right then. All his mind could seem to wrap itself around was Tyler Bowden.

He kept picturing Tyler's face. He wanted to feel righteous anger, but he seemed to have none left. All that was left was a slow, seeping resentment that sat on his stomach like cinderblocks. And more than once on that short helicopter ride, Lee thought to himself, *Maybe I should just give him the goddamned GPS.*

But he knew that he wouldn't. He couldn't. Simply not the way this machine was wired. There was another fight to be fought, another battle to charge into. And Lee was an incredibly stubborn man. He only knew two things: First, someday, his fight would be over; second, that day was not today.

Not today.

One more time.

You're almost there.

In the cabin of the Black Hawk, a dull red light came on. It bathed everyone in blood. Lee, and five other men. Carl sat beside Lee, a crewman's headset on his head, speaking to the pilots. Across from them, Rudy, Mitch, and Morrow sat in quiet focus. Morrow's large, expressive eyes were staring out the side window of the helicopter. The three operators had donned small helmets that didn't cover much of the head, but seemed more useful for mounting their NVGs. On all of their short-barreled rifles, Lee could see they'd attached suppressors. He could also see the infrared laser aiming devices on the quad rails of the rifle— invisible to the naked eye, but brilliant when you were equipped with night vision.

He wondered if Kensey's Marines had night vision.

Maybe. Hopefully not.

Lee pulled on the same helmet that the others were wearing. Carl and his men had packed mission bags full of gear that they kept stored in the Black Hawk. Carl had outfitted Lee out of his own bag, telling him, "This is your fight, I imagine you want to be in on it." The gift included the helmet and the rifle.

A few adjustments to the helmet and it fit Lee's head snugly. The optics were already attached, as well as a mouth- and earpiece for their squad comms. Just like the others, the rifle Lee had been given from Carl's gear bag was fitted with a suppressor and an infrared aiming device.

"What about you?" Lee had asked.

Carl had slung his submachine gun on his back and was holding a bolt action rifle that Lee was not familiar with. It was all rails and ergonomics, nothing left for aesthetics. It had a substantial rifle scope mounted on it, as well as a suppressor. The rifle scope looked like it was equipped with a night-vision attachment. Carl seemed proud of it. "I'll hang back. Give y'all some overwatch."

To their credit, the Delta boys made no negative reaction to the fact that Lee was going in with them. It was never comfortable to do an operation with a new guy, but in Lee's experience, Delta operators tended to be more open to working with others than most other special operations forces. Besides, they'd seen for themselves that Lee was solid.

Lee had night operations equipment in his bunkers, but hadn't had the time to grab it at Bunker

#3, so he accepted the borrowed equipment gracefully. The rifle was in the M4 platform, though it was chambered for .300 AAC. Lee was familiar enough with it to be comfortable using it in a real-world application. All the mechanics were basically the same. Along with the rifle came four spare magazines, loaded with subsonic ammunition.

He felt the helicopter begin its descent, as the sound in the cabin changed.

Again, Lee wondered where the nervousness was. He knew he should have been feeling it right then, but it was not there. Just Tyler Bowden. Tyler and his betrayal. Tyler coming after the one thing he knew that Lee wouldn't give him.

You stupid motherfucker, Lee thought. *Now you've gone and started this. You've pushed me into a corner. You've forced me to hit you back. And I'm gonna hit you hard.*

He looked across from him. Rudy, Mitch, and Morrow were already facing out to the doors. On each side, one of them slid over and pulled the sliding doors, staging them open for the landing. Wind erupted into the blood-red cabin. Outside, there was nothing. Emptiness. Space.

Morrow staged the door and leaned out, looking at the ground. He held up three fingers. Then two. Then one. Then he was sliding out. Mitch followed, and then Rudy, out the starboard side of the helicopter. Lee came out last. They huddled beneath the roar of the rotors as the helicopter dusted off over their heads and then tilted away into the night sky.

There it is, Lee thought as he felt his heart finally start knocking. *Time crunch.*

They were in a nasty situation. The hostage situation required that they have stealth when coming in. But the helicopter insertion required that they be dropped where Tyler and Kensey's crew couldn't hear. And the helicopter couldn't stay aloft all night. They were quickly approaching the hour that they needed to return to Fort Bragg for fuel.

They knew where they were. Just west of Highway 61. And they knew where they were going: four miles to the intersection of Herron Road, where there was an old grain mill. That, apparently, was where Harper and Julia were being held.

The night was dark around them. The sound of the helicopter had already faded. Lee could hear wind in the grasses, and when he looked down he knew that he was in an old farmer's field. Unharvested wheat, it seemed, grown over and weed infested, now dry and brittle and whispering as the stalks rubbed together.

Lee lowered the monocular over his right eye. The world became a bright, pale green landscape shot through with streaks of light. The streaks of light meandered back and forth, scanning, jumping, looking this way and that. Each was blooming from one of their rifles—the infrared aiming device doing its job. The monocular was a fusion system, overlapping light intensification and thermal imaging, so that everything appeared bright and contrasted, and hot things—such as warm bodies—stood out in orange and yellow and red.

Lee scanned around, saw the glow of his own

aiming device, saw the blobs of molten colors that were his comrades. And through his left eye, he could still see the real world. It was disorienting, and it took a little practice to alternate focusing on real-world and night-vision-world. But Lee had done it many times before, and he fell into it with familiarity.

"That's Highway 61," he said, gesturing to a thin gray line across their vision, about three hundred yards to their east, running approximately north to south. "We need to move with it until we see the grain mill. We good?"

Out of one eye, he could barely see some shadows moving. Out of the other, his orange-blob companions lifted thumbs up to indicate that they were ready.

"Let's move, then."

The designated point man moved out ahead of them. The others waited until he was barely inside of their vision, just to the point that they would be able to understand his hand signals, and then they started to follow. The wind through the dried-out wheat stalks covered most of the sounds of their movement, and they took up a good pace, trying to close most of the distance. The stealth approach would be necessary only for the last several hundred yards as they drew in close enough to be seen and heard, if anyone was watching or listening.

They will be, Lee told himself. *Of course they will be. The only question is whether they are expecting this to happen or not. Are they ready for us?*

The pace picked up to a slow jog at points, and

then sometimes just a fast walk, depending on the terrain. They stayed in a single-file line, the six of them spread out over a hundred yards or so. Lee kept seeing flashes of color in the green—hot things moving in the woods around them, and sometimes in the grass at his feet. His heart would seize every damn time and his rifle would swing in that direction, his mind immediately thinking, *Infected!* But the shapes would disappear. They did not appear to come any closer. He thought that maybe they were deer.

They hit a section of woods. The wind hissed at the treetops, bending the trunks and creaking the trees. Their feet crunched quickly through the dry leaves—there was no avoiding that. But they kept scanning for anything warm-blooded, anything that might be watching them.

Halfway into the woods, they stopped.

Lee heard the quiet whisper in his ear: "Contact. Contact. Three o'clock. A hundred yards."

He knelt into the leaves and spun to his right. Mitch was directly behind Lee. He had been the one to call the stop. His short frame was even shorter, knelt down in a compact ball, rifle resting on his knee. He was facing west, deeper into the woods, and up a small hillock. Lee saw nothing with his naked eye, but he raised his rifle and focused through his right, and he could see two, then three, then four shapes, huddled at the top of the woods. They were spread out in a line, like a mirror image of Lee's column.

"Everyone hold," Mitch said breathily. "If they come toward us, put 'em down."

Nobody asked the question as to whether they were infected or not. It was not that everyone was so sure of what they were, but that it simply didn't matter. If the ghostly, glowing shapes at the top of the hill started to descend on them, sane or not, they needed to be taken out.

"Counting one, two, three, four," the electronic voice whispered. "Rudy takes far left. Morrow takes far right. Me and the captain'll take the two in the middle." To Lee, Mitch said, "You're left, I'm right. Rog?"

"Rog."

They knelt there in the cold, dry leaves for a long time. Long enough for the sweat to start chilling on their bodies. Lee's heart was making an appearance again. His adrenal glands stretching their legs once more.

Slowly, the two shapes on the outside crept farther over the hill. And here Lee could see them for what they truly were. Not in any detail, but just from the way they were crouched low to the ground, moving so stealthily forward on all fours. *Definitely infected. A pack. Or maybe hunters...*

He closed his left eye, seeing only the strange vision of illuminated night lands and boiling hot heat signatures. He watched the dot of his aiming device bounce and zigzag up the hill and then hover around the second heat signature from the left, waiting for it to start moving closer with the others. Lee breathed steadily, trying to lower his heart rate.

And then the two on the outside that had been

moving forward suddenly slipped away, back behind the hill.

Lee looked in each direction rapidly, and then when he looked back up at the hilltop, the two middle ones were gone as well.

His heart slapped his rib cage.

His breathing became tense again.

Dammit ... where the hell did they go?

They switched to 360-degree coverage, trying to make sure that they weren't being flanked and surrounded. But after another minute or two of hushed breathing and rustling leaves, there was still no sign of the infected.

"Let's get moving again," Lee transmitted quietly.

The column started moving again. Slowly, at first, and then picking up speed again.

After another minute or two, they emerged into a clearing. They looked in all directions, but there was nothing. They continued through, into the other side of the woods. More valuable minutes passed by as they picked their way through the forest. When they emerged on the other side, they stopped again.

Lee took a knee and waited. Far up ahead, the little blur of orange heat at the edge of the woods was the point man, scoping things out. After a moment of stillness, his voice crackled in Lee's ear: "Eyes on target. Six hundred yards southeast."

"Copy," Lee said. "Everyone hold what you got. Carl—it's on you."

Carl acknowledged. "Copy. Moving."

The sound of Carl's movement was slight, but still audible, as he moved eastward in the woods, toward the roadway. There was some slight high ground just north of the grain mill that he was heading for. Carl had estimated he'd need about five minutes to get there and get in position.

"The rest of ya'll, let's maintain that three-sixty," Lee said. "Don't want those fuckers sneakin' up on us again."

Minutes passed by.

Slow traffic in the fast lane.

Frustrating.

Lee's mind turned to Tyler again. He might know that they were coming. But did he expect them so soon? And did he know how they were going to make contact? No. There was no way he could know these things. He might suspect, and he might have his lackeys on heavy watch, but that wouldn't stop what was coming for him. Lee felt a stir of anger as he thought this time, but it was quiet. It was controlled. There was no rage to what Lee was doing. Just the smooth glassiness of inevitability.

Carl's voice on the squad comms: "I'm in place. I've got a visual on four. Granary is...medium-sized complex. Six-foot chain-link perimeter fencing. No barbed wire. There's a large barn in the center. Metal siding. Painted white. There's a door on the northern side of the building. Two men are standing outside that door. The other two are stationary. One on the north fence. The other I can just barely see between the buildings, but I think he's on the south fence. Break."

The radio cut off.

Lee waited in silence, breathing steadily.

Carl picked up again. "I think our target building is going to be the barn. One of the two outside the door just stepped inside, then back out. There's definitely other people inside, but I couldn't get much detail. Looks like you'll have plenty of concealment and maybe even some cover if you come in from the southwest corner. Stand by for gear intel."

Another long pause.

"Okay. All four subjects that I can see are armed. M4 and variants. Full chest rigs. Body armor. Only one is wearing a helmet. The others have soft covers, including the sentry on the south corner, which is the one you'll probably have to take out. From what I can see, none are currently equipped with night-vision capability. Still, keep your IR off until it's go time. Just in case."

It didn't need to be said, but it didn't hurt, either. Anything infrared could be seen if you were looking through night vision. Including their laser aiming devices. If they were blazing as they tried to sneak up, and one of the targets was enterprising enough to throw on a pair of NVGs, each of them would look like a beacon and surprise would be out the window.

"By the way, I can also see what looks like a Little Bird sittin' pretty in the middle of it all. Think that might be your boy. It's unoccupied. Looks cold. I have nothing further right now. Four total. All armed. The only one with the helmet is standing outside of the barn. On your initiation, I'm taking the sentry on the north side, and the two standing outside the barn, if possible. Keep the channel clear once you're in so I can tell you what's up. Go ahead and move."

They moved.

They skirted the edge of the woods, staying low. The sky above them was still overcast, blocking out any trace of moon and stars. There was some bare ambient light coming off the sky, but it was only enough for them to see a few feet ahead by naked eye. They met a few farm fences that bordered properties and negotiated the barbed-wire tops carefully, then kept moving. They were less than three hundred yards out, and Lee could almost see the tops of the silver grain silos in the muted light.

The woods became thinner and thinner until it was nothing.

They were in the backyard of some large farmhouse, directly across Highway 61 from the grain mill. They stopped there, in the blackness of the overhanging trees, huddled close to cover and concealment. The point man was scanning the farmhouse and the barn out back. Lee closed his left eye and observed the farmhouse for a time.

The slightest of whispers over squad comms. "Possible contact. Heat signature inside the farmhouse…"

The night exploded.

EIGHTEEN

RESCUE

LEE DOVE FOR THE WOODS.

The sound of projectiles splitting the air near him and peppering through tree branches just above his head. The clatter of rifle fire, both incoming and outgoing. In his left eye, there was blackness with strange half-lit geometric shapes, blooming with fire, but in his right eye, he could see heat signatures, big impressionistic blurs of orange and red, his team scrambling for cover in the woods, and other heat signatures in the windows of the farmhouse.

He hit the ground hard on his side, felt nothing. He tumbled over onto his back, and then onto his hands and knees, behind a large pine. He brought his rifle up and watched through his right eye as a half-dozen infrared aiming devices crawled over the farmhouse. He found a window where an orange blob of a man had been and he squeezed the trigger as he watched his infrared dot settle onto the window. The rifle in his hands chattered—muffled but not silenced.

"Contact! Contact!" someone was yelling over the squad comms.

Lee keyed his PTT and addressed the grenadier with the M32. "Morrow! Level that fucking house! Rudy, keep their heads down! The rest of you on me!"

Then Lee started running, crosswise, with the farmhouse to this left.

He didn't see Morrow shoulder the six-cylinder grenade launcher, but he heard the heavy *whump-whump-whump* of the 40mm rounds going out, and only a second later the sound of them smashing into the farmhouse and exploding in white-hot flashes that lit the night only for milliseconds at a time.

Lee tried to see where the hell he was going, but the NVG over his right eye was destroying his depth perception and he kept having to slow down to negotiate fallen logs so that he wouldn't trip over them while he ran.

"Carl," he called breathlessly on squad comms. "Cover's blown! We're hitting now! Initiate!"

Carl's voice came back tight. "Roger."

The darkness of the trees drew back like a curtain. Ahead of them was the roadway. On the other side, the grain mill. Lee scanned it once with his NVGs, but saw no heat signatures lurking in the shadows. He sprinted out of the woods, into the clear, onto even ground where he could run full bore.

"Shamus!" he yelled as he ran, using the helicopter's call sign. "Assaulting now! We need cover fire from air support! Get inbound now!" Lee reached the other side of the road. He leapt across the drainage ditch, hit the other side oddly on his bad ankle, but kept going. He hit the tree line and stopped.

"Shamus copies. Inbound. Two minutes."

Lee looked behind him. The farmhouse looked like a heap of ruins, a fire burning inside, smoke billowing out of it. The Delta team was crossing the road behind him, Rudy bringing up the rear.

From inside the grain mill, he could hear randomly spaced shots, strings of automatic fire, shouting and screaming.

"Morrow, blow the fence," Lee called as the grenadier's big frame came huffing up.

"Rog." Morrow sprawled himself on the ground. "Everyone get low. We're in close."

Everyone mimicked him, getting low on the ground. The fence was only about fifty yards away from them, and they could still catch shrapnel if they weren't careful. Everyone buried their faces in the dirt, keeping their helmets aimed toward the fence, hoping the rest of their bodies wouldn't catch molten steel fragments.

Whump.

BOOM.

Lee looked up at the fence. Morrow was an excellent grenadier and had splashed the round right at the base of the fence. The explosion had ripped a hole more than big enough for a man to fit through.

"We're good! Move!"

Lee surged to his feet, ran for the breach in the fence, then forced himself to slow down. Slow down. *Slow is smooth. Smooth is fast.* A heavy hand landed on his shoulder and stayed firm there. He could hear one of the operators' voices behind him.

"We're with you. We're good. Move. Move."

Lee swept the breach again, made sure there was nothing to trip him. In his right eye, the jagged ends of the chain-link fencing were still glowing orange in the greenness of the nighttime. Past that, he looked right and left, his rifle following, the infrared laser flickering as it passed over the chain links and tattooed the yard beyond. No heat signatures.

Lee stepped through the breach.

Carl's voice: "Two down. Two moving in your direction, coming around both sides of that silo at your eleven o'clock. Right there! To your left! Your left!"

Lee moved laterally to his left, rifle up. The big, round, stainless steel can of the silo sat there, tree branches touching its tops and leaving the southern side in blackness as they shadowed it from even the muted ambient light that was coming from the cloud-covered stars. But he didn't need light to see heat.

Orange on the left side of the silo, peeking out.

Lee fired, kept moving. He realized his stomach was in knots. Not for fear of being shot or hurt, but a sudden terror that the drawback of thermal imaging was a lack of target identification. What if Harper and Julia had managed to escape? What if that was who Carl had seen moving to that silo? What if Lee just shot one of them to death by mistake?

Too late, rounds are downrange . . .

But he pulled his finger off the trigger, and kept edging off the angle between himself and that heat signature. And when he'd taken four more steps, he got his answer. The heat signature leaned out and Lee was closer now. He could see the rifle. He could see the heaviness of the gear that was strapped to the figure. And the rifle was coming up.

Shoot him shoot him shoot him.

Lee cranked off rounds reflexively and got the hell off his target's line of fire. The target's muzzle bloomed white in his right eye. He felt something bite his shoulder, felt the slap of a tiny sonic boom against his face. He was moving to his right now, and so was the orange-red target, both of them circling each other, firing.

Lee went low. The white blaze of his infra-red aiming device settled into the center of the orange-red shape, and he let off a burst of fire. He could actually see the mist of blood in the air, like hot gasses erupting out of the man, registering a muted ochre color in his right eye. The orange-red shape jerked and the knees wobbled, and Lee's burst of rounds tracked up and destroyed the face, toppling the whole thing to the ground, where in a few hours it would take on the same greenish, background quality of all the other cold things that lay scattered around the grain mill.

There was another boom and a flash of light, a billow of dust and smoke.

Lee flattened himself up against the silo. He looked at his arms, his legs, his chest, but couldn't find a bullet hole. *I'm fine. I'm okay. Not hit.*

A chatter of suppressed gunfire, answered by the crack of unsuppressed rifles, back and forth through the grain mill. Footfalls behind him. He glanced back, saw Rudy just a few feet behind him, running with a hitch, sweat beading on his bald head.

"You hit?" Lee asked.

Rudy nodded quickly and put his back to the silo. "Leg. Through and through."

Lee gave the man a once-over with his naked eye. He was close enough to see the damage to the man's upper thigh and the dark wetness of his pants leg. Another round had almost punched through his gut, but the ceramic plate had caught it. There was a hole in one of his magazine pouches, and Lee could see the magazine looked like it had exploded, springs and plastic sprouting from the pouch.

"You got a tourniquet?"

"I'll be okay for another minute," Rudy said with a grimace. "Keep moving."

Lee nodded and turned back to his objective.

Find the barn. Find Harper. Find Julia. Find Tyler.

He edged out from the silo, pie-ing off bigger and bigger angles of the grain mill. All green. No orange shapes—then two of them, moving laterally, away from Lee. He could see their infrared designators on their helmets. Delta. They were moving for cover behind a large piece of farm equipment. Perhaps some sort of cultivator.

Incoming rounds clattered and sparked off of the metal, just over the heads of the operators as they slid into cover like they were stealing a base. Lee tracked the gunfire back. He couldn't see a heat signature, at least not from a body, but he could see the muzzle flashes coming from the door of a large, square metal building. Kind of like a barn.

"Carl, Carl," Lee called out. "We're taking fire from that building right there, you see it? Is that the barn you were talking about?"

Pause.

"Yeah, yeah. Affirmative. I have not put eyes on them directly, but I'd avoid putting rounds into that building."

Lee did a quick scan of the compound. His team was accounted for. No other heat signatures. At least two enemies in the farmhouse, but he didn't know whether they were still in the fight. Carl had taken two. And then the two on the silo. Lee had taken one of them, and he assumed the other had been taken by the Delta operators now huddled behind the farm equipment.

Six bodies so far. How many more? Maybe a couple more. At least one, obviously, since he's shooting at us from the barn.

"Guys behind that tractor equipment," Lee called to them. "You guys copy that? Don't return fire into that building. Continue drawing fire, but don't shoot into it. How copy?"

Lee was watching them as he spoke and he could see in the thermal imaging one of their heads bobbing. "Solid copy. Don't shoot the building."

"We're gonna move around the back, see if there's another entrance."

Lee took a glance behind him at Rudy. He pushed himself off of the silo and readied his rifle.

"You good?" Lee asked.

"Good to go."

Lee crossed, rifle up. Looking for something. A heat signature. A muzzle flash directed at him. Anything to show that the attention had turned in his direction. But whoever was shooting from the door was just laying it down on the tractor equipment, slow and steady, evenly spaced rounds meant to keep heads down.

If they're trying to keep heads down, they might be trying to move.

Lee made it to the side of the barn. He could hear voices inside, shouting, and it sounded like they were shouting at each other, though he couldn't be sure. He tried to listen for Harper or Julia, but he didn't think their voices were in the mix. The gunfire kept going. Slow and steady.

Lee moved to the back corner of the building and pied it off. Nothing. Just empty space.

"Clear," he whispered, hoping not to be heard by the people inside, despite their yelling and gunfire.

"Moving."

"Move."

Lee hit the corner, kept himself a few feet off the metal wall, but traveling parallel to it. A sliding garage door, it looked like. Well-worn gravel acted like an arrow, drawing Lee's attention to it. He stepped up to the edge and inspected the latching mechanism. Which was basically nonexistent. Unlocked. At least from the outside. Perhaps barricaded from the inside, which could be disastrous if he went yanking on it thinking it was going to open for him.

Pop…pop…pop…

The suppressive fire went on and on. Eventually they would realize that no one was shooting back and begin to suspect that they were being flanked, if they didn't already suspect it. Whoever was in there—more than one, and possibly three—they knew damn well they were sitting in a tin can with only two points of entry and exit.

Lee looked down at his feet and saw light coming from inside the barn.

There was a gap between the gravel and the door. Maybe a few inches at the most.

Lee dropped to his belly and pressed his face against the gravel. He could hear the words of the voices now, their individual owners, though he couldn't see anybody just yet. What they were saying made no sense to Lee.

"Back the fuck off!"

"Get outta the fucking way!"

"Guys, I don't…"

"Just keep fucking shooting! Let me handle this shit!"

"Kensey, listen to me…"

Lee felt his skin contract, electricity on his spine. The last voice had been Julia; he was positive. She was still alive. And so was Sergeant Kensey, apparently. He thought he heard three individual male voices inside. But he couldn't get quite enough of a view of the inside from the small crack at the bottom of the door.

He stood back up and held up the appropriate number of fingers: "Three hostiles inside, at least one hostage. Couldn't get a visual. You ready?"

"You want me to bang 'em?"

"Can you get it over the top of this barn and onto the other side?"

Rudy leaned back and judged the height of the building above them, his tongue sticking out and touching the bottom of his mustache. "Yeah, I can do that." He was already shucking the cylindrical "flashbang" grenade out of a pouch on his chest, a finger slipping into the pull rings. "You ready?"

From inside the barn, Lee heard the sound of a gunshot, different from the others. Smaller caliber. Maybe a pistol. This one was inside. And then someone was shouting, screaming curses. It sounded like Julia.

Shit...

Lee put a hand on the sliding door and prayed to God that it would open when he pulled it. "Send it."

A yank. Safety lever and all, Rudy stepped out and flung it sideways like he was making a hook shot. Lee didn't watch the grenade, just kept his focus on the door and hoped that the grenade reached the other side of the barn, roughly where the open door was.

Rudy shouldered his rifle again, his stance poised and ready.

Lee waited for it.

BOOM!

Lee yanked the door.

It opened.

He flowed through, rifle up.

Inside was brighter. Orange glow from a fire. White glow from a lantern. Lighting faces still cringing from the blast of the grenade. Lee wasn't looking for Julia and Harper. He was looking for who *was not* Julia and Harper. He found someone he didn't recognize, registered nothing about them, not age or race or gender. A body standing in the door. Probably the one laying down suppressive fire. He pulled the trigger five times, ending that person.

Beside him, Rudy let out a burst at almost the exact time as Lee, but aimed at a second subject, this one standing in the middle of the room. The burst caught the man in the shoulders and chest, and maybe one of them hit the back of his skull, Lee couldn't be sure. The body went head over heels, sideways, and was still.

There was another body in the room, but it was already dead. Or dying.

Lee moved across the room for the body he'd killed. He put a boot to it, making sure it was dead. It flopped like meat. He turned to Rudy, who was standing over the target he'd taken. There was no need to check that body for life—the brains were littered out the back in a scattered, pink-white trail.

"Clear?" Lee asked, looking around and his eyes landing on Julia, tied to a wooden post.

"Clear," Rudy called, then keyed his radio. "Barn's clear. Barn's clear. We have one hostage recovered. One hostage recovered and one outstanding."

Lee kicked the rifle out of the hands of the

body at his feet and then crossed quickly to Julia. Her wrists were bound, and then bound again to the wooden post. He knelt beside her, pulling his knife from his rig and sawing through the bindings. "Julia, you okay? Are you good?"

Her eyes were fixed at the body that was lying close by, the one that had already been dead when they'd come through the door. Lee cast a sidelong glance at it. A light-skinned black guy.

Julia sounded out of it. "He was trying to help us. Trying to keep Kensey from taking us."

"Taking you?" Lee asked, finally cutting her free. "Taking you where? And where the hell is Harper?"

Julia finally looked up and met Lee's eyes. She seemed to suddenly realize it was him and she grabbed him by the shoulder and by the back of the neck, a desperate grasp of appreciation. "I can't believe you're here. Oh my God. Oh my God."

"Julia," Lee said, pulling away. "Where is Harper?"

She blinked rapidly, like she was struggling to clear her head. "Major Bowden. He took Harper and his pilot..."

The radio cracked in Lee's ear. Carl's voice: "Lee, I got three on the move! I don't know how the fuck they got away, but they're almost to the helicopter now. You need me to take 'em out?"

NINETEEN

LOSSES

LEE ALMOST SAID NO, but held off for long enough to think about it. "One of them is a pilot. If you can positively ID the pilot, take him out. I'm on the way." Lee gave Julia's shoulder a squeeze and stood up quickly. "Julia, I'll be right back. Don't move from here."

Lee burst out of the barn and heard helicopter rotors. For a moment, he thought it was Tyler, escaping in the Little Bird, but then saw the big black shadow of the Black Hawk swoop overhead. Lee heard a muffled rifle report—just the sound of the bullet breaking the sound barrier. Lee looked right and left and realized that he didn't know which way to go.

"Pilot's down," Carl said over squad comms.

"Carl, where are they? Where am I going?"

"Lee, he just ducked inside one of the silos. It's north of you. To your right, from where you are. One, two silos...the second silo on your right."

Lee started running for it.

"The silo has a hole in the side of it. They ducked inside."

"I copy," Lee said breathlessly. "That's Tyler. Tyler and my man Harper."

"Rog, I think I know who is who."

This time Lee did say it. "Don't shoot!"

"I can't even see him."

Lee rounded the first silo and saw the second standing there in the darkness, a gaping hole in the side of it, and beyond that hole, just blackness. Lee lowered the NVGs over his right eye again and peered into the hole from twenty yards away. He could see the miniscule glow from body heat coming from inside, but not the bodies themselves.

In front of the silo, a body lay on the ground, squirming. The pilot, Lee assumed. His arm was still moving, the fingers grinding into the gravel, but if he had any time left to live, it was just seconds, and Lee could do nothing for him.

He scanned around. He was looking for some cover a little closer to the silo. He didn't want to stand at the thin metal wall that bullets could so easily penetrate. And he wasn't going into that silo. Not with Tyler inside, probably using Harper as a body shield. Lee would find himself at a distinct disadvantage trying to go in there. But that was Tyler's only card. He had to know he was trapped. What did he hope to accomplish with this?

Lee spotted a pallet of what looked like large drainage rocks. He slipped around the silo and crouched behind the pallet. He needed to speak to Tyler, but he couldn't do it with the Black Hawk hovering over their heads. "Shamus, go ahead and pull off. I can't hear with you overhead. We got a hostage situation and I need to talk."

Before the helicopter could acknowledge, Carl took the radio. "Lee! He's runnin' out the other side! He's heading for the fence!"

Lee stood up and saw an orange blob filling the empty space of the hole in the side of the silo. He addressed it with his rifle and started moving toward it, but after crossing a few feet, he could see that it was a man, hunched over, stumbling out of the silo, no weapons, no gear.

"Harper!" Lee shouted at him.

Harper looked up, his eyes alarmed.

Lee ripped the NVGs up that were covering his face and recognition dawned on Harper as the two men closed the gap. Harper looked like he was about to collapse and Lee scooped an arm up under his shoulder to steady him and keep him from hitting the dirt. It was only then that he saw the front of Harper's body, slaked in blood.

"Holy fuck," Lee breathed as he felt Harper's legs go out and the man's entire weight was on his shoulders. He slowly lowered the man to the ground. "What happened? What did he do?"

Harper grimaced. "Fucking gut-shot me. Shitfire."

Why? Why would he do that?

Even right at that moment when Harper told him, his mind wanted a different explanation. He wanted the man that had shot Harper to not actually be Tyler. To be someone else that was impersonating Tyler. But there was a certain cold logic to it, and Lee realized, feeling suddenly sick to his stomach, that Tyler and he were two peas in a pod. Everyone had changed, it seemed, and not for the better. Perhaps Tyler had never wanted to believe the things that he'd been told about Lee. Perhaps Tyler had thought to himself, *Lee would never do those things*. But Lee had changed. And apparently so had Tyler. Because Tyler knew he had no way out, not with his helicopter pilot dead and the entire compound of the grain mill swarming with Delta operators. And he knew that he had to run, and that his best chance of getting away on foot was to distract Lee, to distract him with a dying body.

Cold, cold, cold, he thought. *Just like your goddamned self.*

Lee held Harper's head with one hand, keeping it from hitting the gravel. "Oh man, Harper. I can't believe this. I can't fucking believe this. I'm so sorry. I'm so, so sorry." Lee's other hand found the hole in Harper's stomach. Right in the middle. Right where all the important stuff was. The type of injury that needed a real trauma hospital. Not a corpsman's skills while lying in the gravel and dirt.

"What the hell are you doing?" Harper growled, his eyes filling with tears from the pain. "Go get that motherfucker."

In Lee's ears, he could hear Carl once again: "Lee, he's at the fence. He's climbing over."

Lee had questions, but they withered and died, half-sprouted. What good would those questions do him? Tyler was not the man that Lee had once known. And Lee was not the man that Tyler had known. Perhaps they had both miscalculated each other. Lee had tortured Tyler's man for information, and Tyler had shot Lee's man to get away. The both of them were morally unfettered.

Now, kneeling there in the middle of the grain mill, with a friend bleeding out in front of him, Lee had no more questions of Tyler. The man he'd once considered a friend was a friend no more and had not been for a very long time, though Lee had just not realized it. He had no questions. No desire to confront Tyler anymore.

With bloody fingers, Lee depressed his radio button. "Take him out, Carl."

There was no response from Carl, other than the distant *whump* of the suppressed rifle, and the *snap-crack* of a single round travelling at 3,000 feet per second. Lee heard the *smack* of the round finding soft flesh and destroying it, and along with it the sound of breath coming out of someone's lungs as their entire body was put into shock.

"He's down."

Lee had abruptly forgotten about Tyler. It was strange how all the way in he'd forgotten that Harper and Julia were the reason he was here. He'd been so consumed with Tyler that he couldn't picture anything but taking the man down. Vengeance. Answers. He had been forced to endure pain, and it had felt like the time was ripe to shift that onto someone else. To pay back a little of what he'd received.

Now he had a friend in his arms.

Did I fuck this up?

No, don't think about that. Think about how to fix him. How can you fix him?

"Roll onto your side, buddy." Lee pushed Harper's shoulder. He searched Harper's back for an exit wound. Often the exit would bleed more than the entrance. He needed to find that and stop it. In the darkness, though, he couldn't seem to see anything. The blood from the front had soaked through into the back, so everything was just a mess of sopping clothing.

Do something!

Stop the bleeding. That's what you can do.

What if it's worse? What if it punctured an organ?

No. Just find the exit. Stop the bleeding.

"Ah, fuck!" Harper cried out as Lee started ripping the man's clothing off.

"I need a fucking light!" Lee shouted out. "I need some help over here! Help!" He was trying his best to keep pressure on the entry wound and simultaneously pull Harper's clothing off and search for the exit wound. It was just too dark to see.

White light came swaying in, jangling their shadows left and right and splaying them out like dead bodies.

Lee looked back, his thoughts filled with panic now. *Josh Miller Tango Tango Tango and the Petersons and Bus, Bus, Bus, I'm losing everyone, everyone—*

"*Everyone around you dies.*" Angela's phantom voice rolled crystal clear through his head.

"Not you. Not you." Lee was speaking to Harper, though Harper didn't know it. *Not Harper. Not this. Not again. Don't forget Lucas, you fucking killed him, you motherfucker, he was trying to help and you killed him but you didn't know, you couldn't have known. And Abe, your best friend, the last friend, you fucking killed him, too, didn't you? And LaRouche is gone, and so the fuck is Wilson and Father Jim and Jacob and everyone else. Jesus Christ, they're all dead! They're all fucking dead and here's Harper...*

What could I do to change this? his mind screamed over the cacophony of recrimination. *What could I have done differently? Is this my fault?*

"I can't..." Lee's voice was shaking with frustration. He looked behind him, to the source of the light.

Julia was limping up, arm around one of the Delta operators—Mitch, it looked like, by the small frame. He held a rifle, and she held the gas lamp from inside the barn. "Oh my God," she choked out. "Harper...Harper, are you okay? Is he okay? What happened?"

Lee didn't answer her. Couldn't answer her. He turned back to Harper, used the light to search his bare back. "I can't fucking find it! God damn it!"

Harper was starting to shake badly. "It's fucking inside of me."

"What?"

"It didn't go through," Harper said, as though he could feel it lodged somewhere in him. "The bullet. It's inside of me. Just get it out. Get it out of me."

Lee couldn't do that. There was no point in getting it out. That would be ripping and tearing blood vessels and Harper didn't have the time or the blood pressure to withstand that kind of extra trauma. "No, I gotta stop the bleeding. I need to get you stabilized first. Then we can get you to the field hospital in Fort Bragg."

"What? Fort..." Harper shook his head. "Okay. Okay. Do what you gotta do."

I do what I have to do. I always do what I have to do. That's the fucking problem.

"Roll back. Roll back and try to let me work here." Lee put Harper onto his back. The hole in his gut just kept bubbling out. It wasn't stopping. Lee raised his voice. "I need a medic or something! I need some fucking...some gauze or something." He turned to look behind him. Julia was leaning up against Mitch still, her face blank with shock, tears in her eyes. Mitch had doffed his helmet and was ripping through his pockets, looking for something. For once, his face seemed completely serious.

"Here," he said, producing a green foil package. "Combat gauze."

Lee snatched the package and ripped it open with his teeth and his left hand, keeping his right depressed onto Harper's belly. Lee started unfurling the gauze, which was treated with a blood-clotting agent. "Get on the radio. Get that bird on the ground right-the-fuck-now. He needs to get to your field hospital."

"Roger." Mitch relayed the request.

Harper was groaning and mumbling incoherently now.

Lee scooped one hand under Harper's head and tilted his face up to meet his eyes. Harper's face was getting pale, made even more washed out by the white light of the gas lamp. His eyes looked strange. Glazed, but still there. There enough to feel the pain.

"Harper? You with me?"

"Uh-huh..." Harper struggled to nod.

"This is gonna suck, okay?" Lee wadded the combat gauze in one hand. "But it's gonna help you, so you gotta let me do it."

"A'ight...a'ight..." Harper sucked in a few shallow breaths. "Okay. Do it."

Lee felt Harper's body tense beneath his hands. He shoved the gauze into the hole of the wound. Harper's body contorted beneath him. Lee bore his weight down, trying to stabilize Harper. "Hold still! This is gonna help you! This is gonna help!"

"Harper, hold still you stupid sonofabitch!" Julia yelled from behind Lee.

Despite Harper's writhing, Lee managed to get the gauze plugged into the wound. Overhead, Lee registered the sound of rotors beating. "Okay, he's plugged up. You okay? Harper?"

Harper looked at Lee like he didn't recognize him. His eyelids fluttered and his hands kept lazily trying to get past Lee's to touch his own wound. Lee didn't know how "there" he was anymore.

"Harper, stay with me. Say something, buddy. We got the helicopter and everything, we're gonna get you to a hospital..."

Harper's body went limp.

"Hey!" Lee shook Harper by the shoulders. "Hey! Wake up!"

In response to this, Harper's chest hitched up only once.

"Aw shit." Lee's hands flew about, trying to find something to do. "Aw shit, shit, shit!"

"Harper!" Julia was screaming at him. "Wake the fuck up!"

Lee pressed two blood-sticky fingers against

Harper's carotid artery and felt a feathery pulse that might have been his own, throbbing through his fingers. Harper's chest wasn't rising and falling anymore. The air above Harper's nose and mouth wasn't steaming.

"He alive?" Mitch asked, coming down to his knees on the other side of Harper and leaving Julia to balance herself on her own. "He got a pulse?"

"Pulse, I think," Lee said. "No breath."

"Breathe him," Mitch said firmly.

CPR, Lee realized.

He bent over and sealed his lips over Harper's. He pinched the nose shut and breathed out a steady breath, watching the chest. A gulp of air and another breath. The chest rose an inch or two. There was the sound of something sloshing around inside of Harper. Lee tried to pull back, but he wasn't quick enough. Bile and blood filled his mouth.

Lee reared backward, coughing and heaving, Harper's blood and vomit trailing out of his mouth. He tilted off to the side and let out one giant heave, purging himself, then managed to choke the next one off. The world was a blur through tears. His stomach was still trying to rebel, but he made himself control it. When you put air into a body, sometimes other shit came out. That was the name of the game. It was Harper. It was his friend.

Lee blinked away the tears and saw the clumpy white vomit and ribbons of blood spilling out over the side of Harper's mouth. "Tilt him," he croaked, then coughed. He managed to get back onto his knees and pulled Harper onto his side so the vomit and blood could spill out and not block his airway. Lee shook him a few times.

"You good?" Mitch reached across Harper's body and grabbed Lee's shoulder. "You ready to do it again? I've got no pulse right now. No pulse."

Lee turned his head and vomited one more time. Then he wiped his mouth with his hand, wiped it off on his pants, and then used the sleeve of his jacket to rub the sputum from around Harper's mouth. *Two breaths*, Lee told himself, battling an almost overwhelming sense of revulsion. *You can give him two fucking breaths.*

He put his mouth to Harper's again and breathed. One breath. Chest rising. He pulled back. The chest fell. Another breath. Chest rising. Then falling.

"Go," Lee said, struggling not to gag again despite the taste in his mouth.

Mitch bent over Harper's bloody chest and put his hands to the breastbone and began to do compressions, counting them out loud. "One, two, three, four..."

When he got to fifteen, he stopped and leaned back.

Lee gave breaths.

But every time he did, Harper's mouth would pool with the contents of his stomach and they would have to tip him over and drain it out. And the contents began to look less like vomit and more like just blood. Blood, blood, and more blood. Filling Harper's stomach. Filling his throat.

Leaking into his lungs. Leaking into every cavity inside the man's chest. Making everything futile.

It was the fourth time when Lee felt a little bit of that welling blood touch his lips again that he finally leaned away from the body, spitting and swearing and coughing. He pulled Harper onto his side to once again drain his mouth, but then he didn't lay him back out again. He sat there on his haunches, head bowed, eyes on the bloody, wet gravel as his own saliva mixed with Harper's blood and poured from his lips in long, silvery pink streams.

He spat and stood up. Then he turned quickly away from the others. He couldn't look at Julia. He could hear her behind him, but none of the words she was saying made any sense to Lee. He had none for himself. None but curses.

What do you do?

What the hell do you do?

And all he could think was, *Too much, too much, too much.*

He walked. Into the darkness. The darkness that roared and screamed and sounded like men shouting and helicopters landing. The darkness that held nothing for him but pain, but it was a smaller pain than the one at his back. A more manageable pain.

He walked until he could see fencing and he stopped there. His gaze traveled along it until he saw the body of Tyler, sprawled out flat in the weeds that had grown and died at the edge of the fence. Lee watched that body for a long time, but it never moved.

Lee turned around, his back to the fence. Now he was at the point of a triangle, bisected in the middle by a dilapidated silo. At the point to his right lay Tyler's body, alone and unmourned. At the point to his left, there was lantern light and men, and Julia crying out for a friend that lay at her feet.

But at Lee's point in the triangle there was only darkness.

He tottered on rubbery knees and fell into a sitting position in the gravel and tall, dry weeds. He kicked his legs out and slouched. He could not see over the tops of the weeds, and he could not be seen. He doubled over on himself and felt like he was shrinking, collapsing, getting so small that he couldn't contain what was inside of him anymore.

But he just closed his eyes tight, and shut his mouth.

He could do nothing else.

What's done is done. You don't need to wrap your brain around it now. You don't have the time. Right now, you need to put it away. Stuff it down. Don't think about it. You have other things you need to do. You're so close. You're so damn close, don't fuck it all up now…

With unsteady hands, Lee snatched up the handset from the manpack still attached to his chest rig, tuned to the Camp Ryder command channel. He stared at it, clutched in his hands, and he felt ashamed at the tremble that was working through them, no matter how hard he gripped it.

He waited, still kneeling in the tall weeds,

refusing to stand up and face what was out there. He felt guilty for being on the radio, for worrying about those other things that demanded his attention. But he knew, in that ever-practical side of his brain, that no amount of thought and concern, or weeping and gnashing of teeth, would bring Harper back to him.

The dead were dead. It was best to focus on the living. And there were still living people that needed his help. He needed to focus on the big picture. The details would only break him down.

He took deep breaths and hoped the shake in his voice wasn't apparent on the radio.

Then he keyed up. "Lee to all elements on the command channel. Sitrep."

Nate's voice was the first to respond. "Nate to Captain Harden." His voice was tense but controlled. "We're moving, everything looks successful right now, but...but it's kind of hard to tell how much of the horde is following us. When we get to high ground points I can see at least...several thousand. But I'm just hoping the rest are following. We've slowed down to a creep right now. Walking pace. They're still following but it's not an avalanche like it was when we first made contact. Break."

The radio clicked off, then on again.

"We're holding up fine, though. We're going slow, but we're closing in pretty close to Smithfield. Fuel is looking good. Haven't taken any shots yet, just keep stringing them along, and they just keep following. We got the team ready up in the hospital yet?"

Lee closed his eyes again. *Focus. Big picture.* "Yeah, hold off on that for just a second. What's your time estimate for arriving at the hospital?"

"I'd say we're there within forty minutes. Approximately."

"Okay. Paul and Junior," Lee addressed the eastern bait truck. "Sound off for me."

The older Paul came on the radio. "Yeah, uh... We're pretty much in the same boat, but we might be hitting Smithfield a few minutes after them."

"I copy that." Lee opened his eyes again. "Tomlin, what about you?"

"Just got word back from Brinly," Tomlin said. "He says they're in position and he was contacted by Staley about an hour ago and told that the sorties were complete. All the bridges have been blown. We're completely cut off from the north."

Lee wanted to feel relief, or exultation. But everything in him just felt like cold stone. Besides, feeling good about anything seemed like foolishness at this point. They still had a long way to go before they could take the time to wipe the sweat off their brows and slap themselves on the back. And a lot of things could go wrong between now and then.

A lot of lives still hung, uncertain.

"Good," Lee managed. "Excellent. How about you guys?"

"We got the hospital on lockdown," Tomlin replied. "Haven't seen much activity 'cept maybe a few packs skirting the edge of the city. No horde activity. It's dark, we can't see anything out east just yet, but I'm sure as hell hearing something.

Something big. Might be Nate and Devon's tag-alongs." Tomlin cleared his throat. "Nate, once you get a little closer, you hit me on the radio. I got a big-ass fire to light that'll hopefully hold their attention while we take potshots and piss them off." Tomlin took a deep, audible breath over the airwaves that communicated well the knot that was in his gut. "Lee, you got a ride out of here ready for us?"

Lee stood up out of the grass. "Yeah. This Black Hawk just needs a refuel, I think, and then we're on our way. Forty-five minutes, I'd guesstimate. You pretty confident that you can hold out that long?"

A slight groan. "Yeah. Forty-five minutes. Check."

Lee started walking for the Black Hawk. He refused to look right, to Tyler's body. He refused to look to the ground in front of him at Harper's body. *Not now. Not right now. I can't do it right now. I've got things that need to be done. I'm so damn close.*

"Mac, Georgia, or Brett, or anybody in Newton Grove manning the radios, gimme a sitrep."

The sound of empty airwaves.

Beating helicopter blades.

His feet crunching through gravel.

"Anybody in Newton Grove," Lee said, a little firmer. Irritation and concern twining themselves together. "Mac, Georgia, or Brett. Newton Grove. Sound off."

No response.

Sonofabitch.

Lee put one leg up into the cabin of the Black Hawk and looked behind him at Julia. Carl had appeared from out of the darkness. His face shined with sweat, despite the cold. Breath plumed out of him in rapid breaths. He held the big sniper rifle in one hand and regarded him with something akin to concern. Or the closest thing that one could expect from a man like Carl.

"We gotta roll," Lee said hollowly. "Right now."

Carl nodded quickly. He chattered something into the squad comms. Lee couldn't hear because he'd removed the earpiece. Then Carl climbed up into the Black Hawk, and a moment later, the three other operators came out of the shadows and clambered up into the cabin.

Julia remained, staring down at Harper's body.

"Julia!" Lee shouted, a little harsher than he intended. Didn't she see? Didn't she understand? No, of course not. She turned around and looked at him, blank-faced and bleary-eyed, and she could not comprehend why Lee was so cold, why the death of a true friend had no effect on him. She would not understand that Lee couldn't let it touch him. He couldn't let it get its fingers through the crack in the door, because it would rip him to shreds. *Don't worry, Julia. It'll get me. It always does. But right now, I can't let it. I've got to hold out for a little longer.*

Maybe she saw the hurt in his eyes, or maybe she just decided that Lee was a lost cause and there was no point in saying anything to such a cold-hearted bastard. But she turned away from Harper's body with one last look, and she let Lee and Carl help her into the cabin of the Black Hawk where they situated her on the bench seat.

"We're good," Lee shouted. "Let's move out."

"What about Harper?" Julia demanded.

Lee gritted his teeth. "We'll come back." Then he nodded to Carl, who gave the command over the squad comms. Lee keyed the Camp Ryder command channel and spoke one more time. "Anyone from Newton Grove, can you copy this radio?"

Still, no response.

Lee looked at Carl. "What's the fuel situation?"

"'Bout an hour's flying time," Carl reported. "What do you need?"

A rock in a vise. That's what Lee felt like. He was either going to hold underneath the immense pressures, or he was simply going to shatter into dust. For now, he was holding. He could hold for a little while longer. "I need you to take a fly by Newton Grove. It's only a little out of your way from Fort Bragg. They're not answering their radio."

Carl compressed his lips, but relayed the information to the pilots.

Lee keyed the radio again. "Tomlin, you still got comms up with the Marine artillery unit? Have they checked in yet? Did they make it through Newton Grove?"

Tomlin came back a little confused. "Yeah, Lee. They checked in at their position about two hours ago. I'm not really sure why Newton Grove ain't answering their shit."

Lee wasn't sure whether that made him feel relieved or even more concerned. He was so busy blocking everything right now, even the sensation of fear was getting pushed away. Everything was feeling dreamlike and unreal, because he refused to let it get in to him.

That's how psychopaths are made, Lee thought to himself. *If you keep killing your sense of humanity, eventually it doesn't grow back. But maybe it's too late for that. Maybe I've chopped a little close to the root already.*

A new voice came over the radio. He'd been avoiding it. It proved to him that things were still getting through that door in his mind, no matter how tight he thought it was shut.

Angela…

"Lee, this is Camp Ryder." Hesitation. "I've got Marie with me. Did…did you…?"

Lee stared at Julia, who was looking over the side of the helicopter as they started to ascend. Staring down at the body they'd left there on the ground. She looked about as empty as Lee felt. They were always alike in that way. Julia allowed herself a little more leeway, but in the end, they always shut it down before they let it hurt them too much.

Lee's voice was flat and monotone. "We got Julia," he said. "She's safe."

Then he clipped the handset back to his rig before Angela or Marie or anyone could ask questions about Harper.

TWENTY

TIMING

TOMLIN STOOD ATOP THE Johnston Memorial Hospital. He was leaning up against the roof abutment, facing east and straining to see out into the darkness. There seemed to be no stars or moon tonight, except in small slits in the cloud cover, like a stage curtain that sways open every so often to reveal the set beyond.

He couldn't see them. But he could hear them. In the distance. A sound like nothing he'd ever heard before. He could compare it to many things—rushing water, the distant rumble of a train, the roar of the shamal that would blanket Middle Eastern villages in fine yellow dust. It was all of these things, and something completely different.

It was the sound of legions. The sound of a host. Millions of feet pounding the ground, millions of throats barking and yelling and screeching, all of it distant so that it blended together into one strange noise that he could not only hear, but feel in his chest and in the balls of his feet and the palms of his hands. Distant, but still too close for comfort.

The hospital suddenly seemed a very flimsy thing to be standing on.

And not as tall as he would have liked.

He looked behind him. Jared was standing on the other end of the roof, looking out to the west. Tomlin realized his mouth was going dry and he worked some saliva into it. He glanced over to the southern-facing abutment of the hospital roof. There was a massive stack of trash there—anything that looked like it could burn—about seven feet high and twice that wide. It stank of the diesel fuel they'd doused it with. A pyre. A signal fire for the night. A beacon for the men in the bait trucks who were probably scared shitless. And also a beacon for the infected that followed.

Millions of infected, Tomlin thought, not truly comprehending it, but fearing it all the same. *Are there really that many of them? What's that gonna look like? I've never seen that many people before. It'll look like a medieval battle. We'll be completely fucking surrounded.*

He swallowed the small amount of stale spit he'd been able to muster onto his tongue.

Fuck me. I can't believe I'm doing this.

Jared turned around and looked at him, full-fledged panic glimmering darkly in his eyes. "Where the fuck are they? I can hear them, but I can't see them. How many do you think it is? And where the fuck are they? How long?"

Tomlin took a breath and spoke on the exhale, trying to sound more even-keel than he was. "They'll be here soon enough." He nodded to Jared. "Do me a favor and go downstairs. Get Joey and Brandy. Do a double-check on all the doors and windows and make sure our barricades are solid. And then get all of our shit and bring it up here." He almost tried for a confident smile, but thought that if he didn't fake it convincingly enough it might hurt more than it helped. "It's fixin' to be a long night, my friend."

Jared nodded stiffly and fled for the stairs.

Tomlin walked over to the diesel-stinking pile of rubbish. Three road flares on the ground, ready to be lit and tossed in to start the pyre. He stared at the whole mess with vacant eyes, mind going elsewhere. Lee's words bothered him. Newton Grove not answering.

He picked up the radio that the Marines had given him. He keyed the mic. "Smithfield to artillery." He almost said "Steel Rain," but caught himself. Some wire in his mind crossed with old memories. For simplicity's sake, they were using mostly plain speak on the radios these days. "Smithfield to artillery."

"Smithfield, you got the arty." Tomlin recognized the voice before it was introduced. "This is First Sergeant Brinly. Go."

"Hey Sarge, this is Captain Tomlin. Just got word from Captain Harden that Newton Grove ain't responding to hails on the radio. Everything looking good from your end?"

A pause.

"Yeah. We're in position and ready. Can't tell you about Newton Grove. Haven't seen them in several hours. They were fine when we rolled through."

"Copy that." Tomlin looked out east. "Nothing further on that. Get your big guns loaded. The bait trucks are almost here."

"We copy, Smithfield. Artillery is loaded and ready. You give the word."

Tomlin still couldn't work the queasiness from his stomach. "Roger. Smithfield out."

He hung the radio back on his rig and clung to his rifle, staring east and waiting for the first sign of headlights in the darkness.

LaRouche waited in the cold dark, in the cold leaves, surrounded by shadows and fear and determination and the sickly nervous thrill of impending violence. He lay in the leaves, his stomach clenched hard to ward off the chill, to force the blood to keep moving in his system so that he wouldn't start shivering. His abdominals ached with the force of it.

He was about twenty yards into the woods, looking out to the edge and beyond, where bright halogen lights burned in the night and lit up a collection of military hardware. He watched the men, just silhouettes against the lights, moving back and forth, unloading crates from the trucks, what looked to him to be shells for the big guns they'd towed in. There was a perimeter guard, but he had already passed by twice and not noticed LaRouche. How could he? LaRouche was flat on the ground, buried in leaves and brush, twenty yards into the shadows of the forest. He was invisible to them.

He looked to his right and to his left. He could not see the others, but he knew that they were there. And behind them, there were more. And on the other side of the clearing where the Marine

artillery had made camp, there were even more.
The Marines were surrounded. They just didn't
know it yet.

But what the hell are they doing here? LaRouche
had to wonder. Why set up an artillery unit in the
middle of an overgrown farmer's field? With no
legitimate objective anywhere within firing range
of those guns? When he'd first caught wind of
the artillery coming out of Camp Lejeune, he'd
assumed that it was meant for the Followers. But
if they were looking for the Followers, they hadn't
looked very hard, and their guns were pointed in
the wrong direction.

We'll find out why they're here. Later.

It was almost time.

Nate kept having to tell himself to slow down. He
kept wanting to hammer down on the accelerator.
He would get fixated on the rearview mirror and
the strange images behind him.

His taillights were just a dim red glow, and
at the very farthest reaches of them, he could see
the ghosts of faces scrambling behind them. The
noise of the engine and the noise of the roaring
horde behind him sometimes melded into one, and
the result was disorienting.

And then those demon faces would disappear
into the hellish darkness behind him and he would
look down at his speedometer and realize he was
breaking thirty miles per hour, leaving the horde
behind.

Slow down, slow down!

He would take his foot off the gas and they

would coast. He didn't want to press the brakes. He had this thought that just tapping the brakes would cause the whole fucking system to lock up and then they would be stuck, stranded, alone in the dark with millions of hungry mouths...

He knew it was unreasonable. But he still refused to touch the brakes or pull to a stop. The things behind him never seemed to tire. The whole damn way they'd been behind him, keeping pace, never flagging. A ninety-mile road march without a stop or break.

Maybe the individuals were tiring and falling back, only to be replaced by more from the back ranks. But it didn't matter who it was directly behind them. It didn't matter whose faces were illuminated by the red glow of his taillights.

The *horde* was keeping pace.

And it was maddening, having them so close behind him when all he wanted to do was run.

The darkness went by, unending. The endless noise of the infected behind him created a chamber in which Nate could hear nothing else. A sort of sensory deprivation chamber made of sound. He kept praying to God that Smithfield would come soon, that this would be over soon, but then he thought about what was lying ahead of him, and it was no relief. His stomach only sank deeper.

The hospital. Stuck on top with Tomlin's crew. Surrounded by a sea of these things.

"Lord give me strength," Nate said aloud, though he could barely hear his own voice. He hadn't gone to church since the last time his parents dragged him when he was fifteen years old.

But if there was ever a time to rediscover faith, it was now.

"That's what we do, God," Nate said louder, trying to hear himself, trying to be loud enough so that God could hear him over the sound of the disaster closing ranks behind him. But then he just finished the thought in his head: *We put you aside until we figure out that we really need some help. And I need some help right now. I need it bad. Because I'm scared out of my mind right now.*

Nate didn't know whether it was an answer to his prayers or a promise that things were only going to get worse, but out of the gloom his headlights reflected off of a dirty green sign: *SMITHFIELD CITY LIMITS – CITYWIDE SPEED LIMIT 35 MPH UNLESS OTHERWISE POSTED.*

Nate felt both elated and terrified. But he knew what he had to do, regardless of how he felt. He turned around, projecting his voice through the open back glass of the pickup truck where Devon was sitting in the bed, looking cold and nervous.

"We're here, Devon! Hang on!" Nate grabbed the radio handset and transmitted: "Nate to the Smithfield crew. We've just entered the city limits. Go ahead and light that fire!"

Tomlin was quick to respond from the top of the hospital. "Nate, I copy you. We're lighting the fire now."

Nate realized he was leaning forward in his seat, searching the horizon ahead of him for a burning bonfire on top of a building. Perhaps ten seconds passed before he registered a slight glow that was hanging in the middle of the darkness ahead of him. And then that glow suddenly erupted into a visible flame. They were closer than he thought.

"Okay," Nate said to the radio. "I see you guys right now. We're gonna be coming in hot! Keep that fire burning!"

"Roger, we're ready for you."

Then Nate stomped the gas pedal and broke the citywide speed limit.

The noise of the horde suddenly faded just a bit, enough for him to feel like he was breaking free of them. Mixed in with his panic to get away from the horde was a sense of suddenly having blown the whole thing. What if he broke line of sight with them and they stopped pursuing? What if they didn't give a shit about the fire? What if he just crippled the whole fucking plan?

Nate knew which way he had to take to get through the city streets of Smithfield—he'd been there a few times and had reviewed the maps of the safe routes religiously the night before taking on this mission of being a carrot on a stick. He knew he had just merged onto Highway 210 from Highway 70 and he slowed as he reached the sign for Second Street. He made a left turn and then he was going north.

What if what if what if?

The most dangerous question, and yet the one that needed to be asked.

He blew through intersections without hesitation, heading north for Hospital Road.

Two blocks from Hospital Road, he saw something spill into the street ahead of him.

"Oh shit!" He didn't think it was possible for

his heart to simultaneously drop into his guts and jump into his throat, but that was exactly what it did.

The roar of the horde was suddenly loud again.

Right on top of them.

He could barely hear Devon in the bed: "Oh fuck! Oh fuck!"

Nate pushed the pedal to the floor. Both hands on the wheel. Elbows locked out. His whole body cringing behind that steering column. He watched the needle of the speedometer climb in a steady arc. *Go go go go go!*

"Nate!" Devon screamed from the back. "Nate, stop! Stop!"

Can't stop! Can't stop!

In the flash of his headlights, Nate could see thousands, filling the land to the left of the roadway. They were stumbling into the street, then changing directions, trying to run for the vehicle that they saw roaring toward them. They clogged the left lane, and then the center, and then the entire right lane, so that only the narrow gap of the shoulder remained.

Multitudes of faces, pale and contorted, faced him and lunged mindlessly for him. These were not like the packs, not like the hunters who knew that they could not get to the meat inside the vehicle. This was like one being, and it seemed to know by some collective knowledge that it could smash anything by its sheer numbers. It could stop vehicles and get to what was inside. It was fearless in its insanity.

Nate shot for the gap on the right shoulder of the road.

He felt the tires hit grass and dirt. The back end loosened.

From the bed, Devon started shooting. The light flashed onto the side of the pickup, the sound of the gunshots battering at Nate's head and ears. Something hit the side of the vehicle. Not just a single body. Nate felt the entire pickup truck jerk violently like it had been rammed by an immense creature. The steering wheel jerked in his hand and Devon toppled in the back, nearly flying out of the bed.

The tires spun in the loose shoulder.

Nate shouted wordlessly as he felt the pickup turning, starting to spin out.

Get me to the hospital, dear God, please, dear God just get me to the hospital!

The pickup lurched, then found asphalt again and charged forward. Something hit the front bumper and the truck jumped, running it over. Devon was in the back, screaming.

Hospital Road.

He yanked the steering wheel to the right, slamming the brakes so he could make the turn, and then accelerating again, tires spinning out, chirping, sending up white smoke. Up ahead, the signal fire on top of the hospital was burning brightly, very close to them now. Something tumbled around in the bed.

Two gunshots.

"Nate! Help!"

In the rearview, he could see something in the bed with Devon.

Pale flesh and bones sticking out.

Devon screamed. Then fired another volley of shots. Two of them smashed through the back glass, one of them destroying the truck's console and the other passing an inch or two from Nate's head and out the windshield.

"Devon! Devon! You okay?"

Devon screamed again, but then it became words: "I got him! I fucking got him!"

Nate's mind worked in overdrive. They were supposed to have more time. More of a gap between their arrival and the infected horde. Now there was no time at all. And the window of opportunity for both bait trucks to get into the hospital was closing rapidly. If the hospital got surrounded before Paul and Junior arrived in their bait truck, they wouldn't be able to get in.

Nate fumbled with the radio. "Tomlin! We need that ground-floor door open for us when we get there. They are right on our ass! And Paul, you need to hurry the fuck up! Our horde might hit the hospital before you can get in! You need to get there, man! Does everybody copy that?"

Tomlin answered first. "I copy. The door'll be open. Paul and Junior, are you guys gonna make it?"

In the background of Paul's response, Tomlin could hear their engine screaming to get them there. "We're trying!" Paul shouted into the radio, his voice sounding garbled. "What happens if the hospital is surrounded?"

"Then pull off," Tomlin responded quickly. "If you can't get in, then just find a clear road out of town and get gone! Nate, I got Joey and Brandy on the way down now to open the door for you. Get here, brother, and get here quick...I think I see you coming."

Nate dropped the radio. No response was needed.

Up ahead, the parking lot of the hospital sprawled out. They had never removed any of the barricades that had been erected by the National Guard and FEMA. The place was still almost entirely surrounded by Jersey barriers and barbed wire. All but the narrow entrance on the south side of the hospital.

Nate didn't let up. He barreled for that little gap at almost eighty miles per hour, and if he chipped some skin off the side of the pickup truck, then oh fucking well.

"We're almost there," Nate said to no one in particular. "Almost there..."

They burst through the opening, missing the cement barriers by inches and careening into the parking lot. Nate slowed just enough to be able to cut a left turn without rolling the truck. The building rushed up at them, the burning fire standing right over their heads. Nate slammed on the brakes, hoping Devon didn't take a dive.

The front end of the truck stopped just a few feet short of the cement wall. Nate took the half second to put it in park, but left the keys in and left it running. He really didn't give a shit what happened to the truck at that point. He was out of the car before it stopped rocking on its suspension.

Devon climbed awkwardly out of the truck, favoring his right side.

Ahead of them, the emergency exit attached to the ground-floor stairwell opened up and Joey was standing there waving and shouting at them. "C'mon, c'mon! Get inside!"

Joey disappeared inside as Nate scrambled through the door. He could hear the earth-trembling roar of the horde behind them, but couldn't see them yet. The emergency exit door was open just barely wide enough for them to squeeze through. Nate got in, then waited and pulled Devon through the door and slammed it closed. The floor of the stairwell was crammed full of various bulky items that looked like they'd had a long, violent trip down the stairwell. There were hospital beds, machinery, computers, and some chairs.

Nate and Devon both heaved air.

Brandy was on the flight of stairs above them. "You guys okay? You all right?"

"We're good," Nate said breathlessly, then looked at Devon. "You good?"

Devon waved a dismissive hand and headed for the stairs.

Joey locked the doors. He and Nate started pushing the heavy equipment back in place. Nate supposed this was what counted as a barricade. Hopefully the locks would hold, and if they didn't, hopefully all the trash piled in the doorway would at least deter them for long enough that they could get the hell off the roof.

"Wait!" Nate grabbed his head. "What about Paul and Junior?"

Joey shook his head. "Tell 'em to pull off! It's too fucking close!"

Nate grabbed a stair to get out of Joey's way and keyed his radio. "Paul! Junior! Pull off! Get the fuck out of here! You ain't got time to get inside!"

Their response was filled with static. "What? We're almost there!"

Nate found himself shouting at the mic, like he knew he shouldn't. "Pull! Off! You're not going to get inside the hospital! Pull off!"

"There's no . . . Shit!"

The transmission ended.

Joey yelled at Nate, pointing at the stairs, and Nate realized that the sound of the horde had engulfed them again. Nate felt suddenly claustrophobic. A foot of cement between him and death. Extinction was just outside the door.

He charged up the stairs.

They made it to the second landing before the walls of the hospital started to shake.

TWENTY-ONE

─────

MESSY

WHEN THE GOING GETS *tough, the tough get going*. That's what Tomlin believed his entire life. No matter the situation, he was always moving, always acting, always fighting. But as he stood there in the red-orange glow of the signal fire, looking out over the edge of the Johnston Memorial Hospital's roof, for the first time in his entire life Tomlin found himself paralyzed.

The world below him had turned into hell, and he stood on an island in the middle of it all.

Firelight bathed a sea of faces three stories below him, so tightly packed that he could not see the bodies attached to the heads. The sea extended out into the darkness, unending, more than could be counted, more than he had seen or ever imagined to see. Beyond the reach of the firelight, the darkness boiled and squirmed. The stench of millions upon millions was horrendous. The sound of them was deafening. And this was no horde, not like any that he had ever seen before. They did not behave like the other infected. This was a *hive*, and they pushed and scrambled aggressively, but unlike the smaller hordes that he'd seen in the towns and small cities, these seemed to act with a complete lack of individual thought. They swarmed over barricades and over barbed wire and trampled everything to the ground. They reached, and climbed, and climbed on each other, and they didn't shy from pain but allowed themselves to be crushed and then continued on, mindlessly, where other infected would have retreated. The whole mass of them seemed to have only one objective in mind: the priority of getting to whatever was hiding in the firelight at the top of that building and ripping it to shreds.

Tomlin watched Paul and Junior's pickup truck try to punch through the sea of bodies, layered two and three deep in some places, undulating and bulging like waves and swells. He'd caught the first part of Nate's transmission before the noise of the hive had engulfed him. He could still hear it in his periphery, just an electronic noise, yammering against his eardrum, the quality of it the only thing that pierced the heart-freezing sound all around him. But despite Nate's warning, Paul and Junior had tried to make it through. The pickup truck stopped like it had hit a brick wall. Tomlin watched the bodies in front of the grill compress, the faces painted white in bright headlights. Others climbed over the crushed ones, onto the hood, onto the car, blanketing it. Maybe Paul and Junior were screaming, but he couldn't hear them.

"Oh, man," Tomlin said, his own voice just a small vibration in his head. "Oh...Jesus."

The pickup truck lifted, tilted, then toppled

onto its side. A single headlight stabbed out into the gloom, illuminating a cone of writhing not-quite-humans that just kept going until the head-light could illuminate no further.

When Tomlin felt the hospital tremble under his feet, his senses came back to him.

He turned and ran to Jared. He grabbed the man by the shoulder, put his mouth next to the other man's ear, and shouted to be heard: "Start shooting at them! Slow and steady!"

They'd already been over the plan. Hang over the edge and take evenly spaced potshots. Doing damage wasn't the concern. Keeping the infected's attention was.

Jared nodded, though his face was pale and sheened with a greasy-looking sweat. He ran, looking a little fumbly, to the edge of the roof and looked over. He froze there for a moment. Tomlin raised his own rifle and cracked a round off into the air. The gunshots were still loud enough to be heard, and it snapped the hypnosis of fear. Jared stuck his rifle over the edge and started firing.

Tomlin ran for the roof access and the stair-well. He opened it and nearly cranked off another round when he saw the four faces lurching toward him. Then he recognized Nate and Devon, and then Joey and Brandy coming in behind them.

Tomlin coughed out the breath that had caught in his chest and simply pointed to the roof, to where Jared was keeping attention focused on him. Slow and deliberate fire. Maybe one shot every thirty seconds, or so they had planned. The foursome ejected themselves from the stairwell, back into the nightmare beyond. Tomlin slipped in and closed the door.

It was anything but quiet in the stairwell, but it was quiet*er*. Three levels below him, the sound of a dozen fists banging endlessly on the emergency exit doors echoed up at him. He hoped to God that the doors on the ground level held, or they were going to be really and truly screwed. There wasn't enough ammunition or rifles in every bunker in this damned state that was going to save them if it came down to a fight.

Tomlin keyed the Marine radio. "Smithfield to artillery, we got a whole mess of bad guys knocking on our doorstep right now. I hope you're loaded up and ready."

Brinly paced the line of artillery pieces, the radio up to this head, followed by the younger Marine with the manpack strapped to his back. A larger and bulkier thing than he'd seen the Coordinators use, but that was to be expected. The Coordinators were Army, and Army always got the good shit. Marines got whatever cobbled together equipment they could scrape up and steal. It was not a point of contention, just a point of fact.

His world was light and dark. The bright halogen beams from the trucks and worklights cast a whitewashed glow over everything, but they also cast black shadows, and beyond the reach of the lights, the world was dark and threatening.

His left ear—the ear that he had held the radio handset to—rang with the brutal noise that had just come through it. Captain Tomlin was hailing from Smithfield, but the sound in the background made the hairs stand up across Brinly's body, from his neck to his arms and down his back. A screeching, tremulous, roaring sound unlike any he had heard before, and yet he was immediately able to identify what it was, what he knew it had to be.

That's what a million infected sound like.

"...I hope you're loaded up and ready," Tomlin was saying. "Y'all copy me?"

Brinly waited a half beat and then transmitted. "We copy you, Tomlin. The guns are ready to rock. We're just waiting for your signal. You got an ETA for your pickup?"

"I'll have it in a minute," Tomlin said, his voice strained and distracted. Brinly could hear rifle shots in the background, very slow and deliberately paced. "I'm juggling two radios. Stand by."

"Roger. Standing by." Brinly felt his heart kicking into gear. He stopped on his pace down the line of artillery pieces, hand still holding the radio handset. He raised his voice to be heard over the sound of the idling trucks. "Everyone get on your guns! Time is short and we got a city to level!"

There was a loud crack, and then the radio handset was jerked out of his grip.

He turned, half in annoyance, and saw the radioman jerking around on the ground, spitting blood and clutching a bloody hole in his neck.

Someone shouted "Contact!" just before the air filled with the sound of rifle reports and bullets splitting the air.

Brinly didn't wait to figure out what was going on. He snatched up the Beretta M9 at his leg.

All around them the dark woods twinkled with muzzle flashes. He could hear men crying out in pain and surprise and he knew that it was his own men. He started shooting his pistol at the muzzle flashes, stooping quickly down and grabbing ahold of the shoulder strap of his radioman's rig, and then dragging his thrashing junior backward. He kept firing his pistol until the slide locked back.

Brinly pulled the dying man behind the wheel of one of their trucks. "In the fucking trees!" he shouted out to his Marines as they dove for cover and tried to orient themselves to where the threat was coming from. But it was all around them. "Someone get on the fifties!"

The words were barely out of his mouth before the one just over his head started thundering.

The radioman was flailing, grasping at Brinly's lapels, his eyes bulging out of his sockets as he struggled to get air past all the blood pouring into his lungs. His fingernails scratched at Brinly's neck, just trying to grab something.

Brinly put one hand on the Marine's head and fended his grasping fingers away with the other. "I got you, buddy, I got you. You're okay. You're okay," he said, though he knew that the man wasn't. But he'd been here before. And he knew what a dying man wanted to hear. As he held the man down and spoke gently to him, he looked out and tried to get a better grasp of the situation.

It wasn't good.

Brinly reeled the radio handset in by its cord and put it to his head. "Smithfield, Smithfield, we're in fucking trouble out here! I don't know what kind of help you can get us, but we're gonna need it as soon as you can get it!"

LaRouche kept himself pressed to the dirt behind a large hardwood tree. All around him the .50-caliber rounds from the Marine truck were chewing through wood and dirt and smashing through flesh, killing men before they could even cry out. He just lay in the dirt, wishing to be smaller, wishing to be flatter, and praying to a God that he still didn't believe in that one of those rounds wasn't going to find him and cave him in.

Then, suddenly, the heavy machine gun fire was raking away from him.

He took a big breath that stank of gunsmoke. Dirt and bits of bark and leaves peppered his tongue. He spat them out and then pulled his face out of the ground, wide-eyed and animalistic, flashing glances all around. In the darkness of the forest he could see very little, but the lights from the Marine trucks cast a silvery edge on everything and he could see faint outlines of his men, some of them moving from cover, others rolling around, injured.

Another .50-caliber M2 was opening up from another one of the Marine trucks, and LaRouche realized that taking the Marines by surprise had been the easy part. The hard part was going to be carrying it through. He knew the type of men that he was surrounded by—the Followers were not a military force; they had little to no discipline and plenty of avenues of retreat. The Marines were disciplined, experienced, and their backs were to a wall. LaRouche knew without a doubt that if too many of his men died, the rest would run.

LaRouche hiked himself onto one elbow, looking across a space of maybe ten feet to the next man that had crawled up behind a tree. "Concentrate on the machine guns! Get them when they're turned away from us!" he shouted. "Pass it on!"

The man ten feet away stared back like he didn't quite understand.

LaRouche growled a curse at him, and then propped himself up against the tree and sighted down the barrel of his rifle. He saw the blaring muzzle of the M2 swinging in his direction again. *Shit.*

He pulled the trigger three times. His rounds sparked off the armored plating on the trucks, but something must have caught the gunner because the muzzle of the gun tipped up and spat flame at the sky. He felt relief, but mostly still the black feeling in his chest he was so familiar with, so hot that it was cold, terror and rage mixed together and bursting inside of him like a Molotov cocktail.

He rolled out of cover and scrambled to his left, where most of the men had been killed by the last pass of machine gun fire. He needed to get a better angle on the other gunner. The fire was focused away from LaRouche's position and the opportunity felt sudden and ripe. *Kill him, fucking kill him.*

High-minded thoughts of countrymen and allegiances were far from him now. He didn't care who he was shooting at, only that he needed to kill them. A predator's mind-set wherein there was no stopping until someone was dead. Kill or be killed, men turned to beasts and fighting to the death. This was the place where LaRouche felt strangely natural, though afterward the thoughts would come and the realization of death would loom. Always after.

He popped up behind a stump—rotted out and probably not worth much cover, but it was what he had. He strained to see past the glaring lights on the fronts of the Marine trucks, but they dazzled his vision and he couldn't see the second gunner. And now a third was opening up. He couldn't see it, only hear it thundering on.

A shape leaned out from behind the bumper of one of the trucks.

LaRouche fired at it. It fired back, but the rounds went high. LaRouche was at an advantage: the man behind the bumper could not see LaRouche, but LaRouche could see him. At least the shape of him. The Marines were being forced to shoot at muzzle flashes in the night.

LaRouche shot again and the shape jerked back behind the bumper. Maybe hit. Maybe not. LaRouche couldn't be sure. He crawled quickly on all fours, changing his location. Constantly moving. You couldn't just sit in one spot, no matter how comfortable it made you feel. You had to be where they didn't know you were.

Another tree. Large enough to stop rounds.

LaRouche leaned out and sought the gunners again, but still couldn't see anything past the lights. *The fucking lights...*

I need to go the other way.

The trucks were oriented so that their lights illuminated the workspace behind the artillery pieces. The pieces were pointed west, and LaRouche was in the southwest corner of the clearing. The best angle was going to be behind the trucks, where the lights would silhouette the Marines but not blind LaRouche and his men.

Rounds splattered the tree branches above his head.

He ducked momentarily, then began to run back the way he'd come, plunging a little deeper into the woods to avoid fire while he moved. The rounds seemed like they were chasing him, but he just ran faster. Branches lashed his face and tried to grab his legs and arms. He pushed through them and stumbled into a small ravine.

It was crowded with bodies.

LaRouche stood there, panting and looking around as the faces turned.

"Are we retreating?" someone asked in a supplicating voice.

LaRouche snapped his head in the direction of the voice. "Who the fuck said that?"

One of the men, lying with his back to the ravine and the rifle clutched ineffectively to his chest, looked up at LaRouche, fear in his eyes. "They're killing us with those machine guns!"

LaRouche wasn't sure what came over him. He laughed in the man's face. The whole situation just seemed so ridiculous. "Motherfucker, you think you're gonna live through all of this shit? You think you're going to reach old age in this fucking world? You're either a killer or you're being killed, and eventually even the killers get killed. Because if you live by the sword, you die by the sword, isn't that fucking right?"

The man glared back. "We know about you, Crazy LaRouche. We know you got a death wish, but the rest of us don't."

Do I have a death wish? LaRouche wondered, but the smile didn't leave his face. He just shook his head. "Run then, you fucking cockroach. Go fucking hide. Scrape a few more days out of your worthless life."

The man just stared.

LaRouche leveled his rifle at him, the smile finally leaving his mouth. "Run. Before I shoot you down myself."

Half of them ran, not doubting for a second that Crazy LaRouche would in fact shoot them down, and not having the balls to push back though they outnumbered him. He watched them go, feeling suddenly light-headed with the dawning of imminent truth.

Maybe I am crazy. Maybe I do have a death wish.

He looked at the remaining few men. The Followers of the Rapture. Really just a bunch of people as dumb and lost as he was, tagging along for a ride because they didn't know what else to do with themselves. It was better in their minds to be with the wrong group than to be totally alone, because all they wanted was to live. But LaRouche was not encumbered by beliefs. He knew what he was. He knew what he deserved. And maybe this seemed like the best way to make it happen. In some twisted way, in his twisted, fucked-up heart, it was best to go down fighting, no matter who you were fighting for.

"The rest of you gonna man the fuck up and come with me?" he asked almost absently, not really caring what they did in the end.

But they rose to their feet.

LaRouche turned his back on them and didn't wait to see if they were following. Over the edge of the ravine, he could hear the firefight reaching that point after the initial clash of guns, where the people embroiled in it were slowing down, reloading, choosing their shots. Gunfights had a rhythm to them, one that LaRouche knew quite well. They lulled and then quickened, up and down, up and down.

He made his way quickly through the ravine, picking up stragglers as he went. Some came; others stayed hunkered down in fear. LaRouche paid them no mind. Projectiles thrashed through the woods and sprinkled bits and pieces of branches and bark down onto their heads. LaRouche couldn't tell how much return fire the Followers were giving, but it didn't matter anymore.

He bellied up to the side of the ravine and looked over. Now they were about fifty yards into the woods, and he could see the glow of the Marine encampment; rays of light were coming through the trees, catching in the haze of spent propellant. They'd worked themselves into the eastern corner of the clearing, and he could see the back of the trucks now. There were five trucks, and three of them had manned machine guns working against the Followers' assault. But the gunners were backlit and struggling to maintain suppressive fire in the entire 360-degree attack.

"We can do this," LaRouche said, more to himself than anyone else. He turned and looked at the ones that had gathered to him. There were maybe a dozen. Maybe enough. Maybe not. They would have to see.

He pointed toward the clearing. "We need to close the distance here." He raised his voice to be heard. "We're gonna work to the edge of the woods. Concentrate your fire on the machine gunners. Put them down. When the guns go down, we move in. That clear?"

No one responded verbally. A few nodded.

LaRouche climbed the edge of the ravine, then stopped, kneeling in the leaves. He turned to look behind him, frowning as a new sound reached him.

"What?" someone asked. "What's wrong?"

It came upon them fast and low. One second it was just a buzz in the background, and then it became a whirlwind roar, shaking the trees and thundering just above the tops. LaRouche looked up and couldn't see the helicopter itself, but he could see the twin blooms of fire coming off its sides as the two door gunners opened up with the M240s.

LaRouche and every man with him tried to flatten themselves out, but the rounds found them anyway, punching down through the trees and smashing through their backs and chests. He listened to the rounds impacting the ground all around him and finding the flesh of the men that were following him, but they didn't find him.

The helicopter passed.

Those that were still alive began to scream and run. The gunfire was suddenly cut in half, as scores of the Followers cut and run at the sight of the bird over them, chewing through their ranks and demolishing their positions.

LaRouche rolled onto his side and watched the men flee, cursing and yelling, some of them hobbling along, injured. There was a dark sense of amusement that crept over him. Fear, most certainly, but he couldn't stop the laugh again. That black, abysmal laugh that forced its way out of him with almost a painful violence.

"Run, you fucks!" he wheezed, drawing himself up off the ground. "Run the fuck away! I don't fucking need you!" He stood there in the night, with the guns crashing behind him and the light casting about at weird angles through the trees, as the limbs and branches shook and rattled. He could just barely see the running men's shapes in the woods but he watched in fascination as they began to fall. Sprawling on the ground like they'd been snared by some chest-level tripwire, and the sound that accompanied this odd dance was a muffled *chack-chack-chuck* sound that for a brief moment seemed utterly alien to LaRouche, and his brain didn't quite piece it together.

Not until one of the fallen men started screaming, clutching his belly as another *chack* put him down, did LaRouche realize what it was. He'd been an infantryman, not any sort of special operations soldier. He'd never been issued a suppressor for his weapons and had never even fired one. But somehow he knew the sound. He knew that's what it was.

Those aren't regular Marines…

LaRouche ducked behind a tree and got low.

The helicopter circled around again, the guns chattering more sporadically. He could hear screams of wounded men and calls from others to pull back, to run; everyone was splitting and running, just like he knew that they would.

I should have told Chalmers this was a horrible idea.

But he'll figure it out.

He put his back to the tree and put his butt on the ground. He wasn't sure if they'd seen him yet. He wasn't even sure who *they* were. But the shooting had been too quick, too accurate in the gloom of night, for these to be regular grunts shooting through peep sights. They had suppressors, and their shooting made it seem like they were seeing perfectly fine in the dark. *They've got NVGs.*

He leaned out, just an inch or two, just so he could look into the woods, into the darkness, and see if anything was moving. And he could see them. Four of them. Just black shadows moving quickly over the forest floor, scanning the bodies as they stepped over them, calling things back and forth.

"These three are down," one said.

Another stood over a wounded man and finished him. "All clear."

The first shadow to speak straightened and seemed to look to his left, where the other two shadows were moving quickly through the dead and dying. "Hey, Harden, we're all clear. Moving."

A few seconds stretched into what seemed like several minutes. The name rattled around in LaRouche's head like a hard opening shot from a pinball that ricochets around inside the machine before finally rolling toward the paddles. Half of his brain knew damn well what the name was— *Harden, as in Lee Harden, you dumbfuck*—but the other half wanted to remain obstinate—*Lee's gone. Along with Camp Ryder. The radios. No one was answering the radios and what the hell do you think that means?*

Lee's gone. Probably dead.

This is a different Harden.

Different. It's got to be different. There's just no possible way.

He settled back behind the tree and realized he was shaking badly.

Why? Why am I shaking? Why do my guts feel like liquid right now? His heart was thundering like it hadn't in a long time. Not since he'd been with Wilson and Father Jim. Not since the time when he actually cared whether he was alive or dead. Not since the time when he thought he deserved a bullet. Now his heart seemed to be trying to prove that it was still alive, thrashing around in his chest, uncomfortably hard.

What if it is Lee? What if he knows what you did?

What the fuck does it matter if he knows? Am I a fucking kid? Am I in trouble with my father? Fuck Lee and fuck his goddamned missions! He's the one that put me in this situation. He's the one that saddled me with all of this stupid shit when I wasn't FUCKING READY. Go blow the fucking bridges?

*Go take on the goddamned world? Go do what I say,
and by the way, everyone's gonna die if you don't
succeed!*

But if he's alive…

He's not. It's not THAT Harden.

But if it is…

Then the mission. The mission. Maybe…

Maybe there's still a chance.

"Heads up!" someone yelled.

LaRouche jerked his head in the direction of
the call.

One of the shadows was standing not fifteen feet
from him. The muffled *chack* of the suppressed
rifle was much louder when it was so close—and
pointed right at him. LaRouche didn't have time
to react. He saw the wood on the side of the tree
splinter, and felt something rip through his side,
and the first weird thought that came to him was,
Fuck! I got a splinter!

Then the pain was there, quite suddenly, and he
knew it wasn't just a splinter in his side.

He cried out and toppled, clutching his side, not
quite sure why he wasn't fighting to the death. It
was strange how, despite the fear, he could still feel
ashamed, still feel disappointed that he hadn't kept
up his plan… *Oh my God, this fucking hurts.*

*I should fight now. Get myself shot dead before
I can just bleed out and die shitting my pants in
pain…*

But in desperation, what came out of his mouth
was "Lee! Captain Harden!"

Maybe that was the only reason they didn't
shoot him dead right there. He couldn't even

understand why he hadn't taken the death that he knew he deserved. He should've just taken it when he had the fucking chance...

He felt sick and faint. His hands on his side were wet and sticky.

They got me, they got me good.

One of the shadows was standing over him. It had some contraption covering half of its face, but LaRouche knew the other half of that face just as well as he knew anyone's face.

Lee Harden lifted the night-vision monocular from his eye and looked down at LaRouche, confusion on his face, the muzzle of his rifle still looming in LaRouche's vision.

"LaRouche?" he said, the words like steel dragged over gravel. "Is that you?"

TWENTY-TWO

CROSSING THE RUBICON

LEE DIDN'T KNOW WHO was more shocked, himself or the man below him. Lee wasn't even sure that it was LaRouche at his feet. He hadn't responded to Lee's question. But he damn well looked like him, though his face had grown gaunter than Lee remembered, and his beard was longer than LaRouche typically kept it. The eyes didn't lie, though. Hard and cold and sometimes even wanton, but they could be kind when they wanted to be. They were strange eyes, and they belonged to only one man that Lee knew.

Lee didn't move the muzzle of his rifle, and he didn't take his finger off the trigger. "What's your name, motherfucker? You better say something quick."

"LaRouche," the man beneath him mumbled. "My name's LaRouche. Jesus...Lee..."

Both of them tried to comprehend, and failed.

Lee realized his mouth was working like he had words to say but couldn't get them out. "What the fuck...what...what...?"

The haggard, mad-looking man below him seemed caught in his own dilemma of confusion.

But Lee could see there was something more to it. This was not just confusion. This was LaRouche wanting to say something, but not having the guts.

"Wilson said that you disappeared!" Lee said.

LaRouche seemed to wilt at those words. "Did Wilson...did they blow the bridges?"

Lee's eyes narrowed. "Wilson is fucking dead. And what the fuck are you doing here, LaRouche?" He glanced around them, not wanting to believe, but knowing, because the truth was not coy. It was blatant. Oftentimes you don't want to acknowledge it, but that is the working of your own brain. Truth is not relative. It simply *is*. "Are you...?"

LaRouche grimaced and laid his head back into the dirt, struggling with the pain in his side. "Lee, you know damn well what I am. That's why you used me. Just like they used me. Don't try to play ignorant now."

Lee's jaw worked. "What happened? What happened with your group?"

LaRouche's eyes were glistening, but Lee couldn't tell whether it was from grief or pain. Maybe some of both. Maybe he would've been able to keep one locked down, but not both. He blinked rapidly through the tears, straining, his teeth grit, his hands plugging his wounded side.

"I killed Father Jim," LaRouche belted out very suddenly. And it was like watching a building implode, all the structures taken out in microseconds. The demolition of a man. He writhed onto his side, his face twisting up in grief now rather than physical pain. He tried to speak, but just coughed and spluttered, senselessly.

"You did what?" Lee asked, though he'd heard perfectly well. The words were just space filler for his inability to formulate some other question.

"I fucking killed him!" LaRouche bellowed. "I did it! I did it! I don't even fucking know why I did it! We were arguing and then we were fighting and then I just...I just...fuck!" LaRouche leaned up onto his elbows, looking accusingly up at Lee. "What the hell do you want from me? What do you want?"

Lee looked down, his nose wrinkled like he'd smelled something bad. But he had no words. Behind them, coming from the clearing, they could hear whoops and cries of victory. The gunshots were still coming, but they were sporadic now. Lee was well aware of the time restraints. Well aware of the fact that Tomlin was sitting at the top of a building, surrounded by infected. They didn't have time for prisoners. They didn't have time to figure out why LaRouche was here, apparently on the wrong side. Lee could feel the anger that he'd felt when Tyler Bowden had held Harper and Julia hostage, the same anger he'd felt when he'd realized that Tyler had gunned down Harper to get away. But what good was it? What did it do for him? It was an impotent raging, and nothing more.

Lee felt disappointment, sudden and harsh and deep. "Oh, LaRouche. Oh, you..." He clenched his fist and his teeth at once and let the rest of the words burn out in a hiss of breath.

LaRouche laid his head back into the leaves and closed his eyes. "Just fucking kill me," he said quietly. "Do it. Fucking kill me."

And perhaps Lee was just being his usual stubborn self, but that sealed it. He just couldn't do it again. Whether it was LaRouche's words that had flipped the switch, or Lee's own actions—all the violence that he'd added to himself, all the decisions that never seemed to desensitize him, but rather just kept compounding on him.

He bared his teeth and shoved the rifle further into LaRouche's face, trying to wrap his brain around what LaRouche had said. And what LaRouche being here meant. *He killed Father Jim. He killed him, and then he abandoned his group, and maybe if he hadn't abandoned his group, Wilson would still be alive. And now he's here. Now he's here doing what?*

You know damn well what he's doing here.

What he's become.

"You're one of them," Lee said. A simple accusation, but accurate enough. "You're a piece of shit, LaRouche. I don't fucking believe you. You stupid motherfucker, have you ever stood for anything in your fucking life? Or do you just follow fucking orders?" He wanted badly to pull the trigger. But he didn't. He just pulled the rifle away.

LaRouche's eyes widened. "What are you doing? Why don't you fucking kill me?"

Because it's what you want. Because it's what you deserve.

Lee knelt down in the leaves, next to LaRouche.

Mitch looked around, antsy. "Captain, we need to get a move on. Followers have been pushed back. Helicopter's running low on fuel."

"I fucking know," Lee said shortly. He turned

his attention back to LaRouche. "Did you know that Harper's dead?" he asked suddenly. "He was killed. Not two hours ago. By a man who was supposed to be a friend of mine. Because he knew that I was going to kill him if I caught him. And he figured that if he shot Harper in the gut, it would distract me long enough for him to get away. And you know what the fucking problem is, LaRouche? The problem is, that made perfect sense to me. And I think that maybe I would have done the same thing myself. And that is not acceptable." He stood up. "But loose ends fucking bite you in the ass, don't they? They always do. So now I wonder if it's the right thing to do to kill you or not. I don't know. I don't fucking know anymore."

"You want me to fucking kill him?" Morrow asked.

"No," Lee spat out. He pointed a finger right into LaRouche's face. "It doesn't matter what the fuck you've done. Everyone knows wrong from right. And if you wanna die, that's fine. I think you fucking deserve it. I really do. There's a million different ways for you to get yourself killed, if that's what you really want, LaRouche. But it ain't gonna be from me. I've got the bridges blown along the Roanoke River and a couple million infected that have made it across before I could get that done. And I've got people that are waiting for me so that we can solve this fucking problem. That's what I'm going to do, LaRouche. I don't know where the fuck you went wrong, and I don't even fucking care anymore. I don't have the time to deal with you. You chose your path, and I chose mine. I don't know what you're going to do, but I know that I'm going to walk away from you. And I don't want to see your fucking face in the light. As far as I'm concerned, you were dead when you split from Wilson. And now you make some god-damned choices when I walk away. And maybe you make the right ones, or maybe you don't. That's up to you. But I'm fucking done."

Then Lee stood up and turned away from LaRouche, leaving him sitting there at the base of the tree. He'd walked maybe three paces before he heard a nasty crunch behind him. He turned and looked and saw LaRouche, lying limp against the tree, blood pouring from his nose.

Morrow turned and jogged back up to Lee. "Didn't want him shooting us in the back. He'll wake up in a couple minutes. Now let's get the fuck out of here."

Lee jogged a little closer to the edge of the woods and stopped, holding up a hand. Between the columns of tree trunks he could see the bright encampment that the Marines had made, work-lights and headlights from the trucks shining on the artillery pieces, casting long, dusky shadows across the clearing. There were still a few people shooting, but it sounded like it was coming from the opposite end of the clearing. The last few, hard-charging Followers, trying to keep the faith while the rest of them ran.

The Black Hawk was circling the clearing at a slow, steady speed. At random intervals one or both of the door gunners were spitting out bullets at targets in the woods that only they could see.

The door gunners had the same thermal hybrid night vision that Lee and the Delta men had. Lee and the three men with him had IR designators on their helmets and torsos so that the gunners could differentiate them from the enemy.

But the Marines wouldn't be able to see that.

Lee shoved the headset of Delta's squad comms off of one ear and brought his other radio handset up, transmitting to Tomlin over in Smithfield. "Hey, Brian, this is Lee, can you copy me?"

First he heard a horrible roaring noise, and then Tomlin's voice, almost faintly: "Yeah, I got you five-by-five, but it's a little fucking noisy over here." Tomlin stopped transmitting, but not before Lee heard a rifle shot. Then Tomlin came back, sounding strained. "Lee, I'm not gonna lie to you, buddy, it's gettin' a little dicey over here. What's it looking like on your end?"

Lee rubbed his hand over his face. Smelled dirt and gunsmoke clinging to his skin. "We're working on it. I'm in the woods looking at the Marines right now. We've pushed the attack back. It was the Followers, if you can fucking believe that shit. I need you to get on the horn with Brinly and tell him we're coming out of the woods. Don't let his men shoot us down."

"Okay, I copy you. I'll tell them to hold their fire."

Less than a minute passed before Lee could hear someone in the Marine camp shouting, "Cease fire! Cease fire!"

"He says you're clear to come through," Tomlin relayed after another few seconds.

Lee rose to his feet and jogged out of the woods. The Black Hawk had finished its last revolution and was coming into a hover and descending. Out of the shadows behind a cluster of Marine trucks, Lee could see First Sergeant Brinly's form striding out to meet him. He extended his hand and Lee clasped it, the two sharing an oddly familial hug.

"What the hell?" Brinly said, still out of breath. "I had 'em right where I wanted 'em and you scared 'em off."

Lee's mind was so consumed with the cluster-fuck of things happening that it took him a half second to realize that Brinly was joking. He recovered with a haggard smile. "I figured a Marine wouldn't thank Army boys for saving his ass."

"Seriously, though," Brinly said, "I'm glad you guys came."

Lee was already angling for the helicopter as it began to settle onto the ground. He gestured for Brinly to follow him. "That was the Followers, did you know that?"

Brinly nodded grimly. "Yeah, I figured it out."

"How's your situation? You still operational?"

"Yeah." Brinly looked over his shoulder. "Got a few wounded. Three dead. But we can still fight. And we can still shoot them big guns."

"Good, because we're gonna need it. The plan actually worked."

"You sound surprised."

"If you had my luck, you would be, too." Lee directed his attention forward and saw Carl slide out of the cabin of the Black Hawk as it touched the ground. Behind him, Mitch was helping Julia climb out.

"Lee!" Carl shouted, waving him on. "Let's fucking go! We got maybe thirty minutes before we're running on fucking fumes!"

Lee swore loudly. "That's not enough time!"

"No shit," Carl said, coming alongside Lee.

Lee faced him. "Carl, I can't leave them on the fucking building."

"You got some fuel hidden around here?"

Lee gathered a wad of spit in his mouth that tasted metallic and dirty. He spat it onto the ground at his feet. "We're gonna have to play it by ear. By which I mean I fly out to pick up my people. And maybe we have to land this bird someplace else."

"What?" Carl shook his head. "This is my only working chopper. I'm not landing it in a field somewhere and leaving it."

"You can come back to it," Lee said stubbornly. "I can't leave my people on the building. I can't do it. We have to pick them up. And if we stop fucking around and arguing about it, we might just have enough fuel to get there and back."

"Not possible."

"If you drop weight, you might make it. Drop the guns, drop the gear, and kick the copilot," Lee said, firm to the point of insistence. "Just me and the pilot."

"Fuck." Carl turned away, and Lee could see the realization of facts coming over him: The time they were spending here arguing was only making the situation worse. The window was narrow, but if they took enough weight off the bird, then it was just inside the realm of possibility.

"Your men are needed here, anyway," Lee said. "They need to watch the Marines' backs to make sure those fuckers don't try to push again."

Carl whipped around suddenly. "Fine. Go. Get on with it."

Lee didn't wait for further approval. He turned to Mitch and Morrow and pointed at the Black Hawk's cabin. "Help me dump everything. Guns, ammo, gear. If it's not bolted down, dump it." Lee stopped and turned, taking a moment to reach out and touch Julia's arm. "You okay?"

She looked horrible and was being propped up by Mitch. But she nodded. "I'm fine, Lee. Go finish this. Harper would lose his shit if he saw you sitting around jaw-jacking with me when all of this was going on." She smiled a wisp of a smile. " 'Shitfire,' I think he'd say."

Lee felt it in his throat and chest, the thick heaviness of loss. He turned away before Julia could make the cracks and fissures go deeper into him. He grabbed the radio handset and transmitted to Smithfield. "Tomlin, we're on the way, buddy. You copy?"

On the northeastern side of the hospital, Tomlin was leaning out over the edge of the roof and firing down at the parking garage. The entrance was heavily barricaded, but it was the weak spot. Due to the construction of the parking garage, the infected would have to turn their backs on the hospital to rise to the next level, repeatedly running *away*, which was apparently counterintuitive to them. But though the infected didn't seem like they were going to run the parking garage to get to the top, they seemed willing enough to climb it, and there were enough ledges and steel cables to serve as handholds. And they were starting to figure that out.

First one started to climb, but after Tomlin shot him down, another took his place, and then two more, and then three. Tomlin remained calm the first time, breathed deep the second and third time, but the fourth time, when three of the things lurched up and found impossible handholds and began to scale the sides of the parking garage, Tomlin could feel fear and dismay brewing up in his stomach and leaking through his system like radioactivity.

"They're climbing the parking garage!" he screamed out behind him, trying to be heard over the din of the millions below them, but his own voice was barely audible, and certainly not to the others spread out across the roof, trying to tend to the four walls.

They can't hear me. Do I run and shout it in their ears or stay here and focus on the task?

He heard an electronic buzzing next to his left ear and realized it was the radio squawking at him, though he couldn't hear the words. He leaned over the edge again. There were two of them now; one had dropped off or disappeared somewhere inside the parking garage. Tomlin forced air in and out of his lungs, no matter how badly his body wanted to seize up, and he fired, one, two, three, and took the two climbers down.

He leaned back in and grabbed the handset. He let his rifle hang on his chest and he pressed the radio to his ear with one hand, plugging his right ear with the other. "Lee, is that you? I can't hear shit right now! Talk loud!"

Lee's voice yelled into the mic, garbling the words, but at least they were loud enough. "Tomlin, we're on the way right now. Are you holding out?"

Tomlin glanced over the edge again. There were four infected climbing now. And what about the backside of the parking garage? What about the two sides of the structure that he couldn't see? *Shit, shit, shit...* "Lee, you need to hurry the fuck up! They're climbing the parking garage right now! I don't know how long we're gonna be able to hold them off!"

"I copy, we're goin' as fast as we can."

Tomlin dropped the handset, not worrying about reclipping it. He fired a volley of shots, clearing the wall below him of climbers, and then sprinted to Jared. He slapped the other man on the back and yelled at him. "They're climbing the parking garage! Go to that side!"

Jared nodded and ran for the north wall.

Tomlin went to Joey and Brandy and relayed the same message.

Down below, the main entrance had been breached. Tomlin could see them pouring inside. But there was no way up except for the locked stairwell doors. And those would be tougher to breach. He hoped. Dear God, he hoped.

He went back to the northeastern wall. The

other three were hanging over, firing faster now at the climbers.

"Choose your shots!" Tomlin yelled, sighting in his rifle on the torso of one as it managed to haul itself onto the second level. He fired once, toppling it back to earth. "Conserve your ammo!"

Lee, hurry your ass up...

TWENTY-THREE

ABSOLUTION

LaRouche walked through dark woods, through blackness. There were dead men along the way. And the dying. The retreat had clustered around the southern side of the clearing, everyone trying to make it back to the staging point. Guns and ammo had been strewn along the way, along with bodies that had dropped and bled out, and some that were convinced they couldn't go on.

They called out to him as he passed, but he ignored them.

He had dropped his rifle. It was heavy. But he kept his Beretta M9. The old piece-of-shit pistol. The one that he hated so much. The one that he'd used to murder Father Jim. He held it in his right hand, his strong hand, and with his left hand, he gripped the oozing hole on the right side of his body.

It was more than a flesh wound; he could tell. It was bleeding a lot. LaRouche ignored that, too, because it did him no good to dwell on it. No one would be able to put the blood back in him, and he had nothing that could stop the bleeding at this point but his own dirty fingers. And besides the bleeding, there were things that it had ruined inside of him. He could feel them, and the pain was excruciating with every step. The entry wound was just above his right buttock, and the exit was close to his navel. There were some important things between those two points, he was pretty sure.

But he was capable of walking. So he walked.

In the darkness, he heard his own name being called, and he finally stopped, because none of the other wounded had called to him by name. He turned to the sound of the voice and could just barely make out the shape of someone, huddled against a tree.

"Clyde?" LaRouche rasped.

The man extended a hand. "Help me."

LaRouche went to him slowly. It was Clyde, as he'd thought. The man's hand remained outstretched, but LaRouche stopped a few feet from him. Clyde had no weapon. His chest was a bib of blood that poured from bullet wounds to the chest and snot and spit that ran out of his nose and mouth.

Clyde coughed, retracting his hand to cover his mouth reflexively.

"This is kind of like how we met," LaRouche observed quietly, speaking barely above a whisper. "But reversed. Now you're huddled in the dark and it's me who found you."

Clyde regarded him with glistening eyes. "LaRouche...don't..."

LaRouche sniffed. "What'd you think when you found me, Clyde? Who did you think that I was?"

"I thought you were a killer."

"Yeah." LaRouche shrugged painfully. "There's some truth to that. But I wasn't always this way, you know? I was a good person, once. I think. And you know what? It doesn't matter what you've done, everyone still knows the difference between right and wrong."

"LaRouche, would you shut the fuck up and help me?"

LaRouche watched his heavy breathing cloud the air in front of him. "What side do you think we're on, Clyde? You really believe we're in the right? Or is it just more convenient to trick ourselves? Because that's what I think. I think we're just real good at tricking ourselves."

"I'm dying here."

"Nah. You're dead." LaRouche looked away from him. "So am I. Just a matter of time. But I ain't gonna help you live. I've got a bit of time left to do some right things. And letting you die, well that's the first right thing I've done in a while."

Clyde bared his bloody teeth. "LaRouche, you cock…"

LaRouche took another painful step, bending down and slipping the pistol into his pocket. Then he used both of his hands, one to clamp over Clyde's mouth, and the other to pinch his nose closed. Clyde started to struggle, but he was farther gone than LaRouche had even realized. He was weak and fading fast, and his clawing hands couldn't get LaRouche's hands off of his face as the oxygen burned out in his lungs.

"You're a rapist and a murderer. Everyone in

this fucking gang of yours is another rapist and another murderer. And you encouraged them, you brought them up, you taught them everything they know. You deserve to die. I do, too, but I've got some shit to do before I go." LaRouche leaned in further, putting his body weight into Clyde's face.

Clyde's eyes bulged wide and his struggling increased, but it still wasn't strong enough.

LaRouche had nothing else to say to him. So he just held him there for another minute, until the movement stopped, and then he held it for another minute more, to make sure. With each passing second, the fire in his side and in his guts was growing, becoming unbearable. When he was sure that Clyde was dead, he released him, and then struggled back to his feet.

The pain roared through him, but seemed to abate when he was standing again. It felt better to be standing. He continued on through the forest, heading south, following the lines of retreat, back to the staging point.

The Black Hawk ripped over nothingness. Even the sky above had some ambient glow to it. But the earth below them was just solid black, until Lee pulled the NVG monocular over his eyes and it turned green again. Green, but at least he could see the trees blurring by underneath them, the streets extending out like pale veins across the countryside, the clusters of houses and buildings. Sparks of warmth bursting here and there in his vision, but he couldn't tell what they were.

He pulled the NVGs off his eye and leaned up into the cockpit, where the pilot sat alone, steering the bird toward Smithfield. "How far out?" Lee asked, scanning the dials and trying to find which one showed their fuel. He'd been in plenty of Black Hawks in his time, but that didn't mean he knew how to fly one.

"We got five minutes to the hospital and twenty minutes of fuel."

"Fuck me," Lee murmured. He stayed there, hanging over the pilot's shoulder.

The pilot had a different pair of NVGs on than the rest of them. These were a full set of goggles. They provided better depth perception, a necessity for someone piloting a multi-million-dollar war machine in tight tolerances. The pilot leaned forward in his seat, looking like he was craning his neck.

Lee felt the helicopter rise. "You see something?"

"Yeah, I think I got eyes on that signal fire. Hold on..."

The helicopter ascended suddenly. Lee felt it pulling him down, and then it leveled off.

The pilot seemed to shrink back into his seat. "Holy fuck, man."

"What?"

The pilot pointed straight ahead, his voice quiet with awe. "Look at this shit."

Lee could see the twinkling of the signal fire far ahead of them, like a star below the blackness of the horizon. But everything else was just empty space. He flipped down the monocular again. The image that came through froze him solid. All that came out was a breathy, nonsensical syllable: "Ohhh…"

If he didn't know what he was looking at, it might have seemed beautiful.

They were flying over something that Lee had never seen before. Directly below them there were countless pinpoints of light, little figures that looked like blobs of white and orange and yellow. But the closer he looked to Smithfield, the denser they became. And ahead of them, the town of Smithfield was a shimmering mass of heat signatures. Like a beating, throbbing heart, and all the roads leading into the town and branching out through its suburbs were burning arteries. In the center of it all, Lee could see the signal fire burning at the top of the Johnston Memorial Hospital. The rest of the town had caught fire. The heat signatures clustered around the hospital, so dense that they seemed like one undulating mass. Like the hospital was a fissure in the earth's crust, and lava was boiling out. In yards and parks and forested areas, they twinkled like stars, but in the streets and open places the heat signatures were shoulder to shoulder and packed in tight. An ocean of them. A sea that had been set aflame.

And in the middle of that burning sea, the hospital was just a lonely island, and it seemed that it was going to be washed away.

They're swallowing the fucking city.

Lee coughed to clear himself and keyed his radio. "Tomlin, Tomlin, this is Lee, how copy?"

Gunshots, and panic in Tomlin's voice. "Go, Lee! I hope you're fucking close!"

"I'm right here, buddy, I'm looking at you and we're coming in quick, so get ready!"

They'd ripped the parking garage barricades to shreds and were storming through. It only took a few of them to figure out where they needed to go to ascend the parking garage, and then the rest began to follow. Still others were climbing up the sides of the parking garage. The entire structure had just become scaffolding for them to reach the top of the hospital.

Tomlin and his small team weren't shooting them off the walls anymore. They were down to their last few magazines per person, and they were picking targets as they came over the top of the parking garage now, choosing to take out the ones that were closest and the most threat.

The top level of the parking garage was still one level below them, but Tomlin doubted that would hold the horde off for long. They would climb on each other's shoulders, trample their brethren down to create a staircase of bodies if they had to. They were singularly minded.

He fired his rifle haphazardly with one hand. The targets were pouring into the top level of the parking garage in such great numbers, Tomlin didn't think he could miss. With the other hand, he keyed the radio back to Lee. "We're fucking ready now! Just get here!"

He dropped the radio again and ran to Jared and Joey, who were beside each other. "When the chopper lands, I want you two to grab Brandy and get on it first. Then you cover for me and Nate and Devon. You got that?"

"I got it!" Jared said, the pitch of his voice raised in fear.

Tomlin took a few shots, then crossed quickly to Nate and Devon. "Nate! We're holding while Jared and Joey and Brandy get on the bird! It's almost here! When they're on, they'll cover our retreat! Got it?"

"Okay!" Nate shouted back, not even bothering to look back.

Devon kept firing, but yelled at Tomlin in a shaking voice. "I'll hold them for you guys! Let me do it!"

"Shut the fuck up and do what I tell you to do!" Tomlin yelled back in the kid's ear. Was he fucking serious with this hero bullshit? This wasn't the time or the place . . .

Devon spun suddenly and Tomlin could see his eyes were wide with terror and wet with tears. "I got bit! In the fucking truck! I got bit!"

Movement over Devon's shoulder caught Tomlin's eyes. He looked up, saw the horde pouring into the top level of the parking garage, wall-to-wall bodies. It seemed like shooting at them was pointless. Trying to empty the ocean with an eye dropper.

He got bit.

Tomlin was processing.

The sound of helicopter rotors beating the air over their heads. The feeling of the air buffeting down onto them. A sudden explosion of lights. Tomlin turned and squinted. The massive signal fire on top of the roof just barely lit the outline of the helicopter in flickering oranges, and the pilot had switched on the helicopter's lights.

Nate was yelling something at Devon. Devon was yelling back. They were both shooting.

Tomlin started shooting with them. The radio handset flopping on his shoulder was squawking mindlessly—Lee yelling at them to get the hell on the helicopter. He kept shooting down into the crowd of insanity below him as it suddenly crushed itself against the wall eight feet below them, and the infected began to climb, to claw over each other. Never ending. Never stopping. He stood between Nate and Devon, the three of them spread out along the northeastern wall of the roof, trying to hold the line just long enough . . .

He glanced over his left shoulder.

Jared, Joey, and Brandy were sprinting for the helicopter.

They should've been in that shit already! My God, keep us alive . . .

A filthy, gnarled hand grasped the lip of the roof, the fingernails overgrown and black underneath. Tomlin grit his teeth and stomped one boot down onto the hand while he stuck his rifle blindly over the edge and fired. He felt the hand moving underneath his foot, and then it slipped away.

"They're climbing over!"

Madness, madness, madness, don't die in this madness.

Tomlin looked over his shoulder again, and this time the three others were climbing into the cabin of the Black Hawk, and Tomlin could see Lee there, rifle strapped to his chest, hauling them up onto the aircraft as it hovered just a few inches off the ground.

Tomlin turned back and faced the hundreds, the thousands, the uncountable faces. He was screaming. He was shooting. He started moving backward away from the wall. Nate held for a half beat longer, then followed suit. Devon did as well, but then stopped and held his ground as dozens of spidery arms reached over the edge of the roof and began to straddle their way over.

Nate was screaming for Devon.

Tomlin grabbed Nate by the shoulder, getting a good firm grip on his jacket, and started dragging him backward as he heard the sound of gunfire taking up cadence behind him, the bullets whizzing over their heads.

"Let's go! We gotta go! We gotta..."

At the edge of the roof, Devon took another step back and then stood again, firing to his left, then his right, and then something got a hand on him and ripped the rifle out of his arms, and then pulled him to the ground as bodies crawled over the edge and piled on top of him, ripping him to shreds in a frenzy.

Tomlin turned to face the helicopter, still dragging Nate behind him. Lee jumped down out of the bird and grabbed the other shoulder, hauling the screaming man on board, and then climbed on top of him to pin him down.

Tomlin could feel the infected at his back; he could feel them grasping at his heels; he could feel their breath on his neck. He had one leg into the cabin of the helicopter.

Lee was shouting, "Go! Go! Go!"

Tomlin leaped and sprawled himself onto the

cold metal of the floor, rolling as he did and feeling the sudden down-thrust of the helicopter erupting off of the roof, faster than he'd ever felt a helicopter take off. It flattened him onto the deck and pressed at his chest. He looked out, trying to see Devon, but only caught the top of the flames from the signal fire, and then even that disappeared.

The helicopter banked, and Tomlin looked down into moving, thrashing darkness, the signal fire the only point of light in it all, and it illuminated the building around it that looked like ants swarming a mound.

"Tomlin!" Lee yelled at him over Nate's wails. "Tell Brinly to send it!"

Tomlin fumbled with the Marines' radio, but managed to bring it to his mouth and key it with numbed fingers. He realized he was completely out of breath and had to take a few before he could speak: "Smith...ah...Smithfield to artillery! Brinly! Send it! Send it! Level this fucking town!"

Julia stood leaning against one of the Marine trucks, her mind scattered into a million different places, pain coursing through her, and grief pressing down on her chest. One of the Delta men stood by with her, though she told him that she was fine.

She heard Tomlin's voice on the radio, shouting for Brinly to "Send it! Send it!" and she could even hear Lee in the background, yelling, "Tell them to expand the radius! Expand the radius!"

Brinly heard the command over the radio and

nodded to the Marine artillery commander. Then he turned and looked at Julia. "This is gonna be loud."

She stared on numbly, not bothering to plug her ears, though a few of the men around her did.

The artillery commander turned and barked in the direction of the gun crews: "Battery...fire!"

Julia felt the earth shake and the air pound against her chest and her ears, almost deafening her. She closed her eyes, letting the devastating noise wash over her, letting it spark her anger back to life, like breath blown on embers.

Kill those motherfuckers. Kill 'em all.

The sky spat flame. Lee watched the first volley erupt in the night, maybe a few hundred yards from the base of the hospital, shattering concrete and bodies in clouds of billowing black-and-gray smoke, eviscerating, incinerating, demolishing.

Tomlin shouted into his radio: "Splash! Right on target! You got about a mile radius from that point. Fire for effect."

Lee didn't need to tell the helicopter pilot to get them out of there. They were already banking sharply, heading south, trying to make the run to Fort Bragg. Lee watched out the open cabin doors of the helicopter. Even from inside the helicopter, he could hear the distinctive warbling noise of the incoming rounds, the jarring explosions as they crashed down. The dark world below them became a flashing, strobing cloud. A massive thunderhead that grew out of nothing. The dust cloud climbed on itself, billowing up and up. In the heart of it, the rounds kept striking, and the cloud of dust and smoke flashed like lightning. It just kept growing, kept building, compounding on itself, consuming everything. It struck down buildings and flattened houses, though Lee could not see this happening. He only could see the ever-expanding cloud, swallowing everything whole, destroying in seconds what had taken decades to build, and smashing everything to blood and dust and rubble. In that black cloud, in the strobing light of high explosives and fragmentation, all those warm bodies were being burned, incinerated, ripped to shreds. In the distance, the artillery was thundering, and the rounds just kept coming, unending, unsatisfied. A god of war with a bottomless hunger. Lee's mouth hung open at the spectacle of it. An image of destruction. Apocalyptic and wrathful.

Lee had no words. Only a feeling. Like falling. Like vertigo.

From the cockpit, an unpleasant sound blared through his shock and awe.

Lee came up to his feet, wanting to know what it was.

The pilot answered before he could ask.

"Fuel's almost done," he shouted. "I don't think we're gonna make it back."

The feathery feeling of vertigo—almost giddy—solidified into a brick. Lee could think of only one thing as he felt the aircraft shudder. He flipped down the NVGs and looked below them. Heat signatures in the trees, in the streets. Not the sea of fire he had seen, but still hundreds of them.

"There's a lot of infected down there!" he called out. "We're still over top of the horde. You need to get us a little bit farther!"

"I don't know how much farther we're going to go." The pilot sounded irritated. "One second this goddamn fuel gauge says we got twenty minutes of fuel, and the next it says we're empty. Trust me, brother, you don't want this thing to crash."

"Just get us as far as you can," Lee said, then turned to the others. "Everyone strap in and grab ahold of something."

"Are we gonna crash?" Joey stammered, while Brandy started swearing.

Jared and Tomlin and Nate dragged themselves into the available seats and started strapping themselves in, their faces set like rocks.

"I don't know," Lee said, grabbing one of the seats for himself and fumbling with buckles. "I hope to hell not..."

The helicopter shook and dropped.

"Aw, fuck," the pilot yelped from inside the cockpit. "Everyone hang on!"

Lee felt the bird plummet what must have been a few yards.

This was the risk we had to take. Maybe we'll make it.

"Everyone grab something and make yourself small!" Lee demonstrated by seizing the side of the seat he was strapped into and tucking his legs, arms, and head in tightly, almost to a fetal position.

"I think I got it," the pilot yelled back. "It's gonna be hard, but I think...I think..."

The helicopter's lights were still blazing. One second Lee saw the tops of trees flashing through the bright lights. Then it was the ground. He closed his eyes and clenched his teeth, every muscle in his body tensed.

This is gonna hurt...

TWENTY-FOUR

―――――

CRASH

LEE REMEMBERED THE IMPACT, but vaguely. His brain jarred around inside of his skull, unable to fully comprehend what his senses were telling him. The impact felt like an explosion and Lee recalled thinking, *I'm gonna die because of this.*

Then things were fuzzy.

Even nonexistent.

He felt hands on him.

Infected… No… He could hear someone yelling.

"…somewhere between you and Smithfield!" It was Tomlin's voice. "Just get a fucking truck on the road and I'll try to guide you in!"

Another voice, much closer. "I got you, man."

Lee could tell his body was flopping around, but it felt very numb. Almost insensate.

Oh my God, I'm paralyzed.

Lee felt the ground moving beneath him. Peripherally, he felt his heels dragging. He looked up and saw Nate's face, straining as he pulled him out of the darkness. Lee looked back to his feet. They looked normal. He'd half-expected them to be all mangled up and twisted. They were just now exiting what was left of the helicopter's cabin.

Lee felt his lungs suddenly burning. He tried to intake a breath, but it didn't want to go. He coughed out instead. His ribs erupted in fire. Felt like they were cracking and recracking every time that he tried to breathe.

Tomlin was suddenly there, hovering over him. "Breathe. There you go. You're just jammed up, that's all. Take a second and breathe."

Lee tried again, felt a little more air get past his shocked diaphragm. He grimaced around the pain in his side, then coughed again, which only made it worse. He managed a few words: "Others? The others?"

Tomlin just shook his head. "I need you to get up, buddy. Please tell me your shit's still working, because we just made a fuck of a loud boom and there's a lot more things in this woods than you really want to think about. Please tell me those legs are still working."

Lee felt his vision crossing. He blinked rapidly to clear it. "Naw...I...just...concussion."

"You can live with a concussion. But I need you on your feet!"

Lee's awareness was gradually expanding. Past his feet, about ten yards, the helicopter was a mess of disjointed parts. Flames and gouts of smoke were issuing out of the cabin. Lee could hear the sound of the engine ticking loudly, still groaning, though nothing seemed to be moving. A heavy booming in the background and then the feeling of the earth shaking underneath him.

Artillery, that's the artillery. They're still going.

Lee managed to rise up onto his elbows, drawing in breaths, and each breath a little more steady than the last. "I'm good," he said. "I'm good. I got it. Where the fuck are we?"

"No fucking idea," Tomlin said, heaving Lee up so that he was in a sitting position. "C'mon, buddy, let's get you to your feet."

Nate and Tomlin pulled Lee to his feet. For a second they felt awkward and ungainly, but the moment passed quickly and the feeling started to return to his limbs. And it wasn't good. They hurt like a motherfucker. Not broken. But banged the hell up, that was for sure. And being upright put more strain on his side, and the pain compounded there.

"Are they dead?" Lee pointed to the helicopter.

"Left side of the helicopter didn't do well," Tomlin said.

The guns in the distance continued to boom. The earth kept shaking. Somewhere in the darkness beyond them, something howled and screeched.

"Okay," Lee said, forcing some feeling back into his fingers—at least enough to grip his rifle. "Do we know which way is south?"

Tomlin pointed in the general direction that the helicopter seemed to be pointing in. "My guess would be somewhere in that direction."

Something crashed through the brush, very near to them.

"Let's go." Lee turned in the direction that they'd determined to be south and started his unwieldy legs running.

* * *

LaRouche staggered into the clearing where they'd staged their vehicles. The wound in his side would not stop bleeding. The pain kept needling through him with every step. He pressed through the trees and suddenly found himself there, under the sign of an old gas station that had long since been abandoned, probably even before the collapse. They'd parked their collection of trucks and vans and Chalmers's camper behind the boarded-up business.

About a dozen of the men from the assault had made it back to the staging area. LaRouche was sure that there were more, but whether they were turned around back in the woods or deliberately avoiding the staging area, LaRouche did not know. Perhaps they were unsure of how Chalmers would react to this catastrophic failure. Perhaps they had deserted.

LaRouche stood there, just out of the woods for a moment, trying to catch his breath, but never quite able to. The dozen men in the staging area had not noticed him yet. They looked nervous and twitchy. A group of them was arguing outside of Chalmers's camper, all puffed chests and rapid gesticulations. The camper was dark, but LaRouche thought he could hear yelling coming from inside, and the camper was rocking back and forth violently.

The other men inside the staging area were spread out in a few pairs, but their attention was on the camper.

LaRouche scanned the area and found the

flatbed truck with the wooden cage in the back, the huddled forms of women under blankets, trying to stay warm. Then he looked back at the camper. Scanned back and forth, wondering what he should do, wondering what was best, what was the right thing to do. Finally, he lurched into motion again and cut around the outside of the staging area, the woods to his left and the vehicles to his right.

He made his way to the passenger's side of the flatbed truck. He opened the door and peered inside, looking for the keys. In the back, a few of the women stirred, but no one made a noise. LaRouche held a breath and grimaced against the pain. He climbed up into the cab of the truck. His clumsy, bloody hands ripped through the dash-board and center console. He couldn't find the keys.

Exhausted, he leaned against the seat and looked out the driver-side window. Still, no one had noticed that he was there. The dome lights of the truck were turned off, so opening the door had not lit them up. He was sitting there in shadows.

He closed his eyes and when he opened them he had a moment of fear, thinking that he'd fallen asleep. But when he looked back out, all the men in the staging area were in the same spots they'd been. He didn't think much time had passed, if any at all.

He craned his neck, looking through the back glass into the wooden cage on the flatbed.

A single face was staring back at him. Pale skin and wide, green eyes, sharp and bright even in the darkness. She watched him intensely, but didn't move.

LaRouche shoved himself out of the cab and stumbled to the back. She watched him as he rested an elbow against the wooden side of the cage, the pistol dangling from his hand, the other hand still holding his side.

"Where are the keys?" he rasped.

"What are you doing?" she whispered at him.

LaRouche raised the pistol in a warning fashion. "Just tell me where the fucking keys are."

Her gaze narrowed for a brief moment. But then she turned and looked over her shoulder. "Dolf, or whatever the fuck his name is. They call him that. The big blond guy over there."

LaRouche peered through the gap between the cage and the cab of the truck. He could see the man that she was talking about. He was maybe six foot six. Pale with almost white-blond hair. Very Nordic features.

LaRouche grunted in acknowledgment then thrust himself off the cage. "Just shut up. Don't say anything else."

He was aware of his loss of motor skills. His feet felt clumsy. His legs were rubbery. His arms like a straw man's—sleeves just stuffed with nothingness. But like a drunken man, he didn't really register how bad it was. Didn't want to admit the truth to himself, though the thought was circling his head in the background. The cawing of a bird frightened from its nest: *You're dying. You're dying. You're dying…*

He walked around the front of the flatbed truck

and straight for the man she called Dolf. He was standing with another man, away from all the others. Dolf seemed fidgety, like he was nervous about what was going on inside the camper—Chalmers's wrath, no doubt—and fearing that he would be next.

LaRouche made it to within a few yards of him before his scuffing feet drew Dolf's attention. Dolf jerked back, but then seemed to recognize who was standing there. He frowned. "Crazy LaRouche? I thought you were dead."

"Not yet," LaRouche said. "You got the keys to the truck?"

Dolf was confused, his eyes tracking down to LaRouche's lower body and the caking of blood that coated it. But even as his mouth worked for an answer, he held up a pair of keys. "Yeah," he said. "I got them right here."

The fear that everyone had of him, of the incredible violence that Crazy LaRouche had displayed, was obviously still potent, no matter how wounded and near to death he appeared. Because he just reached out and grabbed the keys from Dolf, and the big man said nothing.

LaRouche gripped the keys in bloody fingers and turned away, thinking, *Just let me go, motherfucker. Just let me go.*

He made it about five paces back toward the truck before he heard Dolf call out, "Hey, what the hell are you doin', man?"

LaRouche ignored him. Kept walking.

Rapid footsteps behind him. "Hey, you're in no shape..."

LaRouche spun around. Extended the pistol right into Dolf's face. The body stopped aggressing; the eyes went wide. But LaRouche was not here to take prisoners. So he pulled the trigger and Dolf's face disappeared and his body crumpled to the ground.

LaRouche turned away from Dolf and tried to quicken his pace to the flatbed truck. But instead of running, he was just hobbling along. Someone behind him shouted, but he wasn't sure who they were shouting at. Maybe they were just shouting. He tried to figure his chances, but that type of math was beyond him now.

I gotta do this. I have to. This is the reason I'm here. This is why I stuck around.

Do something good, LaRouche. Do something right for once in your goddamn life!

He hauled himself up into the driver's seat of the flatbed truck. He forced himself to focus on manipulating the keys, aware of how numb his fingers were, aware of how the adrenaline in his bloodstream might make him fumble. He very deliberately took the ignition key and slammed it in. Then he cranked the engine to life.

Somewhere outside a voice called his name: "LaRouche, you sonofabitch, what the hell are you doing?"

He looked up. Bleary-eyed. Swaying, even in his seat. Feeling hot and cold on his head and the sensation that he might pass out at any moment. The only reason he was still conscious was pure force of will. *I have to do this. I have to do one good thing.*

Outside, Deacon Chalmers was standing there. His fists were balled at his sides, his face a mask of rage and partial confusion. But the men standing with him were confused, too. And their rifles were readied, but not aimed at LaRouche. They didn't know what was happening.

"You'll figure it out," LaRouche mumbled to himself and yanked the shifter into drive.

The man that had been standing with Dolf seemed to be the only one that knew what LaRouche was doing. He'd been the only one to see LaRouche kill Dolf, and he jumped in front of the flatbed truck and raised his rifle, shouting words that LaRouche couldn't understand.

LaRouche ducked down so his body was behind the engine block and slammed on the gas.

The engine roared. He heard the sound of gunshots, felt the bullets striking the truck. The windshield spidered around three holes, but he just kept lying down behind the engine block and kept the gas pedal pressed to the floor. He felt something big striking the front of the truck, then the whole thing lurched as the tires rolled over it. They clipped the side of one of the other vehicles, but they kept moving.

LaRouche used the steering wheel to jerk himself back upright, despite the incredible pain in his side. He made it up just in time to steer left before the truck flew across the road and into the trees on the opposite side. He barely missed the dark gas station sign, though it took one of the sideview mirrors off. The truck skidded nastily and leaned heavily to the right as it cut the sharp left turn, and he thought it was going to roll. But then it was pointed down the road and LaRouche righted the steering wheel.

He felt the truck fishtail in the backend. The women were screaming in terror and surprise, but when he looked into the rearview mirror, he could see Claire was there, determinedly holding on to the wooden bars of her cage. Her mouth was set, eyes squinted almost closed.

LaRouche spared a glance behind them to see if he had pursuit. He could see the dark shapes of men running out into the roadway, but they weren't shooting, and he didn't see any vehicles. Then the road turned and he could no longer see them.

He drove on for another five minutes and came out to Highway 701. He stopped at the intersection and felt the light-headedness washing over him. He tried to focus on the task at hand. He could not continue to drive the vehicle. He was almost done. He felt it coming over him like a warm blanket. That was the shock, he knew, and it flooded his veins with chemicals that told him everything was going to be okay. But he knew it wasn't. And that was the icy undertone to everything.

You're dying. You're dying and you know it.

Still stopped, he threw the truck in park. Shoved open the door and slid out of his seat. His legs were barely capable of carrying his weight. He almost collapsed when his feet hit the ground but he managed to hold himself up long enough to lock his knees.

You have to do this. Get it done.

You gotta do it quickly. No time for a pity party.

Claire was yelling something at him, but he wasn't paying attention. He hobbled along the wooden cage to the back where that little gate was positioned. Padlocked. He stared at the lock for a second or two, trying to think of what to do. Shooting the padlock was a bad idea; he knew that much. It wasn't as effective as your average movie watcher was led to believe.

"The keys!" Claire was yelling at him. "The keys are on the keychain! Are you listening to me?"

"What?" He looked up at her, squinting like he was looking into a spotlight.

She pointed to the cab of the truck. "The keys to the padlock are on the same ring as the truck keys!"

"Oh. Fuck." LaRouche growled and hitched himself back to the cab of the truck. He had to stop when he got there to take a breath. Try to get some blood circulating into his head.

Blood pressure's dropping.

He turned the truck off and snatched the keys out of the ignition. Then he went back to the padlocked gate. Claire was there, hand extended through the wooden bars.

"Here," she said, grasping at the air. "Let me do it. Just let me do it."

LaRouche handed the keys to her, almost dropping them in the process.

Claire snatched the keys. Quicker than LaRouche ever could have done it himself, she had them in and the padlock disengaged. She plucked it off and dropped it. The lock clattered onto the concrete. She shoved the door open and jumped off the bed of the truck.

"Okay, let's go," she said, pointing for the truck bed.

"Wait..."

"They're gonna come after us!" she said insistently. "Let's go!"

"Listen to me!" It took a lot of energy to raise his voice. But at least she stopped talking and looked at him. He pointed to the highway in front of them. "Listen carefully. This is Highway 701. You need to make a right. Go north. Just keep going north until you hit Highway 301. Take it south. Or it might be west. Can't remember. South or west. Take it to Highway 27. Go west on 27 toward Coats. You're looking for Camp Ryder. Do you know Camp Ryder? They'll be right there at Highway 27 and Highway 55. Right in that area. It might take some looking. But if you don't find them, they might find you."

Claire was shaking her head in confusion. "Just come with me! Show me how to get there!"

LaRouche shook his head. "I can't go back there. It's on you. I'll keep 'em off of you guys."

"Are you...?" Claire shook her head. "Fine! Fine! Okay. Highway 701 to Highway 301. Take that south or west. To what?"

"Highway 27, west toward Coats. You're looking for Camp Ryder. Around 27 and 55."

"Okay. I got it."

"Then go," he said, pointing to the cab with his pistol. "Get the fuck out of here."

And she went. One moment she was standing there with LaRouche, light from the headlights and taillights illuminating the night, and then she was gone. LaRouche blinked and wondered if he'd hallucinated the whole thing, but he could still smell the diesel exhaust. He must've just blanked out for a moment. He wondered if she'd said good-bye to him, or thanked him.

He supposed it didn't matter anyhow.

LaRouche was alone on the dark roadway. He stood on the concrete, forcing his mind to stay awake, his body to stay operational.

He heard the sound of an engine growling through the night. He turned himself to face the noise. A twinkling of light as a vehicle raced down the highway, the headlights shining off trees and old road signs. LaRouche took one big breath and held it. He could still feel his heart beating, so that was good. He spread his feet so he wouldn't wobble so much. Took his left hand off of his side and used it to support his gun hand. He waited.

The pickup truck came around the corner. He registered the shape of men in the bed of the truck. It was traveling quickly. It straightened out, heading right for LaRouche. Whether or not they saw him was a moot point. If they did, they weren't stopping. Maybe they intended to run him over.

As it bore down on him, he lifted his pistol, aiming just above the driver's side headlight, and he fired three times. Windshields were notoriously bad for the trajectory of bullets, and he wasn't sure whether he actually hit the driver or not, but the truck swerved and lost control, the back end coming around in a spin, the tires screaming.

LaRouche thrust himself to the side, the tailgate of the truck missing him by inches. He saw men in the bed of the truck, trying to hold on for their lives. The truck made a complete one-eighty and then slammed down into the ditch. The men in the back were flung out of the bed, and LaRouche could hear their bodies crashing violently through the trees.

He stood there for a moment. Shocked that he was still standing.

He raised the pistol again, pointing at the passenger side. He knew damn well who it was that was coming after him. And he wouldn't be in the bed of the truck with the common soldiers. He'd be in the cab, pulling the strings, probably yelling and flying into one of his rages.

"Chalmers!" LaRouche tried to yell, but it just came out a wheeze.

Through the passenger-side window, LaRouche registered panicked movement. A gun went off from inside. LaRouche watched the rounds burst out of the door, one after the other. He felt the first zip by his head, but the next found its mark, low in his body, punching into his lower abdomen, and then another found him in the chest, just to the left of his heart, and dead on into his lung.

But LaRouche kept coming, and the rest of the rounds went wide.

He wanted to stop. The pain was incredible.

He could feel things wrong inside of him, wrong in ways that were frightening, panic-inducing, because he knew that they could not be fixed. They were broken. They were in shambles. He could taste blood in the back of his mouth, feel his stomach muscles spasm as his innards leaked and ruptured.

But there was a certain clarity to it as well. The pain solidified him, sharp and poignant. It brought his fading mind back. He forced himself on, because time was short, and his enemy was out of ammunition, and he would not die at the feet of Chalmers. He refused.

He ripped open the door.

The dome light came on.

Chalmers was crumpled, half in the passenger seat, and half on top of the center console. The driver was dead or unconscious, his head bashed against a broken window. Chalmers's eyes were wide with the fear of a hunted animal. He was trying to reload a pistol but couldn't quite seat the magazine. He screamed when LaRouche opened the door, a high-pitched, cowardly sound.

LaRouche pushed his pistol into Chalmers's gut. "We're gonna go together," he said, then pulled the trigger three times in rapid succession. As the third bullet ruptured through Chalmers's midsection, the man cried out and flailed, striking the pistol out of LaRouche's hand.

Then Chalmers had no breath left in him. He clawed at LaRouche and tried to suck in air, but only made gurgling noises. He dropped his own pistol from clumsy, unwieldy hands and clutched his guts as blood started pouring out of the holes in his stomach. He writhed and somehow managed to slide out of the cab of the pickup truck.

LaRouche turned unsteadily to follow, and then lost his legs. They buckled under him and he slid down into a sitting position, back against the side of the truck. He tried to breathe but his lungs rattled when he inhaled. When he exhaled, blood came out of his mouth.

Chalmers stood there, a few yards from the truck, his feet moving around, like he wanted to run but wasn't able to pick them up enough. He was staring down at his wounds, his mouth gaping. "You...you..." Chalmers croaked.

LaRouche spat blood. Felt it dribble over his chin and onto his chest.

Chalmers tried to take a step backward away from LaRouche, but lost his balance and went down to his knees.

Now they were at eye level with each other.

LaRouche held his gaze. "I'm not goin' without you," he said.

"I dunno..." Chalmers winced and doubled over. "I dunno why you did this."

"Just die," LaRouche said. "So I know that I killed you."

"I can't..." Chalmers was shaking his head, and then his whole body was shaking. His eyes rolled up, showing the whites, and he toppled to the ground, heaving for air that would do him no good. His body rolled and hitched. Fingers scratching in the dirt. Legs working like a dog in a fever dream. His voice came out in breathy grunts, no longer able to say words.

LaRouche held on, watching and waiting.

Just a little longer. The pain's not so bad now. But that's probably not a good thing.

Just a little longer . . .

TWENTY-FIVE

BEFORE THE DAWN

THEY RAN STRAIGHT DOWN a two-lane road. They ran to the sound of booming guns. Explosions in the distance, flickering just out of sight like a far-off lightning storm on the horizon. Lee could hear the rounds whistling overhead as they rocketed toward their points of impact. The darkness surrounded them, and the night was alive with sounds.

Not just from the sky, but from the woods. The hooting and screeching of their pursuers. Behind them as well. When Lee glanced behind him, he could sometimes see the dark shapes coming out of the woods, one or two at a time.

Lee could barely breathe. His lungs burned for oxygen. His ribs screamed in pain every time he had to inhale. But it was either run or die. And running required breathing. The pain was bad, but Lee just kept thinking about fingers ripping into him, teeth tearing him apart, feeding on him while he was still alive. He couldn't stop. No matter how bad the pain was, he couldn't stop.

You're almost there, he kept telling himself. *You've run the race. You're almost done. Don't stop now.*

Tomlin had the radio handset up to his head again as they came up to an intersection. He was yelling, hoarse and out of breath. "It's...it's State Road One-Zero-Zero-Nine. I keep seeing that number on a sign. That's got to be what it is. I think we're going south. Where the fuck are you guys?"

Lee couldn't hear the response on the radio. He turned to look behind them. A shape was scuttling out of the woods and onto the roadway. Lee's chest was heaving so hard, the blood pumping so swiftly through him, he could barely stabilize the rifle long enough to take the shot. He fired three rounds and wasn't sure he hit it. He turned and started running again.

Screeches and howls. They sounded close.

His legs burned. Ached. His feet stung like pins and needles for some reason. Every muscle in his body was cramping, seizing up, and he was painfully aware of how long it had been since he'd drunk any water. His mouth felt like paper.

Don't give up now.

The only easy day was yesterday.

Keep those feet moving. Keep 'em moving.

"Devils..." Tomlin gasped for air, still running. "I dunno. Devils Racetrack something. That's the road name, I think. I don't fucking know!"

Lee's world was shrinking. His heart rate had reached the point where his vision was becoming spotty. His peripheral vision was almost completely gone. He had to turn his head to see Nate, lagging to Lee's left, and slightly behind.

"C'mon." Lee reached out a hand and grabbed Nate by the shoulder. He barely had strength enough for himself. But he wasn't going to let Nate fall behind. Not on top of everything else. *No one else, please, God, no one else!*

Straight ahead, Lee spotted shadows.

Tomlin must have seen them as well. He popped his rifle up quickly, firing on the run. Lee didn't know where his rounds went. Tomlin had to slow almost to a walk, and he fired five more rounds before they saw one of the shadows falter and hit the ground. They were close enough then that Lee could see it was two males, younger, stripped naked and looking like nothing but skin and bones.

The one twisted in circles on the ground, spraying blood.

The other kept coming. Lee and Tomlin concentrated their fire and put it down.

They didn't stop. Just ran right past the bodies while they were still moving.

Lee realized his rifle was empty. He ejected the magazine and simply let it drop to the pavement. Chalk it up to a loss. He grabbed the only magazine left in his pouch and slammed it home with more effort than he wanted to admit, then sent the bolt forward.

"Last mag," he huffed.

Neither Tomlin nor Nate responded. They were too busy running. Too busy trying to keep moving. Lee had let go of Nate to fire his rifle and reload it. He checked to his left again and saw that Nate was there, still pushing.

"They're comin'," Tomlin gasped as he ran. "They're comin'."

Headlights bloomed over the roadway, far ahead of them.

"That's them!" Tomlin called out when he saw the lights. "We're almost there!"

Nate let out a cry of pain and determination.

Lee just put his head down and ran.

Get it in. Do the work. You're almost there. It's almost over.

The relief he felt at the sight of the headlights was almost giddy. There was the usual part of him—the negative part, the one that claimed "realist" when in fact it was very much "pessimist"—that told him those headlights were only more enemies, more bad guys, maybe the Followers. But in that moment, Lee needed something to hold on to. Something to give his feet a reason to keep moving. He didn't let himself believe the bad. Just the good.

It's them. You're almost there.

The headlights grew closer and closer, but not fast enough for Lee. Every time he looked up, he thought they would have covered more ground, then he would look back down at his pounding feet, hear the calls of the infected in the woods behind them and all around them, flanking, following, trying to surround them, and when he looked back up at the headlights, he would think the same damn thing: *Fuck, why aren't they closer?*

And then one of those times, the headlights were there, and Lee could hear the roar of the engine over the rushing of his own blood and the heaving of air in and out of his parchment-dry throat. And when he looked up, the headlights turned, angling in the roadway, and Lee saw fire burst out and the deep, bone-jarring sound of the .50-caliber M2 mounted on top, thumping away into the night, the rounds whistling menacingly over their heads. Menacingly, and yet the most beautiful thing he thought he'd ever heard in his life.

It was an LMTV, and as Lee reached the open backend, he grabbed the handholds and might've failed to have the strength to pull himself up, if someone from inside hadn't reached out and grabbed a hold of the straps of his chest rig and hauled him into the bed.

Lee looked up, saw Marine digital camouflage.

He turned back around and reached out a hand, pulling up Tomlin, and then Nate. The M2 drowned out anything anyone could have said, and Nate's boots had barely left the ground before the LMTV was moving again, roaring down the road, the wind buffeting in their ears.

Lee collapsed onto the bed of the LMTV, trying to get air. He felt sick. If he had anything at all in his stomach, he might have ejected it. His throat was so dry and constricted, it felt like it was triggering his gag reflex.

The M2 fell silent, and it was just the wind and the engine, taking them down the night road.

He felt something cool touch his hand.

Lee leaned up partially. It was a canteen that had been placed in his hand. He looked past the canteen and could see the person that had put it there. Julia was sitting on one of the fold-down seats, her wounded leg stretched out straight. She was regarding Lee with a look that was so many things. There was grief, but there was also a great relief, an expression of anticipation.

Lee uncapped the canteen and guzzled water. It was painful at first, but he kept drinking it. When his throat and tongue had moisture on them again, he pulled the canteen away from his lips. "What the hell are you doing here?"

"I wanted to make sure you were okay," she said back.

The Marine that had pulled Lee up into the truck let out a bark of laughter. "Yeah, she wouldn't take no for an answer."

Julia leaned closer toward Lee and put a hand on him, her face tense with a hard sort of expectation. "Did it work? The artillery? Did you see if it worked?"

Lee nodded, then coughed a few times. He managed a wan smile. "It worked, Jules. Better than I thought. You should've fucking seen it. It would've made you smile."

Julia seemed shell-shocked. She leaned back, almost limp. Her face was no longer intense, but lax. But that only lasted for a moment. Then her hand came up and covered her mouth, and Lee could see her eyes clenched as tears started to come out of them. Not tears of happiness or relief. Just sadness. Just the great, gigantic cost of it. The losses that could never be recouped.

She turned her face away from them and she wept loudly.

Lee's own sense of relief was drooping as well, like the wind was scouring it away. But instead of grief, he just felt nothing. What the hell was he supposed to feel? He wasn't sure. He knew he should feel elated. He should feel enraged. He should feel joy and sadness. He'd lost and he'd won. He'd survived and he'd died. In a million different ways, he felt a million different things, and in the whirlwind of them all, he felt absolutely nothing.

He looked to his right and found Tomlin and Nate, both leaning back against the walls of the LMTV, their chests still rising and falling rapidly, while the rest of their bodies seemed like they were trying to be as motionless as possible, their muscles turned to slag. But they looked back at him.

Nate closed his eyes, and tilted his head back.

Tomlin nodded to his friend and partner. *Good job. You did it.*

Lee's eyes fell away from him. *Yeah. Sure.*

He looked back up at Julia. He saw her, and he thought about Harper. He thought about their team, the one that had gone into small cities and towns with packs of claymores and bags of deer guts. The ones that had cleared out the hordes and established the observation points that would keep the Camp Ryder Hub safe. There'd been Julia, of course. And Harper. Father Jim. LaRouche. Wilson. They ate together, slept together, fought together, bled together. That small group, responsible for so many things. And the weight of that responsibility had crushed them down and brought them all closer together.

And of all of those in that original group, who was still alive? Just Lee and Julia.

When he thought about it like that, he felt

incredibly alone. Without Father Jim there to keep him on track. Without LaRouche there to fight tooth and nail over anything that could be fought over. Without Harper there, always with sound advice. Without Wilson there to be everyone's friend and mitigate the frequent disagreements.

Where were they all? Where did they all go?

Swallowed up. Gone forever.

Lee picked himself up, noticing how incredibly cold it was for the first time that night. Feeling the chill of it seeping deep into him. He sat down next to Julia and he put an arm around her and drew her in. "It's just us now, Jules," he told her. "Just you and me."

The night was long and frightening. It dragged on to the sound of thunder in the distance that was so faint, Angela wasn't sure whether she had imagined it or not. Perhaps it was the artillery booming. The sound of victory. Or maybe it was the sound of a million feet, drawing closer. Hordes so large they swallowed the countryside, and consumed everything.

Fort Bragg could scrounge only one bus to transport the men and women of Camp Ryder back to the safety of their gates. Cramming the thing full of people and their belongings, Angela had estimated it was still going to take three trips. And it looked like she was going to be right. The bus had already come and gone twice, with two gun-truck Humvees escorting.

Angela looked out into the murky darkness to the northeast and saw no blush of dawn, no hope of the night ending just yet. She had sent Abby and Sam on with the others, and Deuce had accompanied them. Sam remained quiet after what had happened. His emotions seemed locked down.

Angela had decided to be the last one out of Camp Ryder. Bus's words still worked their way through her brain: *Take it, you have to take it.*

I did the best I could, Bus, she thought. *But now we have to leave it.*

The last group to go was smaller than the previous two. Marie had decided to stay with Angela, along with Old Man Hughes, who sent most of his people from Dunn on before him, except for two men that refused to leave without him. The rest was just a smattering of single men and women with no children, no families. Less than a dozen all together. They milled about eagerly at the gate, eyes constantly looking out, hoping for the glimmer of headlights coming down the gravel drive to Camp Ryder.

It was strange to see the place so desolate. Almost everyone that called the place home had gone, and what was left seemed little more than a trash pile without the warmth of humanity living in it. No fires were burning. There was no sound of people talking or murmuring in the confines of their shanties. It was strange and empty. Like a ghost town.

"I see headlights!" someone called out.

There was that long moment where everyone craned their necks, hoping it was the bus from Fort Bragg, and not some wayward element come to attack them at their weakest possible moment. Less than a dozen of them, standing around laden with everything they owned in the world and only a few rifles and pistols among them.

The trunks of the barren trees to either side of the gravel driveway glinted and glimmered with white light. Two headlights and the sound of a diesel engine roaring down the path. A very familiar sound to Angela now. The sound of a Humvee, which seemed very distinct in her mind.

Only one.

"Something's wrong," she murmured, stepping toward the gate, and then wondering if that was wise.

The Humvee came in quick, then ground to a halt in the gravel, just in front of the reinforced gate. Someone inside hit the horn twice, and it sounded oddly weak despite the heavily armed vehicle it was coming out of. The passenger-side door opened, and in the reflection of the vehicle's own headlights, she could see the passenger.

One of Carl's men.

"Angela!" He waved. "Open the gates!"

Angela pointed to Old Man Hughes's two men that were manning the gates. "Open them."

They grunted and slid the heavy thing out of the way. Angela jogged through, scanning around out of cautious habit, her mind bouncing around in a thousand different directions, wondering what had happened, what had gone wrong. *Something always goes wrong...*

She went to him on the passenger's side of the Humvee. "What's wrong?"

The man was young, and clean cut, which was odd. Most of the men had given up on shaving and cutting their hair. His rank was a black, triangular emblem that Angela knew meant he was a "specialist." His name tag labeled him as *LITTLEJOHN*, but he'd introduced himself as Bryce.

"Nothing, I don't think," he said with a shrug. "Got something up at the top of the road that you might want to see. We're gonna leave this one up to your judgment."

He motioned for her to get in the back and she did, after a brief hesitation and a glance back at Marie and Old Man Hughes. But then she closed the door and the Humvee turned around and roared back down the gravel drive, heading for the roadway beyond.

Specialist Bryce didn't bother telling her what he meant by any of what he'd said. And she didn't ask. She craned her neck around the front passenger's seat to see out the window. The headlights bounced off trees as they took the few small turns in the mostly straight gravel drive, and then she could see the roadway up ahead. The bus, sitting a ways back, and the other Humvee, stopped in the middle of the road, its turret facing another, unfamiliar vehicle.

"Who the hell is that?" Angela demanded.

Bryce shook his head. "No fucking idea. It's a truckload of women."

As they drew closer, Angela could see what he meant. The unfamiliar vehicle was an old flatbed truck, and the bed had been enclosed by a series of two-by-fours and some makeshift carpentry to create a sort of cage. Inside this cage were at least ten women, maybe a few more. They stood at the walls of the cage and their eyes glittered in the light of headlamps and they looked desperate and despairing.

A few of Carl's men were standing in the roadway, their weapons addressed, but not so aggressively that Angela felt there was immediate danger. There was a female stranger standing in the middle of the road, next to the cab of the flatbed pickup truck. Her hands were raised up. The driver-side door of the pickup was hanging open, and Angela intuited that she had been the driver.

Their Humvee stopped just a few yards away from the scene.

Angela and Bryce stepped out and walked up quickly, stopping between Carl's men and the strange woman. Angela put her hand on her pistol's grip and regarded the stranger with a cautious, untrusting eye.

Her initial perception had been one of a *woman*, but this was a girl. Little more than sixteen, maybe seventeen. Her hair was in oily tangles; her face looked unwashed, her clothes worn for too long without washing. But she was not like the women that huddled in the back of the flatbed truck. Though she was plain, her eyes were sharp and measuring and when they fell on Angela, she knew that she was being sized up as well.

"What is this?" Angela demanded, nodding toward the flatbed truck. "Who the hell are you and why do you have a truckload of women in a cage?"

The girl with the sharp eyes kept her hands up and made sure not to move too much or too quickly. "Is this Camp Ryder? I'm looking for Camp Ryder. LaRouche sent me here to find Camp Ryder."

Angela almost choked. She took a few steps forward. "LaRouche? LaRouche sent you?"

"Yes."

"When? How long ago?"

"An hour, maybe?" She looked pained. "I don't know."

Questions rampaged through Angela's brain. It took her a moment to pick and choose the most pertinent ones. "Is LaRouche alive?"

The girl standing in front of her looked unsure. "I don't know. He was . . . he was hurt pretty bad."

"How . . . how the hell?"

"I know LaRouche was from here. From Camp Ryder. But he was captured by the Followers. That's where we came from. The Followers. We were all prisoners. LaRouche worked with them. But I don't think that he wanted to. Because . . . because he came back for us. He got us away from the others and told us where to go. Told us to come here. To Camp Ryder."

"The Followers?" The facts were like an unsolved jigsaw puzzle scattered about. She tried to put them in logical order. "You came from the Followers?"

The girl looked frustrated. "Look, there's a lot to explain. I'm sorry. I know. But we just got away." Tears sprang up in her eyes and she looked behind her. "I don't know whether they're still coming after us or not. LaRouche stayed behind to try to stop them, but I don't know if they killed him or not. It was Deacon Chalmers and a few others. I think most of them died attacking the Marines, but...but...do you know the Marines? Do you know them?"

"What?" Angela rubbed the side of her head. "I...uh...yes. We know some of them."

The girl's hands dropped and reached out. She took a hopeful step toward Angela, her voice straining and for the first time, those sharp green eyes breaking down a little bit. "Do you know John Staley? Colonel John Staley?"

Angela's mouth worked for a moment as she wondered whether she should answer that question. But the words came out after a moment of indecision. The girl standing in front of her just seemed so suddenly desperate, and her need to have an answer to that question was palpable and genuine.

"Yes. I've met him."

The girl started to shake. Her face twisted up in some mix of relief and horror, like coming out of a long, long nightmare. "I'm Claire Staley," she choked out suddenly. "Colonel Staley's daughter."

The next hours of Lee's life passed by in a fog. When the adrenaline waned, when his heart was no longer pumping at its maximum capacity, the exhaustion took hold of him hard. He operated in a daze and later would only remember bits and pieces of it in a disjointed fashion, rather than in a continuous time line. In the darkness, with his mind split in a million directions and his body beaten down, time stretched and contracted in an odd, dreamlike fashion.

They were taken back to the Marine encampment. Smoke hung over the entire clearing. The guns belched fire into the sky, time after time; endlessly they went on. The smell of the guns permeated him, the sound of them, the feel of their impacts. The booming guns hijacked all of his senses.

Sometime around dawn, the last gun crew fired their last round. It rocketed out into the night and somewhere far in the distance splashed down inside of Smithfield, inside of the mile radius surrounding the Johnston Memorial Hospital. As the sky turned to gray all around them, Lee could look northeast and pinpoint where Smithfield was by the black smudge on the horizon. What had once been an American town, now reduced to smoking rubble.

The silence felt strange and empty. His ears rang. His body ached.

He wanted to feel some measure of triumph, some sort of victory. But he was overwhelmed. Shorted out. Everything inside him felt like static. No signal. Empty.

He stood out of the way of the Marine crews as they worked to hook the artillery pieces to the trucks that would tow them. The Marines were dirty and bedraggled, their faces and hands filthy with grime and dirt and carbon scoring. They looked about as exhausted as Lee felt.

Carl appeared next to him, or perhaps he'd been standing there. Lee felt out of touch with himself.

He glanced in Carl's direction, swayed a little on his feet, and shifted his weight to cover it up. "Sorry about your helicopter," Lee said quietly.

Carl's lips were a flat gash across his face. "I don't give a fuck about the chopper. Dale was a good pilot."

Lee nodded. Had nothing to say. There were words that floated around in his head, but he was so discombobulated, he feared that they only sounded good there, and if he dared to say them they would come out sounding completely different. It was best to stay quiet.

"Brinly's agreed to take a stop off at Fort Bragg," Carl said, his tone clearly saying that he was changing the subject. "I figured I could afford to give the Marines some fuel for their birds. Not like we need it so bad anymore. Plus we need a ride back to Bragg."

Lee just nodded again.

Carl regarded him. "You okay?"

Lee raised his eyebrows. "Am I okay?" His mouth hung open for a moment. "Fuck if I know. I'm just taking it one minute at a time. I'm here. But I don't feel like I'm here."

"You sound dead on your feet."

"Yeah."

Tomlin, Nate, Julia, and Lee were all shoved into the same vehicle. They sat side by side on the bench seat in the back of an LMTV, along with a half-dozen Marines. No one talked. Everyone was too damn tired. This LMTV was covered, though, so the wind didn't get them as bad. They had a little room to spread out, but they stayed together because it was warmer. Julia was next to him, and Lee clasped her hand in his. He didn't think twice about it, simply wanting to comfort her and take some comfort himself from the presence of human contact.

He was too tired to stay awake, and too keyed up to sleep.

So he just closed his eyes and drifted.

TWENTY-SIX

MILES

LEE AWOKE ON A cot. Cold wetness on his hand.

He was disoriented. He didn't know where he was, or why he was there. He leaned partially up off the cot and saw that he was in a crowded barracks room, and the first place his mind went was basic training. But the other people in the barracks room were not soldiers or recruits. They were men and women and children, jumbled in together. Some of them slept, and some of them were walking around.

Homeless camp, he thought to himself. *I'm in a homeless camp.*

For a second, the disorientation caused a little spark of fear. He pulled himself into a sitting position and swung his legs off the cot. It was only when he turned that he realized he was not alone. The brown-and-tan dog that he had named Deuce was huddled next to the cot, looking up at him with his curious golden eyes, his tail slapping the ground.

Tomlin was seated in a chair next to Lee's cot, slouched over and asleep.

The disorientation evaporated. He remembered

where he was. He remembered arriving at Fort Bragg. The massive, organized confusion of it. Carl's men had sent a giant bus for Angela and Camp Ryder, and by the time that Lee and the Marines pulled into the center of Fort Bragg, they were still trying to get the people from Camp Ryder settled into some barracks.

Which was where he was.

He rubbed Deuce's head, earning himself an even harder tail wagging. Lee smiled down at the animal. "Hey, buddy. I'm glad you're here." The dog hung its tongue out and laid its head against Lee's leg, seeming relieved that Lee was finally awake. Lee turned his attention to the man sleeping across from him.

He reached out and touched Tomlin's knee. "Brian."

Tomlin sniffed and jerked, then woke up, blinking rapidly. "Shit. I need a full eight hours."

Lee rubbed his face. "I think we need a full twenty-four. How long have I been asleep?"

Tomlin looked toward a window. Beyond, the sunlight was bright and golden. An early sun. "Not that long. It's still morning."

The medics from Fort Bragg had been triaging the injured as they came in. Lee recalled them pulling him off to the side and doing a quick patch job on the lacerations on his face and wrapping his broken ribs tightly. Unfortunately, there wasn't much else that could be done with broken ribs.

Just remembering them brought the pain back and he winced.

"Yeah." Tomlin smirked. "Three broken ribs. How's that feel?"

"Don't remind me."

Tomlin rubbed the sleep out of his eyes. "Carl's sending fuel back with the Marines. When they can get some birds in the air, they're gonna do a visual recon of the Smithfield area. See how bad the damage is. See if any of the horde survived."

Lee nodded. He felt the burgeoning of something. Hope? Relief? Maybe. But his mind wouldn't let him believe that it was over. How could it be over? It was never over. "I'm sure some of them survived." He met Tomlin's eyes. "I know you saw them. But you should have seen them from our perspective. Flying over with the thermal imaging. Damn. There were a lot of them. I think that artillery made Smithfield dust. But I wouldn't be surprised if a decent amount of them managed to get away. Scatter out into the countryside."

Tomlin leaned forward and put a hand gently on Lee's shoulders. "Hey. You did good. You did fucking great. I'm sure a few of them got away. But we knew there was gonna be cleanup. And they won't be in the millions anymore. There'll be pockets of them. And we can deal with that. We'll hunt 'em down. Do whatever needs to be done. Carl's a part of this now, and I don't think he has any intention of kicking us out on our asses. He's already talking about using Fort Bragg as a central staging area to reclaim the rest of North Carolina. I think he recognizes that we're in this together."

"Maybe. We'll see." Lee looked around them. Most of the people in the barracks were Camp Ryder folks. When they saw him looking, they nodded to him. But they steered clear and left him alone. Which he supposed was best.

"I talked with Carl about what happened with Kensey and the Marines. And Tyler."

"Oh." Lee felt his stomach sink, steadily, like a boat hull filling with water.

"Hey, you did what you had to do," Tomlin said earnestly. He shook his head. "Man, I can't believe that shit. Briggs..."

"Yeah." Lee looked down at his feet. He hadn't bothered to take off his boots before lying down for his hour or two of rack-out. "I don't...fuck, I don't know."

"It's gonna be a goddamn cluster," Tomlin said quietly. "But Carl's always been against Briggs. We've got his backing one hundred percent. And I think what's gone down over the course of the last few days has solidified Colonel Staley and First Sergeant Brinly. I think they're with us." Tomlin brightened. "Which, by the way, you didn't hear, but Angela found Staley's daughter."

"What?"

"Yeah. Her and a truckload of the women that were being held captive by the Followers. They managed to escape and ran into Angela as they were leaving Camp Ryder. Almost got shot up by the escort, but Angela told them to hold their fire. Good thing, too." Tomlin's face darkened. "What those fuckers did..."

"Any word on them?"

Tomlin shook his head. "I haven't talked to her. Or any of the women. Most of them are in bad shape. A few malnourished. All of them dehydrated. Stuck in the back of a fucking cage. Like animals." Tomlin's jaw clenched. "If any of those fuckers are still rolling around..."

"We'll find them," Lee said. "Just like we'll find the rest of the infected."

Tomlin nodded.

Lee thought of something else. "Brian, have you heard anything about Abe?"

Tomlin's face grew serious. "I, uh...I'll show you where he is."

They found Abe Darabie recovering in the same field hospital as the injured Marines and Rudy, who'd caught a round that almost killed him and suffered through the night. Just as Lee and Tomlin gained access to the hospital, they were settling an unconscious Rudy back into the room after emergency surgery. The medics looked exhausted. The patients looked terrible.

The doorway into the room was guarded, but the soldier standing watch either knew who Lee and Tomlin were, or he didn't care that they were coming into the room. He let them pass with nothing but a solemn nod.

A few feet into the room and Lee choked on the smell of it. The smell of sickness and injury, lurking beneath heavy antiseptic. He hated that smell. It made the hairs on the back of his neck stand up. He'd never had a problem with hospitals in his life, but seeing beds filled with men close to death and in pain . . . that was never a pleasant thing to behold in any of your senses.

Lee could see Abe. He was lying down in the far corner of the room, asleep, apparently. Or maybe just resting. His hair was wild and greasy; his jet-black beard was matted and wiry and out-of-control. From the way the sheets were draped over him, Lee could tell there was very little left to him.

Tomlin spoke quietly. "I asked the medic about him when they were triaging everybody coming in. They knew who he was. He's the only reason the guard is here. They got him locked down to that gurney he's on. But he's fucked up, the doc said. Said they had to go in and take the bullet out and he nearly died of blood loss."

Tomlin cleared his throat. "Apparently the doc had to beg for blood. Nobody wanted him to use their supply on Abe. Doc managed to get him two units of blood and kept him from dying. Got the bullet out. He's been awake, they say, but on and off. He's still real weak."

He was only trying to escape, Lee thought. *Just like any of us would have done.*

But he kept it to himself. He was not surrounded by sympathetic ears.

He looked at Tomlin. "You coming?"

Tomlin shook his head. "Nah. I'm . . . I'm a little mixed up about all this."

Lee reached out, wincing at the pain in his ribs, and gave Tomlin a squeeze on the shoulder. "All right, buddy. I'll get up with you. We're gonna be busy over the next few weeks."

"Yeah. I'm gonna grab some sleep." Then Tomlin left.

Lee looked at Abe and walked slowly to the bed that he lay on. He stood there at the foot of it for a time and he watched Abe's eyes flickering underneath his eyelids, the heavy, rattling breaths. But they were steady and even. The sound of deep sleep.

Lee went to the side of the bed. There was a bucket upended at the bed. Lee didn't know whether it was a makeshift stool or not, but that's what it would be for him. He sat on it and looked at his old friend, resting one arm on the sheets beside Abe, wondering if he should wake him or just let him rest. He wondered if he truly had anything worth talking about, or if he just wanted Abe to be awake so that he would know he was okay.

His frazzled mind was working through things. Processing them little bit by little bit. He didn't yet have a full comprehension, but still there came flashes of clarity. The magnitude of what had been done. The horrible odds of the gamble that Lee had made, anteing up with other people's lives. But what he'd done, what he'd accomplished... couldn't he be proud of that? Or had the cost been too great?

His mind swirled, capturing glimpses of emotions and trying to knit the whole thing into some massive patchwork. All the shock and the grief and the overwhelming relief, the loss of friends and the realization that he'd saved his people and countless others from complete annihilation, the rage and the resentment, the feelings of betrayal, the hard coldness of revenge, righteous anger, justice, and guilt for his own sins—they were all scattered parts, put together into some great, unfathomable thing. Like the blind man at the elephant, he could not realize it in its entirety, but could only sense the parts.

He found himself short of breath and realized that his chest ached and his throat was tight.

You're done. You did it. You finished the race.

So why did it feel like he had miles and miles left to go?

He felt cold, dry fingers touch his.

He looked up and saw Abe, his eyes watery and only half-conscious.

Lee took the other man's hand and held on to it, like it was keeping him from slipping off of the edge of the world and falling into oblivion. Abe's lips were parched and cracked and peeled, but they smiled the slightest hint of a smile, one that was born with such exhaustion, but through that exhaustion it was genuine.

Abe spoke and his voice was a dry whisper. "Hey, brother."

Lee clutched his friend's hand with both of his, then he lowered his head and wept.

Sam stood in the barracks, beside the cot where Abby was lying, passed out in an almost unwakeable sleep. He watched her for a time, staring at her and seeing many other things. But always he would blink and she would be there, and she seemed peaceful.

He could not sit. Not here in this strange place,

no matter how many faces around him were familiar. He kept standing, and he clutched his little rifle. The small caliber. The tiny little bullets, of which he had only thirty more. The tiny bullets that could do so much. And had.

He looked away from Abby and cast his gaze, young and hollow, over the people he knew. The survivors from Camp Ryder. Somehow family, and somehow complete strangers to him. He found himself looking for the kids from the camp that had pushed him away, the ones that didn't want to talk to him because they could see the weirdness in him. But he didn't see any of them in this barracks. He wished they were there, though he didn't know why.

He started at the sound of the barracks door swinging open.

A man came through the door. Tall. Balding head. He looked dirty all over, but his face. His face looked like he had washed it. He had a trimmed beard and eyes that scanned and analyzed, collecting data, it seemed. Judging everyone. But not in an unkind way. Like he was making a tally. Counting numbers in his head.

Sam shifted, slightly, so he was facing the man.

The man with the analyzing eyes stopped by and spoke quietly to a pair of younger guys that Sam knew from camp. He could not tell what they said. The man spoke, and the young men listened. Then they nodded. Shook hands.

Sam watched the man continue through the barracks, speaking to people. The young men. The young women. The able-bodied of them. The only common thread that Sam could see among them was that they did not have children with them. They did not appear to be families.

Sam watched him until he had made his way around the entire room, had talked to seven different people, and finally came to stop at the foot of Abby's bed.

The man looked at Sam, held his gaze for a long time. More numbers rolling behind his eyes. Then he looked down at Abby, who still slept. He looked at her and something else went on in his head besides the analyzing. Then he blinked rapidly and looked back at Sam. Up and down. Fixed on the rifle.

"Small rifle," the man observed.

Sam looked at it. "It works."

A faltering smile flashed over the man's mouth, then it was back to straight. He nodded toward the sleeping form on the bed. "You know her?"

Sam considered. "My sister."

He, dark-skinned and Middle Eastern. She, pale and blond.

"Hmm," the man said. "Parents here?"

"Her mother."

"You?"

Sam shook his head slowly.

The man scratched his beard. "What's your name, son?"

"Sam."

"I'm Sergeant Carl Gilliard." He extended his hand.

Sam hesitated, then took it.

"How old are you?" the man named Carl asked.

"Thirteen."

Carl nodded steadily.

"Why?" Sam asked.

Carl looked away, as though seeing things beyond the walls of the barracks. "We got a lot of work to do around here, Sam. Miles of fencing that needs to be patrolled. Need people. Now, you're young, but...that's the way it is now. I think you know what you're doing. Am I wrong?"

Sam looked at him. Then at Abby. "No, sir."

Carl reached out and squeezed Sam's shoulder. "Good man."

Angela was sitting on his cot when Lee returned. She sat with her knees together, elbows braced, chin resting on her hands, looking off into no particular direction. Her eyes were intense but unseeing. Her mind was not in the present, but milling over things come and gone and things still to be. It was a troubled look.

Lee stopped in the doorway of the barracks, still not seen by Angela. It was not as crowded as it had been thirty minutes prior, and the people that remained were sticking to their individual bunks, taking stock of what they had and what they had lost. Lee looked at the things stuffed beneath his cot, and atop it, and the woman that sat on it, and his mind ventured in the same direction.

He stepped through the door, but it wasn't until he stopped beside Angela and his cot that her eyes came back to the present and she straightened from her pensive slouch. She looked up at him, for a moment seeming surprised to see him there. Then her expression softened into something more familiar. The look she gave him wasn't quite a smile. Her lips were pressed together, the corners of her mouth just slightly downturned, as though her mouth wanted to summon a smile but couldn't quite find the energy.

They regarded each other in silence for a moment, both trying to find words.

Lee broke it first, looking away. "It's a madhouse out there."

"Yeah. Carl's people had free barracks that they're putting us up in." She looked around. "I know this was considered spartan not so long ago, but everybody is pretty happy just to be sleeping on an actual bed, in an actual building. It's been a while since we've had that." She sighed. "But of course, keeping everyone organized is like herding cats."

Lee spared a smile. "Well, you seem to have a knack for it. You're a good cat herder."

"Thanks." She turned and grabbed a pack that was sitting next to her, undoing two buckles and pulling the main flap back. "I brought something from Camp Ryder. Grabbed it before we left. I didn't know...uh...didn't know whether you even wanted it, considering everything. But..." She shrugged and reached into the pack.

Lee recognized it before she had it completely pulled from the pack. There was no mistaking the bloodred and dingy white stripes. She'd folded it in a haphazard square, and this was how she handed it to him. He hesitated for a moment, looking at the folded banner that was hanging in the air between them. But then he reached out and took it from her.

She looked at him warily. "I understand if you don't want it."

Lee ran his fingers over the stitching, his face blank. Then he took the folded flag and put it under his arm, almost protectively. He looked at Angela, his feelings difficult to put into words. "Why wouldn't I want it?" he said quietly.

Perhaps he hoped that Angela had some better insight into his head than he did himself.

She glanced between his eyes and the flag under his arm. "Because of everything that's happened. Our government betraying you. The acting president..."

Lee shook his head. Then he took a seat on the cot, next to Angela. He sighed as he sat, a sound that was worn to the bone, like the sound of an old cave carved by eons of wind and water. He pulled the flag around, placed it in his lap, regarded it for a time.

"Yes. I feel betrayed," he said. "I can't deny that. But America is not its government. It's not something that's held together by politicians and bureaucrats. So it doesn't matter to me who comes along and tells me I'm not a patriot, or tells me that I'm committing treason because I'm not following them down their rabbit hole." He looked at her, intensely. "This is my flag. It's not his. He never fought for it. And I refuse to let him take it from me. Not after everything I've done. Not after everything I've been through. He can claim the presidency all he wants, but what I'm doing will never be a secession. What we're doing will never be treason. So thank you for bringing this to me, Angela. Because no matter how much Briggs tries to hijack the plane and attempt to convince everyone that he's the captain, I'm not ever calling myself anything but an American. And this is the flag I'm gonna fly."

Angela nodded, then smiled wanly.

After a moment, her face fell into thought again. She seemed to have something that she wanted to say but was having difficulty with it. Finally, she seemed to give up. She rose from the cot, touching Lee one last time on the shoulder, almost a forlorn gesture of affection.

As she turned away from him, he spoke quietly. "I'm sorry that things..."

She stopped and looked back at him.

"I'm sorry for how things turned out," he said. "For us."

For a flash, she almost seemed angry with him. Her hands clenched and unclenched. But then there was a sadness in her eyes that seemed to overtake her. She swallowed hard and a visible tremor went through her.

She spoke suddenly. "Yesterday Sam killed Jenny."

Lee wasn't sure how to react, but he could see that Angela wasn't done.

She looked up at the ceiling, her eyes wet. "She was sick. Infected, I mean. Not the flu. I don't know how it happened. I was just trying to get everybody packed up and ready to leave. And then I heard a gunshot. And when we came around the corner of the building, Sam was standing there with Abby. He said that Jenny had tried to attack them and he shot her." Angela touched her head with a finger. "Right there. And he was…he was broken up, Lee."

Angela shook her head. "I wanted you to know that when I saw him standing there, shaking and holding that rifle of his, I understood why you did the things that you did. Because when it comes right down to it, surviving is more important. And making sure that the people that rely on you stay safe…that trumps everything. I understand what was going through your head. And no matter what happens going forward, we're always going to need you, Lee. And others just like you. You were right. Sometimes…sometimes you have to do the ugly things to keep everyone safe. And we can't condemn the people we have that are willing to do those things. Or we're gonna fall apart before we even get started." She pointed at him, almost sternly. "We need you. So don't go anywhere."

Lee sat there, holding the flag of his father, and of his youth, the flag that would eventually see him to his willing grave. He clutched it tight and nodded to the woman standing in front of him. "I'm here. I'm not going anywhere."

EPILOGUE

LEE STOOD IN THE center of the lonesome two-lane road. The very same stretch of abandoned highway where he'd crouched beneath an old elm tree and waited, rifle in his hands. Now the roadway had become just a whitewashed channel through this section of woods, all the trees and branches to either side crusted in ice and snow.

This was the first snow of the winter, and it had come in early January. It hadn't snowed a flake before that, but now North Carolina weather seemed to be playing catch-up. It was dumping everything it had, as fast as it could. All the previous night and into this morning. No sign of stopping.

Early January.

A half a year, people said.

They'd made it a half a year.

Lee glanced behind him at the two gun-truck Humvees that idled there. He made a quick cutting motion across his neck. The engines died. In the absence of their growling, the stillness of the snow-covered wilderness around him seemed vast, almost infinite. He listened to it. Felt it chill him to the bone, more than the cold air ever could have.

Silence in the woods. Silence on the road.

Deuce leaned against his leg. Lee watched the breath plume from the dog's wolflike muzzle, his golden eyes scanning through the tree line all around them. He was as still and quiet as the rest of the world.

Lee looked forward again, to the object of his interest.

One mound in the road, covered by snow.

His eyes tracked up, further in the direction that the two Humvees were heading, and he could see another lump hiding there beneath the snow, like a body beneath a sheet, and the thought went through him, no matter how illogical—*waiting to jump up and attack us.*

Behind them, in the direction that they'd come, a few more white lumps.

No sign of tracks. They'd been there all night.

They're not gonna jump up and attack you, he told himself. But still, he gripped his rifle a little tighter, his ungloved hands aching in the cold.

He stepped up to the nearest lump in the snow and he pointed his rifle at it—logic be damned— and then he nudged it with his foot. It felt like ice. Frozen solid. He hit it harder, a solid kick this time. Then scuffed some of the snow off with a hesitant toe.

A woman lay beneath that layer of white coldness. Her skin was grayish blue. Eyes closed. She looked almost beatific. It was a peaceful way to go, he'd been told once. Freezing to death. Well, peaceful once the shock and hypothermia took over. Once you got through that part, it was supposed to be peaceful.

She was naked, not a stitch to keep her warm. Not that she would need it now. Hands curled into her chest, but Lee could see the longish, clawlike nails, the dark gore and dirt that were gummed up beneath them and also covered her arms up to the elbow like gauntlets. Around her face and neck and chest was more of the same. Filth. Blood.

All frozen solid.

Quiet crunch of boots through snow.

Lee hadn't even heard the Humvee doors open or close, but when he turned, Tomlin was standing there looking down at what Lee had uncovered. He seemed to consider it for a time, soak it in, make the necessary connections. There wasn't much reaction. Lee didn't feel much reaction, either.

Tomlin spat into the snowy road. "Well, shit."

"Yeah." Lee nodded slowly. "All along these roads."

Tomlin knelt down and inspected the body more closely. "Not hunters."

"No," Lee agreed. "But from how many we've seen, I'd guess they were bits and pieces of the horde out of Smithfield. Still floating around out here. Until last night, anyway."

"Hm," Tomlin grunted, then stood. "Wonder if the horde kept them warm. All those bodies packed in tight. Kinda create a bubble of warmth for themselves."

"Maybe."

"We've been thinning them out pretty good, so..." Tomlin trailed off.

"Maybe," Lee repeated.

"But not the hunters."

"No, not the hunters."

As if on cue, Deuce growled low. As if he'd heard Lee and Tomlin talking about them, and the mere mention of the hunters was getting his hackles up. But Lee knew better than that. Deuce only growled when they were around. When he could smell them.

Lee put a hand on the dog's head and scratched behind the ears. "Good boy."

Somewhere deep in those woods, all still with ice and snow, something howled. A distant sound. And an answer, as the first call faded. Both of them a good ways away, though. Not enough to get Lee running just yet. And besides, if they were close, Deuce would be losing his mind.

"No," Lee said, sounding a little tired. "Those things seem to be doing just fine."

Tomlin slapped him on the shoulder. "Come on. We got places to be."

They arrived in Camp Ryder by midmorning. Or what had once been Camp Ryder. Now more like *Outpost* Ryder, though everyone still called it by its original name from force of habit. It was different, though. Shantytown was gone, razed, the materials used for other things. No fires burned in the complex, no smoke trails against the gray-white sky. No families lived there anymore. Just soldiers. Soldiers, and militiamen.

The pass colors were shown and the gates were slid open and the gun trucks rolled in and parked on the hard-packed dirt and gravel. Doors opened, and the occupants came out. Lee first, from the front passenger side of the lead Humvee. His driver was Tomlin. And Abe, coming out last from the backseat, still moving a little slow as he continued to heal, but refusing to stay under care at Fort Bragg.

Lee felt lucky, in a way. Surrounded by men that he knew, men that he trusted. Good friends. Good advisors. Good warriors.

From the second Humvee came Nate, Julia, and Carl. They hesitated a bit and Carl waited at the back door, holding it open and looking inside, patiently. Claire Staley emerged a moment later, spindly in her teenage youth, with her homely features but intensely green eyes.

She looked around the camp, unafraid. She was never afraid, it seemed. Like that part of her had been excised long ago. She'd probably been asleep in the back of the Humvee. Lee was told that she slept like the dead.

She was not a part of Lee's regular team, as everyone else in the Humvees was.

But she was needed for today, as she had been a few other times for similar things.

In the middle of the Square, Lee was met by Rudy. He gave Lee a firm handshake and shared a quick brotherly embrace with Carl.

"Where are they?" Lee asked.

Rudy nodded toward the Camp Ryder building. "Inside. Where it's warm."

Lee looked at the building for a moment, then looked over at Carl, and then to Claire Staley.

The young woman was also staring at the building, her breath hanging in the air. Then she turned and saw Lee watching her. She straightened a bit. Getting down to business. Her green eyes tacked over to the building again, and she started walking with the slightest shrug.

The group entered the building, a silent procession. They shook the cold and snow off themselves, stomped the ice from their boots. Rudy led them around the corner, around the metal stairs that led to the office that had once been Lee's home, and he took them to the utility closet under the stairs. The door was closed and locked. Rudy glanced back at the men following him, and then opened the door.

There was no light inside. Lee's eyes took a moment to adjust.

Two forms sat huddled in the cold darkness, shivering, with their arms wrapped around themselves. They did not immediately look up when the door was opened, but took a moment and then seemed to gradually realize that they were being looked upon.

Two men. One that Lee didn't recognize. Another that he did.

Lee's jaw worked. He felt...what did he feel?

Anger? Indignation? Rage?

No. Not that anymore.

He sniffed, smelled the scent of humans long unbathed. Watched the two captives for a moment, fixating on the face that he knew. "Brett," Lee said quietly.

The man didn't react to his name being called. He just kept staring up at them, his face numb. He must have known what was coming. He must have known where his choices had led him. The dark path that he'd chosen. The murders, the betrayal...they always come back to bite you in the ass.

Lee stepped out of the doorway and made room. Claire sidled up next to him, arms crossed over her chest, hands holding her elbows defensively. This was difficult for her, they knew. But it was necessary. Accusations could not simply be leveled without proof. That was a dangerous way of doing business. But she was a witness. She knew faces that the rest of them did not.

Lee spoke slowly: "Claire...do you recognize any of these men?"

Claire looked at them for a long time. They did not bother to hide their faces. She took her time, studying each one, knowing what lay on her shoulders—more than any young person should have to have leveled on them. Finally, she nodded, seemed very confident. "Yes. They were both with the Followers. That one killed all of your people at Newton Grove. The other one..." She stared at him for a moment more and a small shiver worked through her body. "...the other one is their leader. Pastor Wiscoe."

Lee looked each man in the eye. Neither denied what was being alleged. Neither had anything to say. He reached over and put a hand on Claire's shoulder. Then he pulled her gently away and closed the door behind them, locking it again.

"You did a good job, Claire. Thank you."

She stared at the closed door, then turned away.

Lee looked at Rudy. He leaned in close to the other man and spoke quietly, gravely. "You know what needs to be done."

Outside the building, Lee stood on the steps, taking in the unfamiliar view. Looking out over what had once been Shantytown and was now just a big barren area. Lee knew that all these people were now in Fort Bragg, that the barracks and mess halls there were teeming with life, that they were fighting, they were pushing back, and they were surviving. But still...seeing the evidence of what had been left him with a sort of melancholy that he could not explain. Like walking the halls of an old high school. The amount of time he'd spent in Camp Ryder had been only a little over three months. And yet it had been such a strange and cataclysmic time that those fast-moving months had stretched into decades in his mind.

Claire moved past him, hands stuffed into the pockets of her jacket. She stepped quickly away from the building and stood in the middle of the Square, face lifted to the snowing sky, and her eyes closed as the flakes settled softly onto her face and held for brief moments before melting. She seemed to need to be away from the enclosure of the building, needed to be in the open.

Abe stood next to him, stiff left arm held close to his side. He favored it, and there was no doubt in Lee's mind that the bones and sinews that had been destroyed by that bullet had not finished knitting themselves together. But Abe still managed to pull his own weight. He avoided doing anything with that arm, but there had been times when it had been required, and he had done it, using that arm to grab the arm of a wounded comrade and drag him to safety. When he'd done it, he'd just grit his teeth and none of the pain had shown through his bearded visage, but rather a panicked sort of anger, like his body was a reactor, converting agony into rage. Nobody mentioned his arm, because even with his barely healed limb, Abe did more work than the average man. So no one could really complain.

Abe watched Claire for a time through narrowed eyes. "This has got to be rough on her."

Lee rubbed his nose. "Can't really tell anymore."

"How many more?"

"However many more it takes." Lee cleared his throat. "By her own estimates, there were only a dozen or so men that held rank. The rest were just thugs. Going along for the ride."

"We can't chase every single one of them down."

"Oh, I know." Lee looked at his friend. "We haven't hunted any of them. But when we, or any of our people, happen across them, I certainly intend to make things right."

Abe held up a hand. "Hey, you don't have to explain shit to me, buddy. I'm on board. It feels like it's been ages since everything went to shit, but it hasn't been that long. It's still a very violent place out here. And it requires us to be violent, too. And that isn't gonna change for a long time." He nodded to their charge. "I just worry about Claire is all."

"I know," Lee said. "I do, too. But when she's ready to call it quits, she will."

"Sometimes you keep doing things far past when you're ready to call it quits."

Lee was silent.

Abe put a hand on his shoulder. "We should get back. Important things are happening today. Wouldn't want to miss them."

Lee stood at the back of the crowded auditorium, near the door. He could feel the icy air slipping in through the cracks. Cold and ice lay outside. Wet and miserable. Inside, it was hot from burning kerosene heaters and from the hundreds of bodies packed in so tightly together. The vast majority of the people inside of the auditorium were observers. Concerned citizens, in a way.

But the front section of the auditorium nearest to the small stage had been roped off, and in there sat only the representatives. There were four distinct groups, only one of which Lee was very familiar with. That was the North Carolina group. The other three were from South Carolina, Georgia, and Florida, respectively. Each group was comprised of representatives from small and large groups alike. And from each of their groups, they had elected a chairman, who would speak for the entire state.

At the front, and all the way to the right, the group from North Carolina sat. Civilian representatives from Fort Bragg and Camp Lejeune, as well as several smaller groups. Camp Ryder was well represented. Marie was there. And Angela sat as the chairman for North Carolina.

She didn't want it, but she got it anyway.

News of how Camp Ryder had fought back, stood their ground, not only against the hordes coming out of the north, but against Briggs, had spread across the state. Even among the other states represented, North Carolina seemed to hold a special spot—the northernmost state, the line in the sand. And Camp Ryder was credited with much of that.

Angela had been a shoo-in.

She glanced backward, perhaps feeling someone's eyes on her. She met Lee's gaze and gave him a bewildered smile. These were large things to discuss. Big decisions. He nodded back to her, his face very serious.

Amid the rumble of subdued conversations, Angela turned away from him, and then she rose, somewhat stiffly, straightening her jacket. For what was being referred to as a "congress," everyone was dressed much alike. There was no room for suit jackets and nice dresses. They all wore what they normally wore—jackets worn out and patched, guns still slung on their hips and backs. But you did not need suits and ties to feel the gravity in the air, the seriousness of what was about to be discussed. All the representatives and state chairmen might be dressed as normal, but what they were discussing was very unusual.

As Angela took the stage, the crowd quieted. People in the back craned their necks to see. People in the front jostled for position. But the quiet swept through and people watched, and people listened, because the words that were spoken would push them onto one unstoppable path or the other.

Angela stared out, still incredibly uncomfortable with the position that she'd found herself in. She alleged she was deathly terrified of public speaking, but all she showed now was some hesitation, maybe a little bit of nerves, but nothing debilitating. Lee knew that she was stronger than she gave herself credit for. She would find that out. But it would be on her own.

She cleared her throat, and her voice sounded small in the auditorium.

Silence in the crowd, everyone straining to hear. There were no microphones or speakers to amplify the voices.

"Thank you everyone for coming," Angela said, eyes cast downward at the podium as she addressed the hundreds of faces in front of her. "I know that the weather is not very nice outside. The fact that so many of you showed up today is proof to me of the importance of today's discussion, and how seriously we're all taking it."

She paused for a moment—gathering her thoughts or overcoming her nerves; Lee wasn't sure which. "We're on the cusp of something we never anticipated seeing again. Our country has changed. Physically, emotionally. Spiritually. Borders are being drawn up, and for the first time in almost two hundred years, we live in a nation that is militarily divided against itself. Acting President Briggs sits on the other side of the Appalachians, and we all know his position. We know what he claims. And we know that he is eventually going to come for us, those eastern states that he abandoned so many months ago. I don't think there's any denying that. Every account we have from those that have left Colorado says the same thing. He is there, and he is gathering his strength, and he intends to unite America again. Which includes us.

"I know this is difficult, and it should be. We should not approach this lightly. I believe that most of us consider ourselves to be patriots of this country, and it is part of our identity that we see ourselves as one nation, and not separate states. But we have to be careful of blind loyalty. We have to guard against accepting anyone's version of America simply so that we can feel safe and protected. That's what we're here to discuss. And I intend to make my position, and the position of those people from North Carolina that I represent, very clear right from the get-go.

"Many of you know Captain Harden, or you know of him. And if he'll let me, I'd like to tell you all something that he said to me when our group first arrived here from Camp Ryder." She found him again, in the back of the auditorium, and offered him a quick smile. Some of those in the audience followed her gaze and glanced back at him, but then they focused on her again. "This was after we'd managed to cut off the hordes from the north. I brought him an American flag that had been hanging in Camp Ryder. I took it down before we evacuated. I didn't know whether he wanted it or not, because of everything that had happened with President Briggs. But he took it and he told me, 'America is not its government.

It's not something that's held together by politicians and bureaucrats.' And I think that we need to come to that realization once again."

She paused for another moment, and Lee could feel her nervousness about what she was going to say. But when she spoke, it was firm, and it was forceful. "Knowing what I know now, and having been through everything that I have been through, everything that my family, that my group, that my entire state has been through, I can only give you advice as you move forward in these deliberations. And my advice would be this: Do not love your country. Love your God-given freedoms. Don't fight *for* a government, but rather fight *against* anyone who would threaten your liberty, and your right to be alive. Government does not exist to be served, but to serve, and to be a physical manifestation of common ideals. And to protect those ideals through the forceful hand of the people that espouse them."

Half of those gathered applauded, aggressively.

The other half mumbled among themselves, unsurely.

Split, right down the middle, Lee thought to himself as he scanned the crowd.

Then he looked to his left. Standing with him was his small team, all wet and snow-crusted, and they watched with concentration, and perhaps some trepidation, but if they agreed or disagreed, they did not say. Nate glared on. Julia was more relaxed, though her face was tight—perhaps from the pain in her freshly healed leg. Tomlin and Abe were whispering in quiet conference together. Carl stood stone-still against the wall, arms crossed. He glanced at Lee, and his lips pursed.

Agree, or disagree? Lee thought, but Carl was remaining enigmatic, as usual.

Suddenly, Lee needed to be out of that auditorium. Away from all of those people. Away from their opinions and the things that they thought they knew, and all of the arguments that those opinions would spawn, and all of the shouting and yelling that was only minutes around the corner, as soon as people realized how divided they were when it came to this ultimate decision. And in the end, it was not his decision to make.

As Angela continued to speak, Lee turned away and pushed out of the door. The cold, white-washed world met him. Deuce had stayed close to his legs inside, but once outside he ran and began sniffing the wind. Lee stood at the entrance to the auditorium for a moment, acclimating himself to the cold.

He heard the door open and close behind him.

Abe stood next to him again, shrugging against the wind. "Not interested?"

Lee scratched at his beard, grown a bit longer now. "No, I'm interested." He looked behind him at the closed door of the auditorium. "But it ain't up to me. I've done my job. I got them here. I'll keep them safe while they decide what to do with themselves." He hiked a thumb behind him. "That's government in there, Abe. That's what we were supposed to rebuild. And there it is. So I guess..." Lee shrugged. "I guess mission accomplished."

Abe stayed quiet for a moment, then just: "Hm. Mission accomplished."

Lee looked at him with a quirked brow. "What?"

"That's bullshit and you know it." Abe blew warm breath into his cupped hands. "Our work is never done, my friend. They'll always need us to keep them safe. And we'll always do it. Because it's what we do. It's the way we're wired. We're always looking for the good fight." He worked his injured shoulder a bit, grimacing. "You think you want to rest, but you'll just spend it wondering when the next battle will come along. We can't help ourselves. It's in the blood. We do the right thing, not because it serves us best, but because it is *right*. And without rightness, without honor? There's just every man for himself. And that's just anarchy.

"Trust me," Abe said, some finality in his voice. "Our work is never done."

Lee's expression was tired, but accepting. "Yeah. I know."

The man walks to the edge of the open field, the dog by his side. Acres upon acres, covered in brilliant white. The snow will melt, the ground will thaw, and the seeds will be planted. But for now it lies dormant. Just promises, waiting to be fulfilled.

The snow clouds thin, and the sky breaks. The sun is muted coming through. It is not exactly the moment in the sun that he wished for so long ago, but it will just have to do. He closes his eyes and looks skyward. Behind his eyelids, he sees red. His own blood. Behind his eyelids, he sees loss and gain and struggle. Endless struggle.

When he opens his eyes, he sees the dog is no longer with him.

His eyes follow the tracks in the snow that cut a wide circle, following the edge of the open field. He spots the brown-and-tan shape, moving swiftly and deliberately. The dog is doing what he was bred to do. Patrolling the perimeter. Nose in the wind. Smelling for the next threat. Searching for the next fight.

Always watching.

Always ready.

extras

meet the author

D. J. MOLLES is the bestselling author of the Remaining series. He published his first short story, "Darkness," while still in high school. Soon after, he won a prize for his short story "Survive." *The Remaining* was originally self-published in 2012 and quickly became an Internet bestseller. He lives in the Southeast with his wife and children.

introducing

If you enjoyed
THE REMAINING: EXTINCTION
look out for

THE LAZARUS WAR

Book 1: Artefact

by Jamie Sawyer

In the twenty-second century, mankind has spread out into the stars, only to find themselves locked in eternal warfare with the insidious Krell. On the farthest edges of known space, a stalemate has been hard won, and a Quarantine Zone is being policed by the only people able to contain the Krell menace: the brave soldiers of the Simulant Operation Program, an elite military team who remotely operate bioengineered avatars in the most dangerous theaters of war.

Captain Conrad Harris is a veteran of the Sim Ops Program, a man who has died hundreds of times running suicide missions inside his simulants. Known as Lazarus, Harris is a man addicted to death, and driven by the memory of a lover lost to the Krell many years before. So when a secret research station deep in the Quarantine Zone suddenly goes dark, there is no other man who could possibly lead a rescue mission.

CHAPTER 1

There was something so immensely *wrong* about the Krell. I could still remember the first time I saw one and the sensation of complete wrongness that overcame me. Over the years, the emotion had settled to a balls-deep paralysis.

This was a primary-form, the lowest strata of the Krell Collective, but it was still bigger than any of us. Encased in the Krell equivalent of battle-armour: hardened carapace plates, fused to the xeno's grey-green skin. It was impossible to say where technology finished and biology began. The thing's back was awash with antennae—those could be used as both weapons and communicators with the rest of the Collective.

The Krell turned its head to acknowledge us. It had a vaguely fish-like face, with a pair of deep bituminous eyes, barbels drooping from its mouth. Beneath the head, a pair of gills rhythmically flexed, puffing out noxious fumes. Those sharkish features had earned them the moniker "fish heads." Two pairs of arms sprouted from the shoulders— one atrophied, with clawed hands; the other tipped with bony, serrated protrusions—raptorial forearms.

The xeno reared up, and in a split-second it was stomping down the corridor.

I fired my plasma rifle. The first shot exploded the xeno's chest, but it kept coming. The second shot connected with one of the bladed forearms, blowing the limb clean off. Then Blake and Kaminski were firing too— and the corridor was alight with brilliant plasma pulses. The creature collapsed into an incandescent mess.

"You like that much, Olsen?" Kaminski asked. "They're pretty friendly for a species that we're supposed to be at peace with."

At some point during the attack, Olsen had collapsed to his knees. He sat there for a second, looking down at his gloved hands. His eyes were haunted, his heavy jowls suddenly much older. He shook his head, stumbling to his feet. From the safety of a laboratory, it was easy to think of the Krell as another intelligent species, just made in the image of a different god. But seeing them up-close, and witnessing their innate need to extinguish the human race, showed them for what they really were.

"This is a live situation now, troopers. Keep together and do this by the drill. *Haven* is awake."

"Solid copy," Kaminski muttered.

"We move to secondary objective. Once the generator has been tagged, we retreat down the primary corridor to the APS. Now double time it and move out."

There was no pause to relay our contact with Jenkins and Martinez. The Krell had a unique ability to sense radio transmissions, even encrypted communications like those we used on the suits, and now that the Collective had awoken all comms were locked down.

As I started off, I activated the wrist-mounted computer incorporated into my suit. *Ah, shit.* The starship corridors brimmed with motion and bio-signs. The place became swathed in shadow and death—every pool of blackness a possible Krell nest.

Mission timeline: twelve minutes.

We reached the quantum-drive chamber. The huge reinforced doors were emblazoned with warning signs and a red emergency light flashed overhead.

The floor exploded as three more Krell appeared— all chitin shells and claws. Blake went down first, the largest of the Krell dragging him into a service tunnel. He brought his rifle up to fire, but there was too little room for him to manoeuvre in a full combat-suit, and he couldn't bring the weapon to bear.

"Hold on, Kid!" I hollered, firing at the advancing Krell, trying to get him free.

The other two xenos clambered over him in desperation to get to me. I kicked at several of them, reaching a hand into the mass of bodies to try to grapple Blake. He lost his rifle, and let rip an agonised shout as the creatures dragged him down. It was no good—he was either dead now, or he would be soon. Even in his reinforced ablative plate, those things would take him apart. I lost the grip on his hand, just as the other Krell broke free of the tunnel mouth.

"Blake's down!" I yelled. " 'Ski—grenade."

"Solid copy—on it."

Kaminski armed an incendiary grenade and tossed it into the nest. The grenade skittered down the tunnel, flashing an amber warning-strobe as it went. In the split second before it went off, as I brought my M95 up to fire, I saw that the tunnel was now filled with xenos. Many, many more than we could hope to kill with just our squad.

"Be careful—you could blow a hole in the hull with those explosives!" Olsen wailed.

Holing the hull was the least of my worries. The grenade went off, sending Krell in every direction. I turned away from the blast at the last moment, and felt hot shrapnel penetrate my combat-armour—frag lodging itself in my lower back. The suit compensated for the wall of white noise, momentarily dampening my audio.

The M95 auto-sighted prone Krell and I fired without even thinking. Pulse after pulse went into the tunnel, splitting armoured heads and tearing off clawed limbs. Blake was down there, somewhere amongst the tangle of bodies and debris; but it took a good few seconds before my suit informed me that his bio-signs had finally extinguished.

Good journey, Blake.

Kaminski moved behind me. His technical kit was already hooked up to the drive chamber access terminal, running code-cracking algorithms to get us in.

The rest of the team jogged into view. More Krell were now clambering out of the hole in the floor. Martinez and Jenkins added their own rifles to the volley, and assembled outside the drive chamber.

"Glad you could finally make it. Not exactly going to plan down here."

"Yeah, well, we met some friends on the way," Jenkins muttered.

"We lost the Kid," I said. "Blake's gone."

"Ah, fuck it," Jenkins said, shaking her head. She and Blake were close, but she didn't dwell on his death. *No time for grieving*, the expression on her face said, *because we might be next*.

The access doors creaked open. There was another set of double-doors inside; endorsed QUANTUM DRIVE CHAMBER—AUTHORISED PERSONNEL ONLY.

A calm electronic voice began a looped message: "Warning. Warning. Breach doors to drive chamber are now open. This presents an extreme radiation hazard. Warning. Warning."

A second too late, my suit bio-sensors began to trill; detecting massive radiation levels. I couldn't let it concern me. Radiation on an op like this was always a danger, but being killed by the Krell was a more immediate risk. I rattled off a few shots into the shadows, and heard the impact against hard chitin. The things screamed, their voices creating a discordant racket with the alarm system.

Kaminski cracked the inner door, and he and Martinez moved inside. I laid down suppressing fire with Jenkins, falling back slowly as the things tested our defences. It was difficult to make much out in the intermittent light: flashes of a claw, an alien head, then the explosion of plasma as another went down. My suit counted ten, twenty, thirty targets.

"Into the airlock!" Kaminski shouted, and we were all suddenly inside, drenched in sweat and blood.

The drive chamber housed the most complex piece of technology on the ship—the energy core. Once, this might've been called the engine room. Now, the device contained within the chamber was so far advanced that it was no longer mechanical. The drive energy core sat in the centre of the room—an ugly-looking metal box, so big that it filled the place, adorned with even more warning signs. This was our objective.

Olsen stole a glance at the chamber, but stuck close to me as we assembled around the machine. Kaminski paused at the control terminal near the door, and sealed the inner lock. Despite the reinforced metal doors, the squealing and shrieking of the Krell was still audible. I knew that they would be through those doors in less than a minute. Then there was the scuttling and scraping overhead. The chamber was supposed to be secure, but these things had probably been on-ship for long enough to know every access corridor and every room. They had the advantage.

They'll find a way in here soon enough, I thought. A mental image of the dead merchant captain—still strapped to his seat back on the bridge—suddenly came to mind.

The possibility that I would die out here abruptly dawned on me. The thought triggered a burst of anger—not directed at the Alliance military for sending us out here, nor at the idiot colonists who had flown their ship into the Quarantine Zone, but at the Krell.

My suit didn't take any medical action to compensate for that emotion. *Anger is good.* It was pure and made me focused.

"Jenkins—set the charges."

"Affirmative, Captain."

Jenkins moved to the drive core and began unpacking her kit. She carried three demolition-packs. Each of the big metal discs had a separate control-panel, and was packed with a low-yield nuclear charge.

"Wh—what are you doing?" Olsen stammered.

Jenkins kept working, but shook her head with a smile. "We're going to destroy the generator. You should have read the mission briefing. That was your first mistake."

"Forgetting to bring a gun was his second," Kaminski added.

"We're going to set these charges off," Jenkins muttered, "and the resulting explosion will breach the Q-drive energy core. That'll take out the main deck. The chain reaction will destroy the ship."

"In short: gran explosión," said Martinez.

Kaminski laughed. "There you go again. You know I hate it when you don't speak Standard. Martinez always does this—he gets all excited and starts speaking funny."

"El no habla la lengua," I said. You don't grow up in the Detroit Metro without picking up some of the lingo.

"It's Spanish," Martinez replied, shooting Kaminski a sideways glance.

"I thought that you were from Venus," Kaminski said.

Olsen whimpered again. "How can you laugh at a time like this?"

"Because Kaminski is an asshole," Martinez said, without missing a beat.

Kaminski shrugged. "It's war."

Thump. Thump.

"Give us enough time to fall back to the APS," I ordered. "Set the charges with a five minute delay. The rest of you—cállate y trabaja."

"Affirmative."

Thump! Thump! Thump!

They were nearly through now. Welts appeared in the metal door panels.

Jenkins programmed each charge in turn, using magnetic locks to hold them in place on the core outer shielding. Two of the charges were already primed, and she was working on the third. She positioned the charges very deliberately, very carefully, to ensure that each would do maximum damage to the core. If one charge didn't light, then the others would act as a failsafe. There was probably a more technical way of doing this—perhaps hacking the Q-drive directly—but that would take time, and right now that was the one thing that we didn't have.

"Precise as ever," I said to Jenkins.

"It's what I do."

"Feel free to cut some corners; we're on a tight time-scale," Kaminski shouted.

"Fuck you, 'Ski."

"Is five minutes going to be enough?" Olsen asked.

I shrugged. "It will have to be. Be prepared for heavy resistance en route, people."

My suit indicated that the Krell were all over the main corridor. They would be in the APS by now, probably waiting for us to fall back.

THUMP! THUMP! THUMP!

"Once the charges are in place, I want a defensive perimeter around that door," I ordered.

"This can't be rushed."

The scraping of claws on metal, from above, was becoming intense. I wondered which defence would be the first to give: whether the Krell would come in through the ceiling or the door.

Kaminski looked back at Jenkins expectantly. Olsen just stood there, his breathing so hard that I could hear him over the communicator.

"...and done!"

The third charge snapped into place. Jenkins was up, with Martinez, and Kaminski was ready at the data terminal. There was noise all around us now, signals swarming on our position. I had no time to dictate a proper strategy for our retreat.

"Jenkins—put down a barrier with your torch. Kaminski—on my mark..."

I dropped my hand, and the doors started to open. The mechanism buckled and groaned in protest. Immediately, the Krell grappled with the door, slamming into the metal frame to get through.

Stinger-spines—flechette rounds, the Krell equivalent of armour-piercing ammo—showered the room. Three of them punctured my suit; a neat line of black spines protruding from my chest, weeping streamers of blood. *Krell tech is so much more fucked-up than ours.* The spines were poison-tipped and my body was immediately pumped with enough toxins to kill a bull. My suit futilely attempted to compensate by issuing a cocktail of adrenaline and anti-venom.

Martinez flipped another grenade into the horde. The nearest creatures folded over it as it landed, shielding their kin from the explosion. *Mindless fuckers.*

We advanced in formation. Shot after shot poured into the things, but they kept coming. Wave after wave—how many were there on this ship?—thundered into the drive chamber. The doors were suddenly gone. The noise was unbearable—the klaxon, the warnings, a chorus of screams, shrieks and wails. The ringing in my ears didn't stop, as more grenades exploded.

"We're not going to make this!" Jenkins yelled.

"Stay on it! The APS is just ahead!"

Maybe Jenkins was right, but I wasn't going down without a damned good fight. Somewhere in the chaos, Martinez was torn apart. His body disappeared underneath a mass of them. Jenkins poured on her flamethrower—avenging Martinez in some absurd way. Olsen was crying, his helmet now discarded just like the rest of us.

War is such an equaliser.

I grabbed the nearest Krell with one hand, and snapped its neck. I fired my plasma rifle on full-auto with the other, just eager to take down as many of them as I could. My HUD suddenly issued another warning—a counter, interminably in decline.

Ten...Nine...Eight...Seven...

Then Jenkins was gone. Her flamer was a beacon and her own blood a fountain amongst the alien bodies. It was difficult to focus on much except for the pain in my chest. My suit reported catastrophic damage in too many places. My heart began a slower, staccato beat.

Six...Five...Four...

My rifle bucked in protest. Even through reinforced gloves, the barrel was burning hot.

Three...Two...One...

The demo-charges activated.

Breached, the anti-matter core destabilised. The reaction was instantaneous: uncontrolled white and blue energy spilled out. A series of explosions rippled along the ship's spine. She became a white-hot smudge across the blackness of space.

Then she was gone, along with everything inside her.

The Krell did not pause.

They did not even comprehend what had happened.

PFC MICHAEL BLAKE: DECEASED...

PFC ELLIOT MARTINEZ: DECEASED...

PFC VINCENT KAMINSKI (ELECTRONICS TECH, FIRST GRADE): DECEASED...

SCIENCE OFFICER GORDEN OLSEN: DECEASED...

CORPORAL KEIRA JENKINS (EXPLOSIVES TECH, FIRST GRADE): DECEASED...

WAITING FOR RESPONSE...WAITING FOR RESPONSE...WAITING FOR RESPONSE...

CAPTAIN CONRAD HARRIS: DECEASED...

This was the part I disliked most.

Waking up again was always worse than dying.

I floated inside my simulator-tank—a respirator mask attached to my face—and blinked amniotic fluid from my eyes to read the screen more clearly. The soak stung like a bitch. The words scrolled across a monitor positioned above my tank. Everything was cast a clear, brilliant blue by the liquid filling my simulator.

PURGE CYCLE COMMENCED...

The tank made a hydraulic hissing, and the fluid began to slough out. It was already cooling.

I was instantly smaller and yet heavier. Breathing was a labour. These lungs didn't have the capacity of a simulant's, and I knew that it would take a few minutes to get used to them again. I caught the reflection on the inside of the plasglass cover, and didn't immediately recognise it as *my* reflection. That was the face I had been born with, and this was the body I had lived inside for forty years. I was naked, jacked directly into the simulator. Cables were plugged into the base of the device, allowing me to control my simulant out there in the depths of space. My bio-rhythms, and those of the rest of my squad, appeared on the same monitor.

All alive and accounted for. Everyone made safe transition.

I had been operating a flesh-and-blood simulation of myself, manufactured from my body tissue. These were called simulants: simulated copies, genetically engineered to be stronger, bigger, faster. Based on the human genome, but accelerated and modified, the sims were the ultimate weapon—more human than human in every sense. Vat-grown, designed for purpose. Now, my simulant was dead. *It* had died on the *New Haven*. *I* was alive.